Dark Money

A JACK BRYANT THRILLER

Larry D. Thompson

STORY MERCHANT BOOKS
LOS ANGELES / 2015

STORY MERCHANT BOOKS

Also by Larry D. Thompson:

Dead Peasants – The Jack Bryant Series
The Trial
So Help Me God
The Insanity Plea

Dark Money

A JACK BRYANT THRILLER

Larry D. Thompson

www.larrydthompson.com

Story Merchant Books
400 South Burnside Avenue #11B
Los Angeles, CA 90036

www.storymerchantbooks.com

Book cover/interior design
©2015 Leslie Taylor, www.buffalocreativegroup.com

Los Angeles / Larry D. Thompson

ISBN 978-0-9969908-0-6
Printed in the United States of America

For my friends in Fort Worth, particularly Arlington Heights High School, who have now become my faithful readers.

PROLOGUE

The convoy of three troop trucks made its way through the northeastern part of Saudi Arabia on their way to join with other American troops in Dhahran. Jack Bryant, a lawyer from Texas who was called up from his practice in Beaumont, was riding shotgun in the front truck. He was a Sergeant First Class and the senior NCO in the convoy. They passed through several villages deserted or nearly so out of fear of the rapidly moving Iraq army. The convoy approached another village, apparently abandoned, when Jack raised his hand.

"Stop. I saw a glint of metal in a balcony about a hundred yards ahead on the right and then it disappeared. I'm getting out my side and will use the door as a shield. Open your door as quietly as possible. Go back to the men and tell them to maintain complete silence. I don't even want to hear the click of a cigarette lighter until I signal."

The driver was a young private named Walt Frazier, also a Texan from the small town of Wharton. He nodded as he opened the driver's door and dropped from the truck. He made his way back to the other vehicles, delivering the message. Jack propped his rifle on the open window ledge and watched the balcony, occasionally flicking his eyes around the rest of the village but seeing no movement. Walt returned and settled into his seat. "See anything, Sarge?"

"Not yet, but I think he's there, just waiting to ambush us when we pass. We can outwait him."

Seconds turned into minutes. Jack continued to focus on the balcony. After twenty minutes the driver was thinking that his sergeant must have been imagining something when a head slowly surfaced above the wall on the balcony. Jack waited until he could see the mouth and fired one round, striking the Iraq sniper directly between the eyes. The enemy soldier dropped from sight.

Bryant climbed back into his seat and told his driver they could now move out.

"You sure, Sarge? Could be you only wounded him."

"Trust me. I don't miss from this distance. He's dead. Let's get going. I hope we'll still have a little light when we get to the barracks."

The convoy stopped in front of an abandoned oil field warehouse close to dusk on February 25, 1991. The concrete reflected heat of 104 degrees as the American troops piled out of the trucks to assemble around their sergeant. The men were young, around twenty, many younger, a few slightly older. Most of them had joined the National Guard, expecting to spend a weekend every month with units close to their homes as a means of paying college tuition or supplementing income from their regular jobs. Very few ever expected to see combat. That was before Saddam Hussein invaded Kuwait and President Bush began Operation Desert Storm.

Sergeant Bryant waited until they quietened before he spoke. A part-time soldier himself, he was not much for military formalities. "Listen up. This warehouse has been converted to a barracks. It's not air conditioned, but there are large fans that will cut the temperature by ten or fifteen degrees, and it's February; so the temperature tonight ought to drop to around eighty. You'll find cots inside and they're setting up a chow line. Latrine is around back. Enjoy the luxury. It'll probably be the last night you'll have a roof over your head for a while, and it'll damn sure be your last hot meal until we're finished with this son of a bitch."

"How long is this war going to last?" one of the men asked.

"The flyboys have been pounding the hell out of the Iraq forces. The ground war started yesterday. We'll be heading to the front tomorrow. The word from General Schwarzkopf's head-quarters is that they can't hold out much longer."

"Sarge, I hear they're using Scuds. Is that going to be a problem?"

The sergeant shook his head. "Shouldn't be around here. This area is protected by Patriot missiles. They've been damn success-ful in knocking Scuds out of the air. Now, grab your gear and pick a bunk." He glanced at his watch. "Chow line should be open in fifteen minutes. After that, clean your weapons one more time."

"Come on, Sarge. Mine are cleaner than a fresh washed-ba-by's butt."

"I hear you, but one more time, just for good measure. Then, get a good night's sleep. It may be your last for a few days."

By eight o'clock the chow line was closed and weapons had been cleaned. Some of the men were playing penny-ante poker, using a bunk for a table. Some were writing letters back to wives, girlfriends or moms. Others had taken off their boots and lay on top of their sleeping bags, fully clothed, packs and weapons close at hand. Six of the troops were members of the National Guard from Texas, including Sergeant Bryant, the "old man" of the out-fit at thirty. He had served in the 101st Airborne after finishing college and was beginning a law practice in Beaumont when President Bush came calling. The Texans bunked close to each other. Bryant had struck up a friendship with Frazier. He was one of the guard members who planned to serve his six years, mainly on weekends, as a means of paying his tuition at the local college.

They talked about their families, the just completed football season, and soon ran out of topics as, one by one, they closed their eyes, knowing that four o'clock the next morning would come far too soon. Walt was drifting into sleep when he heard a whistling sound and someone shouted, "Incoming!" Walt dove under his bunk, as if that would provide any protection from the missile that crashed through the metal roof and exploded, slinging fiery shrapnel from one end of the warehouse to the other.

Next came screams of pain as smoke filled the building. Then the beams that supported the ceiling buckled and, along with the jagged, tin roof, began to fall on the troops, inflicting more injury and death. Walt crawled from under his cot and witnessed the devastation. He tried to pull another man from under a cot across the aisle by tugging on his leg. Horrified, he realized that the leg was not attached to a body. Dropping it, he looked around. Some men were lying motionless, probably dead. Others were holding gaping wounds in their abdomens. Still others were trapped under beams and pieces of the roof, begging for help.

Through all the screams and yelling, somehow Walt heart Jack, speaking in a surprisingly low voice, "Walt, I need some help here."

Walt turned to find his sergeant's leg trapped under a beam.

"Can you get this thing off me?"

Walt considered his options and dropped to his back on the floor. "Sarge, I'm going to try to get my feet under it and push it up with my legs. If I can get it up a few inches, you think you can scrabble out from under it?"

Jack nodded. "Give it a try."

Walt positioned his feet and strained so hard that the blood vessels in his temples were bulging. The beam didn't budge. "Let me rest just a few seconds. I'm going to move my feet down a little and try again."

This time when he drove his legs, the beam started to move.

"One more inch, Walt, and I think I can get out."

Walt shoved the beam again and the beam moved a few more inches. Jack was having to force himself through the pain shooting throughout his leg, but he made it. Walt lowered his feet and sucked in a breath. After a few seconds, he got to his feet. "Can you walk?"

Outside he could hear sirens. Ambulances were on the way. "Not without some help."

"I'm going to pull you up. Put your arm over my shoulder."

Jack screamed as Walt pulled. "I'm all right. Just get me out of here."

Walt sized up the devastation around them and started picking his way through debris and bodies. Some of the men cried to him for help, fearful that another missile might land at any minute. "I'll be back as soon as I get Bryant out to the ambulances."

When he arrived at the door, someone was opening it from the outside. "Here, let me help." They moved Jack to a blanket where they lowered him to the ground. "I'm a medic. Let me have a look at that leg."

The leg just above the knee and the knee itself was crushed. "Any other injuries? How about your head?"

"No, just my leg," Jack replied through the pain etching his face.

"I'm going to get you something for that pain. Just lie still and an ambulance will take you to the base hospital. You'll be on a flight to Landstuhl in the morning. They have surgeons in Germany that can deal with this."

"If I pass out, tell them not to cut off my leg."

The medic nodded. Walt was listening to the exchange. "I'm going back inside." He turned and walked back to the door and into the building. Over the next several hours he made ten more trips, returning each time with a seriously wounded soldier. After the ones who were still alive were rescued, he was part of the team that retrieved the bodies. When daylight broke, he dropped to sit against a truck and buried his head in his arms as sobs wracked his body.

ONE

Jack Bryant turned his old red Dodge Ram pickup into the drive-way of the Greek revival mansion at the end of the cul-de-sac in Westover Hills, an exclusive neighborhood in Fort Worth. He was amused to see Halloween ghosts and goblins hanging from the two enormous live oaks that fronted the house. The driveway led to wrought iron gates that permitted entry to the back. A heavy set Hispanic man with a Poncho Villa mustache in a security guard uniform stood beside the driveway near the gates, clipboard in hand. He was unarmed.

Jack stopped beside him and lowered his window. "Afternoon, officer. Fine autumn day, isn't it?"

The guard sized up the old pick-up and the man wearing jeans and a white T-shirt. "You here to make a delivery?"

Jack reached into his left rear pocket and retrieved his wallet from which he extracted a laminated card. "No, sir. Name's Jackson Douglas Bryant. I'm a lawyer and a Tarrant County

Reserve Deputy. My friend, Walter Frazier, is part of the Governor's Protective Detail. Said Governor Lardner is attending some big shindig here tomorrow night and asked me to lend a hand in checking the place out before he hits town. My name should be on that clipboard."

The guard took the card, studied it closely and handed it back to Jack. He flipped to the second page. "There it is. Let me open the gates. Park down at the end of the driveway. You'll see another wall with a gate. Walk on through and you'll find your way to the ballroom where the party's being held tomorrow. I'll radio Sergeant Frazier to let him know you're on your way."

The gates silently opened, and Jack drove slowly to the back, admiring the house and grounds. The house had to be half a football field in length. Giant arched windows were spaced every ten feet with smaller ones above, apparently illuminating the second floor. To Jack's right was an eight foot wall. First security issue. Not very hard to figure out a way to scale it. Fortunately, cameras and lights were mounted on fifteen foot poles that appeared to blanket the area.

Jack parked where he was directed and climbed from his truck. Before shutting the door, he took his cane from behind the driver's seat. He flexed his left knee. It felt pretty good. He might not even need the cane. Still, he usually carried it since he never knew when he might take a step and have it buckle under him. Better to carry the cane than to fall on his ass.

He found himself in front of another wall. He was studying it when Walt came through the gate. Walt was ten years his junior, six feet, two inches of solid muscle. He bounded across the driveway to greet Jack. They first shook hands and then bear-hugged each other like the old army buddies that they were.

Walt pulled back and looked at Jack. "Damn, it's good to see you. Been, what, about three years since you were in Austin for some lawyer meeting?"

"Could have been four. I think I was practicing in Beaumont

then."

"Still carrying the cane. That injury at the barracks causing you more problems?"

"No worse, not any better. Every once in a while the damn knee gives out with no warning. I may have to put an artificial one in some day. Meantime, the cane does just fine. I've got a collection of about twenty of them in an old whiskey barrel beside the back door of my house. This one is my Bubba Stick. Picked it up at a service station a while back."

Walt's voice dropped to just above a whisper. "Follow me into the garden. There are some tables there. We can sit for a few minutes while I explain what's coming down."

They walked through the gate. Beyond it was a garden, obviously tended by loving hands. Cobblestone paths wound their way through fall plantings of Yellow Copper Canyon Daises, Fall Aster, Apricot-colored Angel's Trumpet, Mexican Marigold and the like. Walt led the way to a wrought iron table beside a fish pond with a fountain in the middle, spraying water from the mouth of a cherub's statue. The two friends settled into chairs, facing the pond.

"This is what the help call the little garden. In a minute we'll go around the house to the big garden and pool that fronts the ballroom. You know whose house this is?"

"No idea."

"Belongs to Oscar Hale. He and his brother, Edward, are the two richest men in Fort Worth. Their daddy was one of the old Texas wildcatters. The two brothers were worth a few hundred million each, mainly from some old oil holdings down in South Texas and out around Midland. Life must have been pretty good. Then it got better about ten years ago when the oil boys started fracking and horizontal drilling. Counting proven reserves still in the ground, word is they're worth eighty billion, well, maybe just a little less now that we have an oil glut."

"Edward still around?"

One of the servers in the kitchen had seen the two men and brought two bottles of water on a silver tray.

"Thanks…Sorry, I forgot your name."

"Sarah Jane, Walt. My pleasure. Let me know if you need anything else."

Walt took a sip from his bottle as Sarah Jane returned to the house. "Yeah. His legal residence is still in Fort Worth, and I understand he and his wife vote in this precinct, only they really live in New York City. He always kept an apartment there. When the oil money started gushing, he upgraded to a twenty room penthouse that I hear overlooks Central Park. He's big in the arts scene up there, opera, ballet, you name it. He's also building the Hale Museum of Fine Art here in Fort Worth."

Jack nodded his head. "Okay, I know who you're talking about. My girlfriend is thrilled about another museum in Fort Worth. She's into that kind of thing. When I moved here, she took me to every damn one of them. The western art in the Amon Carter museum was really all that interested me. So, the Hales play with the big boys, and the governor's coming. From what I read, Governor Lardner travels all over the world. Never seems to have a problem. What's the big deal here?"

"Fundraiser. One of those damn PACs, Super PACs, Leadership PACs, dark PACs. I can't keep up with all of them. Far as I'm concerned, they're just ways for the super-rich to buy themselves a politician. Both parties have so many, nobody can keep track. The one tomorrow night is a 501 (c)(4), something like that. Name is Stepper Official Strategies, SOS for short. It's what they call a dark money organization. It can even take unlimited money from any damn billionaire, even from big corporations. Lardner is the keynote speaker, only the money doesn't go directly to him. There's a guy named Kevin O'Connell who runs SOS and its sister Stepper PAC. It's all hush-hush. O'Connell doesn't even have to disclose who contributes. That kind of lid on who contributes makes those big corporations and billionaires very happy. With another presidential election just over the horizon, I hear he's expecting pledges in excess of a hundred million tomorrow."

"So," Jack said, "must be that you've got a few of those new oil billionaires coming."

Walt nodded. "Guest list of two hundred and fifty."

"What's your security?"

"I'm the team leader of five detail members. Technically, I'm called the lead advance, but I call all the shots. You've seen they have a few rent-a-cops. And three off duty Fort Worth officers are lined up. Pretty standard for an event like this."

"You expecting trouble?"

"No, but there will be a lot of politicians here along with all these rich folks, even a United States Senator. Just being cautious."

"What do you want from me?"

"Another pair of eyes to make sure I haven't missed anything. You had an eye for spotting problems in Desert Storm. Remember that sniper on the road to Dhahran? Since you're living in Fort Worth, I wanted you to take a look-see. Let's head over to the ballroom."

The two men walked through the garden and turned the corner of the house. Jack now understood why where they had been sitting was called the little garden. The one they walked through was four times the size of the other with an Olympic size pool in the middle and a waterfall cascading from one end. Ten double French doors were open to the autumn air as people swarmed inside and out to make ready for the party. Jack pointed to the wall. "You see the problem there, don't you?"

"Yeah. Easy to climb. I'll have one of the security guards out here all evening. And, I have given orders that these doors are to remain locked. You know what's beyond the wall?"

Jack turned around slowly to get his bearings. "Yeah. Woods on the other side, some type of nature preserve. Shady Oaks Country Club is on down the hill."

Walt motioned Jack into the ballroom. Jack surveyed it for a moment. He estimated it was a hundred by forty feet. Carpenters were constructing a stage at the end farthest away from the main house, right in front of the ballroom delivery entrance. On the other end there were three double doors that permitted entry through a screened and covered breezeway from the house. A second floor balcony surrounded the ballroom, displaying what Jack presumed were very expensive paintings. Even from the main level he recognized a Rembrandt, a Picasso and several Remington and Russell western classics. He figured that Colby, his girlfriend, could probably have named most of the rest without a program.

"You going to be able to secure the balcony? I'm sure that Hale would like to show off his collection, but I'd recommend against it."

"I've made that request. That's all I can do."

Jack studied the four sides of the balcony, the doors and the giant windows. "Big room but a helluva lot of people. I'd put some of your folks up on the balcony. I guess you'll be with the governor up on the stage once things kick off."

"Yeah, me and two of my detail. I'll have one more at the back of the room."

"Thought you said you had five?"

"You're right, only we always leave the limo driver out by the governor's Suburban. It and the follow car will be parked just out the delivery entrance behind the stage. And there's one more thing. This is a Halloween fundraiser. Everyone is required to come in costume. Masks are encouraged. O'Connell wants to emphasize that no one has to reveal himself or herself after showing credentials and the invitation at the front door."

Jack stared at Walt, not sure what to say at first. "Shit, Walt. Everybody in Halloween costumes with, I presume, fake guns and knives and swords. Your metal detectors will be working overtime at the door."

Walt shook his head. "No metal detectors. Governor's a strong right-to-carry guy. He even demanded that people with a permit can carry their guns into the state capitol a while back. Someone has a permit, he wants them to know that guns are okay around him. Hell, he'll even be armed himself. I gotta tell you, the whole set-up has me a little spooked." He smiled sheepishly. "No pun intended."

"It's Hale's house. Couldn't he overrule the governor?"

"Could, but won't. He believes in the Second Amendment just as much as the governor. He is going to permit security at the entrance to ask if a guest has a concealed handgun. That's it. We can write down a name, but can't even ask to see the weapon."

Jack grabbed a chair from a worker who was wheeling a stack by the two men and sat in the middle of the ballroom, letting it all sink in. "Look, I'm not saying anything is going to happen. Probably everything will go off like clockwork, but you're looking at potential trouble. Did you try to talk the governor out of attending? Couldn't you have him on closed circuit on a big screen?"

"I tried. He and his staff wouldn't hear of it. Staff said there would be too many big money boys here. He needs to shake their hands in person. It's one of the most frustrating parts of this job. I get into arguments all the time with his staff about the risks he's exposing himself to. Waste of time. Security always loses to politics. Hell, he's even wearing a Lone Ranger outfit and carrying six-shooters on a belt around his waist. And he's making all of us wear masks and six shooters, too. They're all real, even the governor's. I've told the detail to still carry their Sigs in shoulder holsters just for good measure. I've got an extra mask. You want to attend?"

"Hell, no." Jack shook his head. "We plaintiff lawyers are Democrats. I wouldn't be caught dead around your governor and all those fat cat Republicans. Give me a call in a couple of days and let me know how it went."

TWO

The young woman with the mane of black hair left the convenience store on the edge of Pecos, Texas, hollering, "I'll open at seven in the morning." She was dressed in a form-fitting yellow T-shirt, Wranglers and Nike running shoes. The logo on the T-shirt said, *Don't Mess With A Texas Woman.*

She walked to a dust-covered pickup and was stopped by a lean man, wearing a pearl-button cowboy shirt, jeans and boots. "Hey there, Miriam. How you doing?" His name was Johnson and he managed to stop by the store for something almost every day when it was her quitting time. "Why don't you let me buy you a beer before you head out to the compound?"

"Thanks, Jeb, but my dad called and is waiting for me. Maybe some other time." She smiled, climbed into her truck and started the engine. Next she tuned the radio to a country station and was pleased to find they were playing songs by Lukas Nelson, one of Willie's offspring who was developing a name as a country rock singer. She adjusted the volume and pulled out of the driveway, heading her pickup north on U.S. 285. There was nothing visually appealing about her commute. The terrain was flat desert with a few barely discernable low hills. It was covered with a sparse population of shrubs, range grasses, cacti and an occasional mesquite tree that managed to survive with virtually no water.

When she turned right onto Ranch Road 302, and passed over the county line into Loving County, she was reminded why her father had chosen this desolate corner of the world to establish the compound. The sign at the county line announced Loving County and proclaimed it to be the least populated county in the country. Only eighty-two hardy souls lived in 677 square miles. Of course, that didn't count those who lived in the compound. They wouldn't allow census takers past the front gate. If they had, the population might have swelled to around one hundred and thirty.

When she neared the Pecos River, she turned onto a dirt road and was faced with six foot barb wire fencing and a locked gate. Above the gate was a wooden sign, proclaiming it was the home of THE ALAMO DEFENDERS. Beside the gate, wired to the fence, was another, warning, TRESPASSERS WILL BE KILLED! On a pole to the right of the gate was a flag with a black star, an old cannon and the motto, *Come and Take It*, a copy of the banner made famous in one of the first battles of the Texas Revolution at Gonzales.

Miriam Van Zandt dropped to the ground from her pickup, walked to the gate and twirled the combination lock until it clicked open. She pushed the gate open, climbed back into her pickup and drove through, stopping on the other side to shut and lock it. About a hundred yards past the gate were the beginnings of a replica of the Alamo. Years before, her father and other defenders had built the façade, complete with four Spanish-style pillars, a large window over the main door, and flanked by four arched windows. They completed the signature scalloped roof line and abandoned the project in the heat of one summer, promising each other every year that they would complete it.

Down the road was a shooting range, suitable for a small army post. Across from the range were a three level ropes course and a shed where weights of various sizes were scattered among benches on a concrete floor in the shade. All were well maintained and obviously regularly used. As Miriam approached the Pecos River, she saw her father's double-wide with multiple single and double-wide trailers positioned haphazardly within a hundred yards of her father's trailer. Her own single-wide sat over closer to the river under a lone scrub oak that managed to survive within a few yards of the Pecos. In the center of the compound was a building with a gabled tin roof and concrete block walls. Antennas of multiple shapes and sizes dotted the roof. A sign over the front porch stated it was the Town Hall. A small window unit whined and cried as it struggled to keep the temperature inside below eighty-five.

Her father was Richard Van Zandt, who called himself Colonel. He had bought this barren hundred acres years before with the help of a Texas veterans land program. He also readily accepted a monthly disability payment for injuries he suffered in Vietnam. Otherwise, he wanted nothing to do with any government, local, state or federal. After he bought the land and moved his double-wide to it, he placed a much smaller sign beside the dirt road at its intersection with the highway, the first announcement that this was now the home of The Alamo Defenders. Over the years he had attracted a group of about forty men and women, along with a few children who were homeschooled at the Town Hall. Some with similar beliefs sought him out. Some drifted by in old pickups and meandered in, having no place better to go. And, there were others who were wanted by the law and saw The Alamo Defenders as a way to avoid arrest. The Colonel interviewed anyone who showed up at his doorstep. Few were turned away. Once he approved a new member, he arranged for a down payment on a used trailer in Pecos. When the fracking boom hit, most of the men had caught on with oil companies in the Permian basin.

As the small band of rebels grew, he called them together on Sunday morning, not for a prayer service but to rant about the ways that the government was invading lives of ordinary people, reinforcing his beliefs that the day would come when they would be attacked by the feds and they must be prepared to defend themselves like Colonel Travis and his small band of Texans did at the Alamo.

Miriam had been the product of a brief encounter with a bar-maid in Pecos. When she was born, her mother appeared at the compound, as Van Zandt now called it, handed the infant to him and left for California. At least, that's what she said. Van Zandt named her after his mother. Having no idea how to raise a daughter, he turned to two women who lived in the compound with their husbands. They showed him how to prepare formula, feed Miriam, change her diapers, and such. Once he caught on to the basics, he thanked them for their help and took over his daughter's care. Having no roadmap to raise a girl, he treated her as a boy. He put a .22 rifle in her hands when she was five and taught her to shoot, first at beer cans and later they ventured into the desert, shooting rats and other varmints. She was homeschooled to shield her from any liberal influences that might come from the outside. He was determined to teach her his ways. And he was successful. As Miriam grew older, her dad took her on hunting trips to the Davis Mountains to the west. Deer, bobcats, and an occasional mountain lion or bear were their prey. She could kill a deer running full speed at a hundred yards with one shot. In fact, she knew she would incur her father's wrath if it took a second. The ropes course was originally designed for Miriam. At first, it consisted of a tightrope strung two feet off the ground between two posts. As she grew so did the course.

Other than leaving the compound to work, the men were like Colonel Van Zandt; they, too, insisted on being left alone. They spent their free time at the firing range or on the ropes course. As the compound passed its thirtieth year, they had assembled an armory of weapons. Most of the defenders were crack shots with all of them. The ropes course and weight shed were used to hone their strength, coordination and agility. They expected that some government force would raid their compound, if not this year, then the next or the next. They would be ready, just like the defenders of the Alamo. *Come and Take It!*

Miriam spotted her father, rocking on the front porch of the Town Hall. A ceiling fan languidly revolved above him, doing little to cut the scorching air that permeated the compound and nearly every square inch of land within a hundred miles. A shotgun leaned on the wall beside him. Van Zandt was lean with blue eyes that peered through bushy, gray brows and a messy beard that covered his face and dangled down to his overalls. Periodically, he would lean over and spit tobacco juice into a Styrofoam cup. When he saw Miriam's pickup park in front of him, she had barely turned off the engine before he said, "Baby girl, come over here and sit. I think I have a job for you."

Miriam took a bottle of water from the center console and walked to her father where she bent over to give him a kiss on the cheek before settling into a rocker beside him. She knew what was coming. Since she was sixteen she had been one of the two primary sources of money for weapons. By then she could outshoot any man, take down any of the defenders in a fight by using her quickness and agility to overcome their strength, and run twice as far through the desert as her closest rival. Shortly after her sixteenth birthday, Van Zandt told her he had a proposition.

"You've been killing since you were five. There's not an animal alive that gets in your sights that you don't bring down with one shot. We need to be adding to our armory. Rifles and shotguns won't cut it anymore. I've been reading about the arsenal of weapons that the FBI, ATF and DEA have at their disposal. I've lectured to our defenders about what they did at Ruby Ridge.

The feds didn't hesitate to kill innocent civilians, even children. When they come for us, we might as well be using BB guns. I got a call from a woman in El Paso, someone I knew in my younger days. Not sure how she found my number, but she's been abused by her husband and wants him killed."

"Pa, there's got to be plenty of hit men in El Paso. Why can't she use one of them?"

"The husband's a rich lawyer. Represents a bunch of the drug dealers. She figures that if she goes to someone local, chances are good it'll get back to him. She wants someone who can sneak into town and get out without being noticed. It's worth a hundred grand to us. I'll set up an account for you in the Caymans. Your share is $25,000. They damn sure won't be expecting a sixteen year old girl. You have any problem with killing a man?"

Miriam gazed off into space while she considered the proposition. "I guess not, particularly if he's a wife beater. Besides, we need the money."

Van Zandt nodded. "I'm going to drive you to El Paso. Here's the plan."

Thereafter, once or twice, sometimes three times a year, Van Zandt would get a call from places as far away as California, Florida and New York. He never knew how the word spread, but he certainly didn't discourage it. And he turned down little jobs. If a caller wasn't willing to get into six figures, Van Zandt told the caller to look elsewhere. Once he negotiated the money, he chose Miriam or one other sharpshooter in the compound to handle the contract. Over the years Van Zandt had brainwashed his daughter into thinking that killing a human being was no different from killing an animal. Besides, she knew she was helping to fill their armory to aid in withstanding the attack that even she agreed was imminent.

As she sat beside her father, she already knew the topic of conversation. "What's up, Pa?"

"Had a call from an old army buddy of mine. You'll recall that he's sent me some jewelry from time to time that I sold to some of the cartel members. In fact I bought those diamond earrings for your last birthday from him. He's like us. Doesn't like what's happening in our country. Doesn't give a damn about the government or any of the politicians. He's been approached about doing some shooting in Fort Worth at a Republican fundraiser. Wants to know if we're interested in the job."

Miriam stared at the flat horizon where heat waves drifted above the landscape. "I'm listening."

"The target's a rich guy. We may want to create a little collateral damage as a decoy."

"What kind of fee did you quote?"

"$150,000. If you're interested, you get $50,000. I figure that we'll use the rest to keep stocking up on more ammo before Obama shuts down all the gun dealers. The day's shortly coming when we'll need all we can get our hands on."

"Why not one of the guys on this one?"

"Miriam, we've talked about this before. You're the best pistol shot we have. Anything you get in your sights within fifteen yards is done for. And this shindig is indoors. Figure you won't be more than ten, fifteen, twenty feet from the target. Besides, a woman's less likely to be noticed."

Miriam stood to face her father. "Look, old man, I know you're holding back. You say $150,000, and I can see it in your eyes. There's more. At least $200,000, maybe three. I want a hundred grand. You do that, and then we'll talk specifics."

Van Zandt was silent while he mulled through the numbers.

Finally, Miriam spoke. "Pa?"

"You have a deal. The money will be wired to my account in the Caymans ten days or so before Halloween. I'll wire your share as soon as the money hits. You can check it yourself before you take off for Fort Worth. Come over to my trailer and let's take a look at Google Earth. I've already zoomed in on this mansion."

Van Zandt's trailer was surprisingly neat. The kitchen was

spotless. Books on warfare lined a bookcase against one wall. His computer was open on the kitchen table.

"Here's the mansion, right at the end of a cul de sac. Place is walled, but it only looks to be about eight feet. I've seen you on our ropes course. Figure you can scale it. Some kind of wooded area is behind it. Once through the trees, you're on a golf course."

"Where's the party?"

"In a ballroom, right about here." Van Zandt pointed to the back of the house.

"Someone on the inside will supply you with a key to get in one of the patio doors. The governor is going to be there. So that means at least four members of his protective detail will be with him. As it gets closer, we'll be given more intel on cops, security guards and so forth."

Miriam nodded.

"And I almost forgot. This is going to be right before Halloween. Everyone is coming in costume, including you."

Miriam pushed a hand through her hair. "Well, I expect that I'll be attending as a cat burglar. I've got time to make my own costume. Now, tell me about the target."

After she finished talking with her father, Miriam walked to a single-wide that was on the edge of the cluster of trailers. A solidly built man about her age with bushy brown hair and matching trimmed beard was sitting at a picnic table under an awning extending from the trailer. His name was Manford Donley, called Manny by everyone. He sipped on a beer as he watched her approach. She bent over and kissed him before sitting on the bench opposite.

"Well," she said, "aren't you going to get me a beer?"

He grunted and walked to his trailer, returning with one in his hand. He handed it to her and returned to his side of the table.

"I've got a job to do in Fort Worth around Halloween. It's going to be my last. Pay's a hundred thousand. I figure with what we have saved, that ought to be about enough to buy that land outside of Alpine, build a house on it, buy some cattle and start a family. We can take my trailer to live in while the house is under construction. Pretty country down there. Ought to be a good place to raise some kids. You ready for it?"

Donley smiled. "Ready as I'll ever be. You told your pa?"

Miriam shook her head. "Not going to until we're ready to leave. He'll accuse me of abandoning him. He'll be right, but that's just how life is." She walked around the table and pulled him to stand in front of her. She nuzzled her breasts into him and pulled his mouth down to hers. Her tongue flicked between his teeth. He wrapped his hands around her butt and squeezed her closer. "What say, we go inside and start working on that family?" Manny asked.

"You're reading my mind, cowboy. Last one naked has to clean the kitchen tonight," she grinned as she turned to race up the steps to his trailer.

THREE

Jack showered and dressed quietly so as not to disturb Colby. Today he put on one of his lawyer suits, a red tie, and black shoes that he had shined the night before. Looking in the mirror, he had transformed himself into a distinguished attorney, six feet or so in height, just past fifty years old with brown hair brushed back to reveal a widow's peak. The Kirk Douglas cleft in his chin had been passed down for generations. He smiled when he thought that he had even passed it on to J. D., his son and potential All American tight end with TCU.

Jack leaned over the bed and lightly kissed Colby, still sleeping nude on her side of the bed. She stirred, pushed her auburn hair out of her face and pulled him to her as she blinked open her emerald green eyes. "My, you're a handsome looking lawyer. I like your blue eyes. Did you tell me you were going to court this morning?"

"Yeah," Jack smiled. "You just forgot. I've got a hearing for Ike

Irasmus about that rapper that stole his songs. First encounter with those Los Angeles lawyers that represent T-Buck. I'll call you afterwards to let you know how it went."

Colby smiled as her eyes slowly closed. Today, he would leave the pickup in the garage. If he happened to be spotted by the Los Angeles lawyers, he wanted to be seen in the gray Bentley.

Jack had grown up in Fort Worth and became rich as a plaintiff lawyer in Beaumont. Once he had a hundred million in the bank, he moved back to his hometown of Fort Worth when his son completed a four year hitch in Marines, including two tours in Iraq and Afghanistan, and announced that he was going to walk on to the Horned Frog football team. Jack soon discovered that kicking back with nothing to do was not fitting his type-A personality. So, he moved his armor-plated RV to a vacant lot on North Main and put a sign in the window that read, "Lawyer-No Fee." Before long, he was helping people as a pro bono lawyer, just like when he was representing folks who had been badly injured or lost a loved one because of the negligence of a corporation. The difference was he did it for free.

Ike was waiting in front of the RV when Jack pulled up. He was in his sixties with white hair and a neatly trimmed goatee. This morning he wore a freshly starched white shirt, a black bow-tie and spit-shined shoes. Jack lowered the passenger window.

"Morning, Ike. Hop in."

"Nice wheels. I thought you just owned that red pickup."

"That's my favorite, but I've got a few others. I'll show them to you sometime."

"I heard you calling that old truck Lucille. How come you gave your truck a name?"

"I've had that truck a long time. Just figured she was part of the family."

Ike nodded and buckled his seat belt. Jack pulled back out onto North Main to make the short drive to the courthouse complex on the bluff overlooking the Trinity River.

"Can I ask a question about your RV?"

"Fire away."

"You put all that armor on it to set it up out here in the barrio?"

"Naw. I had a big case down in the valley a few years back. It was going to take several months to try. Rather than rent office space and stay in a motel, I bought the RV to be my office and home. I was worried about drug violence along the border; so, I had that retractable armor installed. Worked well then and certainly protects the RV in this neighborhood, too."

"You ever charge folks for representing them?"

"Not any more. I made more money than I can ever spend. Call it payback or whatever you want. I like helping folks."

Ike shook his head. "Then, all I can say is thank you."

"That's all I ask." Jack smiled.

Jack and Ike were the first ones in the courtroom in the Tim Curry Criminal Justice Center. For some reason, Judge Jamison had temporarily moved there, something about asbestos in the old red courthouse. Jack didn't like the courtrooms in the Center. They had about as much personality as a hospital room. Jack told his client to take a seat at the table while he opened his briefcase and removed the file. A few minutes later a lawyer with silver hair, carefully coifed, and a matching mustache, entered, trailed by two younger partners and a paralegal. He set his briefcase on the opposite table and stepped over to introduce himself.

"Nicholas Whatley," he said, his hand extended.

"Jackson Bryant. Pleased to meet you. You figure you got enough fire power there?" Jack continued, motioning to the team behind Whatley. "I don't expect to take more than half an hour."

Whatley ignored the jab. "We came a long way. Just want to make sure we have all of our bases covered. I presume that this is Mr. Irasmus."

Ike nodded at the mention of his name. What followed was a small flurry of activity as the court reporter took her seat and the bailiff confirmed that all persons necessary for the hearing were present. He picked up the phone on his desk and advised the judge that everyone was ready to go. Almost immediately, he announced, "All rise. The 452nd District Court, the honorable Gladys Jamison presiding, is now in session."

A distinguished black woman, wearing a pearl necklace, a black robe and gold wire rimmed glasses took the bench. "Be seated." She smiled. "Now would any lawyer who expects to say something in this hearing, state your name and who you represent."

"Jackson Bryant, for the plaintiff, Ike Irasmus, Your Honor."

"Welcome back to my court, Mr. Bryant. I haven't seen you in a few months."

"My pleasure, Judge. And may I introduce Mr. Irasmus."

Ike rose and nodded at the judge.

"Your Honor, I'm Nicholas Whatley from Los Angeles, representing the defendant."

"And a welcome to you and your team, Mr. Whatley." Judge Jamison turned to Jack. "I understand we have an injunction arising out of the rights to a song. Not very often I've had to deal with singing in my courtroom. Let's move it along. Mr. Bryant, call your first witness."

"My only witness is Mr. Irasmus. Ike, please approach the bench so that you can be sworn." After he swore to tell the truth, Ike took the stand.

"You're Ike Irasmus?"

"Yes, sir."

Jack chose not to hold anything back. "Mr. Irasmus, how are you employed?"

Ike spoke softly. "I, I, uh, do some panhandling on North Main, me and my dog, Trousers. We live in a homeless shelter close by there. Not exactly what I expected to be doing in my old age."

"At one time were you a jazz musician and song writer in

New Orleans?"

Ike's face lit up. "Yes, sir. After Vietnam, I moved to New Orleans and within a couple of years started my own band. Wrote most of the music we played."

"You do well?"

"Probably too well. I got involved in drugs, got hooked on heroin." The witness hesitated.

"Go on."

"Killed a man in a fight over a woman. We were both high. I did it and pled guilty. Did twenty-five hard at Angola. Make no excuses for what I did. It was wrong and I apologized to everyone involved. Did my time. When I got out, I learned that my sister had gotten my trunk from my old apartment. Found all my old music and was starting over when Katrina hit. I was told to get on a bus and ended up here in Fort Worth. My sister said my trunk was washed away in the flooding. I was too old and too tired to start over again. So, I've been living in homeless shelters ever since."

"Did you write a song called *We Was Doing All Right*?"

"Yes, sir. Thirty-five, forty years ago."

"How did you learn that T-Buck had recorded it as a rap song, and it hit number one on the hip hop charts."

"Saw him on Jimmy Fallon. He was singing my song."

Jack flipped through a pile of papers and pulled two sheets from them. "T-Buck claims he wrote it, not you. Do you have a way to prove you're right?"

Ike smiled. "I could sing the entire song right now, if the judge would let me."

Judge Jackson looked over her glasses. "Let's not do that. Do you have some other way to prove you wrote it?"

Jack rose. "Judge, if I can approach, I'd like to hand the witness Plaintiff's Exhibit One. Can you identify that, Mr. Irasmus?"

Exhibit One was a faded and water stained copy of the song. Ike looked at the exhibit and turned to the second page. "This is one of the original copies of the sheet music. After you agreed to represent me, I got on the phone and started chasing down my old band members. Finally got hold of one who had this from forty years ago. It's in my writing, every word and every note. I signed and dated the bottom of both pages."

"Did you ever authorize T-Buck to record your song?"

"No, sir. He never even asked me."

Jack thought a moment and said, "Pass the witness."

Whatley rose. "Mr. Irasmus, just to make it clear, you're a convicted felon, pled guilty to murder, correct, sir?"

Ike glared at the lawyer. "I done told you that already. I did it and I'm sorry for it. I'll go to my grave with that weight on my shoulders."

"You expect the judge here to believe a murderer?"

"I'm telling the truth. That's long in my past. I, I wish I could change what happened, but I can't."

"So, you're telling the judge that you wrote one song and now you're trying to get rich off of what T-Buck has done."

"No, sir. In fact, I wrote all of the songs on that album your client made. My lawyer said that we should just take this a step at a time."

Whatley glanced back at his team who had blank expressions, knowing that there would be more to come.

Whatley looked the judge. "Your Honor, if the plaintiff has nothing more, I would like to offer an affidavit from my client. In it he swears that he wrote the lyrics and the music to *We Was Doing All Right*."

"I'll accept it as an exhibit, Mr. Whatley. Do you have anything else?"

"No, Judge. Defense rests."

Jack stood. "Judge, I have one more thing. It's a pauper's oath, confirming that Mr. Irasmus cannot put up a bond for the injunction we seek."

"I understand, Mr. Bryant. I heard his testimony about living in homeless shelters. You seek an injunction, requiring any future funds from this song be placed in the hands of a trustee until we can have a jury hear evidence. Am I correct?"

"Yes, ma'am."

"Mr. Whatley, I must say that it's a little disappointing that you show up here with two other lawyers and a paralegal; yet, your client apparently thought that this was not important enough for him to attend."

Whatley leaped to his feet. "Not so, Your Honor. He's on tour in Australia at the moment. I presumed that his affidavit would be sufficient."

The judge looked sternly at the lawyer. "Maybe in Los Angeles, but not in Fort Worth. I'm granting the motion. I'll appoint a trustee by tomorrow, probably a local bank. And, Mr. Whatley, when we go to trial, I suggest that your client should be present."

Jack thanked the judge and asked to be excused. He knew it was best to get out quickly when he had just won a major motion. He dropped his client off at the shelter and decided to call it a day. Driving back home, his cell chimed.

"Jack, Walt here. It's worse than I could have imagined. I drove over here to do a final advance check. Someone has put black crepe around the doors to the patio. Same crap is hanging from the ceiling. Streamers come down to about six feet from the floor. And on top of that, they put out cocktail tables, the four foot ones that people can stand around. I knew those were coming. But, they have black helium filled balloons attached to them. One of them popped while I was checking under the stage. Sounded just like a gunshot. I can already see drunks popping some of those balloons. Shit. This just doesn't feel right."

Jack turned into his driveway. He detected an unexpected note of alarm in his friend's voice. "Calm down. What do you want me to do?"

"I know you don't like Republicans, only I need you over here this evening."

"Why me?"

"I feel like we're understaffed. I could get Hale to bring in some more security guards, but you don't know what you're getting with one of those services. Can't get more off-duty cops on short notice. I trust you. Besides, you're a Tarrant County reserve deputy. No one can give me any flack for involving a deputy sheriff."

Jack shook his head as he turned into his driveway. "Okay. Since it's you, I'll be there. Just don't tell my Democrat friends."

"And, Jack, come armed."

Jack clicked off the phone and opened the automatic gate with his remote. He drove around the house and parked the Bentley in its usual slot in the garage. As he exited and lowered the garage door, he saw Colby, dressed in shorts, T-shirt, and running shoes, weeding her fall garden on the second level of the back lawn below the house. She rose and smiled.

"How'd the hearing go?" she asked as she raised her head for a kiss.

"Judge is requiring all future revenues from Ike's song to be placed in trust in a bank she will name by tomorrow. Good as we could get. Once that's done, I'm going to amend our petition to add the rest of the songs on that album. If it's okay with you, I'd like to invite Ike to a TCU football game before the season is over. He's heard me talking about J.D. He's really a decent man. I'd like to get him out of that world that revolves around the homeless shelter and his street corner. You'd like him."

Colby smiled her agreement. "Now, Fort Worth's best pro bono lawyer, what can I fix you for dinner?"

"Why would you limit it to Fort Worth? How about Texas or the whole country?"

"Then, maybe the best pro bono lawyer in the world, but answer my question."

"Actually, I'm going to have to grab something early and help out Walt Frazier over at this fundraiser in Westover Hills."

"I thought you said you wouldn't be caught dead among all of those Republicans."

"You heard correctly, but Walt is nervous about the event with costumes and revelers with guns. There's an edge in his voice that has me worried."

Colby stepped back. "Didn't you tell me that he has PTSD?"

"Had would be the operative word. He says it's been gone for years. After he returned to the states, he drank too much and stayed in his room at his parents' house. Hardly ever went out. He finally saw a psychiatrist who put him on anti-depressants and anxiety medications. That helped some. When he married, his wife had to put up with his nightmares. He told me he used to wake up, drenched in sweat, shouting, "Incoming." For a while he wished that he had died in that barracks. Walt gives Mary the credit for getting him through the PTSD. He claims he hasn't had a panic attack in years. He must be doing okay. He got a job as a cop in Wharton while he worked his way through college. And the DPS would have given him a battery of psychological tests to be working on the governor's detail.

Colby nodded her understanding. "Did you say guns at this party?"

"You heard me right. Governor's a right to carry man. If someone has an invite and a concealed handgun license, he can walk right in with his sidearm."

"Walt saved your life. Go help your friend. It's the least you can do. And make sure you have your own gun."

FOUR

Every afternoon when she got back to the compound, Miriam took her Glock 26 and several boxes of ammo to the range. Since most of the men now had found steady jobs in the oil patch, she usually had it to herself during the week. She was already a superior marksman, but still worked to improve her skills before each contract. Perfection was her goal. She started at ten yards and within a couple of days could put all eleven rounds in a cluster no more than three inches in diameter. Then she started moving back five yards each day. At twenty-five yards the cluster grew to twelve inches with a couple of rounds beyond that. After two weeks, she had moved to fifty yards and was hitting the mark, but there were no guarantees that any one shot could do anything more than wound a man. Still, she was satisfied since she did not expect to be more than fifteen or twenty feet or so from her target.

One evening she stopped at the Walmart in Pecos to buy

black cloth, sequins, and a pair of black slippers. She visited the optician shop at the front and was fitted with a pair of dark, almost black, contact lenses to conceal her distinctive sapphire blue eyes. Last, she bought the biggest fanny pack available, also black. After that, she spent evenings in her trailer, sewing her cat burglar costume. She sewed stockings to the slippers and fashioned them to look like calf-length boots, with an inch of sequins at the top. Next, she constructed a holster of cardboard, covered with black cloth and sequins to attach to her calf. All of this, including the gun and her mask, had to fit into the fanny pack for the mission.

Five days before the party, Miriam put her truck up on blocks at the compound and changed the oil. Various people walked by and inquired if she was taking a trip. She smiled and said that she was going to visit a sick friend. Four days before the party she confirmed that the money was in her Cayman account, loaded her pickup, kissed her father on the cheek and drove slowly out of the gate. When she got to Pecos, she pointed her truck east on I-20 for the long drive through West Texas to Fort Worth. She stopped twice for gas and twice at McDonald's before hitting the western edge of Fort Worth at about dusk.

She made her way over to Camp Bowie Blvd., a major four-lane street that ran almost to downtown. It only took her five minutes to spot a restaurant with a parking lot that overflowed with vehicles. She paused on a side street, looking for cameras or a security guard. Seeing none, she entered the parking lot and searched until she found a pickup with an empty space beside it. Checking once more for restaurant patrons and seeing none, she dropped from her truck with a set of screwdrivers. She moved to the front of the other pickup and took only the front license. She figured that someone was less likely to miss a front license and with the one still on the rear, it was less likely to attract the attention of a cop. In less than three minutes, she was gone.

She had already spotted a Hampton Inn on the internet just

off the freeway and not far from Westover Hills. She made her way through back streets to the inn, pausing under a street light to trade her back license for the one she had just stolen. When she got to the motel she looked for cameras. At the entrance there was only one; so she turned under the port-cochere so that the camera could record only the stolen license. Having done several similar missions, she knew to pay cash for four nights and, of course, used a fake driver's license for identification. She also put the new license number on the registration. Once on her floor, she stopped to get a Diet Coke from the machine and went to her room where she turned the air conditioning on high and drank the Coke with a protein bar for dinner. Then she was asleep.

The next morning Van Zandt read the *Fort Worth Star Telegram* while she enjoyed the inn's complimentary breakfast. There was nothing about the upcoming party, which didn't surprise her since she presumed that a bunch of Republican fat cats wouldn't want publicity. After breakfast, she checked her GPS and within five minutes was at the edge of Westover Hills. The first thing she noted was that the community had its own police force. That told her that she could not wander the streets forever without someone noting an old pickup without lawn tools or something similar in the ritzy neighborhood. Having a good satellite image of the area and a GPS, she located the mansion at the end of the cul de sac. She paused at the driveway and took pictures with her cell phone when she peered through the archway and down the driveway to the back. Beyond the driveway, she could make out the woods behind the house. Slowly turning in the cul de sac, she started driving the surrounding streets, memorizing their complicated paths as best she could since they seemed to twist and turn for no apparent reason. She amused herself by being the sole judge for best Halloween decorations. She had been in the neighborhood about a half hour when she passed a patrol car. She waved and smiled and then elected to leave the area, at least until late afternoon when there would almost surely be a shift change.

Next she drove to Roaring Springs Road and followed it to the entrance to Shady Oaks Country Club. She told the lady at the guard booth that she was applying for a job in maintenance and was waved through. She drove the parking lots, noting surveillance cameras and parked to study the fairways. Concluding that she could not leave her truck in the club parking lot, she left and continued on Roaring Springs until she found herself on Alta Mere where she saw Ridgmar Mall in the distance. Miriam circled the mall several times, locating most of the cameras. She finally decided that there was one back corner that would be near perfect to park her truck. She estimated it would be about a mile and a half jog back to Shady Oaks. From there she would figure out the fairways that would lead into the trees behind the mansion. She would test the route before sunset tonight and again tomorrow night when it was completely dark. For now she was ready for lunch and a nap. She chose Pulido's Mexican Restaurant, the original one on a street named after the historic restaurant near Fort Worth's rail yard, and arrived there in less than fifteen minutes.

Four hours later she was parked once again at the mall in the back corner. She circled the mall in a slow jog and turned onto Alta Mere. The traffic was a hassle until she made it to Roaring Springs. When she arrived at the country club, she paused in the parking lot of some condos that faced it and looked for guards. Seeing none, she crossed the street to the closest fairway. She moved in the direction of the mansion, dodging sprinklers as she went. When she got to the woods, she slowed to a walk and picked her way through trees, shrubs and bramble bushes. It was clearly a nature preserve where nothing was cut or cleared. Even in daylight it took her twenty minutes to find her way through the woods to the back wall of the mansion. The wall was of cut stone. She found a couple of cracks to use as hand holds and scaled a few feet until she could grab the top of the wall and hoist herself so that she could look over the top to confirm that she was in the right place. She was. Facing her across the patio and pool area was a ballroom with ten beveled glass French doors. No doubt this was the place. She took a minute to survey the surroundings, including spotting a potted plant next to the last door on the left where the person on the inside was supposed to leave a key. She didn't know who her accomplice was and wouldn't ask. All she wanted was for that person to leave the key, as planned.

FIVE

Jack showed up at five o'clock in his Bentley and was waved through the gate by the same guard who told him to park where he had yesterday. "Different outfit and ride," he noted. Jack had told Walt that his costume would be that of a plaintiff lawyer, dark suit, white shirt and tie, no mask. Walt met him as he exited his car.

"Thanks, Jack. I owe you."

"Naw. This is just a minor payback for what you did for me. What do you want me to do?"

"For now, just walk around the ballroom. Check the outside. They start letting people in at six-thirty. Then, I'd like you to man a post at the back of the ballroom. I'll have Wyatt Kamin from our detail back there, too. Just observe the guests when they come in. Radio me if you see anything that looks out of order."

Jack did has he was told and wandered the premises. He found the kitchen, talked to the cooks and observed the preparations.

He made his way through the house to the front entrance. It was a pleasant evening with no chance of rain; so, the security guards had set up tables on either side of the front sidewalk. He noted that each table had a clipboard with handwriting on the top sheet, *Concealed Handguns*. That was the closest thing to common sense he had seen. When costumed guests started lining up at the front, he made his way back to the ballroom, introduced himself to Wyatt and stood to the left of the doors while Wyatt took a similar position to the right.

Walt Frazier stood at the corner of the balcony behind the stage so that he could analyze the guests as they entered the ballroom. It was strange to be wearing a black mask and have a pearl-handled six shooter strapped to his waist. Somehow, it didn't fit with the business attire that was his normal evening wear when on the job. At least, he was not the only one feeling out of place. Jeff Foster and Ryan Fitzpatrick positioned themselves at other balcony vantage points, also wearing coats, ties, masks and six-shooters. At least he had drawn the line when the governor wanted them in full Lone Ranger attire. Earlier in the day they had escorted the governor and his wife to a suite on the second floor that Oscar Hale reserved for visiting dignitaries. The detail could observe the activities below until eight-thirty when they would go upstairs to escort the governor and his wife to the party.

At six-thirty the doors opened like floodgates and the guests streamed in. It was then that Walt realized that his nightmare was coming true. "Holy shit," he said into the microphone on his cuff. "Roger that," the others said almost simultaneously.

"Walt, how the hell are we supposed to do our jobs?" Wyatt asked.

"You just do the best you can with the cards you're dealt. Can't do anything more," Jack drawled.

The intent was that the Hale brothers and their wives would receive the guests as they entered. Oscar Hale was dressed as

Elvis. Ellen, his wife of thirty years, was wearing a comfortable witch outfit. Edward dressed as Captain America. His trophy third wife, Maria, filled a tigress costume very nicely. Once the doors were opened, many chose to forego the receiving line in favor of getting to the bars more quickly.

Walt watched the costumed guests fill the room and head to bars located against each wall. *Batman* entered, escorted by an obviously female *Robin*. Both had weapons strapped to their sides. *Darth Vader* followed, light sabre in hand. Through the other doors came the scarecrow and tin man along with Dorothy from *The Wizard of Oz*. No weapons on them unless the tin man's oil can contained pepper spray. A zombie sheriff followed, gun strapped to his side. "Jeff, keep an eye on that zombie sheriff. Ryan, here comes a terminator. He's yours for the evening. Wyatt, there's a female cop with a tiny halter top and short shorts. She's carrying a gun. Watch her."

"Walt, this is all we **need**," Ryan said. "Annie Oakley just arrived, rifle over her shoulder."

When Annie Oakley entered, she raised her gun in the air and fired off a shot that echoed through the ballroom. Walt froze for a moment, not sure what to do until he realized that the gun contained blanks. Still, he could feel his blood pressure climbing. "I've got her, Walt," Jack said. "She seems harmless. Talking about how she can outshoot any man or woman within a hundred miles." As the room continued to fill, Walt said, "I count six pirates, three male and three female, all with swords and a couple with blunderbusses. And there are five tigresses, three who can wear those skin-tight outfits and a couple who could have found more appropriate costumes. Then there's the *Incredible Hulk, Captain America, Spiderman,* the *Black Widow* and a usual assortment of naughty nurses and schoolmarms."

"Walt, I see a couple of army rangers. Remind you of your old days?"

"I prefer to forget those days. And, finally we have three or four Draculas and vampires, all with knives."

The room was overflowing. One evil clown, an unlighted cigarette dangling from his mouth, was trying to get a door to the
patio open. Walt called Al, one of the security guards on the first
floor. "Go tell that guy that the doors can only be opened with a
key. He's wasting his time."

As the crowd mingled, complimenting each other on their
costumes, waiters and waitresses drifted among them, serving food and drinks. Walt had arranged for several of the security guards to be part of the wait staff, available in the event
of a problem. When the bartenders broke out the champagne,
corks started exploding around the room. Every cork caused the
detail to pause a split second to determine if it was a shot or a
champagne bottle. Walt's eyes began to dart nervously around
the room. The members of the detail were trained and had been
on the job for at least ten years. When the governor arrived, they
knew that the split second to figure out whether a noise was a
bottle or a balloon or a gun could be a life or death moment. Shit!

By eight-thirty only one vampire had drunk too much and
was escorted by a guard to a den where he was served coffee and
observed for the remainder of the evening. Walt saw both Hale
couples making their way to the stage. As they walked, Maria
Hale turned to her sister-in-law and said, "Can you believe how
many women are in tigress costumes? If we ever do this again,
I'm going as the queen of the jungle."

The Hales were followed by a clown with a star on his chest, a
Power Ranger and *The Terminator*, also with stars on their chests.
Walt knew that the clown was Kevin O'Connell, the fundraiser-
in-chief. The other two were Tom Sinclair, the state's first black
Republican Senator, and Alberto Sanchez, a Congressman,
along with their wives. The stars indicated that they were
allowed on stage.

Walt surveyed the scene below him one more time and said,
"Okay, guys, it's time. Let's get Lone Wolf and Petal, that damsel

he rescued from the bar in Abilene. It's time for their grand entry." Lone Wolf and Petal were the detail's code names for the governor and his wife. "Jack, stay where you are. Radio me if you need to."

SIX

Robert C. Lardner was a born politician, which was good since
that was his sole occupation once he left the Air Force thirty years
before. Six feet tall and lean, he could have been a Hollywood
leading man. Instead, he married his college sweetheart, Susan,
and ran for the legislature, seeking to represent the rural area of
West Texas where he grew up. He won and was on his way, next
as Commissioner of Agriculture and then Lieutenant Governor
before climbing to the governor's office ten years before.

Along the way, he had become a multimillionaire although
he never held a job that paid more than $150,000 a year.
Knowledge was his key to fortune. As a young legislator and later
as Agriculture Commissioner, he could borrow, say, a couple of
hundred thousand dollars from a friendly banker who might
need a favor down the road, with interest a few percent, then
turn around and loan it to his campaign at twenty-five or thirty
percent. When questioned about the interest rate over the years,

he would laugh off the question and reply, "Have you looked at the interest on your credit card lately?"

As he climbed the political ladder and accumulated money, he also had access to where freeways were going or dams were being built. Once he was certain a freeway was going to be funded, he would send out his friends to buy land along the right of way, wait a few years and sell it for ten times what he paid. And, if a lake was going to be created in the water-starved state, it was manna from heaven. Once he was sure of its location, he and his colleagues would buy hundreds of acres in an area prime for a residential development and again, wait a few years before cashing in.

Lardner never did anything illegal. It was just the way that politicians in every state and, particularly, in Washington, supplemented their salary for public service to make the living they were certain they deserved. Nothing new about it, particularly in Texas where President Lyndon Johnson set the standard. He never held a job except as a small town school teacher and in politics; yet, he left a multi-million dollar estate when he died.

And Lardner understood money and politics. He had his own PACs that he could dip into for almost anything, even family vacations. Did it pass the smell test? Maybe not. But following the *Citizens United* decision from the United States Supreme Court no one cared. Politicians on every level had two missions: First was to advance as far up the political ladder as possible. The second was to use the system to make sure when he or she finally got shoved aside, millions were socked away in savings and the stock market. If, along the way, he or she did something good for the country, that was a bonus. It was probably no different from early in the country's history or even back to Roman times. Only, now there were so many more ways for a politician to make money. On top of that, judges and election officials looked the other way. Even on the Federal Election Commission, there were members who believed that the First Amendment's mandate about freedom of speech was so powerful that no law could restrict campaign contributions since money, in their eyes, equaled speech.

As fpr Lardner, he had not faced a serious opponent for ten years. Still, businessmen seeking access to him fed millions every year into his various PACs. He didn't need the money to be elected in a solid red state, but he could take those same millions and pass the money out among his conservative friends in other states, knowing that his largess would create a due bill that he could call in as he moved into position to run for president.

That, of course, led to Kevin O'Connell, the clown in charge of the fundraiser. O'Connell had not started life as a rich man either. He toiled behind the scenes in various Republican races over the years and had actually served in the White House when the last Republican was elected president. If there was one person anywhere who understood how the various PACs worked and how to move money from one to another to the advantage of his candidates and their causes, it was O'Connell. On top of that, he had practically memorized the *Citizens United* and *McCutcheon* opinions. He was comfortable being the man behind the throne, the master puppeteer, pulling the strings. Only the stakes were higher for him in this election cycle. His efforts had not produced big winners in the last three national elections. People were saying that he had lost his touch. When the Tea Party came along, he lifted his nose to the wind, sniffed which way it was blowing, and began raising funds for Tea Party candidates.

That was where the goals of Lardner and O'Connell merged into one. O'Connell saw the strength of the movement and wanted to take advantage of it. Lardner, on the other hand, was a true believer. He wanted everyone to carry a gun, wanted no woman to be allowed an abortion, hated Obamacare, wanted Christian values taught in schools, tougher immigration laws and fought for government to come from statehouses not Washington. He was a power to be reckoned with by anyone, Republican or Democrat.

He attended the event because he knew that big money would be in the room. He wasn't sure that he even needed O'Connell to raise money, and had expressed that opinion on more than one occasion. Still, tonight he was making nice with everyone. O'Connell was not quite as smitten with the ultra-right; only, he was a practical politician and figured at least for now the Tea Party was forging to the lead among Republicans. He needed to be in the front of that parade, baton in hand, like Professor Harold Hill in *The Music Man*.

Governor Lardner was dressed in a full Lone Ranger outfit: White hat, black mask, gray long-sleeve pullover shirt and matching pants, a bandana tied around his neck, black boots, and two six-shooters strapped to his waist. Susan played the part of a bar maid, looking like Miss Kitty in *Gunsmoke*, only with a red mask. When the doors opened, the detail allowed the governor to momentarily stand in the center, waving both hands to the crowd before they closed around him. Walt took point with Ryan and Jeff on either side of the couple. Walt looked at the crowd and suddenly felt tightness in his chest. His breath became rapid and shallow. *Am I having a heart attack?* He couldn't force his legs to move. Wyatt took his position at the back of the ballroom, nodding to Jack as he did so. Finally, Jeff said, "Walt, you okay? We need to get to the stage?"

Walt looked at Jeff and at the crowd as the panic attack dissipated. "Yeah, I'm good. Let's go."

They started moving deliberately through the crowd, having to pause frequently when the governor stopped to shake hands and make small talk with potential donors. Walt glanced at the balcony, pleased to see no one but the two Fort Worth policemen who had taken their place. The third was at the front, scanning the partiers as they entered. It took a half hour to traverse the one hundred feet of the ballroom. Walt's breathing had returned to normal. The three detail escorts scoured the room as the governor walked through the crowd, praying that they would get him and Petal through the freaks, unharmed. While Walt looked ahead, he also was watching the hands of everyone who came close to Lardner. After many years on the detail, he had learned that hand movement was the potential tell, not the eyes.

Miriam Van Zandt had taken a late afternoon nap. When she awakened, she made coffee in the percolator in her room. No food on her stomach until the mission was complete. She showered and laid out her costume and checked the Glock one last time. When she was satisfied, she dressed in the costume with a green T-shirt over the top. She slipped on her Nikes and placed the slippers, the sequin-topped stockings, her Glock, the holster and cat mask in her fanny pack. At the last minute she remembered a pocket knife that she also put into the holster. After she inserted the black contact lenses, she checked herself in the mirror and pronounced herself ready for the party. She thought through potential contingencies. She always had an extra sweatshirt and pants in the back seat. She checked everything off in her mind and left the room.

She drove to the side street beside the mall and duct taped the front and rear licenses just in case her truck was spotted on surveillance cameras. Maybe it was belt and suspenders, but she was successful in her avocation because she was meticulous. Satisfied with the job, she went to her chosen space. There were no cars parked within fifty yards. She strapped on the fanny pack and traced her steps in a slow jog down Alta Mere to Roaring Springs and through the fairways. She already knew that getting through the woods with the brushes and brambles was going to be difficult. Clouds filled the sky. With virtually no light, it was going to make the trek through the woods even more precarious. She waited until her eyes were as accustomed as possible to the dark and took her time walking to the back of the mansion. Once there, she identified a live oak tree she knew she could spot from the other side. She changed from her running shoes and removed the T-shirt, buckled on the holster with the Glock and the knife, and folded the shoes and shirt into the fanny pack which she placed at the base of the tree. Taking a last look around, she scaled the wall until she could peek over to get the lay of the land. One guard was sitting in a chair, texting someone. He would have to be eliminated. The cat burglar dropped silently to the other side and eased over the patio stones to the guard. She had her knife in her hand. With one slice across the neck, both his carotid arteries were severed. She walked to the last door on the left to retrieve the key from the pot. It wasn't there.

Van Zandt fished around in the dirt. Nothing. She moved to the next pot. Again nothing. She tried two doors. Both locked. She looked around the patio and considered aborting the mission. Only she didn't want to lose her hundred grand. It was to be her biggest payday and she could already picture that land above Alpine with kids playing in the front yard. And, she didn't want to disappoint her dad. She considered alternate plans and walked to the back of the ballroom to the delivery entrance she had spotted on the satellite photo. She rounded the corner and found it not only unlocked, but the doors were open. She straightened her shoulders as if she belonged there and approached the doorway.

"Ma'am, you can't be out here. All of the guests must remain indoors."

She turned to see a man in a dark suit, leaning up against a Suburban. He obviously thought she was a guest and hadn't noticed that she had come from the side of the house. She considered approaching him and again using her knife, but thought better of it. The element of surprise was gone.

"It was a little stuffy in there. I just stepped out to get a breath of air. I'm okay now."

She turned and walked through the doors. When she stepped into the ballroom, she looked as if she belonged. A mask with feline ears covered the top of her head and her nose. Black eyes peered through the mask. The contact lenses concealed their natural color. She wore what appeared to be calf-length sequined boots with her Glock 26 strapped to the right calf. She slipped through the crowd and took a position beside a bar in front of the third patio door, no more than twenty feet from the microphone in the center of the stage.

Governor Lardner bounded up the stage steps, intending to convey the message that he was much younger than his sixty-four years. He shook hands with the Hale brothers, Kevin O'Connell, Senator Sinclair and Congressman Sanchez. After hugging each of their wives, he turned and raised both hands in the air when he approached the microphone. Walt discreetly took a place a few feet to the governor's right. Ryan was in a similar position on the left. Jeff, the body agent, stood directly behind the governor next to the curtains. Wyatt and Jack remained in the back of the room, on the lookout for the slightest awkward movement. Walt breathed a sigh of relief that they had made it through the crowd to the stage without incident.

When the governor raised his hands, the crowd roared, Annie Oakley fired her gun and several balloons were popped in greeting. When that happened, Walt suddenly no longer saw the Republicans, but, instead, the carnage at the barracks in Saudi Arabia. He heard the sound of the Scud whining through the air and then crashing through the ceiling. Bodies were everywhere; the roof collapsed, men were crying and screaming. "Incoming," he said under his breath. He turned to run when Jeff quietly approached and grabbed his elbow.

"Walt, are you all right?"

Walt blinked, looked at Jeff and Governor Lardner and then out to the audience of Republicans. "Yeah, I'm fine. Get back to your position."

Then he did what he would usually do when the governor was speaking. He surveyed the crowd, looking for anything out of the ordinary. As he did, he thought that everything was out of the ordinary. If there was an assassin somewhere out there, what kind of tell would he give in a sea of two hundred assorted freaks. Nothing in his training had prepared him for this. He spoke quietly into his microphone when the crowd started to settle. "Anything?"

He got a chorus of "nothing" from his detail and Jack.

Lardner motioned with his hands for quiet, and the crowd did as he requested. The other guests on stage moved a few feet to the rear to sit on high-backed, ornately carved stools made of Texas oak.

"My fellow Texans, fellow Republicans and fellow Tea Party members, first Susan and I want to thank Oscar Hale for hosting this event and thank Oscar and his lovely wife, Ellen, for sharing their home. We can consider this magnificent ballroom as one tent big enough for all of us."

That brought boos from the Tea Partiers. The barracks flashed before Walt who, this time, was able to blink the apparition away.

For now, Lardner chose to sidestep the gap that was growing between mainstream Republicans and the Tea Party. He hadn't given up on the idea of raising money from the mainstream Republicans. "I know that we can have honest differences of opinion, but we must all remain true to our core values. Consider Texas. Standing alone, our great state would have one of the largest and strongest economies in the world. Businesses are flocking to Texas, making our unemployment rate the envy of nearly every state in the union. No matter which wing of our party you're in, I know you want smaller government."

Cheers.

"No matter which wing of our party you're in, I know you want Washington to get the hell out of our lives."

Cheers.

Someone popped a balloon. Walt jolted and almost jumped in front of the governor before he realized what it was. He caught himself just in time and managed to avoid embarrassing Lardner.

"No matter which wing of our party you're in, I know you want to stop the flood of illegal immigrants streaming across the border from Mexico."

Cheers with more balloons popping. Sweat appeared on Walt's face. He wanted to wipe his brow but didn't know how to do so without showing his nervousness. From the back of the room Jack saw what was happening on stage. He was probably the only one in the room who knew that Walt had suffered from PTSD. Still, all he could do was observe the stage and particularly Walt.

"Tonight we're going to take another step down the road to righting what is wrong with our country. In just a minute I'm going to turn this microphone over to Kevin O'Connell, the absolute best political strategist and fund raiser in the country. He's going to ask you to dig deep into your pockets, deeper than ever before. To win the White House along with the senate and congress, it's going to take billions of dollars. Let me repeat that. I said billions of dollars, more money than has ever been spent in national elections. In fact, we may find that we will have spent more in this one election cycle than in all of the national elections up to this one, combined. I'm confident that Kevin can get it done. Only, we need your help. The oil industry has once again been good to us and we need to spread that wealth around. You remember those old bumper stickers from the eighties, the ones that said, *Lord, just give us one more oil boom, and this time we promise not to piss it away.* Well, the Lord answered our prayer. Now, we've got to make sure that we spend our money wisely and seize control of our country. Here's Kevin O'Connell."

The crowd cheered their governor once more as O'Connell stepped to the microphone. Lardner moved slightly to his right but continued to stand with him. Walt maintained a posture almost like he was at attention with his arms hanging loosely at his side. The detail knew that a transition like this could be potential trouble. They scanned the costumed crowd and could not detect a problem.

Kevin O'Connell smiled through his clown face. "Wow, this

is great. Let me explain what is about to happen. You know that we're going to ask you for donations to a social welfare commitee. It's a very special one I set up under section 501 (c)(4) of the Revenue Code. It's called *Stepper Official Strategies, SOS for short.* The Stepper motto is *Washington is no hill for a stepper.*"

More cheers.

"And here's the most beautiful thing about it. All of your donations are confidential. No one and I mean no one will know who contributed and how much because it's for social welfare." He paused while the crowd laughed and clapped.

"It's so-called dark money. We can spend the money from it to support candidates, to oppose candidates, to support positions like pro-life or oppose positions like immigration. You contribute. Your corporation can contribute. As long as we don't coordinate with the candidates, it's all legal, thanks to our Supreme Court and decisions like *Citizens United* and *McCutcheon.* In fact, that's the reason we decided to have this fund raiser as a costume ball. You all get the symbolism. No one can look behind your mask to see who made a pledge. Further, I can assure you that the wait staff, valet attendants, cooks and security guards all had to pass through metal detectors and turn over any cell phones, iPads, cameras or other recording devices. The media has been barred from this room. In short, what happens in Westover Hills stays in Westover Hills. Now, I'm going to ask our host, Oscar Hale, to step forward to get things rolling."

Hale rose and moved to the microphone. He was a short man, a little dumpy with a fringe of white hair now covered by a black wig with long black sideburns, looking like an old Elvis, but he moved with the power of forty billion dollars. "Thank you, Kevin." He reached into a pocket in his sequined jacket. "We have a job to do. I want to do my part. I have here a check for ten million dollars from Oscar and Ellen Hale. Who's going to match it?"

The crowd roared, applauded and stomped their feet. Walt's

eyes flickered nervously around the room. At one point Jack saw him put his right hand on the butt of his pistol. Annie Oakley fired her gun into the air. That caused a short panic among the detail. Walt was about to pull his weapon until Wyatt said, "It's just Annie. No problem."

"We're having our staff members make their way through the crowd. They have a pad of pledge cards and are waving a gold Montblanc pen with the *Stepper* slogan. You sign the pledge card and you can keep the pen."

"Oscar, over here," a voice in the front hollered. It came from Darth Vader. "I'll match your ten million and raise you five million."

Oscar recognized the voice as coming from Tom Keith, another newly minted fracking billionaire. "Thanks, Tom. Who's next?"

Hands were raised so fast that the staff had trouble keeping up. A screen dropped from the ceiling and a spread sheet appeared. As each pledge was announced, the total changed. The number was approaching $100M when it happened.

SEVEN

Governor Lardner and Oscar Hale were standing together at the microphone. O'Connell had a hand-held microphone and was dancing from one side of the stage to the other as more and more people were signing pledge cards. His eyes were gleaming at the prospect of what he could do with the $100M.

Walt received a call, then spoke to Jack. "Jack, there's some kind of ruckus at the front of the house, a gate crasher who claims he forgot his invitation; only, he's not on the guest list. Our Fort Worth cop who was there has now moved up to the balcony. This guy is getting out of hand. Can you go up there and get the situation under control?"

"Roger, Walt. On my way." Jack nodded to Wyatt and disappeared through one of the doors to the house.

The cat burglar watched for her opportunity and seized it as the noise from the crowd became an almost constant roar of shouts and applause. She reached down to the holster on her right leg and pulled her gun. Before anyone could see what she was doing, she fired. Walt heard the shot. Time froze as he tried to determine if it was a popping champagne cork, a pop gun, balloon or the real thing. In that split second a bullet hit Lardner in the left lower chest. Walt spoke rapidly into his microphone. "Wolf's hit. Repeat, Wolf's hit. Everyone over here. Let's get him and Petal to safety." Then the scene changed suddenly, and he saw Jack lying on the floor in the barracks. He threw his body on top of the governor, hollering, "Incoming," only no one could hear him above the screams coming from the stage and the floor below.

"I see the shooter, Walt," Wyatt said. He pulled his revolver and aimed at Miriam. She ducked behind the bar as Wyatt fired several shots over her head before heading for the Suburban. The bartender fled his post. As calm an assassin as one could ever imagine, she watched for another opportunity. If someone had taken her pulse, it would have been no more than sixty. Her blood pressure would have been steady at 110/70. At first the revelers didn't know what had happened. Then, there was panic as some dove for the floor, some headed for the back doors of the ballroom and some tried unlocking the doors to the patio. Some of the guests had pulled weapons and were also shooting toward Miriam with most of their shots wildly missing the mark and even going in the direction of the stage. Someone in the crowd screamed, grazed by a stray bullet. Oscar Hale was standing at the microphone, trying to convince people to remain calm as the detail pulled the governor down. Ryan ran to the governor's wife and pulled her from her stool to the floor, dragging her across to the stage steps.

Jeff had to pull Walt from his position over the governor's body. "Walt, what the shit are you doing? We've got to get him out of here." Now Walt's mind returned to the reality of what had happened. He jumped to his feet and helped Jeff carry the unconscious body of the Governor down the three steps from the stage, shielding him with their own bodies. Ryan hurried Petal across the stage and down the steps, again making sure that he was between her and what he perceived was the line of fire.

Miriam rose behind the bar and fired twice more. The first hit Edward Hale in the head as he was attempting to follow the detail behind the governor. The second wounded Kevin O'Connell in the arm. Miriam smiled when she saw the results of the two shots. Just as planned. When the policemen in the balcony realized what was happening, they radioed for backup and started shooting in the direction of the bar. By then, Miriam was racing toward the delivery entrance, beating the governor's detail by several seconds. When she stepped out, she saw that the engine in the Suburban was now running and its lights were on. The same male voice shouted, "Stop, lady."

Blinded by the lights, she turned and fired at the sound of the voice, hoping to buy a few seconds. Instead, there was a shot in return that struck her in the right leg. She limped around the corner of the house as the voice said, "I saw her. She just went that way."

"I'll let Jack know. We've got to get the governor to the hospital."

Miriam realized she could no longer scale the wall without help. She pulled a patio chair over, climbed on it and hoisted herself over. When she dropped to the other side, pain shot through her right leg. She leaned against the wall for a moment, hoping the pain would subside and then knew that she had to move. She retrieved her fanny pack from below the tree. Blood was oozing from her leg. She used her knife to cut the stockings from the slippers and slit them long ways. Tying them together, she wrapped the bandage around her leg and tied it the best she could before putting her mask, gun holster, knife and slippers in the fanny pack. After tying on her running shoes, she started through the woods, realizing that the trip back to the truck was going to take much longer than she had planned. She could only hope that no one would spot her.

EIGHT

Wyatt had bolted out a door to the house and met them at the Suburban, pistol drawn. As they were leaving, Walt radioed Jack. "We've got the governor and his wife. He's been shot. Two others are down. We think the killer escaped over the patio wall. Best guess from Hal is it's a woman in a cat burglar outfit. Get back to the ballroom."

Jeff and Walt laid the governor across the back seat. They encouraged Susan to ride in the follow car. She refused, insisting that she would hold her husband's head in her lap. Walt called the Fort Worth Police and asked that the valet service be suspended. The scenes in the barracks were left behind, at least for the moment. Hal drove the Suburban with Walt beside him. Ryan and Wyatt jumped in the follow car. Like all detail members, Jeff was trained in first aid. He pulled the first aid kit from the back and, kneeling on the floor, started checking the governor. Both vehicles turned on lights and sirens as they made their way to the front of the house. Once on the street, they found most of it blocked. They jumped the curb and ran down the sidewalks and over shrubs to get to the next open street.

"Walt, he's losing a lot of blood. Pressure is 45 over 20. Heart is racing at 120 and respirations are rapid and shallow."

Walt called the emergency department at Harris Methodist Hospital to advise that the governor had a chest wound and re-lay the vital signs. As they hurried away, they got a report that Edward Hale was dead and Kevin O'Connell was wounded. Tears came to Walt's eyes as he heard the news. He was overwhelmed with the thought that he and his team had failed.

As part of their preparations, Walt had traced various routes from Westover Hills to Harris Methodist, evaluating the routes at different times of day. It was standard protocol which he had never had a reason to implement in the ten years he had worked on the detail. Not until now. The two vehicles were met at the emergency department by a physician and a nurse practitioner. The team placed Lardner on a gurney and wheeled him into a bay. The emergency physician was a young woman with brown hair and a very professional manner. Her name tag read *DeAnn Fisher, M. D.* She checked his vital signs again. "No real change since you called. He's lost a lot of blood. We need to get a central line and a peripheral. Natalie, get him typed and cross-matched. We're going to need at least five units of blood, maybe more. Get Frank Cisneros in here. I'm going to insert a chest tube." Cisneros had trained under the legendary Red Duke in Houston and was the best trauma surgeon on the hospital staff. "He's going to have his hands full. Meantime, as soon as we can, let's wheel him to imaging. We need a chest x-ray and CT of his chest and abdo-men. I suspect a collapsed lung and spleen injury. This is the gov-ernor, people. Let's move."

NINE

Returning to the ballroom, Jack's mind filtered through an on-slaught of ideas, discarding them until he settled on one. Joe Shannon was the Tarrant County District Attorney and a long-time friend. He pulled his cell and punched in a speed dial number.

"Joe, Bryant here. The governor's been shot at the Hale mansion in Westover Hills. Big fund raiser. Edward Hale is probably dead and some power broker is wounded."

"Yeah, I got an invite. Keep talking."

"Lardner's being taken to Harris Hospital right now. I'm here because one of the governor's detail, Walt Frazier, is an old army friend. Walt left me in charge. There are two hundred or so people milling around in costumes. We think the killer escaped over the back wall. What the hell should I do?"

"First, cut off the valet service. Next, lock down the place. We're going to need to know if others were involved."

"I'm on it."

"There may be some that will find a way out, but there will be a guest list. We'll track them down later. Hold on a minute. I'm hearing chatter on my police band." Joe paused a moment to listen. "Fort Worth cops, sheriff's deputies and state troopers are all on their way. Tell all those people to take off their masks. If they have guns, confiscate them. I'll have several CSI teams from the agencies bring kits to check for gunshot residue. Try to get everyone to calm down. Oh, and ambulances are also on the way for Hale and that other guy. I'll be there in twenty minutes."

"Wait, Joe. Make it three ambulances. There's a guest who may need help, too. One more thing. The killer is probably female. When she left here she was dressed as cat burglar. The governor's limo driver thinks he may have wounded her."

"Got it. I'll get patrol cars on Roaring Springs. The sheriff and Fort Worth Police both have canine units. I'll request them, too."

Jack radioed the city cops and the security guards, telling them the plan. Rather than fight his way through two hundred and fifty or three hundred people, he looped around the ballroom and came in the delivery entrance. Edward Hale was lying on the stage. His wife was sitting beside him, holding his hand and sobbing. Kevin O'Connell had been helped to a chair. Someone had wrapped a napkin around his arm, just above the elbow. He was pale, but conscious. Jack surveyed the turmoil before him and started toward the stage when he spotted the hand-held microphone that O'Connell had been using. Sirens shrieked in the background. Jack hoped they were ambulances. Hale was probably dead, but O'Connell needed attention.

Rather than taking the stage and risk more contamination of an evidence site, he climbed onto a chair. He tested the microphone and found it working. "All right. All right, now. Everyone listen up. I'm Jack Bryant, a Tarrant County deputy sheriff. I've just talked to Joe Shannon, the D. A. I'm instructed to give orders for now; so bear with me. First of all, everyone take off your masks. The party is over. This is now a crime scene."

Slowly, the guests did as they were told.

"Thanks. Now, I'm sorry to say that we have locked down this room and the mansion. No one is leaving until Mr. Shannon gives the okay." Jack paused to think. "We don't have any crime scene tape; so I want some of you men to start grabbing chairs and stools. We need a perimeter of about 30 feet around that bar where I'm told the shooter was all the way up to the stage." Several guests and waiters started moving chairs into position as Jack directed.

Rumbling came from the crowd. These were rich people, not accustomed to being told what to do or when to do it. Tom Sinclair spoke first. "Sir, I'm Senator Tom Sinclair. You have no reason to hold me. I will cooperate fully and will make myself available at any time."

"Yeah, that goes for me, too," Darth Vader said.

Others started chiming in with similar comments. Jack, saw that things were rapidly escalating out of control. "Everyone calm down. Edward Hale is probably dead. Governor Lardner is on his way to Harris Hospital in critical condition. I hope that all of you would understand that some of your time is vital right here and right now. If anyone attempts to leave, that person will be stopped and will go to the top of our suspect list."

"Well, could we at least still get some drinks?" Darth Vader asked. Jack could now see that he was a round-faced, bald man with sweat glistening on his forehead and bald pate. He resembled the *Wizard of Oz* when Toto pulled back the curtain.

Jack thought a minute and then nodded. "Let's get the bar open. I hope to have you all out of here in an hour."

Joe Shannon lived close-by and was there in fifteen minutes, at about the same time that various cops, deputies and DPS officers arrived. Shannon also decided to circle around and enter through the delivery entrance. He surveyed the scene. "Nice job, Jack."

"Thanks. Not exactly what I signed up for this evening, but I'm doing my best."

"I'll take it from here." Joe mounted the chair. "Attention, everyone. I'm Joe Shannon. If you don't know me, I'm the D. A. in this county. Here's what we're going to do. First, enjoy your drinks. I'll have various officers here any minute along with come CSI units. The CSI folks will be taking gunshot residue samples from every one of you. If you have a gun, we will have to confiscate it. Once that's done and we have your contact information, you're free to go. I've got enough teams coming that we should have you on your way in no more than an hour. I see some of the officers with clipboards coming through the doors now. Officers, if you'll pick a table and take a seat, I'll ask these good people to line up and give you contact information. As soon as the lab folks arrive, we'll do the GSR tests. Oh, I forgot one thing. If any of you test positive for GSR, I'm going to arrange for some of the anterooms to be used by detectives from the different agencies. You won't be able to leave until they give the okay. Sorry for the inconvenience."

About as soon as he was finished, Joe saw CSI details entering, test kits in hand. "Officers, if you'll coordinate with the CSI teams, we'll try to get these people out of here."

Joe stepped down from the chair to see that he was surrounded. Roger Culbertson, the Fort Worth Chief of Police, was joined by Randall Meacham, the Chief from the town of Westover Hills and Lance White, Tarrant County Sheriff. He greeted each of them before receiving a call from Colonel Max Burnside, the head of the Department of Public Safety. The governor's protective detail ultimately reported to him. "Joe, Max here."

"Evening, Max. I know you're aware of what happened."

"We'll be taking over. The governor's shot and Edward Hale is dead. I've got Rangers on the way. The DPS will handle it."

"I hear what you are saying, but I've got Roger Culbertson, Lance White and Randall Meacham here. I suspect they may have something to say about that. This is a big house. I'm going to leave a deputy sheriff in charge here. We'll go find a room where we can talk. We'll call you back in no more than fifteen minutes." Joe clicked off the phone. "Jack, you're in charge. I've got to find a place to have a high level meeting."

Joe led the heads of the agencies through the crowd from the ballroom into the house. Halfway toward the front he found a library that was empty. A table in the center of the room was surrounded by six chairs. He motioned for his entourage to follow him and shut the door. "Okay, if you would, please take a seat at the table. I'll get Colonel Burnside on my cell phone speaker." He punched a recall number. "Max, we're in a library. You're on a speaker. Westover Hills police department is in the ballroom, all six of them. Fort Worth Cops are showing up by the car load, deputy sheriffs, too. DPS is turning out in force. Crime scene teams are now on site."

"Joe, gentlemen, this happened on my watch. I don't blame my protective detail, but they have to bear some degree of responsibility. So, I want the DPS and Rangers to run this show. This is likely to turn into a statewide investigation. We've got the best crime lab in Texas in Austin. Our swat team is the best of the best. Besides, I'm required to have a Ranger team do an internal investigation since this is an officer involved shooting. No use duplicating effort."

"Colonel, I hear what you're saying, but I've got about every law enforcement agency around these parts right here already. Tell your Rangers they can come any time, but they're not in charge, not yet anyway. I'll be back in touch shortly." He clicked off his phone. And put it back in his pocket. You heard that. Colonel Burnside wants to be in charge."

"Bullshit. This is clearly an investigation that should be handled by my department," Culbertson said. He could already envision the multiple press conferences, garnering national media, as they tracked down the killer. He liked his current job but had a big ego and ambition to match it. Fort Worth was a wonderful mid-size city, but he certainly could picture himself as chief of police in Houston or Los Angeles, maybe even the Big Apple. "With all due respect to Randall, he's got a fine town police department but only has about a half a dozen officers. He would need to call on us, anyway."

"Just a damn minute, Roger," Meacham replied, his face turning red. "It's true we're small and elite. You forget that I retired after thirty years in Houston to take this job. There's no crime that I haven't investigated. Maybe you just ought to butt out of Westover Hills. I'll call you if I need help."

Lance White was Tarrant County's first black sheriff, a big man with a determined but easy manner. *Speak softly and carry a big stick* fit his demeanor perfectly. "You gentlemen forget that my department has jurisdiction over the entire county, including Westover Hills. We can conduct this investigation and track down whoever did this without calling on any outside force."

Shannon contemplated what he had just heard. Four dogs fighting over a king sized bone. It wasn't the first time he had witnessed jurisdictional battles, but never one of this magnitude, involving the shooting of a governor and the death of a billionaire. "Gentlemen, excuse me a moment. I need to make a call." He stepped out into the hallway and hoped that Jack Bryant could hear his cell over the thunderstorm of noise in the ballroom.

"What's up, Joe?"

"Jack, can you come into the house? Follow the big hall to the third door on the right. I'll be in there with Sheriff White, Chief Culbertson and Chief Meacham."

Shannon returned to the library. The three men were still bickering about who could do the best job. There was a knock at the door and Jack entered, cane in hand.

"I'm sure that you folks either know or have heard of Jack Bryant. Lance, in case you have forgotten, I asked you to appoint him a reserve deputy a couple of years ago. He is the one that single-handedly broke the Dead Peasants serial killings and put Beau Quillen on death row. I have just appointed him special prosecutor on this case. From this point forward, he'll make all the command decisions. Jack, you want to have a seat and discuss how you and I concluded that we can use the combined efforts and resources of all of these departments."

Jack looked at his friend, wondering why he had not been consulted on this appointment, but decided to talk to him in private at a later time. He didn't want to embarrass Joe by declining the request. As far as conclusions, he had none. "Joe, if you don't mind, I'll just take a seat and let you outline where we go from here."

TEN

It had taken Miriam Van Zandt nearly thirty minutes to limp through the woods. Twice she had to lean against a tree to take the pressure from her right leg and relieve the pain. She emerged from the woods to a fairway that led in the direction of the clubhouse. As she surveyed the scene in front of her, she could see a patrol car on Roaring Springs. Both the driver and passenger were operating powerful search lights that illuminated about two hundred yards. She dropped to a prone position when the light on the passenger side swept the fairway in front of her and bounced off the trees. When the patrol car had disappeared around a bend in the road, she stayed on the ground to see if another would be close behind.

As she did so, she pressed the bandage on her leg, hoping to reduce the flow of blood. Of course, she had to change her plan. They now knew the shooter was a woman, dressed in a cat burglar outfit. They also may have guessed that she was wounded.

The idea of jogging in the open back to her car was not only physically impossible, but trying to walk along the road was out of the question. Then another problem hit her. Dogs. It had taken her long enough to get through the woods that they could have dogs on the scene any minute.

She forced herself to her feet and started moving across the fairway to the trees that lined it. Close to the trees, she stumbled onto a creek, placed there long ago by the golf course architect as a water hazard. The creek appeared to line the fairway all the way to a green in front of the clubhouse. Having no way to know how deep it was, she stepped into it, ignoring the chilly water that late October had brought. Fortunately, she found it to be only a few inches deep where she entered. As she made her way toward the clubhouse, twice she stepped into holes and found herself in water up to her waist. Each time, she discovered that the cold water eased the pain in her leg. She paused to allow it to relieve the pain before slogging on. Nearing the clubhouse, she heard dogs barking up the hill, probably behind the mansion. They would surely pick up her scent from the area around the oak tree. With that thought she forced herself to hurry as the creek crossed in front of the green. Once past the green, it flowed into a culvert. Her only choice was to cross the street and pray the creek continued there. Hopefully, the cold water and her wet pants would have stemmed the flow of blood. On the other side, she was relieved to find that the culvert opened onto another creek lining a different fairway. She pushed as hard as she could down it for ten minutes until it flowed into a natural stream, several feet across and flowing to her left. She stepped into it and found herself up to her chest. She started breast stroking with the current, pleased to take pressure from her right leg. The creek flowed around the country club and along Alta Mere. Periodically, she paused to check the heavily traveled street, but saw no sign of patrol cars. And the sound of dogs had disappeared.

The creek ended in a marsh about a hundred yards from the

Ridgmar parking lot. She got to her feet and slogged through the mud to the perimeter of the lot. After checking for patrol cars, cameras and security guards, she hobbled around the outside of the shopping center to her truck. When she arrived at her truck, she satisfied herself that it had not been disturbed. She dumped her gear behind the seat and drove to the secluded side street with no street lights. She grabbed her sweats from the back and, knowing she could not possibly wiggle out of her pants while seated, she opened the door and stripped them off. She cut her soaking T-shirt into ribbons and wrapped the ribbons around her leg before donning her sweatpants and shirt. She stripped the duct tape from her license plates and climbed back into the truck. Now she had to find a twenty-four hour drug store.

ELEVEN

Shannon nodded at Jack and took a sip from a bottle of water. "Randall, as soon as we clear the partiers, I want your men to secure the ballroom, the front of the house and the patio. In case, you don't know it, we found a dead security guard out there. Roger, have your CSI team search for slugs. People think the killer fired several times. We ought to find two or three in the stage or walls behind the stage."

"Joe," Jack said, "I was told that she, if it's a woman, was shooting from the vicinity of the bar over by the patio, the one close to the stage. Should be some casings around there."

"Then, at first light, Roger, I want a team to search the grounds, particularly the patio where that guard was killed." Knowing he had to split up the assignments, he turned to Lance. "Sheriff, give me a half a dozen teams of two men in the woods behind the house at dawn. Tell them to be damn careful where they step. We might get lucky and find a footprint. I'll tell Max to do his usual internal investigation."

"I'm going to head over to the hospital, check the status of the governor and do some preliminary interviews with Walt and his detail," Jack said. He reached into his pocket and extracted three business cards which he handed to the two chiefs and the sheriff. "Joe, we know we'll need to interview Edward's wife and Oscar and his wife as well as O'Connell and the others on the stage. You or I should do that, but not until after the funeral. We'll make a decision about Lardner and his wife later. I suggest that we meet in your office about four tomorrow afternoon for updates. Unless anyone has anything else, I'm headed to the hospital. Call me on my cell at any time, day or night."

Jack parked in the hospital garage and made his way to the front desk. "I'm Deputy Jack Bryant with Tarrant County. Can you tell me what floor the governor is on?"

The lady behind the desk looked at him. "I can tell you, but you won't be able to get past the elevators."

"Appreciate that, ma'am. If you'll just give me the floor, I'll take it from there."

"Ninth. It's the executive floor."

Jack nodded, made his way to the elevators, exited on nine and then understood what she meant by it being the executive floor. The reception area looked more like that of a Ritz Carlton than a hospital. Several sitting areas with leather and oak furniture dotted a light blue carpet. The sitting areas were filled with reporters, observing the comings and goings from the elevators and corridors. No cameras were allowed. A breakfast buffet was set up on a credenza under a window looking out toward downtown. Jack glanced at his watch and discovered that it was nearly six o'clock. He assumed the governor was now out of the PACU. Two corridors led to patient rooms. It wasn't difficult to determine which one had the governor. A large, brown desk has been pulled in front of it. Behind the desk sat a tall, raw-boned, muscular man. His Stetson was on the desk to his side. He was dressed in jeans and a Western shirt. A nametag identified him as Sergeant Willis. The most prominent feature was his badge. It was circular and made from a Mexican five Peso silver coin. The lone star of Texas was cut from the middle. Above it was *DEPT. OF PUBLIC SAFETY.* Below the star was the inscription, *TEXAS RANGER.* The inscription in the middle of the star identified the man wearing it as a sergeant in the Texas Rangers, one of the most elite and respected law enforcement agencies in the country. He looked up at Jack and asked in a deep voice, made more so by probably 30 years of cigarettes, "What can I do for you?"

"Morning, Sergeant. Name's Jackson Bryant, I'm a reserve deputy with Tarrant County. Can I ask if Walt Frazier is down the hall with the governor?"

"He is, Mr. Bryant, but only family, DPS, and a few Fort Worth cops are allowed down there. Wait a minute. You said Jackson Bryant. I think I just got a text about you." He picked up his cell from the desk and studied it for a moment. "You're the special prosecutor. Joe didn't waste any time getting you involved. I figured he'd just let us Rangers take it on. Let me see some creds, and you can go on back."

Jack pulled a laminated card from his wallet, confirming his name and status with the sheriff's department. The ranger motioned down the corridor.

At the end of the corridor he saw several men. Five were dressed in suits with their ties now hanging at half-mast. Another ranger and two police officers stood close by. As Jack approached, one of the officers stepped in the middle of the hall to block the way.

"He's okay," Walt said. "In fact, he's now in charge of this investigation. Name's Jack Bryant." Walt escorted Jack around the officers to where his detail was guarding the door to the governor's room. Two stood beside the door and two sat in chairs on the opposite wall. All of them had blood shot eyes and were desperately in need of sleep.

"How's he doing?" Jack asked, nodding toward the closed door.

Walt shook his head. "They're not briefing us. I think it's still touch and go. They operated for nearly four hours. Took out his spleen and had to repair some major damage to his left lung. Fortunately, the bullet missed his heart.

"Mrs. Lardner?"

"She wasn't hit. She hasn't left his room since the surgery."

"What about you and your men?" Jack asked.

Walt rubbed his face with both hands before speaking. "I screwed up. I should have taken that bullet. That's my job."

"Whoa, just a minute. You didn't create that scene. You were trying to monitor two hundred or so people in crazy costumes. What the hell do you think you could have done different?"

"I can answer that, Mr. Bryant." It was Wyatt Kamin. "There wasn't a goddamn thing we could have done differently, except to lock Wolf in his room until the party was over. We followed protocol to the letter."

"What about Edward Hale?"

Walt hesitated and a concerned look flickered across his face before he spoke. "He, he wasn't our responsibility. Our job was to get Wolf and Petal out of harm's way."

While they were talking, Sergeant Willis walked up to them, briefcase in hand. "Gentlemen, you know the protocol in this situation. I need to confiscate your guns for testing. I've got replacements in the case here. We have more members of the protective detail on their way from Austin to relieve you. Should be here any time now. Until then, you'll just have to hang in here. Coffee's on the house." He allowed a slight grin to show on his face.

The five men unbuckled their six-shooters and handed over their Sig Sauer P229s. Two of them reached for their ankles to retrieve Sig Sauer 936s.

"I'll also have a D.P.S. lab guy here shortly to check for

gunshot residue," Sergeant Willis continued.

Wyatt raised his hands, palms up. "You'll find it on me. I fired several rounds. Unfortunately, I don't think that I hit the bastard."

Jack hung around to try to get whatever information he could extract from Walt and his detail. Walt had frozen out the rest of the world and moved to a straight back chair where he folded his arms and stared at the governor's door, as if trying to block everything around him out. Jack's attempts at conversation were met with grunts and an occasional 'yes' or 'no'. For Walt, it was now sinking in. The taking of their guns was just the first step of a long, frustrating and embarrassing process.

TWELVE

Miriam tried without success to hide her limp as she entered the drug store on Camp Bowie. She smiled at the woman who greeted her and declined her offer of help. She took a blue basket from the stack by the door and went to the back where the pharmacy was now closed and found iodine, large bandages, an ace bandage, and ibuprofen. In the grocery area she added two rolls of paper towels, a package of cloth hand towels, a propane fire starter and a small box of garbage bags. She made her way to the women's hair section and chose bleach and red dye. Her last stop was for a bottle of red wine. She didn't need a drink, but thought that it would help deaden the pain she was about to inflict on herself.

She made her way to the front counter and started taking the purchases from the basket. The clerk stopped her when she reached for the wine.

"I'm sorry, ma'am, but we can't sell wine after nine o'clock.

State law."

Miriam paused and thought. "Point me toward the cold and cough section. I forgot something."

"Back toward the pharmacy, aisle eight. I'll return the wine."

She sized up the cough syrups, finding one that had ten percent alcohol. That would be twenty proof, a better pain killer than red wine. She returned to the front and checked out, paying cash and asking the clerk for several extra bags.

She returned to her truck, placed her purchases on the passenger seat and shut her eyes for a few minutes, hoping the pain would diminish, before starting the engine. Backing out, she looked for cameras and saw none. In ten minutes she was pulling into the Hampton Inn parking lot. By now, she knew where the cameras were and knew to park at the side where she could enter with her card and not have to pass the front desk. Knowing that she looked like she had barely survived a hurricane, she hoped to see no one at the elevator. She was lucky. The elevator was there as soon as she punched the button. Better yet, no one saw her. She exited on her floor, purchases in hand. along with the holster with her gun and knife. The remainder of her gear could remain in the locked truck. She slid the card into the slot and watched as the green light invited her to enter. Inside, she dropped her purchases on the bathroom counter. She knew she had lost blood and needed to rest; only she couldn't risk bleeding on the bed. Instead, she sat on the toilet, and leaned back. Somehow, she dozed and woke with a start since she knew she had to be out before dawn. She glanced at her Timex Triathlon: 12:30 a.m.

First, she opened the cough syrup and downed as much as she could without gagging. It would take her several minutes to make the other preparations. Hopefully, the alcohol in the medicine would have some effect. Next, she twisted off the top of the ibuprofen bottle and swallowed eight pills with water. She stripped out of her sweats and placed them in one of the drugstore bags. Next, she carefully removed the second makeshift bandage and took a look at the hole in her leg with the makeup mirror she retrieved from her purse on the bed. "Ugly wound," she murmured to herself. She took her knife from the holster and washed it in the sink. Next she removed the cellophane from the fire starter. She pushed the button for propane and clicked the trigger. Blue flame erupted from the end. She used the flame to sterilize her knife, moving the flame up and down the blade for two minutes until she was satisfied that it was free of any germs picked up from the guard she killed or from the creeks she had navigated. She allowed a minute for the blade to cool.

She pushed the bathtub curtain back and laid the knife on the tub with the bottle of iodine and mirror beside it. Last, she tore open the package of cloth towels. She had thought this through and knew that she must perform the surgery in the bathtub so that she could wash away the blood and any debris. She stepped in and sat on the side of the tub with her right leg extended toward the faucet. She opened the iodine and poured it over the wound. She almost cried out, but knew the pain would pale in comparison to what she was about to do.

She folded two of the drugstore towels and put them in her mouth, hoping to muffle any sound she would make. She picked up the knife with her right hand and positioned the mirror with her left so she could see the wound. Taking a deep breath, she pushed the tip of the blade into her leg. She had cut herself many times over the years. There was some pain, but nothing like now. It started in her leg and seemed to shoot from there through her whole body to her brain and to her vocal cords. She tried not to scream, but failed. At least the towels muffled the screams. She paused to regain control. So far, she had not encountered the bullet. After a minute, she pushed further with the same result; only this time, she felt the tip of the knife hit metal. She again paused to let the pain diminish and flipped her wrist to dislodge the slug. At first nothing happened. She tried again and pulled the knife out with the slug alongside it. She grasped the slug with her left hand and managed to pour more iodine into the wound before she passed out.

Miriam awoke two hours later, lying in a pool of blood in the tub. The pain was still there, but not as severe as before. She still had the slug in her left hand. She pushed herself to her feet and allowed a minute for the blood to return to her head to overcome the dizziness that enveloped her. When she was somewhat steady, she pulled the shower curtain and turned on the water. She knew it would be cold at first, but thought she needed the shock to clear her head. It worked. She turned the water to warm and let it wash over her. She raised her right leg to allow the water to bathe the wound. She took one of the bottles from the corner shelf and scrubbed. Next she shampooed her hair. The towels that had been in her mouth lay in the tub. She bent slowly so as not to risk passing out and cleaned the tub. When the last of the blood had gone down the drain, she turned off the water and reached for a hotel towel. When she stepped from the tub, she used another towel to dry her hair. Clean once again, she bandaged her leg and wrapped it with the Ace bandage. Feeling slightly better, she made coffee in the room and flipped on the television, hoping for some all night news, She found what she was looking for on CNN. With the Texas governor in the hospital and Edward Hale dead, it was a national story. She confirmed that the governor would live and O'Connell only had a flesh wound in his arm. She retrieved her cell from her purse and called her dad. He picked up on the first ring.

"You okay, baby girl?"

"I'm okay, Pa. Didn't go exactly as planned. I took a bullet in my right thigh, but it didn't hit the bone. I cut it out with my knife, just like you taught me when we practiced on that deer I shot. Mission went exactly as we were directed. Our client should be happier than a pig in shit."

Colonel Van Zandt laughed. "Sounds like you're going to be okay. You heading out of there?"

"In a little while. I bought some bleach and red dye. Any cameras will see a red head leaving the motel. Figure that might throw off the posse for a little while. I may need to spend the night somewhere on the road. It's a long drive and I haven't had much sleep. Expect to see me roll in tomorrow night."

THIRTEEN

By eight o'clock five fresh detail agents arrived from Austin, dressed in shirts, suits and ties that must have just come from the cleaners the day before. They formally relieved the haggard men that had preceded them. Their leader reminded Walt that they had forty-eight hours to unwind before the process would start. It took some persuasion, but Jack finally convinced Walt to spend the night with him before driving to Austin the next day.

Walt had already called his wife in the middle of the night to assure her that he was fine. When they pulled out of the garage, Walt again called Mary to tell her he was going to crash at Jack's place and would probably spend the night. Since they were only five minutes away from the Residence Inn on Seventh where Walt and the rest of the detail were staying, Jack drove him to the motel and waited while Walt checked out. Walt assured him that he could drive the ten minutes to Jack's house. Jack led the way, but watched his rear view mirror for any signs of sleep deprived driving. There were none.

They took Seventh past the museum district to Camp Bowie and followed it west to Hillcrest where they turned right. Taking a left on Crestline, they circled around Rivercrest Country Club, one even older and more prestigious than Shady Oaks. They passed by the club house and turned on Alta Drive. Jack turned into his driveway and waited for Walt to catch up before pushing the remote for the gate. He motioned for Walt to follow him around the mansion to the garage that had ample room for other vehicles to park on the driveway.

Walt climbed from his state issued Crown Victoria and admired Jack's house. "Damn, I forgot what kind of place you had. You told me about it, but I didn't picture this. What is it, 6,000 feet?"

"Something like that. I mainly live downstairs. Colby stays over a good bit. J. D. has a room upstairs and spends the summers and a lot of weekends in the off season. Your room is up there beside his."

"Yeah, from what I read, he may not need to call on his old man for much after this season. Isn't he projected to be a first or second round draft pick?"

Jack nodded proudly. "That he is. The Frogs are five and one this year. They're getting national attention again, and that's helping. He also carries a 4.0 in computer science. Not bad for a kid that just barely got out of high school. The Marines made a man out of him. Maybe we can make a game or two. Sorry to say it, but you know that you're going to be spending a lot of time in Fort Worth during the investigation. I'll give you a key to the house along with the gate and alarm codes."

Colby had seen the two cars turn into the driveway, knowing that the driver of the Crown Vic must be Walt. She rushed out the kitchen door, ignored Jack and gave Walt a hug. "Walt, I'm so sorry. Are you okay?"

Walt nodded his head. "I'm fine, Colby. Worried about the

governor, but it's out of my hands for now. Nothing that a few hours' sleep shouldn't take care of."

"Come on in. You want something to eat? A drink? Water?"

"Maybe a glass of water and then a bed."

Colby led the way into the house and introduced Killer to Walt. "I got him back when someone was trying to kill me."

Walt stooped and scratched Killer behind the ears.

"Now, you've made a friend for life," Jack said. "Here's that water you requested." Jack handed him a tall glass.

Walt took a sip. "If it's okay, I'll just take the water to my room. Point me in the right direction."

Jack led him to the hallway with a curving staircase. "Second bedroom on the left. If you need anything, just holler. One more thing. We have a meeting in Shannon's office at four this afternoon. You want me to get you up for it?"

"Damn right." He turned and made his way to the top of the stairs, glass in one hand and suitcase in the other.

Jack and Colby filled coffee cups. Jack sat at the breakfast table and turned on the news while Colby got a skillet from under the stovetop and loaded it with bacon. Then she returned to the table. "Now, tell me everything."

While Jack brought her up to speed she rose to turn the bacon twice. Once it was done, she placed it on a paper towel covered plate to drain and cracked four eggs that went into the skillet. She continued to listen and put bread in the toaster. Within ten minutes she placed eggs, bacon, toast, grape jelly and butter before Jack and refilled his coffee.

"You not eating?" Jack asked.

"I had breakfast three hours ago. Dig in. Then I think you're going to need a nap before that meeting this afternoon."

Jack ate quietly, allowing his mind to drift back to the night before, again thinking through what he knew in an attempt to make some sense out of it. Walt had told him the governor had a couple of death threats over the years, but nothing that amounted to anything. He knew of no one who wanted Lardner dead. As to Edward Hale, he again had no clue. He and his brother were generous with their money for conservative political causes. No doubt he had made some enemies, but which of them would be so angry as to plot and execute his murder? Jack was beginning to lose focus and couldn't come up with anything. When he finished, he said, "I think you're right. If I'm not up by three, kick me out of bed. Then, I'll get Walt up." He rose, bent over to kiss Colby and walked down the hall to his bedroom. Stripping off his clothes, he was asleep in five minutes.

Colby's cell rang. "Hey, is dad all right?"

"He's exhausted, but fine. He just went to take a nap. He's got a meeting at four. Have you heard that Joe appointed him special prosecutor, and he's in charge of the investigation into what happened last night?"

"Holy shit. He's not a detective."

"Maybe you forgot what you and your dad did three years ago in solving those Dead Peasants murders. I even helped a little. He may not have the badge but Joe thinks he can get the job done."

J.D. paused. "Yeah, you're right. Wish I could get involved, but I'm right in the middle of the season. We're playing Oklahoma this weekend. You think that you and dad can make it to the game?"

Colby smiled. "I bet your dad will figure that the investigation can be put on hold for a few hours on Saturday afternoon. Just remember to score a couple of touchdowns."

"You got it. Tell dad I called."

FOURTEEN

Joe looked across the table at Jack, who was now dressed in jeans and a green golf shirt. Walt sat beside him, wearing his wrinkled suit. Culbertson, White and Meacham rounded out the meeting. "Jack, you're in charge," Joe said.

Jack looked around the table and began. "Sorry, gentlemen, but I've got nothing to report about the investigation. I can tell you that Governor Lardner survived the surgery and is expected to make a complete recovery. Otherwise, after we left the hospital, Walt and I went to my house for a nap. Got up just in time to make the meeting. I'll be back to my old self by morning. Roger, let's start with you."

"We found three shell casings near the bar as you suggested. We retrieved two slugs from the wall behind the stage. Also found various other slugs in the walls, nowhere near the stage. One slug was in one of those expensive paintings in the balcony, a Remington, not the slug but the painting, is what I was told. They probably came from the partiers who started shooting wildly. We have retrieved the slug from the governor's surgery and it's a match with the slug in the wall behind the stage. Preliminary identification is they're from a Glock 26. We're waiting for permission from Ms. Edward Hale to retrieve the one that killed him. Oh, and one of those slugs probably wounded Mr. O'Connell, who is doing fine and was only treated in the emergency room and discharged."

"I can report that we did GSR tests on everyone in the ballroom," Culbertson said. "Found a few with residue. We released them and know how to find them. The consensus is that the shooter was a woman dressed as a cat burglar who was near the bar. So, there's not much point in contacting them right now. A few of the attendees on the guest list managed to get out before we sealed off the mansion. I've got detectives chasing them down for interviews. I don't believe anyone other than the cat burglar is going to be involved."

Meacham let out a low whistle. "You're telling me that this woman fired three shots and hit three men on stage. I suppose I can understand getting the governor, but then pandemonium broke loose and she still fired only twice more and killed Hale and wounded O'Connell. Who the hell is this woman and where did she come from?"

"Both excellent questions," Jack said. "Right now we can't answer either one."

Sheriff White cleared his throat. "I may have something. My deputies walked a grid in those woods behind the house, including two houses on either side and all the way down to the golf course. Just beyond the house wall we found some footprints and blood. You'll remember we had a little rain a couple of days ago. For want of a better word, it looked like a staging area beside a big tree. Two things of note. The footprints were from sneakers and also what appeared to be slippers. And," he paused, "the prints were small, almost surely a woman's. So, that seems to confirm the limo driver's comment that he thought it was a woman. He must have wounded her."

Silence filled the room as the men absorbed what White had said. Finally, Jack spoke.

"So, a woman scaled an eight foot wall, snuck up behind that security guard and slit his throat and entered the ballroom. Then she killed Edward Hale, almost killed the governor and wounded O'Connell. And, on top of that, she was wounded but managed to scale the wall again and escape." He shook his head. "Amazing. Why two pairs of shoes?"

"I'll give you a theory," Walt said. "She jogged from somewhere to the wall, changed into the slippers, which were probably part of her costume, did what she planned and then changed back into her jogging shoes to escape."

"And, we started searching the area within thirty minutes after the shootings," Chief Culbertson interrupted. "We had patrol cars and a dog team. Dogs picked up her scent under that tree. They followed it as far as the creek that runs along the eighteenth hole and lost it. Even with a bullet in her leg, looks like she made a clean getaway."

"Wait a minute," Jack said. "What about the security cameras at the mansion. Hale must have had some focused on the patio."

"He did," Meacham said. "We have the footage from the cameras in the ballroom, and have the cat burglar on the discs, but she's in costume and a mask that comes down to her mouth. We'll be studying the film but I don't expect to identify her. Someone had turned the outside ones off at 3:38 in the afternoon before the party. That's the other issue."

"Raises another question," Shannon said. "Why the hell turn off the outside cameras and leave the ones on inside the house?"

"Maybe whoever did it was not really familiar with all of the switches and thought that he had disconnected the cameras, inside and out," Walt said

"Good a guess as any," Jack said as he put his elbows on the table and rubbed his hands together while he thought. "Then, it looks like our cat burglar had help from the inside. If the cameras were cut, one of those partiers, or the staff, or the security guards, or the cooks and wait staff, one of them must have been in on the deal. Boy, that makes it more complicated. Suggestions, anyone?"

"If the ones outside the mansion were cut off in the afternoon, let's start there," Sheriff White said. "Let's go back a week and study them all. If we're looking for a woman, I'm like you, Jack, a little surprised. Only we shouldn't be. Women are cops. They fly fighters. They are on the front lines of wars. They bolted out of the kitchen a long time ago. All that means is that we may be able to cut our search by half of the population. I'll get discs of the camera feeds and see where we go from there."

Meacham had been quiet up to this point. "Why don't I get the camera info from Shady Oaks for that same week. I know the manager there. Won't even require a subpoena."

"Agreed," Jack said. "Roger, I'd like you to put some cops knocking on doors on Roaring Springs and the streets in Westover Hills. Randall, if you can spare some officers, please assist. They know the neighborhood. Let's see if anyone saw someone walking with a limp around ten that night. Long shot, but worth a try."

FIFTEEN

Walt got up before dawn. After leaving a note, thanking Jack and Colby, he was on I-35 and headed south for Austin. He turned off at the Leander exit. Leander was a bedroom community about twenty miles northwest of Austin. Mary was surprised to see him so early. She made a fresh pot of coffee, and he brought her up to speed on the events of the past two days.

"I'll be put on administrative leave. The Rangers will conduct a full investigation. Any way you slice it, my detail and I failed. The governor was almost killed."

Tears filled Mary's eyes. "Could you lose your job? You don't want to go back to being a street cop. What do I tell the boys?"

Walt rose and pulled his wife into a hug as he also began crying. "I've been thinking of nothing else since it happened. We did as we were trained. Can some Ranger look at the events and find a flaw in our handling of the situation? I suppose. Hindsight's twenty-twenty. Someone may be looking for a scapegoat." He paused. "I don't know. Tell the kids that I'll be spending most of my time in Fort Worth for a while." Walt took a napkin from the table and wiped his wife's eyes, then his. "Hell, and remember I was a damn good street cop."

Mary managed to break into a slight smile. He climbed the stairs and put on a fresh shirt, suit and tie, re-packed his suitcase, retrieved his personal Sig Sauer and kissed her goodbye.

He drove south on 183 to Mopac and cut over to Lamar to the DPS headquarters. He parked in front and entered the building. He showed his credentials at the desk and asked to see Colonel Burnside. The receptionist called Burnside's assistant and told him to take the elevator to the fifth floor. When the elevator opened, an attractive, middle aged woman smiled and led him down a hall to Burnside's office. After twenty minutes, she invited him through the door to find Colonel Burnside standing in front of his desk, hand extended.

"Sergeant Frazier thanks for coming. I'd like to hear a first-hand account of what happened. Thank God Governor Lardner is going to be okay. Have a seat." He motioned to a sitting area to the right of the door with a picture window looking south toward downtown and the University of Texas tower to the left.

Walt outlined the events of the past two days. Colonel Burnside interrupted frequently, searching for more details. When Walt finished, the colonel said, "I know you've thought of little else. Looking back, could you have prevented this?"

Walt shook his head. "No, sir. We did exactly as we were trained."

"How are you doing? I mean you, personally. I've looked through the files on all five of you. I saw what you did in Desert Storm. They should have given you a goddamn Congressional Medal of Honor. I know you suffered from PTSD for several years, but you passed all of the DPS exams with flying colors. This kind of tragedy can cause that to flare up sometimes. You doing all right? Be honest with me."

Walt hesitated just enough that Burnside caught it. "I'm fine, sir. I know I'll have to have a psychological evaluation before I go back to work." He paused again. "I'm not worried about passing."

Burnside drummed his fingers on his desk. "Well, I suppose we'll just have to let the Rangers deal with it. For your sake, I hope you're right."

"One more thing. I presume you've heard, sir, Hal was assigned as limo driver. He saw the shooter. It was a woman dressed as a cat burglar. He exchanged fire and thought he wounded her. Yesterday afternoon I attended a team meeting. Sheriff White's men found footprints and traces of blood in the woods behind the house. Judging from the size, they are almost certainly female."

Colonel Burnside stroked his chin as he absorbed the information. "At least, that ought to narrow down the search. We're looking for a woman who just happens to be a sharpshooter with an assassin's personality."

Walt rose. He took his gun from his holster and his badge from his belt. He retrieved his credentials from his wallet. He placed them all on the table in from of the colonel. "Sir, I know that protocol demands that my team and I be suspended during our internal investigation. Rather than upset my wife and kids with a Ranger showing up at my door, I would appreciate it if you would take these now."

"Understood, Sergeant," Colonel Burnside said as he also stood. "I've already appointed the investigation detail from our Rangers. They may find it necessary to go beyond an internal affairs investigation since Shannon took the criminal investigation away from us. You know this Jack Bryant?"

"Yes, sir. Very well. He was my platoon sergeant in Desert Storm. I was a grunt. He had served his time with the 101st and was called back up when we had to fight Saddam the first time. He was the best. That incident you mentioned. He was the first one I pulled out of there."

"Then, he was the one you pushed that thousand pound beam that was on him to free him. How the hell did you do that?"

"Did what I had to do, sir. Back to Jack, he still walks with a cane sometimes because his leg was crushed. They wanted to amputate it above the knee and he refused. He went back to Beaumont and made a fortune as a plaintiff lawyer before he took early retirement and moved back to Fort Worth where he grew up."

Walt paused.

"Sir, I got him involved in this mess. When I saw what a nightmare it was going to be to protect the governor with everyone in costumes, I called him to assist that night. Maybe I forgot to mention that he's a Tarrant County reserve deputy."

Burnside walked over the window and looked out while Walt continued.

"Sir, I know that I am not permitted to participate in the investigation while I'm on suspension. I'm leaving here and heading back to Fort Worth. I'll be staying with Jack. I'd like to unofficially give advice to him as needed."

Colonel Burnside whirled with a smile on his face. "That's the best idea I've heard today. We'll have one of our guys with the ear of the special prosecutor. You do exactly that. I'll expect you to report back to me from time to time, only no one else in the DPS is to know. Hell, I'm in charge of this outfit and can have a few secrets." Then he wrote his cell number on a yellow sticky and handed it to Walt. "Here's my cell. I'll tell our internal affairs team that you're in Fort Worth and will make yourself available as needed."

SIXTEEN

Walt parked in the driveway behind the house beside another pickup, in a spot beside the six car garage that he suspected had once been the place for the RV. He retrieved his suitcase from the back seat of the Crown Vic that Colonel Burnside had told him to continue to drive as long as it was their secret. Jack met him at the back door and handed him a Budweiser. "I presume you're off duty and can have this?"

"I am. Thanks."

Colby was in the kitchen, stirring spaghetti sauce. J. D. came from the library that had been converted to a media room where he was watching film of the Oklahoma football team.

"Evening, Colby. I hope I won't be an imposition."

"Of course, not. We've got more rooms than we ever use, anyway. When I sold this house to Jack, I tried to talk him into something smaller. He wouldn't hear of it. He wanted to be in Rivercrest and he wanted that view out the back down to the

Trinity River and over across to the old bomber plant where his dad worked."

J.D. walked over to shake Walt's hand. Walt looked at him. "Let's see. Best I remember, last time I saw you was in Beaumont when you were visiting your dad, maybe ten, maybe fifteen years ago."

"Yes, sir. Sorry, but I don't remember it."

"Not a surprise. I've been following your career ever since you walked on to the Frog football team. As I recall, you're six feet, four inches and two hundred and forty pounds."

"He's put on ten pounds at Coach Patterson's request. Still runs a 4.45 forty, though." Jack said.

"Excuse me. I'm going back to watch more film. We've got the Sooners in town Saturday afternoon. I'm still studying their linebackers and defensive backs. Just holler when dinner's ready."

"Ten minutes," Colby said.

"Drop your bag at the foot of the stairs and we'll sit at the kitchen table. Colby likes to hear what's going on."

Walt did as he was told and took a seat. After another long pull from the Budweiser, he said. "Just as I expected, I'm suspended from the DPS."

That got Colby's attention. "Why? They put you in a situation where you couldn't prevent what happened. From what Jack said, it reminded me of that bar scene out of the original *Star Wars* movie."

Walt shook his head but smiled. "I hadn't thought of it that way, but that's a pretty good description. The suspension is routine. The DPS considers it an officer involved shooting, particularly since the governor was wounded. The whole detail that night is suspended while the Rangers conduct an investigation. Fortunately, we still draw paychecks. And here's the silver lining to this cloud over my head. I briefed Colonel Burnside this morning. He asked about you and I told him I was going to be staying here. I'm not supposed to be involved in the investigation, but he was delighted that I would be so close to you. Wants me to keep him informed. I was required to surrender my DPS Sig Sauer; only my personal weapon is identical. Any developments?"

J.D. heard the question and returned to the kitchen. "I want to hear the latest."

"Good timing," Colby said as she placed a giant bowl of spaghetti and a slightly smaller bowl of meat sauce on the table beside a green salad.

After everyone had filled a plate, Jack said, "One thing of interest. I forgot. When you left yesterday, had we learned that the outside security cameras had been turned off?"

"Yeah, I was at the meeting when that came up."

"We had some of the deputies go through the camera discs for the past week. Didn't find anything around the house. However, one of the front cameras caught an old pickup that paused in front of the driveway for a couple of minutes. The camera was directed more toward the driveway than the street. So, we only got the bottom half. Appears to be an F-150, probably white with several layers of dirt on it."

Walt swallowed a bite. "Can I have a look?"

"Sure, I brought a copy of that disc home. If J.D. will let us have the media room for a few minutes, I can put it up on a giant screen."

"I guess the interviews haven't turned up anything?"

"Nothing, yet. A few guests managed to get out before I could get the house locked down. We should have all of them in a couple of days."

"You got any suspects?" Colby asked

Jack shook his head.

"Still, Dad, someone inside the house had to be in on it. Security cameras don't all go out at once, just a few hours before the party."

"J.D. is right. Only we have a house full of people that afternoon. Could have been any one of at least a hundred. We need a break. Can we look at that film, now?" Walt asked. "And, Colby, that's wonderful spaghetti."

Colby smiled. "You have to give Jack a little credit. The sauce is his old family recipe. He swore me to secrecy before he showed me how to make it."

The media room had been a library when Jack bought the house. He bought the largest television he could find, surrounded the room with sound and placed eight reclining and vibrating leather loungers on two levels facing the television. They took four seats on the front row, and Jack handed the disc to J.D.

"This only shows a view of the driveway and the pickup, nothing more."

J.D. pushed "play" and the cul de sac appeared with nothing in it. Then the pickup came into view. The camera angle was such that the license plate was obscured. All that could be seen was the side of the vehicle from the street up to the bottom of the windows. It moved slowly and stopped in front of the driveway. The digital clock counted off two minutes. Jack froze it just before the pickup moved away. "See anything interesting?"

"I think so," Walt said. He moved to the screen that was six feet by eight feet. "See here." He pointed to the right front bumper. "There's a small indentation on it, like the driver must have hit a parking lot pole or something, maybe three inches in diameter."

"Good catch. On the small screens, we had overlooked that."

"Anything else."

"I think the window is down," Colby said. "Little hard to tell. Maybe the air conditioning wasn't working on the truck."

"Or maybe someone lowered the window to take cell photos of the house and driveway."

"Dad, it's definitely a Ford F-150. Old one. My guess is somewhere between 2000 and 2004 model. And definitely white under all that dust."

Jack nodded. "That's not going to be much help. People in Texas drive those pickups until the engine freezes up, somewhere between 250,000 and 500,000 miles. And white is the most common color. Still the dent on the right bumper is something we didn't have before."

SEVENTEEN

"Jack, Roger Culbertson here."

"Morning, Roger, tell me something good."

"Don't really have anything. Between Randall's guys and mine, we've knocked on practically every door in Westover Hills. Haven't turned up any stranger that night. Also checked all those condos and houses off Roaring Springs. Nada. Randall has the video feeds from Shady Oaks. Don't know if he's found anything."

"I'm still at home. Walt is staying with me a few days. I'll call Randall. This afternoon we're meeting with Kevin O'Connell. He's still at the Renaissance Hotel, resting up. Oh, here's one little bit of information. We looked at that video of the driveway and the pickup. Had it on a large screen. There's a small dent in the right front bumper, probably only about three inches across. Not much, but it's all we have for now."

Jack filled Walt in on the conversation, then called Meacham at the Westover Hills Police Station. Meacham had noted his phone i.d. before he picked up the receiver. "You got anything, Jack?"

"Not much. Roger tells me you struck out in the neighborhood."

"Yeah, but I do have the video from Shady Oaks. Did see a couple of pickups that seemed to be out of place."

Jack nodded at Walt. "Can we come by to look at those?"

"Sure, any time."

"We'll be there in ten minutes."

They arrived at a small but attractive police station that had a redwood and stone façade. When they entered the double doors, Jack introduced himself to the receptionist who directed them back to Meacham's office. They knocked and entered. Meacham was just finishing a call and motioned them to have a seat. The office window looked out onto a wooded area with a creek.

Meacham ended his call. "You want to see those two pickups in the club parking lot? I loaded them five minutes ago. Turn your chairs around so you can see the television."

Meacham's office television was about forty-two inches and the clarity was good. "Here's the first, a red Toyota Tundra. We've already checked out the license plates. Belongs to a family on the south side. Appears to be a teenager driving it."

Jack shook his head. "How about the other one?"

"There you go."

An old, white ford came into view, moving slowly through the lot.

"Can you back it up a few frames and pause on that right side?" Walt asked.

When Meacham did so, Walt walked up to the television and peered at it from two inches away. "Can't be sure, but I think that's the dent we saw."

Jack nodded his agreement.

Meacham looked puzzled. "You want to clue me in?"

"Sorry, Randall. That pickup was on video, stopped in front

of the Hale mansion two days before the party. The camera could only see the lower right side. It has a small dent on the bumper, same as that one." He pointed to the screen. "Was that made two days before the event?"

"Yep. You can see the digital clock in the upper right hand corner."

Walt was still kneeling close the television. "Jack, I can't be sure, but I think that's a woman with dark hair driving. Hard to tell. Randall, anything on other cameras? Maybe at a guard house."

"Nothing at the guard house. It's manned during the day. I think the last shift ends at six in the evening. Members decided they didn't want a camera there, recording their comings and goings. And they don't like a lot of cameras in the parking lots. Not what I would recommend, but they don't have a lot of crime at the club."

Jack rose and Walt followed suit. "Would you make a copy of that video? I live just over in Rivercrest. If you'll let me know, I'll drop by the front desk to pick it up. We're on our way downtown to talk with Kevin O'Connell. And would you check with whoever was at the guard house to see if they recall anything about that pickup?"

EIGHTEEN

As they made their way downtown in Jack's pickup, he asked Walt, "What do you know about Kevin O'Connell?"

"Mean, hard-nosed son of a bitch. I've been around him a few times at the Republican Governor's Conference and at other meetings where the Republican high rollers show up. When he's raising money, he turns on the charm, whether it's one on one or in a gathering like the other night. Behind closed doors, he demands that the politicians he supports march to whatever tune he's playing. If they don't, he'll dump them on the side of the road. I hear he pays his employees well, but treats them like crap, fifteen hour days, six or seven days a week. Simon Legree had nothing on him.

"Lately, he's been singing the Tea Party anthem. Had a run of bad luck in the past couple of election cycles, mainly because he was still backing the old school Republicans who wanted to work with the Democrats. He took some pretty good lickings with some of the senatorial candidates he has backed recently. Only, you'd never know it to talk to him. I heard him say they were just a few minor hiccups. Governor Lardner is both an admirer and also a little bit scared of him. Lardner needs O'Connell in his corner if he's going to take a shot at the White House."

Jack turned into the circular drive in front of the Renaissance Hotel, just a couple of blocks from the courthouse complex and stopped behind a chauffeur-driven black Mercedes. The valet handed Jack a ticket. "Now you be sure that you park this pickup in a place where it won't get banged up. It's a whole lot more valuable than that Mercedes."

The valet looked at Jack to see if he was joking. Jack wasn't smiling, but there was a twinkle in his eye. "Tell you what. Just put it over there in that space by the curb. Here's a twenty for you to hold it there for about an hour."

"You got it." The valet grinned.

They were directed to a house phone where Walt asked to be connected to O'Connell's room. When O'Connell answered, he identified himself and was given a room number. Walt led the way to the elevator and punched the button for the tenth floor. They got to room 1042. Walt knocked. The door opened, and they were greeted by a small man, somewhere around fifty, slender with a prominent Roman nose and a receding hairline. His arm was in a sling. *He could never win an election*, Jack thought. *His image would turn too many people off.*

"I think I recognize you," he said to Walt. "Still, I need to see some identification."

Walt handed him his driver's license. Jack leaned on his cane and flashed his reserve deputy card.

O'Connell looked at them and back at Walt. "If you're part of Lardner's protective detail, where's that identification?"

"Protocol. Since Lardner was shot, my detail and I are on administrative leave until the Rangers complete their investigation. I can give you the cell number of Colonel Burnside, the head of the DPS, if you want to check me out."

"I suppose that won't be necessary. Come in, but you need to make this brief. I don't have a lot of time to waste with two local cops. Turn off your cell phones and put them on the coffee table. I don't permit any recordings of my conversations."

The room was a corner suite. O'Connell pointed them to a sofa. He sat in an easy chair opposite them. Before either Walt or Jack could say anything, O'Connell turned to Jack and launched a tirade. "Tell me who you are."

"I'm Jack Bryant. I'm also a lawyer. Here's my card." Jack handed him a cheap card he had ordered on line. Fancy cards didn't impress his clientele.

O'Connell studied the card. "Oh, you're the one, the special prosecutor. You two need to get something straight. How the hell could this have possibly happened? I've held fundraisers all over the country and never had a problem. You guys let one lone shooter kill my good friend, Edward Hale, leave the governor near death and shoot me. Incompetence. Utter incompetence. Mr. Frazier, I'm going to do my best to see that you're suspended permanently. And that goes for the rest of your detail."

Jack had enough. He rose from the couch, trying to control his temper. "Just a goddamn minute. I understand this costume party was all your idea. I doubt if another fifty men could have stopped what happened. They might have caught her after the fact, but the damage would have already been done. Just where the hell did you come up with something so idiotic. Costumes and real guns. They don't mix, Mr. O'Connell. You've got a bad case of dumbass and want to blame someone else."

O'Connell also stood and walked to gaze out the window at the courthouse. When he turned, his face was red with eyes mere slits. He spoke through clenched teeth. "Idiot. I'm not the idiot. Security is not my job. If you couldn't handle it, you needed to tell someone. Don't blame me because you screwed up.

"Do you know what this has done to me? It's devastated my

business. To start, there are no guarantees that those donors at the fundraiser are going to honor their pledges. Since we are not being recorded, I can tell you that I couldn't blame them. Then, this has gotten national attention. I've been sitting in this hotel, calling people I could always rely on for contributions to our candidates and causes. A lot of them are 'not available' and won't return my calls. This was going to be my biggest campaign by far. I'm raising money for several Tea Party senators. If Lardner or someone like him gets the Republican nomination for president, a billion dollars from my efforts is not out of the question. Now I've got to figure out how I can recover from this fiasco. If I can't, there will be more than hell to pay. I'll be suing everyone involved, including you and your detail, Frazier."

"You can do whatever you damn well please," Walt interrupted. "Only, before we leave I need to ask a few questions about that night."

O'Connell nodded, his face still contorted in anger.

"About two hours elapsed from the time the party started until the dignitaries took the stage. Where were you during that time?"

"Working the room. There was a ton of money there that night. Even setting aside the Hales, there were other billionaires. I wanted to get to know all of them better."

"How well did you know the Hales?"

"They helped me get started in this business. Twenty, thirty years ago I worked for a couple of friends of theirs and got them elected to the Texas House. The Hales were wealthy by any measure back then, but nothing like today. They didn't like the way the country was headed. Even George H. W. Bush was too liberal for them. They started small and quietly put their money in political campaigns. Before long, they were swinging a big stick in Washington and state houses all over the country."

"You know anyone who would want Edward Hale killed?"

"I could give you a list of a hundred, maybe a thousand

Democrats who wanted him out of politics. Killed? That's going a little too far."

"How well do you know Governor Lardner?" Walt asked.

"We're professional friends. We agree on what's good for the country. I was hoping he would sign me up as his chief fundraiser. I think he would make a fantastic president."

"Tell us about the party," Jack said.

O'Connell managed a slight grin. "It was spectacular. I had never come close to raising what I did that night. Well, I should say that I never had so much money pledged. SOS and Stepper may never see a penny." His eyes glazed over as if seeing into the future. "I could see it being duplicated in states all over the country." He paused. "Then it happened. The shot was just barely loud enough to be heard over the uproar in the ballroom. The governor went down." He pointed at Walt. "I saw you covering the governor and one of your other guys grabbing Susan. Then there were more shots. I got hit. Edward was trying to follow the governor and was killed, probably instantly. I wondered at the time why one of you guys on the stage couldn't have been shooting at the killer. They called it cover fire back when I was in the army. Might have saved Edward's life." He glared at Walt. "If you were in charge, the goddamn buck stops with you." He pointed to the door. "Now, get the hell out of my room and out of my sight."

NINETEEN

On the morning after the shooting, Miriam bleached her Raven black hair and dyed it red. Next, she took the bandage from her leg, finding that the area around the wound was red and warm. She needed to get back to the compound where they had a medical cabinet ready for a war. It was well stocked with pain pills and antibiotics. She re-dressed her wound and picked up all of the wrappings, boxes and paraphernalia from the night before to stuff in a garbage bag. She put on jeans, her running shoes, and a Dallas Cowboys T-shirt, packed her small bag and took one look around the room. No sign that it had been used as an infirmary the night before. She limped to the elevator and pushed the button. When it opened she was greeted by an older couple. She nodded and turned to face the front. When the door opened on the first floor, she walked to the side exit, doing her best to hide her limp, only to find that it was raining hard. A cold front was on the way, pushing a thunderstorm ahead of it. She opened the door and limped and hopped to her truck. When she turned the key, the gas gauge read half full. Enough to get her to Abilene.

I-30 led to I-20. Traffic thinned the farther she got from Fort Worth. Miriam's leg was aching, forcing her to use her left foot for the gas and brake pedals. She pressed her hand to her forehead to confirm she was running a fever. When she arrived at a rest area east of Abilene, the rain had slowed to a drizzle. She found a parking space with no cars nearby and quickly changed her rear license and dumped the trash bag. Then she was back on the highway. She stopped for gas, food and a restroom break at a combination Shell station and McDonalds in Abilene. She noticed cameras around the pumps but had no choice. Leaving the restroom she paused to pick out a baseball cap, paid for it, and pulled it low over her eyes when she returned to her truck.

When she saw a road sign advising that Big Spring was fifteen miles away, she had to make a decision. It was four in the afternoon. She was tired and her temperature now had to be at least 101. If she stopped at a motel, her infection was going to get worse. She made the decision to get a large, black coffee and continue driving.

She stopped at the compound gate and hobbled to unlock it. She drove through and continued to her father's trailer. He could send someone back to lock it. When she parked, she stumbled from her truck and pushed open the colonel's door and collapsed in a chair. Pa was in the back and came rushing to her.

"You don't look so good, baby girl."

He felt her forehead. "Temperature must be a hundred and three."

The medicine cabinet was kept in last of four bedrooms in his trailer so that he could know when anyone in the compound was sick enough to need it.

"I'll be right back."

He came back with a bottle of Ancef and one of hydrocodone. He poured a glass of water and shoved two of the Ancef and one hydrocodone into her hand. "Now, drink the whole glass of water. Doesn't have to be all at once, but you've been sweating and I suspect you're dehydrated."

Miriam drank about half the water. "Thanks, Pa. I think I told you that the mission went off without a hitch, at least until I got shot. I killed Hale and wounded the governor and that other guy just as you planned."

Van Zandt nodded his approval. "I knew you would do it right. Now, stand up and pull those jeans down to your knees. I want to have a look at that wound."

TWENTY

It was Saturday afternoon, a crisp, sunshiny autumn day in Fort Worth. A cold front had blown through, leaving blue skies and temperatures in the upper forties. Perfect football weather for a Big Twelve battle between TCU and Oklahoma. Just a few years before, such a match-up would never have been considered by the mighty Oklahoma Sooners. TCU was considered a non-conference early season warm-up game by the football powers.

It hadn't always been that way. The Horned Frogs were original members of the old Southwest Conference, a major in every way until it collapsed in the eighties. Most of the bigger schools in the Southwest Conference joined with similar schools from the Big Eight to form the Big Twelve. TCU was left to wander the back waters of college football until Gary Patterson became coach. TCU and Fort Worth committed to rebuilding the Frogs to a major power, and Patterson did it. After Texas A&M left for the SEC, TCU was invited to join the Big Twelve and fought its way to the top. This year the Frogs were five and one, sitting atop the conference with another religious school, Baylor, and were playing for a berth in the final four. It was a long shot, but the number of undefeated schools in the country was down to two.

J.D. Bryant had barely made it out of high school in Los Angeles where his mother moved him after divorcing Jack. after a bar fight where he busted the heads of three guys who assaulted him, to keep him out of jail Jack flew to Los Angeles and struck a deal with the assistant district attorney: Drop the charge to a misdemeanor and Jack would get J.D. to join the Marines, never to be seen in Los Angeles again. Four years and two tours in Iraq and Afghanistan later, J.D. mustered out, now six feet four inches of chiseled stone. He announced to his dad, then a Beaumont plaintiff lawyer, that he was going to walk on the TCU football team. When J.D. made the team, Jack took his last big plaintiff verdict and retired to Fort Worth to watch his son play football.

That was three years ago. J.D. now was a likely All-American tight end who had pro scouts drooling. A slightly smaller version of the Houston Texan's J.J. Watt, he was fast, determined, focused and smart, carrying a 4.0 in computer science. Jack had not missed a game, at home or away, in the past three and a half years. Today was no exception. The investigation could be put on hold for a few hours.

Jack and Walt were sitting on the back patio, waiting for Colby to finish dressing. Jack had been looking for an opportunity to bring up an issue. This was the time. "Look, I wasn't there when the shooting started. You sent me to the front. Only before that I was watching what was happening on the stage. I saw your eyes darting around the room. I saw you reach for your gun. What were you thinking?"

"Nothing," Walt said without hesitation. "I'm always studying the room in that kind of situation. I don't stop moving my eyes unless there is a reason. That's how I was trained."

"What about reaching for the gun?"

Walt's eyes flickered. "I don't remember doing that. I

may have subconsciously done it when one of those damn balloons popped."

Jack leaned forward in his chair. "Walt, I've known you for over twenty years. I was there at the barracks. I know that you suffered from PTSD, flashbacks, nightmares, you name it, for years. Were you having another flashback? Look, you can tell me. It won't go any farther."

Walt sighed and hesitated. "I hadn't had a flashback or any other post traumatic problem for more than ten years. That night when I looked at that mass of people in costumes, it happened again. I, I don't know why."

"You tell the DPS psychologist?"

"Can't. He'd put me on indefinite leave. I can deal with it."

Before Jack could respond, Colby came from the back door. "Okay, you two, let's get going."

Jack looked at Walt, nodded at Colby and they rose to join her. Jack concluded that he was going to have to be Walt's sounding board and confidant. He knew that the worst thing that Walt could do was to keep his feelings bottled up. He would have to watch for other opportunities to continue the conversation. Jack, Colby and Walt loaded into the Bentley. Colby insisted that Walt take the front passenger seat.

"So, you think that the investigation can get along without the two of you for a few hours," Colby asked.

"Yeah," Jack replied. "Even if it couldn't, you know I don't miss a game. So far, we've come up empty-handed. We've expanded the search. Today, we put teams to canvassing motels and hotels as well as shopping centers. If they have cameras, we're going to get their feeds for the week before the shootings and a couple of days after."

"Some people may think that surveillance cameras are infringing on their privacy, and maybe they are, but they have proved to be a giant help in tracking criminals," Walt said. "Now, who's favored today?"

"Frogs by four. That's mainly because of home field advantage. We'll have time to go by the Frog Club and then head to our seats. I can pretty well size up how J.D.'s going to do, just by watching him warm up."

Jack parked the Bentley in a space with his name on it and led the way to a room fronting the end zone with twenty foot windows looking out onto the field. As they entered, he said, "It was right here that I first began to learn a little more about Colby. Folks kept asking her how Rob was. She brushed them off and changed the subject."

Colby blushed. "Rob was my late husband. He had an aneurysm and had been in a vegetative state for ten years when I met Jack. I didn't want to tell him I was married."

"Someone killed Rob and a grand jury indicted Colby," Jack added. "J.D., Colby and I eventually proved that he had been murdered in his bed at the nursing home by a serial killer who will go down in the criminal history books as *The Dead Peasants Killer*. That's a chapter in our lives we're glad is behind us. Hey, I see Joe over there."

Besides being a great trial lawyer, Shannon was an outgoing, gregarious sort, a born politician, who enjoyed mingling in any crowd and pressing the flesh. When he saw Jack, Walt and Colby approaching, he excused himself.

"Let's step over here by the window. Give me an update. By the way, Colby, you look beautiful as usual."

Colby smiled her thanks.

"Sorry to say that we've struck out so far," Jack said.

Joe shook his head. "Damn frustrating. Three people get shot with two hundred others standing around and the shooter gets away. She has to be a pro."

"Good a guess as any," Walt said. "She had everything planned perfectly. Even when she got shot in the leg, she scaled the wall and managed to get away from the dogs, most likely by wading in the creeks. Probably not the first time she has done something like this."

"When the game's over, I'll have someone run all available data bases, looking for a woman who's a hired gun. Should have thought of it before. I wouldn't be surprised if she's former Mossad or KGB. Now we better get to our seats. I want to see J.D. score today. Go Frogs!" When they entered the stadium, Jack was focused on Walt, looking for any reaction to the crowd and noise. Fortunately, there was none.

Oklahoma took the kickoff and marched down the field until the Frogs line held and forced a field goal. TCU returned the favor, only for seven points. At halftime the score was 28-24 in favor of the Frogs. The Frogs had the ball to start the second half. Coach Patterson called an end around, but it was not a wide receiver on the play. The Oklahoma defense and nearly everyone in the stands watched as J.D. dropped back to block, swiveled and ran behind Samuel Killen, the fifth year senior quarterback, who faked a pass long down the field, before slipping the ball behind his back to J.D. With 4.45 speed, equivalent to most wide receivers, J.D. ran for the left hash mark and turned up the field. He sidestepped one tackler and was on the move, all 250 pounds of muscle, barreling down the field. The Sooners had backs equally as fast, but fifty pounds lighter. J.D. stiff armed one of them and kept rolling. As he neared the goal, the safety dived in front of him in a last ditch effort, but to no avail. J.D. jumped the defender and stepped into the end zone. J.D. scored once more on a pass to the flat from the twenty. Final score: TCU 49, Oklahoma 38. TCU was now number four in the nation.

TWENTY-ONE

Jack retrieved his cane from behind the seat as Walt exited the passenger side of Lucille in the Harris Methodist garage. They punched the elevator button for the ninth floor and rode in silence. When they got off the elevator, Ranger Willis was still at the desk, partially blocking the corridor leading back to the governor's room.

"Morning, Sergeant. I hear that Governor Lardner is feeling better."

"Yep. He's about to kick the door in. Doc says another twenty-four hours and he can probably head back to Austin. You can go on down there. He's expecting you."

When they got to the room, two agents, obviously known to Walt, were sitting on either side of the door. "Morning, Walt. You doing okay?"

"Hanging in there. This is Jack Bryant. He's the special prosecutor and a longtime friend of mine."

Both of the agents rose to shake Jack's hand. "Pleased to meet you, Jack. Walt was telling me about you when he called to set up this meeting. Investigation turning anything up?"

Jack grimaced slightly. "Dead ends, so far."

"Walt, just knock on the door. Wolf's expecting you."

Walt tapped on the door with the knuckle of his index finger. "Come on in," the governor said.

They entered the room to find Governor Lardner sitting in a lounger, pushed back to a reclining position with the Wall Street Journal on his lap and the television turned to CNBC. Susan was sitting in a straight back chair on the other side of the bed, a book in her hand.

"Come in, Walt. This must be Jack Bryant."

Jack walked over to shake the governor's outstretched hand. "My pleasure, Governor."

"Have a seat. I convinced the hospital to get me a few extra chairs. Let me mute the volume on this program. First, Walt, I want to thank you for getting Susan and me out of that ballroom."

Walt shook his head. "I'm sorry, Governor. I was supposed to take that bullet. I was wearing a vest."

"Nonsense. In hindsight, I was a damn fool for even being there. I should have listened to you and put my mug up on a big screen. Nothing you could do about that first bullet. Your fast action probably saved my ass. A second bullet would have done me in. Not to mention that you guys got Susan out of there safely. Now, tell me about the investigation. By the way, I'm trying to convince my doctor to discharge me in time to make Edward Hale's funeral tomorrow morning. They postponed it because so many Republicans are coming from all over the country."

"Governor, I just told this to the agents in the hall," Jack said. "All dead ends, so far. We've got a big task force working. I'm still hopeful that we'll get a break."

"Is it true that the killer is a woman?"

"Yes, sir," Walt said.

"I suppose that made it a little easier for her to go unnoticed. No one expects an assassin to be a woman."

"Governor, did you see anything, see her, maybe? She was dressed as cat burglar."

Lardner scratched the several day old stubble on his face. "I've been thinking about it. All I really remember was this sea of costumes that we walked through and that I looked down on from the stage. I understand that she was shooting from over near the patio doors, but nothing caught my attention."

"Not a surprise, Governor. I was right there with you. It was my job to spot her and I was no help. Speaking of the funeral, I'll be there tomorrow, too. You know that I've been placed on suspension until the Rangers do their investigation. So, it will be in an unofficial capacity."

Lardner frowned. "You okay with that? Not your damn fault."

Walt dropped his gaze to the floor and hesitated before he looked again at the governor. "I don't like being suspended. It eats at me every day, but I don't have any choice. That's our protocol. Hopefully, everything will come out all right in the end."

Jack looked at his friend, knowing that he was keeping his emotions pent up. He could only hope they could wind this up quickly so Walt could get back to his work and family before they erupted.

The next day Jack and Walt drove to the First Methodist Church just west of downtown. They got there early and took positions, standing at the back of the church where they could watch the mourners arrive. The church filled rapidly, as if those attending worried that they might not get a seat. Of course they were correct. Thirty minutes before the service was to begin, the sanctuary was at capacity and the later attendees were shuffled off to an adjoining room where they could observe by closed circuit television. The exceptions were dignitaries, politicians and billionaire friends of the Hales as well as family. The first fifteen rows were cordoned off for them. Governor Lardner arrived in a wheelchair just before ten. He and Susan were escorted to the third row. He remained in his wheelchair and Susan took an aisle seat that had been reserved for her. Jack noted that somehow Kevin O'Connell had an aisle seat in the fifth row. Four members of the protective detail took positions along the wall, vigilant to make sure that nothing more happened to the governor. Jack and Walt studied each person who entered. After the overflow room opened, Jack moved there and took a similar position at the back.

The organist stopped, and the minister came from the right to take a seat. He was joined by two other men. Last, Edward Hale's family came from an anteroom to occupy the first two pews. When the service began, Jack slipped out the front door and saw various law enforcement officers. He recognized a couple of them from the investigation.

"Morning, officers. I didn't see anything out of the ordinary. Just your average goat roping."

One of them smiled at Jack's description of the funeral. "No, sir. Looks routine to us. We've got Greenwood Cemetery locked down for now. No one will get in until Mr. Hale is buried. We also got permission to set up temporary cameras at the entrance and in the trees around the grave site. We'll remove them and take them to the station as soon as the service ends."

Jack's cell sounded. "Jack, Lance White here. I figure you're probably at the funeral. I couldn't make it. Can you talk? I think we may have something."

"Go on."

"We've had a bunch of officers from all of the services checking motels, Ridgmar, other shopping centers in the area that might have cameras. We've found two that have images that may be useful, one at Ridgmar and one at that Hampton Inn on I-30."

"How quickly can I see them?"

"You name it."

"Walt Frazier is here with me. Shannon is inside. He may want to see what you have. I figure the service will be over and the church will be clear in about an hour. Doesn't sound like I'll be any help at the cemetery. Let me suggest that you bring them to my house. I've got a giant television with the best clarity available. Here's my address. The gate will be open. Pull around to the back when you get there."

TWENTY-TWO

Jack and Walt were sitting on the front porch when Joe turned into the driveway, followed by Sheriff White. They pulled to the back. Jack and Walt walked down the driveway to greet them. As they approached, the sheriff opened the back door of his car and pulled a backpack from the seat.

"Never liked carrying around a briefcase. Backpack serves me fine." The men shook hands all around.

"Come on in," Jack said. "Colby's home today. I asked her to make us some sandwiches."

Colby was placing a platter of ham and turkey slices on the kitchen table. Jack introduced Lance to her.

"Now, Colby," Joe said, "You didn't have to go to all this trouble."

"Come on, Joe. Cold cuts from the fridge, bread, mustard and mayo, a little lettuce and tomatoes with a bag of chips. Yeah, I really slaved for you. Help yourselves. Who wants tea and

111

who wants water?"

The men loaded plates. Jack led them into the media room and showed which button to push to have a tray pop out when they took seats.

Lance looked around the room. "Boy, you're right about that television. I saw one that size in a sports bar a while back. I may need to borrow it on another case some day."

"It's yours," Jack replied. "Just give me a little notice. If you'll hand me whichever video you want to start with, I'll load it."

Lance reached into his backpack and retrieved two discs. "Start with this one. It's showing the parking lot at Ridgmar before the party and afterwards."

Jack inserted it in the DVD player and returned to a seat. Colby had joined them on the second row.

The light was not good on the video. Still, they could make out a woman in dark pants and a green T-shirt jogging in the direction of Alta Mere. She had something strapped to her waist. The digital clock display confirmed it was the night of the party. The timer read 7:30 p.m.

"Lance, you figure that's a fanny pack?" Walt asked.

"Most likely. If it's our killer, she probably had her gun, a knife and part of her costume in it."

The section ended.

"Jack, if you'll go to the next section, this will start to get interesting."

This time the video showed what appeared to be the same woman. She was headed toward the camera which was placed too high to get an image of her face. She now had a noticeable limp. Her hair appeared to be black. She limped out of view of the camera. The time was 10:08.

"Where in the parking lot is this camera?" Jack asked.

"Southeast corner. About the only time anyone parks in that area is around Christmas when the mall is packed."

"Looks like she scouted that lot and chose a place that would not be visible to a camera," Joe said. "Still, she jogs away and comes back limping, and the times fit. No doubt in my mind that she's our gal. What's next, Lance?"

"The Hampton Inn, three days before the party. Load this one, please."

It showed an old white pickup turning under the port-cochere and stopping. A woman climbed from the driver's seat. Jack paused the video.

"Damn, Lance, you've got a license number on the rear."

"Sorry to say, we've checked it. Belongs to a family with a Chevy truck. They live on the Northside. They had reported it missing the next morning. Best guess is it was parked at a restaurant on Camp Bowie. Their son was using it for a date. Came off the front of the Chevy. Not surprising that he didn't notice it missing. And you know, Walt, that cops aren't really looking for cars with front license plates missing."

Walt nodded his agreement.

"She's a petite woman, black hair, looks to be in good shape. Can you zoom in on her face?"

"I can do better than that. We've got the video at the front desk. Keep it running, Jack."

The next scene was the front desk, immediately to the right of the entrance. The camera caught the top half of the woman with a frontal image of her face. Jack stopped the video while they all studied her.

"Good looking woman," Jack said. "Colby, how old?"

Colby thought a moment. "Somewhere around twenty-five, give or take a year or two. And judging from her make-up and hair, she's proud of her appearance."

"What else do we know about her, Lance?"

"Run the video again."

Jack did so.

"You can see she's paying cash. I suspect she had a fake driver's license and used that stolen truck license on her registration."

"Do we have her leaving the motel any time?"

Lance shook his head. "We've checked out the parking lot. There's a blind spot between surveillance cameras. She's good at picking those out. There's a side exit to the motel. It requires a key card, but it's not monitored. And the camera at the rear of the parking lot had been out of commission for about a week. So, short answer is this is the only video we have."

"Hell, it's a start, anyway. Have you sent anyone back over there since you got this video?" Jack asked.

"We called. The desk clerk who was on duty has been off a few days. He's back at noon today. Name's Alfred Santiago."

"Let me go back to that side view of the truck. We're looking for a dent on the right front bumper."

Jack froze it as the woman was getting out from the other side. "There it is, Walt. Same damn truck for sure."

"Lance, if you'll let me borrow that disc, I'll burn another copy and print off some photos of the truck and the woman at the desk."

Lance reached into his backpack again. "I'm ahead of you. Here are copies of the discs, and I've already made photos." Lance handed them to Jack.

Jack flipped through the photos and handed them to Walt, then turned to Joe and Lance. "Why don't Walt and I take it from here? We'll head on over to the Hampton Inn and visit with the desk clerk."

"Fine with me," Joe said. "I suspect that Lance has a full plate himself. Call us when you leave the motel."

After the two men left, Colby asked, "You mind if I tag along. A woman's eye might pick up on something that you guys could miss."

"And let's go in my Crown Vic. I don't have a light rack, but I do have lights built into the grill and a siren. The license is also a state exempt one."

It was early afternoon. The morning guests had departed and

new ones would mostly start showing up in a couple of hours. They parked in front of the motel and walked to the desk. A young Hispanic man, neatly dressed and sporting a mustache and goatee, greeted them. His name tag identified him as Alfred Santiago. "Afternoon. You checking in?"

Since Walt was temporarily without credentials, Jack took the lead. He put his deputy card on the desk. "I'm Deputy Sheriff Jack Bryant with Tarrant County. This is Sergeant Frazier with the DPS. And this is Colby Stripling." Walt moved his coat slightly so that the clerk could see the gun strapped to his waist. It was currently the best credential he had.

"Is there something wrong, officers?" Santiago asked with a slight tremor in his voice.

"Relax, Alfred," Jack said. "Nothing wrong now. We're investigating a murder, only not here. We want to talk about last week, Monday afternoon. We've got the motel's videos from that day and have made some stills from it."

Colby handed Jack the stills. He started with the photo at the desk. "You recognize this woman?"

Santiago studied the photo with a blank look.

"We could show you the video. It's clear the woman paid cash."

"Yeah, now I remember. We don't get very many guests who pay cash these days. In fact, we keep a separate register, nothing fancy, just a spiral notebook. Let me pull it."

He reached under the desk and came up with the notebook. After flipping a couple of pages, he said, "Here she is. Late afternoon on Monday. Name's Katherine Ward, at least that's what her driver's license showed. I think she was driving an old Ford pickup. Now that I've got a name, let me go to the computer." He turned and pushed a few keys. "She paid cash for four nights. We required a hundred dollars more as a deposit. Doesn't look like she ever claimed it."

"You have a room number?"

"Sure, 308."

"Is it occupied now?"

"Not booked for today. Has been for a couple of nights since she probably left."

"We're going to need a key to have a look," Walt said.

"You got it," the clerk replied. He turned to get a blank card, inserted it into a reader and handed him an electronic key. "Please don't mess anything up." He paused and thought. "Well, it is a murder investigation. If you do, just tell me so I can put it back to our standards."

They rode the elevator to the third floor in silence and turned right to find room 308. Walt inserted the key and they entered a standard and very clean motel room with two double beds, a desk, dresser with a television on it and a side chair. Beside the dresser was a small refrigerator with an ice bucket and a four cup coffee pot in a tray. The bathroom was to their left with the usual soaps and shampoo at the sink and in the bathtub. The room had been cleaned at least twice since their killer had occupied it. Still, they took their time to study every detail.

Jack was on his knees in the bathroom when he called to Colby. "Hon, can you come in here a minute?"

Colby appeared at the door as Jack pushed to his feet, his bad knee popping when he did. "Take a look behind the toilet. I see a few small red spots. Could be blood, maybe wine, maybe something else."

Walt appeared at the door. "Here, use my flashlight." He handed her a small Maglite.

Colby dropped to her knees and then to her stomach while she studied the spots. "I don't think it's wine. Could be blood. You think she might have dyed her hair before she left here?"

"Damned if I know," Jack replied. "Why?"

"If she wanted to go from having black hair to red, it's a two-step process. You have to bleach the black hair first before you apply red dye. Otherwise, you end up with just ugly streaked black hair.

"Well," Walt said, "I suppose we should check the all night drug stores. I should have thought of it before. She was going to need something to bandage her leg. We're going to have to seal this room. I also found a spot on the rug right up against the wall. My guess is it's blood. I think we can establish her DNA from the blood we found in the driveway and the woods behind the house, but we should be thorough just in case we have to track her activities."

"Doesn't the DPS have facial recognition software?"

"It's actually the FBI's, but we have access to it. They have a new software program that is supposed to be the best available. It's updated daily. I'll drop these photos off at the local DPS office and have them run the photos."

"Let me suggest one more thing," Jack said. "I know the DPS has access to traffic camera footage. Can you have your guys check the footage going both east and west on I-30, starting about two a.m. We're looking for that truck and that stolen license number. Maybe we can at least figure out which way she went."

"I'm on it."

TWENTY-THREE

The next morning Jack lingered in bed with Colby. With a last bedroom kiss, he pushed himself away and stood beside the bed. "I hate to leave you, but I need to get going."

"Typical man. You get laid and toss the woman away like a limp rag." Colby was smiling when she said it.

"Come on now. As you can plainly see, it's not a rag that's limp. You wore me out."

Colby put her feet on the floor on her side of the bed and reached for her robe that was draped over a chair. "What's on the agenda today? You expect to have anything back from the DPS?"

"I don't think so. I need to go to the RV and check on the status of some of my other clients."

A few minutes later Jack joined Colby in the kitchen, dressed in his boots, jeans, and a blue and white plaid long sleeve shirt. Colby had prepared bacon and eggs with English muffins. He poured himself coffee and sat at the table while she filled his plate and one for herself.

"What are you up to, today?" Jack asked.

"I've got three showings. The first one is at ten. Housing market is booming." She took Jack's right hand in hers. "And I wonder if that proposal is still open," she said as she looked into Jack's blue eyes.

Jack almost choked on his eggs. "You mean marriage?"

"That's exactly what I mean." Colby smiled.

Jack stood at the table and pulled Colby to her feet, then kissed her.

"Damn right it is. When?"

"Well, I think you need to catch that killer and then we have to get through football season. If TCU lucks out and gets into the championship series, that puts us toward the middle of January. I was thinking, maybe, spring."

"And, Ms. Bryant-to-be, have you considered where you would like to get married?"

"Jack, we've talked about this, I may want to keep my last name. It's got a long history in Fort Worth. We'll see. As to a place, I was thinking just out in the back yard. You love the view from there. Maybe at sunset."

"Done."

"And, one more thing. I'm going to take advantage of this hot housing market and list mine today. I think I'm ready to make this my permanent home."

Jack pulled her to him and kissed her again. "I love you, only now I've got to work on some problems for a few other clients."

"I love you, too."

Jack hesitated. "There's one more thing I need to tell you."

Colby could tell from the look in his eyes that it was something serious.

"It's about Walt. You know that he saved my life and the lives of a bunch of other men in Saudi Arabia."

"Yes. Go on. That was twenty years ago."

"You know he had a bad problem with PTSD for a lot of years after that. He says that he hasn't had any problems for at least ten years. Until now. The events at the mansion have triggered it again. Flashbacks, mood swings, no telling what else. I dragged it out of him, but he won't tell anyone else. He's keeping it bottled up. I'm worried that it might explode. I'm pushing him to open up to me about it."

Colby put her hand to her mouth. "I'm so sorry. Is he getting counseling?"

Jack shook his head. "Refuses. He's worried it might cost him his job."

"What can I do?"

"Nothing, but I just thought someone else should know. When you're around him, just keep a watchful eye and let me know if you see anything unusual about his behavior. That's all we can do for now."

Colby pulled him back and hugged him. "We'll just have to get him through it. We can do that," she said with more confidence than she felt.

Jack turned to the kitchen door and chose a cane with a silver horse's head for a handle. He pitched it in the back seat of Lucille and headed out the gate.

When he arrived at the RV he found the parking lot deserted. Maybe he could have a few quiet hours to work on credit card, mortgage, car loan and the myriad of other issues that poor folks found themselves having to deal with these days. He wrote letters, drafted answers to lawsuits and responded to discovery until it was approaching dark. Finally, he shut down his computer and locked up for the day. He hadn't been to Moe's in a while. It was time for a game of dominoes and a beer. Moe's Icehouse was a throwback. With rusted metal walls, it had two garage doors in front that were open on warm days. A couple of old wooden tables were on the concrete driveway in front. Three more tables were scattered around the inside. With no air conditioning, ceiling fans stirred a decent breeze. A worn and scarred bar ran across the back. The three barstools had seen better days. Behind the bar was a cooler where Moe iced the beer and a few sodas every morning.

Jack walked in, limping just a little. *Must be a change in the weather coming,* he thought. Four men were seated at one of the tables, drinking and loudly slapping dominoes on the scarred surface. Jack knew each anteed twenty-five cents per game. The men were laborers who worked construction, repaired streets and the like, blue collar for sure. Jack lived among the rich in Rivercrest, but enjoyed the company of these men.

As he walked past them to bar, one of them said, "Get your beer, Jack. I need to take a little of your money." Jack enjoyed the games and the comradery, but always expected to lose two or three bucks. Before he could take a sip of his Lone Star, his phone rang. He glanced at the caller i.d.

"Hey, Walt, what's up?"

"We've got a lead on the truck."

"Go on."

"You know where I-30 merges with I-20 west of town, we got her. She went through there at 8:54 on the morning after the attacks."

Jack took a sip of his beer. "Go on."

"Knowing she was headed west on I-20, we next checked the cameras in Abilene and found her going through there three hours later. Didn't pick her up again. Don't know whether she turned off the interstate or what. Of course, the farther you get into West Texas, the fewer cameras."

Jack thought a minute. "Well, that puts her somewhere between Abilene and California. At least we can probably eliminate her being east of the Mississippi."

TWENTY-FOUR

Jack and Walt entered the Fort Worth DPS office. Walt introduced himself and Jack to the officer at the front desk.

"We're here to see Captain O'Reilly."

The officer turned to a phone, spoke briefly and disconnected. "He'll be right out. Have a seat if you like."

Captain O'Reilly came through a door on the side of the reception area. His badge identified him as a Ranger. "Sergeant Frazier, nice to see you again. I believe we met a while back when Governor Lardner was in Fort Worth." O'Reilly was a big man with a fringe of brown hair and a booming voice. "How's he doing?"

"Out of the hospital and expected to make a full recovery."

"Thank God for that. Sorry about Edward Hale. I used to run across him and Oscar at various events around town. They're good men. Well, I'm sorry, Edward was a good man and Oscar still is. They have done a lot for Fort Worth."

"Captain, this is Jack Bryant. He's the special prosecutor in this case and is coordinating the activities of all the law enforcement agencies."

Jack stuck out his hand. "My pleasure, Captain. I understand that the facial recognition software may have a hit for us."

O'Reilly smiled. "I think I've got something. Sorry it took so long, but the feds move at their own pace. Follow me back to the conference room." He led the way through the side door and down a hall lined with pictures of various law enforcement officials from the past one hundred years. The emphasis was on DPS officers and Rangers. O'Reilly opened a door on the right and motioned his guests into a conference room. "Have a seat."

He went to a credenza and picked up a file folder, took a seat opposite them and opened the folder. He passed several photos across the table. "I believe you recognize these."

"We do. They're the photos from the Hampton Inn desk camera. We believe this woman is the killer," Jack said.

Captain O'Reilly next passed several other photos across the table. They were taken with a camera, probably a Canon or Nikon, with a powerful lens. The first showed a woman leaving a convenience store, front view. Next was a close up of her face. The image was identical to the ones at the Hampton Inn.

"That's her," Walt said.

Next was a photo of the same woman getting into an old F 150 pickup.

"And that's her truck."

"And a couple more," O'Reilly said as he handed them to her. "She's getting out of the truck and opening a gate. Appears to be a combination lock."

"You know who she is?" Jack asked, his voice rising slightly in anticipation.

"We do. She belongs to one of these anti-government separatist militia groups. They call themselves *The Alamo Defenders*. Her name is Miriam Van Zandt. She's the daughter of Richard

Van Zandt, the founder of this group of whackos."

Jack sat back and stared at the photos. "I've got a ton of questions bouncing through my mind. Let me think where to start. Obvious one. Where is she?"

"Loving County. You know where that is?"

"Not me," Jack said. "And I grew up in Texas."

"Me either," Walt said. "I've been with the governor to a bunch of our 254 counties. Somehow, we missed that one."

"Not a surprise. It's the least populated county in the whole country. Last census counted eighty-two people. You won't find much but sand, sage brush and cactus, maybe a few mesquite trees. Richard Van Zandt used his G.I. bill from the Vietnam War to buy a hundred acres out there so he could be left alone. His property backs up the Pecos River forty miles or so north of the town of Pecos. It's surrounded by six feet of barbed wire. Behind the barbed wire are bunkers about four feet tall. The dirt was dug out and stacked up with a backhoe over the years. Trenches are now behind the bunkers. Rumor is that they also have tunnels that they can use to get from one place to the other if they were ever attacked. Those are probably also where they stash their weapons."

"I at least know where Pecos is. How did you get photos of the woman?"

O'Reilly rose and walked to the credenza. "I have coffee here. Any takers?"

"Black for me, Captain," Walt replied.

"The same," Jack said.

After serving the coffee in mugs with the emblem of the state of Texas emblazoned on the side, O'Reilly took his seat. "A few years back we started getting worried about these militia groups. The Alamo Defenders aren't the only one. They're scattered all over West Texas and even some in East Texas. We suspected that they were assembling large numbers of military grade rifles, assault weapons, AK 15s and the like, even grenades. There was talk that they would band together and seal off part of that area in far West Texas and declare themselves a sovereign nation. No doubt that we could defeat them, but at what cost?"

"Nowadays they don't stay on the compound. Most of the men started working in the Permian basin when fracking led to our latest oil boom. We decided to start dossiers on them. Built up a file on just about everyone, including photos. Miriam Van Zandt works at a convenience store in Pecos. Word is that she's the best marksman in the whole bunch. Not surprising that she would hire out as an assassin."

"You still worried about them leading some kind of revolution?"

"Can't rule out the possibility."

"Where do they get their weapons?" Walt asked.

"Mexico. Short drive from where they are. The men are making a lot of money in the oil patch. They go across the border at night. There are some low water crossings along the Rio Grande, good for illegal immigrants, drug smuggling and gun running. The cartels have any weapon short of a tank that they want. We also suspect that there may be some bartering going on. The cartels may have some of these guys doing some of their dirty work in trade for guns."

Jack rose and stood behind his chair to stretch his knee. "Sorry, Captain. I've got a bum knee that's aching a little today."

"Saw your cane. War injury?"

"It was. Walt and I met in Desert Storm. I got called back up by Bush, the 41st. If you suspect all of these weapons are in their compound, why don't you just get a search warrant and raid the place?"

O'Reilly shook his head. "We don't need another Waco or Ruby Ridge. That could set off these crazies from here to California. From all outward appearances, they are just ordinary folks who want to be left alone. We don't even get them for traffic tickets."

Jack drummed his fingers on the table while he thought. "Is the woman still there? We know she was wounded."

"Since we have just now identified her, the answer is that we don't know. I'm having hospitals within fifty miles of the interstate between here and there check for a woman showing up with a gunshot wound to the leg. Oh, and you may not have heard this, but those red spots you found in the bathroom at the motel were red hair dye. And that one spot on the carpet is blood, matches the blood on the patio at the Hale mansion and in the woods behind it. She may now be a red head. We'll also be checking the hospitals within a hundred miles of Pecos." He smiled. "That won't take very long."

"Can I make a suggestion?" Jack asked.

O'Reilly nodded.

"Can you put an officer in a private vehicle to stake out that convenience store for a few days? If she's thinking that she got away with it and has recovered, she may have gone back to work. Once we get a warrant for her arrest, you could pick her up."

"Agreed. We're short of troopers out there. I'll have to call Colonel Burnside, but I'm sure he'll give the okay. Not often that the governor's shot."

Walt rose. "Thanks, Captain. Jack and I will head over to Joe Shannon's office, bring him up to speed and get a warrant for her arrest issued. We'll have it in our back pocket when the time comes."

"Here, I've got a set of these photos for you," O'Reilly said as he handed an envelope to Jack. "I'll be in touch in a few days."

TWENTY-FIVE

Jack and Walt drove to the courthouse complex and dropped in, unannounced, on the District Attorney. They had to drink coffee in his reception area while he wound up a meeting. After an hour he came through the door.

"Sorry to keep you waiting. I was in the middle of a meeting with a couple of my assistants about a public corruption investigation. It ought to hit the papers any day now. Come on in."

Joe led them back to his office where they took seats around a coffee table. Joe's secretary appeared to take coffee requests, which were declined.

"We don't want to take up much of your time," Jack said. "Just want to keep you in the loop."

Joe smiled. "I figure you must have something good or you wouldn't be here."

"We've identified the killer," Jack said.

"Son of a bitch," Joe said as reached over the coffee table to shake the hands of his two guests. "Tell me more."

Walt explained the photos and handed them to Joe. The D. A. took his seat and carefully lined them up. "Damn sure is a match. I presume you've got a name."

Jack took him through what they learned from O'Reilly and their current plan. Joe walked to a bookcase and pulled a directory from it. He flipped through it. "There he is. The D.A. out there covers Loving, Ward and Reeves counties, 143rd District. I've run across him a time or two at meetings. There's a lot of crime in that area. They're not on the border but close to it. The population is about eighty percent Hispanic. Cartels are running drugs east and bringing money back from their east coast runs constantly. I hear the sheriffs in those counties are always making arrests, but the D.A. rarely prosecutes. He's a deal maker, usually for some kind of probation or deferred adjudication. Still the people out there keep re-electing him. I could give him a call about this compound if you want."

Jack shook his head. "We're not ready to call anyone right now. We need to let O'Reilly do his surveillance for a few days. Then, from what you say, it may be the sheriff we want to contact and leave the D.A. out of it. For now, we would just like you to get out a warrant for the arrest of Miriam Van Zandt. O'Reilly is emailing you the reports on the blood in the room and from the mansion. You figure that, along with the photos, will be enough for the warrant?"

"Plenty." Shannon looked at his watch. "Come on. It's about lunch time. We can just beat the crowd at Angelo's. Best barbecue in Fort Worth and only five minutes away. Jack, I figure I owe you a lunch. I didn't really think it through the other night when I named you special prosecutor. This is probably taking up nearly all of your time. You're getting paid a daily rate. Not what you're used to making, but it's what the state allows."

Jack rose and leaned on his cane. "I'll take that barbecue as payment. Otherwise, remember I'm a pro bono lawyer. Donate whatever the state pays to Habitat for Humanity."

After lunch Jack dropped Walt back at the house where Walt packed his clothes and left to spend a few days with his family. He also intended to see Colonel Burnside to give him a personal report on the status of the investigation and arrange for an appointment with Governor Lardner to update him now that he was back in Austin. Then he needed to call the Rangers and sit for the required interview for their internal investigation. He knew that the other members of the detail had done so. He was the last. He worried about questions the Ranger interrogator might ask. Still he had no choice. Maybe they would wind up after that so he could at least get his badge back. He knew he had been withdrawn around Mary and the boys. Mary tried to understand, but she tossed and turned as much as he did, worrying about what might become of them. The boys tried to avoid him when he was home since he was now prone to lashing out in anger at the least little thing. It wasn't their fault. He needed to regain control of his emotions. Deep down, though, he knew that there was no hope of his returning to normal until at least they caught the killer and wound up the investigation. And maybe that would help get rid of the nightmares that caused him to wake in a sweat nearly every night.

TWENTY-SIX

Colonel Van Zandt knocked on Miriam's trailer door and entered. It was dusk. He found her lying on the couch with her wounded leg propped up on several pillows, watching a re-run of CSI Miami.

"How you doing, Baby Girl?"

"This damn thing is taking longer to heal than I thought. Temperature is coming down but still around a hundred."

"Just thought I'd tell you that a bunch of us are going to be in the back for a while. We have a shipment coming in."

"I want to go. I'm about stir crazy in here. Hand me those crutches."

"You sure you're up to it?"

"I'll probably just stay in the truck."

"Okay. Come on. We're going to the front gate first to let them in and then back to the landing strip."

Miriam handed one of the crutches to her dad and used the

other one along with the rail beside the steps to get to the bottom. She took the other crutch from Van Zandt and made her way through the twilight to his truck. Once they were both inside, he started the engine and drove slowly to the front of the compound. When they arrived at the gate, they had to wait. Van Zandt grew impatient after fifteen minutes.

"Damn Mexicans. They would be late for their own funeral."

In the distance they saw headlights evolve into a black Suburban that turned into their gravel driveway. Van Zandt used a flashlight to see the combination on the lock and swung the gate open. The Suburban drove through and stopped. Once he re-locked the gate, Van Zandt walked to the driver's side.

"Buenas noches, Senior Van Zandt." He switched to English. "Everything is on schedule. Our plane should be here in twenty minutes."

Van Zandt glanced inside the vehicle and saw three other men. He spit tobacco juice on the ground beside the Suburban. "Just so you'll know, Jose. My daughter's in the truck with me. I'll turn around. We'll take the perimeter road to the back."

Jose nodded his agreement and handed a two way radio to Van Zandt.

Once in his truck, Van Zandt backed up and proceeded down the fence line to the west until he reached the boundary of the property. The road was nothing more than two ruts in the desert hardpack. At the fence he turned to the right and drove slowly to the back. As the two trucks approached the back of the property, he flashed his lights once. Eight other trucks flashed theirs back. They were parked along an eight hundred yard runway, four on each side. Van Zandt had rented a bull dozier some years back when approached by one of the cartels. His men smoothed out the desert and packed it as firmly as possible. The deal was for the use of a landing strip in return for weapons. The cartel leaders loved the arrangement. They had stockpiles of weapons large enough to take over a Central American country if they chose.

This landing strip was literally in the middle of nowhere. On the other side of the fence was a thousand acres of desert, owned by someone in Houston but no one had set foot on it for twenty years. And the cartel leaders knew that The Alamo Defenders weren't about to divulge their arrangement.

As per plan, Van Zandt drove to the west end of the runway and turned his lights on low. Jose drove his Suburban to the other end and faced it away from the runway with the rear red lights on so that the pilot would know where the runway stopped. Then all was quiet with light coming from an occasional lighter that would flame momentarily, followed by the burning end of a cigarette. And they waited under a sky filled with stars, flashing and twinkling in an area with no man-made light. The men had a contest on each of these nights. One point for a satellite sighting; two for a shooting star. The one who scored the most points was exempt from chores on the next weekend.

"Miriam, you've got young eyes. Tell me when you see the plane."

"Got it, Pa. I'm just glad to be away from that damn trailer and doing something. I'm going to get out of the truck and stand a few yards away to get a better view."

"You need any help?"

"I'm okay." She hobbled about ten yards on her crutches and stared out into the western sky until she saw what she thought was a star moving. Satellite or airplane? She watched for a full minute and then hollered. "It's coming, Pa."

Van Zandt turned his lights on high and flashed them twice before returning them to low. Instantly, eight sets of headlights illuminated the runway. The plane seemed to be moving in slow motion as it approached. It was so low when it passed over her father's truck that Miriam ducked out of reflex. The pilot was experienced. He put the wheels down in the first one hundred yards, slowed and taxied to a stop ten yards from the Suburban. He killed the engine, waited for a minute, and then climbed from the cockpit. At the same time, the four occupants of the Suburban were beside the plane. Two carried assault rifles and stood guard. The other two started removing packets of cocaine from the airplane and stacking them in the rear of the Suburban.

While they did so, Van Zandt and Miriam drove down the runway. As they passed each set of trucks, their lights went out. When they got to the end of the runway, Van Zandt killed his engine and waited until Jose signaled that he could get out. Van Zandt understood that what they were hauling was none of his business.

"Well, my friend," Jose said, "looks like another successful operation. The weapons you ordered will be at the usual place beside the Rio Grande tomorrow night about this time. Tell your men thanks. If you'll lead us to the gate, we'll be on our way."

The two vehicles moved back the opposite way on the runway. As they did so, the truck lights were again illuminated. The pilot checked his instruments briefly, hollered, "Clear," and started the engine. The plane pivoted and he revved the engine. Before he got to the last set of headlights, he pulled back on the throttle and was airborne. His next stop would be in a small village on the other side of the river.

TWENTY-SEVEN

After Walt left, Jack and Colby took glasses of iced tea out back and sat in loungers beside the pool. Colby paused to put on a sweater. It was a sunshiny November day, but the temperature was in the fifties.

"I've got some good news," Colby said. "I've only had my house listed for a few days and two buyers have met my asking price."

"Congratulations," Jack said. Then he paused. "What are we going to do with all of your furniture and stuff?"

"I've been thinking about that. After the Dead Peasants killer torched my house, my family heirlooms were destroyed. All of the furniture is new. I don't have any real attachment to much of it. I decorated this place and I like what I did for you. I'll pick a few pieces that I think we can fit in here. Otherwise, we'll donate the furnishings to your favorite charity, Habitat for Humanity."

"Tell you what, most of my clients live in trailers or apartments with furniture that you and I wouldn't even allow in the front door. When the time comes, let me put out the word. We'll let each of them pick out two or three items."

"I like that. You've really become attached to your clients, haven't you?"

Jack thought a minute before replying. "I really have. I suppose they help me recognize how lucky you and I are. As I help them work through problems, I become their counselor as well as their lawyer. Some of them are like family."

"Yeah, I pegged you almost from the first day we met. You put on that tough, trial lawyer exterior, but you're really just a softy underneath. Now tell me about what happened today."

Jack brought her current. "And the good news is that I have a few days while they do some surveillance out in West Texas to spend with you and take care of some of my clients. Of course, we have a game this Saturday. Another big one with Texas. Maybe we can get J.D. and his girlfriend to join us for dinner Saturday night."

It was late afternoon with only a couple more hours of daylight. Jack drove past his RV to Ike's corner where he parked and walked up to his client. Trousers woke from a sound sleep in the sun and bounced around at Jack's feet.

"Afternoon, Jack," Ike said. "Trousers, behave yourself."

"You having a good day, Ike?"

"Not bad. How's our lawsuit coming? Excuse me a minute." A car had stopped and the window rolled down. The woman driving reached over the passenger seat and handed Ike a dollar. "Bless you, ma'am. And Trousers thanks you, too." She smiled as she drove off, satisfied that she had done her good deed for the day.

"Tell you what, Ike, when you quit today, come on by. I'll either be in the RV or at Moe's."

Ike nodded as another car stopped. Jack used a Burger King parking lot to turn around and go the few blocks back to his

RV. He raised the armor and turned off the alarm. He walked a couple of steps before he remembered he had forgotten his cane and returned to the truck. Inside the RV he stripped off his Levi jacket, turned on the lights and retrieved a bottle of water from the fridge before he walked back to his office. Settling into his chair, he turned on the computer. There was an electronic notice from the district clerk's office about Ike's case that brought a smile to his face.

Some clerk must have brought his amended petition to the attention of Judge Jamison. On her own motion she had ordered that all of the funds from the other songs Ike claimed were his were to be deposited in the trustee account, pending the outcome of the lawsuit. Jack figured that she either liked Ike or took a disliking to Whatley and his California entourage. Whatever the reason, all of the royalties from the album were no longer going to T-Buck's account. He was probably a wealthy man, but this was his most popular album by far. It wouldn't be long before he started feeling the pinch.

Next, he turned to his phone to see he had several messages. Most were from potential pro bono clients. Jack wrote down their problems and return phone numbers. The investigation was interfering with his helping these folks. He would fit them in as he could. Otherwise, he would contact them by phone, advise as he could and tell them he would let them know when he could schedule an appointment.

Jack looked at court filings and correspondence and emails on other cases and moved each to its respective file. Last, he checked his stocks and shut down the computer. After putting on his Levi jacket, he stepped from the RV, lowered the armor and set the alarm. The overhead lights would automatically come on at dusk.

He was walking next door to Moe's when he saw Ike and Trousers coming from the other direction. He waited and motioned them to a table on the inside, out of air that was getting more chilly by the minute. Jack declined an invitation to join the domino game. He and Ike took a table. Moe brought them two Lone Stars and returned with a bowl of water for Trousers."

"Much obliged, Moe," Ike said.

They sipped their beers, and Jack began. "Got some good news. Our amended petition has been served."

Ike nodded.

"The good news is that the judge has ordered all of the proceeds from the other songs on that album to be put into the trust account."

Ike let out a low whistle. "That could be a whole bunch of money."

"You got that right. Now, tell me how you're coming with getting some of that old sheet music for those songs."

Ike took another sip of beer. "I've been calling, trying to locate every old band member I can find. Some are dead. Some just can't be found. Still, I've got two, so far, who say that they think they have some of the music in their attics. And I'm still working on locating more. I may have to go to New Orleans and start knocking on doors."

"Ike, this is big. You may be a wealthy man. For damn sure we can get you out of that shelter. I'll pay for your trip back to New Orleans if you think it's necessary. Now, on Saturday, be out in front of the shelter at noon. Get one of your friends to take care of Trousers. We're going to watch TCU play Texas."

The next morning Jack and Colby awoke and lingered in bed for an hour.

"Okay, you pick football tomorrow. Today, it's my turn. We're going to the Kimbell Museum. They have a new impressionist exhibit."

Jack stifled a yawn.

"No, you're not going back to sleep. Breakfast, then the museum followed by lunch. If you want a nap this afternoon, that's okay." She smiled, coyly. "Although, I may be up to some more bedroom time by this afternoon."

Jack jumped from the bed. "Since you put it that way, let's get going."

They arrived at the shelter promptly at noon. Ike was in front, wearing a Horned Frogs sweatshirt and a jacket. He climbed into the back seat of the Bentley.

"Ike, this is Colby, my fiancé."

"Pleased to make your acquaintance, Miss Colby."

"Same here, Ike, only drop the Miss. Colby is just fine."

The game turned out to be much closer than the Frogs wanted. It was supposed to have been a rebuilding year for Texas. The Longhorns had lost four of their first seven games and played like this one was for the national championship. The Frogs pulled it out, but just barely, 42-39. Ike yelled so much that he was hoarse after the game. When Jack dropped him off at the shelter, he said, "I haven't had that much fun since I left New Orleans. If we get some money out of this lawsuit, I'm going to buy a house and fix you some of my world famous gumbo."

Two hours later Jack and Colby parked in front of Bonnell's Restaurant. Jack spotted J.D.'s pickup a few spaces down. They entered the restaurant to find J.D. surrounded by fans who were beseeching him for an autograph. Beside him was his longtime girlfriend, Tanya, a tall blonde and an All American in her own right as a volleyball player. She secretly hoped that J.D. would be drafted by the San Diego Chargers so she could start a professional beach volleyball career. J.D. saw his dad and Colby. He apologized, broke away from the fans and nodded at the hostess who whisked the four of them to a corner table.

When they were seated, Jack ordered a bottle of Chardonnay. J.D. enjoyed wine and beer as well as occasional bourbon, only not during the season. From August until it was over, he was a teetotaler. He said he was fine with water. Tanya asked for the same.

"You limping a little, Son?" Jack asked.

"Yeah, I got my ankle stepped on toward the end of the game. I'll go to the training room tomorrow and ice it. Should be okay by next weekend."

"Tanya, how are you doing? We haven't seen much of you lately."

"Volleyball season runs about parallel with football season. We usually play twice a week. Between games, practices and studies, even J.D. and I have a hard time getting together. But, I might add, that our volleyball team is almost as good as the football team. The conference tournament is coming up. We're seeded number one."

The waiter brought their drinks, explained the specials for the evening, handed them menus and excused himself. Colby sipped her wine and placed it on the table.

With her eyes sparkling, she said, "Jack and I have some news."

"Spill it," J.D. said.

"We're going to be married."

J.D. rose to hug his dad and kiss Colby on the cheek. "Wow, congratulations. When?"

Jack took over the conversation. "We figure we can't do it too soon. Hopefully, you'll be playing for the national championship. Then I've got to round up this killer. That may take a little while. Next, you've got the NFL draft and we'll have to negotiate a contract, assuming you still want me as your agent. We figure in the spring, maybe May."

"Works for Tanya and me. And, of course I want you to represent me. You really think you can wind up this criminal investigation by then?"

"Hoping to. Right now things are going well. Could be in a few weeks even, but I can't tell you anything for now."

TWENTY-EIGHT

Jack had just said goodbye to his third pro bono client of the day when his cell rang. He glanced at the caller i.d.

"Hey, Walt, you enjoying a few days with your family?"

"Actually, I can't seem to get my ass off the couch. My boys always look forward to this time of year because it's deer season; only, we haven't been once. I can't get motivated to do much but flip channels on the television all day." Jack shook his head at that reply. "We've got some news. I suppose I should say, we have a report, nothing really newsworthy."

"I'm listening."

"DPS has been watching that convenience store for four days. She's not been around."

"Hell," Jack said. "I was hoping this was going to be easy. What do we do now?"

"Drone."

"Say that again."

"You've read about them. Also called unmanned aerial vehicles or UAVs. DPS has a long range one. We have an agreement with the Border Patrol to split the cost. When we don't need it for anything else, one of them flies up and down the Rio Grande at about six thousand feet, looking for drug smugglers, illegals and so forth. It's based at Laughlin Air Force Base in Del Rio on the border. That's where the pilot is. Colonel Burnside is arranging for it to be diverted to Pecos and Loving County. They say it's small enough that it won't be noticed at six thousand feet or so. We'll get some good pictures of the compound."

"Sounds good to me. When can we see the results?"

"Instantly, if you want to drive to Austin. We have a room at the DPS headquarters with high definition screens on the walls. The pilot in Del Rio is flying it. There's a feed to Austin. We can watch what he's seeing."

"I'll be there. Tell me when."

"How about ten in the morning. That'll give you time to drive from Fort Worth. I'll arrange for the pilot to have the drone close to the compound around that time, but he won't fly over it until you and I are ready."

"You got it. Give me directions to the DPS office and I'll see you there. And, get your ass off that couch and at least take your wife for a walk, maybe the boys, too." Jack clicked off the phone and gazed out the window, thinking about Jack vegetating on the couch. Clearly, he was still dealing with issues. Jack finally concluded there was nothing he could do for his friend at the moment. Still, he would watch for an opportunity to encourage him to talk.

At a quarter of ten the next day Jack parked Lucille in front of the DPS headquarters, reached for his cane and walked toward the main entrance. Today he wore a long-sleeved, blue dress shirt. Walt greeted him at the front door.

"Follow me."

They went through a door different from the one going back to the Colonel's office. This hall was institutional green with no pictures or decorations on the walls. At the end, Walt buzzed. The door opened and Colonel Burnside stood in the doorway.

"Come on in. You must be Jack Bryant. I've been hearing good things about you. I had some reservations when Joe appointed you as special prosecutor, but no more. We've made good progress." He stuck out his hand.

"Thank you, Colonel. I relied heavily on Walt."

They entered the room to find one wall with a video screen similar to the one Jack had in his media room. In the middle were swivel chairs on rollers with drink holders in the arm rests. The large screen on the wall showed what appeared to be a desert. It took Jack a few seconds to realize that the scene was changing. In the lower left corner was a smaller screen.

A lean, middle aged black man with white hair, bushy eyebrows and a similar mustache could be seen on the smaller screen. He was dressed in jeans and a T-shirt and was holding a control in his hands.

"Jack, this is Colonel Floyd Foxworth. We just call him Fox. He flew fighters for the air force for twenty-five years and retired in Del Rio. We talked him out of retirement to do a different kind of flying."

Fox looked toward the camera. "Morning, Jack. I've got a camera there in your room so I can see you, too."

"Fox, can you give Jack a short demonstration as to what your toy can do?"

"Sure. I flew it up from the border early this morning and have it just circling about fifty miles from your target. What you're seeing now is from the camera mounted on the bottom. I could take it up to ten thousand feet and you could still see a coyote running across the desert. I can also rotate it three hundred and sixty degrees, like this."

They watched as the camera made a full circle, very slowly, before returning to its starting position.

"Then, I can switch cameras to the one facing the front and we can see where it is going, somewhat like the view from a cockpit."

"What's the speed?" Jack asked.

"I can make it hover, which is what it is doing now, or we can get up to sixty miles an hour."

The craft leaped forward and soon the ground was flying by.

"I can also drop it to a couple of hundred feet like this and then pull it back up to the six thousand feet where we were when you walked in."

"Just curious," Jack said. "How long before you have to refuel it?"

"Usually we don't need to. If it's been sitting in the hangar for a while, which it does only for maintenance, we'll recharge it. Otherwise, it has solar panels on the top that continually feed the battery.

"I'm impressed," Jack said.

"It's amazing technology. Not quite as much fun as when I was flying fighters, but it's a great retirement job. And, no one is shooting at me." Fox grinned. "Now, where are we going?"

"North of Pecos," Colonel Burnside said. "By road, it would be up U.S. 285 and hang a right on 302. When you get to the Pecos River, the compound is on the left. Here are the coordinates." He held a piece of paper up in front of the camera. Fox wrote them down.

"Give me a second to program them, and we'll be off." A moment later the drone picked up speed. "This front camera also rotates. I'll set it so we can see the ground and the horizon. You still want it at six thousand feet?"

"You tell us," Jack replied. "We want high definition pictures, but don't want it to be spotted."

"That ought to be about right. You can see that we're passing over I-20 east of Pecos."

The eyes of the three men in the room in Austin were glued to the screen, like kids watching their first model airplane.

"Damn," Walt said. "I can even tell you the makes of the cars on the freeway. Amazing."

"We'll just follow highway 285 until we get to the turn. Won't take but a few minutes."

A different highway came into view and the craft veered right.

"Not much traffic on these roads," Fox commented.

"Yeah, it's one of the most desolate parts of the country. That's the reason these guys chose it," Burnside said.

"Okay, we're coming up on the Pecos. Pretty dry this time of year."

"There it is," Jack said, pointing at the upper part of the screen. "Can you switch to the bottom camera now? You can see a gate."

The camera view changed.

"Now, slow it way down," Jack said.

The drone appeared to be barely moving.

"Damn, look at that. Bunkers and trenches all the way around the place. What's that?" Jack pointed to a partially constructed building.

"That, my friend, is their version of the Alamo. Nothing but the front façade. They started it several years ago but haven't gotten around to finishing," Burnside said.

"There's a bunch of trailers. Must be where they live. I don't see any people," Jack said.

"Word is that the men started working out in the oil fields when the Permian basin took off again. Closest drilling is about an hour from there. I suspect the men leave before dawn and return after dark. They may not want anything to do with the government, but they like money as much as the next guy."

Walt pointed to the upper part of the screen. "Look over there by the river. There's a trailer set off a little from the others. That looks like our killer's pickup beside it. Fox, can you zoom in on it?"

The camera zoomed until the pickup covered nearly the entire screen.

"Now, can you circle around so we can see the right side? That's it. Jack, there's our dent in the bumper. We found her."

"No, we didn't find her. We found her truck. We need to find out if she's still living here. Fox, can we circle around a couple of hours?"

"No problem, as long as you want. I'm going to have her hover for a couple of minutes. I've got to step out to take a leak. Tell me if you see something."

When Fox returned, Jack said, "Can you go over to the northeast part of that property. I want to have a look at it."

Fox pointed the drone that direction.

"You guys, particularly you, Fox, tell me if I'm wrong. Isn't that a landing strip there along the west fence?"

Fox zoomed the camera in. "Looks like it to me. Smoother and flatter than the desert around it. Could be used for some prop planes."

"Probably not related to what we're looking for, but our criminal division will need to be watching that compound more carefully," Burnside said. "Fox, I'll coordinate with the Border Patrol and get you to start regular fly overs of the compound."

"Roger, Colonel," Fox replied.

Two hours went slowly. Jack had to remind himself to focus. Two pickups stopped at the front gate with men in them. Each time a man climbed out on the passenger side and bent over what appeared to be a lock on the gate. Once the truck went through, he re-locked the gate and the truck moved among the trailers where the men separated. At noon the doors of a building in the middle of the property opened and several children came running out, followed by women who must have been their mothers. They played on a swing set and a jungle gym for a half an hour until they were called back into the building. For the most part the women wore jeans, long sleeve shirts and sneakers. Miriam was not among them.

An older man with a long beard, wearing overalls left a double-wide close to the building with a beer in hand. He settled himself into a rocker in the shade of the front porch.

"That must be Van Zandt," Jack said. "Fox, since we're here, can we stay until dark? If her dad is on the porch, she may join him."

"No problem for me," Fox said. "I brought my lunch."

"Speaking of lunch," Burnside said, "I'll have my assistant bring us some take-out menus."

The afternoon wore on. The children were dismissed from the building about three. The sun was drifting toward the horizon. More men were returning. After going in their trailers, they came out with tall boys in hand and stood around the backs of pickups, swapping stories. Jack pointed to the trailer that appeared to be Miriam's.

"There she is," Jack said. A redhead was limping past the pickup, using a cane for support. She made her way to the building and disappeared under the cover where her father was. "Fox, we've seen enough. Thanks for your help. You can go back to patrolling the border."

"My pleasure, gentlemen. Let me know when I can be of service."

"It may be sooner than you think," Walt said. "Colonel, can you burn a DVD of what we've seen today before I leave?"

TWENTY-NINE

Jack called a meeting of the heads of the local law enforcement agencies along with Walt and Colonel Burnside who agreed to fly to Fort Worth for the meeting. He scheduled it for his house because he wanted to confirm the understanding that he was in charge and had the last word. They arrived one by one for the two o'clock meeting. Jack greeted them at the front door and introduced them to Colby who led them into the media room where she had set up a side table with coffee, tea, water and soft drinks.

Colonel Burnside was the last to arrive. So the others talked TCU football as they stood around the table.

"Helluva season we're having," Joe said.

"Any chance we can be in the final four and contend for the championship?" Lance asked.

"Jack, you're the inside expert. What's your take?"

Jack shook his head. "All I know for sure is that J.D. is healthy. Beyond that, what you guys read in the newspapers is about

147

what I know."

"Then, we best win out and see what that damn committee does," Roger Culbertson said. "Don't like to leave it up to the subjective decision of the committee, but that's what we have to live with. They should have put eight teams in the championship round. After all, we have sixty-five teams in March Madness."

"I see Walt's Crown Vic pulling up. He went to pick up Burnside at Meacham field. You guys take a seat. Controls on those fancy chairs are on the right arm rest."

Walt and Colonel Burnside were met at the door by Colby who led them into the room.

"Sorry I'm late, gentlemen. Had to circle around a storm over Waco."

Walt and Burnside both asked for iced tea from Colby and took two seats that had been left for them on the front row.

When they all were seated and Colby took a seat on the second row, Jack started. "Thanks to all of your efforts, we have identified the killer and tracked her to a compound in Loving County, about forty miles north of Pecos. You've seen the reports. She's now a redhead. Still walks with a limp after one of Walt's men managed to wound her. Here's footage, compliments of the DPS, of the compound and specifically identifying her."

He pushed a button on the remote and the footage started with images leading up to the compound, showing the gate, the Alamo, the shooting range, the ropes course with the weight shed beside it and the trailers. The footage went blank and then showed Miriam's trailer with the pickup beside it and her walking with a cane to the building.

"Based on what we found in the motel room, she died her hair the morning after the attack," Jack said. "No doubt she's our gal. So, how do you propose to proceed?"

Silence filled the room as each of the men weighed the options.

"Colonel, is this one of those militia outfits that's armed to the teeth?" Randall Meacham asked.

"We don't know for sure. Only, we have to assume that they are well armed, assault rifles, grenades, probably a couple of snipers."

"Then, Colonel, I have an idea," Lance White said. "I've run across the sheriff out in that county a time or two. He's reasonably honest. Why don't I call him and see if he'll serve the warrant on Ms. Van Zandt?"

"Suppose he agrees and she refuses to surrender. He can't pull his gun. He'll be outmanned about forty to one."

"He's not going to get involved in a gun fight. He either brings her back or he leaves."

"I suppose it's worth a try," Walt said.

"But, we're tipping her off," Jack said. "What's she going to do?"

"I don't think she'll run for it," Colonel Burnside said. "She's going to feel safer there than anywhere else. If we don't at least try, we're in for a fight, risking lives. Chances are slim, but it's worth a shot. Still, I think I better alert the DPS SWAT team. And there's one other potential benefit. If we have to raid the place and there are a bunch of casualties, we can at least tell the media that we tried to arrest her without force."

THIRTY

Jim Bill Davis parked his white Ford F-150 pickup in front of the courthouse in Mentone. It had a red and blue light rack on top and a siren. Both were little used. Mentone wasn't even really a town. No one had ever bothered to incorporate it. Besides, there wasn't all that much to incorporate. At the last census its population was fourteen. The town consisted of a small café, a run-down filling station, an ancient post office that somehow had survived the postal service downsizing, a handful of houses, beaten up by the desert sun and wind, and a boxy, yellow brick courthouse that looked as if it had been designed with a child's building blocks. Each of the buildings was dusted with a thick coating of sand. The courthouse contained the county clerk's office, the sheriff's office and a holding cell that was rarely occupied. On the second floor was a courtroom that was occasionally visited by the judge from Pecos, The town lined maybe a quarter mile of Highway 302. Beyond it on either end was the vast expanse of the desert.

Davis was a lean man in his fifties. He retrieved a straw cow-boy hat and climbed from his pickup. He wore his usual attire of faded jeans and a blue denim shirt. On his chest was a badge. If one got close enough, he could see that Davis was the sheriff of Loving County. Strapped to his side was a Colt 45 that hadn't been out of its holster except for cleaning in more than twenty years. With only eighty-two permanent residents, there wasn't much need for a gun. Still if you were a sheriff in West Texas, you had to have one visible to residents and strangers alike. As he walked into the courthouse, Davis took a toothpick from his shirt pocket and put into his mouth. He started chewing on toothpicks when he quit smoking years before, and now a toothpick was as much a part of him as his badge and gun.

Davis stopped by the clerk's office. Standing in the door-way, he said, "Ruth Ann, this is the first time I've seen your office empty in a while. No land men checking through the deed records?"

Ruth Ann looked up from her desk and smiled. "The day's young. You know what that fracking has done in the Permian Basin. We're on the far west side of it, but those oil guys are check-ing mineral rights and trying to dig up information on some of those old wells that haven't produced in thirty years. Course it may be that the drop in oil prices is having an impact."

"You know, I even had to give one of those guys a speeding ticket the other day. First time I've done that in a couple of years. Mostly, I just let people ignore the speed signs. Only a damn fool would drive seventy on a vacant, stretch of paved road around here. This guy was pushing a hundred; so, I figured I better rein him in a little. Wasn't sure my old pickup could still go that fast. I'm going back to my office and then head over to the café for lunch. You know where I am just in case someone tries to run off with one of your land books." He laughed at his joke and shifted the toothpick from one side of his mouth to the other.

The sheriff walked down the white marble corridor, his steps echoing in the empty hallway. The marble had been installed to upgrade the interior of the old courthouse during the last oil boom in the seventies. His office was small, just big enough for a desk, a bookcase and two guest chairs. The windows had a view to the south and east, if sand and sagebrush and a rolling hill or two constituted a view. The desk was usually empty except for a phone and an old computer that could be used to very slowly dial up the internet. On a middle shelf of the bookcase was an old printer, connected with a cord that snaked down the bookcase, across the floor to the desk and climbed to the computer. Sometimes it worked; sometimes not. Beside it was a fax machine that Davis used a little more often. In fact, he dug into his own pocket to have it replaced recently.

Davis sat at his desk, propped his feet up and stared out the window, wondering how he would spend the afternoon after he had lunch and went home for his afternoon siesta. He was about to doze off in his chair when the phone rang.

"Sheriff Davis, here."

"Sheriff, this is Lance White over in Fort Worth. You keeping busy out there in West Texas?"

"Lance, nice to hear from you. I think we last talked at that meeting in San Antonio four or five years back. Yeah, things are picking up out here. Got a little oil boom underway. More cars and trucks than we've seen in years. Most of them stay in the motels in Pecos or commute from Odessa. They've already poked a few holes in the ground over on the east side of the county. I keep hoping that the oil companies will decide they need to put up a cell tower so I can get service here. I've got a cell phone but it's only good when I get over toward Pecos. What can I do for you?"

"You familiar with an outfit called The Alamo Defenders?"

"Sure. I've known old man Van Zandt since he bought that land thirty years ago. He doesn't get off his property very often, but I run across him in Pecos occasionally. Most of the boys that live there have gotten jobs in the oil patch."

"You ever have any problem with them?"

"Nope, can't say as I have. I hear that they're preparing for the government to attack them. I suspect that they have some illegal weapons stashed somewhere, but they stick to themselves and don't bother anyone; so, I prefer just to leave them be. Why are you asking?"

"I'm sure you saw that the governor was seriously wounded and a billionaire named Edward Hale was killed here in Fort Worth a few weeks ago."

"Yep, saw it on television. Governor's okay, isn't he?"

"Yeah, he's making a full recovery. Here's why I'm calling. We've tracked down the killer. Name's Miriam Van Zandt. You know her?"

Davis took his feet off his desk and sat upright. "Sure. She's the old man's daughter. Works at a convenience store in Pecos." He paused. "I don't recollect seeing her in there lately."

"Sheriff, we've got a warrant for her arrest. You think you can serve it?"

Davis stood and turned to gaze out the window. "Shit, Lance, you're asking for damn big favor."

"Look, I'm not asking you to do anything you don't want to do. I also don't want to put you in danger. Can you get in the compound?"

Davis nodded his head. "I suppose I probably can. I can talk to the old man. If she won't surrender voluntarily, there's not much I can do."

"That's all we're asking. If she won't go peacefully, we did what we could. Next step will be that we'll have to take her by force."

"Whoee. You're not saying the half of it. They'll be armed to the teeth."

"So, what do you say?"

Davis took the now-shredded toothpick from his mouth and replaced it with one from his pocket. "I'll give it a try. Fax me the warrant. And, one more thing. If I fail, I'm the sheriff here and I decide who can try to take her. I won't have any of the feds, no FBI, no DEA. We ain't having another Waco or Ruby Ridge around here. I know the DPS has a damn fine SWAT team, made up of Texas men, most of whom served in the military. I'll let only them into my county. Understood?"

"You got it, Sheriff. Look for the fax in the next few minutes."

Davis turned on the fax machine and walked across the street to the café for lunch. He greeted the few people who sat at the plastic covered tables, calling each of them by name. After all, he was a politician and was up for election the next year. He placed his hat on a scarred wooden rack and took a seat at the same table where he lunched every day. Mable, the owner, cook and waitress, brought him black coffee. He sipped it quietly until she returned with the day's special, meatloaf with mashed potatoes and green beans. While he ate, he thought about Miriam Van Zandt, her father and the men in the compound. He definitely would not cause a ruckus. He would just call Richard and ask him to get the front gate open so he could discuss a matter. He knew in his gut that he would fail, but he would give it his best shot, and it might as well be this afternoon. No use in stalling.

When he returned to his office, the fax was waiting. He sat at the desk and studied it. Miriam was charged with murder, attempted murder and assault with a deadly weapon. He visualized the attractive, petite young woman who always had a smile for him in the convenience store and couldn't imagine her doing something like that. Still, the warrant was in his hand. He picked up the phone and called his wife.

"Hon, I'm going out to Van Zandt's compound to serve a warrant. Just wanted to let you know. If I'm not home by dark, call the DPS."

"You going to be okay?"

He chewed on his toothpick a few moments. "Should be."

He clicked off the phone and found Van Zandt's phone number in a listing in his desk drawer of everyone who lived in the county. He slowly punched in the numbers and the phone rang. After seven rings he was about to disconnect when a voice said, "Yeah."

"Colonel, this is Sheriff Davis."

"What do you want?"

"I need to talk to you."

"That's what you're doing. Go ahead."

"No, Richard. That's not what I mean. I need to drop by for a visit. I'll be there in thirty minutes. Can you get someone to unlock the front gate?"

Silence.

"I suppose. You understand I don't like cops on my property. You best make it brief when you get here."

The phone went dead.

Davis got in his pickup and drove slowly west on 302. He slowed to let a tumbleweed blow across the highway. He saw the gate in the distance. A red Chevy pickup was parked beside it. When he drove closer, he saw a young man with a long black beard leaning up against it. He was holding a shotgun, but the gate was open. He stopped beside the pickup and lowered his window.

"Okay for me to go on in?"

"That's what the Colonel said. Just follow the road."

Davis did as he was told. He noted the embankment and the entrenchment behind it that appeared to surround the property. He passed the Alamo façade on his right. At the shooting range two other men turned when he approached, rifles at the ready. The last time he visited the compound must have been twenty years ago. Back then, the Alamo and shooting range didn't exist. And he didn't remember the shed beside the range. The encampment then consisted of three or four trailers. Now he estimated there were around twenty. The building in the middle also had been added.

He saw two men, leaning against posts on either side of the

building's front porch. Each had a rifle slung over his shoulder. Van Zandt was sitting in a rocker in the middle, shotgun across his lap. As he parked, he made a decision. Having a weapon would not change the outcome. He pulled his revolver from the holster and laid it on the passenger seat.

When he exited his truck, he said, "I'm not armed."

Van Zandt motioned him to the porch with an almost imperceptible movement of his head and pointed to the rocker beside him. Davis sat on the edge of the rocker.

"State your business," the colonel said.

Davis eyed the old man and the two guards. "I'm here to serve this on Miriam." He handed the warrant to Van Zandt.

Van Zandt took it and slowly read to the end. Then he ripped it into small pieces. "She ain't here."

"I've been told otherwise."

Van Zandt rose to face Davis. "Then whatever you were told is wrong. So's them charges on that paper. You did what you came for. Now you need to get out."

Without another word Davis walked back to his pickup and retreated the way he came. After he was off the property, the man at the front closed and locked the gate.

Van Zandt watched him go, then spoke. "Boys, when the rest get back from work this evening we need to have a meeting. Looks like trouble's coming."

THIRTY-ONE

Jack heard from Lance that evening that the attempt to serve Miriam Van Zandt had failed. He told Lance that he wanted to confer with Joe Shannon since it was his warrant. He clicked off the phone and found Colby in the media room, watching NCIS.

"That's who we need. Get Gibbs and his team to Texas. They could handle this in an hour."

Colby paused the television. "I heard you talking to Lance. The high sheriff of Loving County failed in his effort to serve the warrant."

"Not only that, the place was crawling with armed men. Colonel Van Zandt ripped the warrant into little pieces and told him he better get his ass off their property."

Colby rose from her chair and walked to the bar. "Sounds like we both could use a drink." She poured two 10th Mountain bourbons over rocks and added a splash of water, then handed one to Jack who nodded his thanks before sipping it.

"I need to call Joe." He pulled the cell from his pocket and punched in the D.A.'s number.

"You got any good news?" Joe immediately asked.

Jack recounted the events as described by Lance. "What do you want to do now?"

Joe's voice was hard. "We don't have any choice. We're going to have to assault the damn compound and take her by force. That's my warrant and she'll damn sure obey it one way or the other."

Several men and two women, dressed casually but all with sidearms, filled the room where Colonel Burnside, Jack and Walt had watched Fox fly the drone just a few days before. They sat in the chairs and lined the walls. Jack introduced himself to the SWAT team members while they awaited Colonel Burnside. Jack counted twenty-two. Walt had met all of them at one time or the other. They seemed remarkably relaxed, talking about the Texans and Cowboys and their kids in school. When Walt asked Jack a casual question about J.D., a group surrounded him to get his thoughts about TCU making the playoffs. An outside observer would never have concluded that they were about to launch a military mission where lives would be at stake.

The door opened. Colonel Burnside and Joe Shannon walked in. Silence enveloped the room as Joe took a place along the wall beside Walt. Colonel Burnside walked to the front of the room.

He clicked a remote in his right hand and Fox appeared on the screen in the lower left corner. "Fox, can you see and hear us?"

"Perfectly, Colonel."

"Ladies and gentlemen, this is one of the most serious missions our team has had to face. I know some of you saw combat in Iraq and Afghanistan. I believe that this has the potential to be just as dangerous. To get the introductions out of the way, you have all probably met Walt Frazier at one time or another. Beside him is Joe Shannon, the Tarrant County District Attorney. Next to him, the man with the cane, is Jack Bryant, the special prosecutor who has been coordinating various law enforcement agencies. Jack is a lawyer in Fort Worth. You may remember the Dead Peasants killer a few years back. Jack's investigation is what broke that case."

Several of the people in the room looked at Jack with new respect.

"Jack doesn't jump out of planes any more, but in his younger days he was in the 101st Airborne. The reason for that cane is an injury in Desert Storm. Now, I'm going to turn the briefing over to Captain McCombs."

Pat McCombs was a Ranger Captain and leader of the DPS SWAT team. Five feet, ten inches tall, a lean and wiry man with a bushy red moustache and a red flattop, cut so close that his head sunburned in the Texas summers. His manner commanded respect.

"Thank you, Colonel. Our mission is to capture this woman, Miriam Van Zandt."

The photos of Miriam Van Zandt that they had assembled appeared on the large screen. They showed her with black hair, as a redhead, and they had photo shopped her image with hair of various colors and lengths.

"She is a petite woman, just a little over five feet tall. Her size should not fool you. She is a deadly killer, skilled with almost any weapon and could give any of us a real fight in hand to hand combat. You all know about the incident up in Fort Worth a few weeks ago. She killed Edward Hale, almost killed Governor Lardner and wounded a man named Kevin O'Connell before she escaped. Hal Travis, the governor's limo driver, managed to shoot her in the leg. She still was able to scale this eight foot wall and disappear into the night."

Images of the mansion patio and the wall appeared on the screen.

"Captain, if it's just one woman, why will it take our entire team?"

"I'm getting there, Wally. Well, we can do it now. Thanks to the combined efforts of Tarrant County, Fort Worth P.D., Westover Hills P.D and the DPS, we tracked her, primarily through surveillance cameras. Twenty years ago she would have just disappeared, but not anymore. Once we finally got a good photo, we involved the FBI and their facial recognition software identified her. When we figured out who she was, we knew where she was most likely to be."

An image from the drone appeared on the screen, showing the compound. "This, ladies and gentlemen, is the home of The Alamo Defenders, a separatist militia group in Loving County."

"Hell, Captain, I've been around there, nothing but sand, sage and cactus."

"Exactly why these people are in that county. They want to be left alone, and usually are. The DPS learned about them ten, maybe fifteen years ago. We opened a file on the group. We've been doing spot checks several times a year, watching the comings and goings. When we see a new face, we identify it and start a sub-file on that individual. Fox, can you give us a shot of the front of the compound?"

The screen filled with the gate and barbed wire.

"You can see from the sign they don't like strangers. Now, Fox, how about the shooting range."

"Wow, Captain, can we upgrade ours to one like that?"

"In your dreams, Ralph. We have checked the compound over the years and know that Miriam spends more time there than probably anyone else. One thing that may work to our advantage is the oil boom in the Permian Basin. Most of the men have gotten some high-paying jobs working on the rigs, driving trucks and so forth. They haven't been spending as much time on the range. Fox, put up all of the trailers."

"Here's the living area." McCombs used a laser pointer.

"This is the town hall, used for meetings and as a school house. Note the various antennas on the roof. They have very sophisticated electronic communications. The double-wide to the right of the town hall is Richard Van Zandt's. He's the head honcho and appointed himself colonel of the militia. A little beyond his trailer over by the river is Miriam's. As you can see, there are about twenty trailers scattered around. We figure there are about 35 adults and a few kids, living there. Fox, zoom in on Miriam's trailer."

The camera showed a single wide with the white pickup beside it. "This is where she lives. That's her pickup. We were able to identify it on some footage in Fort Worth at the time of the attack. Beyond her trailer is the Pecos River. Not much water in it this time of year, but it's a potential avenue of approach." He pointed the laser. "This bluff is on the west side of the river. The top of it is about twenty feet above the compound. We can set up a sniper and camera here about midway down the side of compound. Then we can have one more on either end. They can approach from the west through the desert from U.S. 285 without being seen."

"What's the make-up of the team, Captain?" Wally asked.

"Six snipers alternating shifts, six on the helicopter to fast rope into the compound, eight, plus a driver and me in the APC."

Jack knew that APC stood for armored personnel carrier. It was a vehicle that held eight members of the team and a machine gunner who would man the turret mounted weapon on top. Its steel armor could withstand anything up to fifty caliber gunfire.

"I had the supply trailer double-checked this morning. Other than your sidearms, all of your weapons are on board, along with the usual grenades. The medical cabinet is fully stocked. Sleeping bags are stored along with meals for a week. I can tell you right now that there's no way we're going to take a week. The APC and trailer will be loaded into the eighteen wheeler this afternoon."

"We'll take the team's RV for a command post. Jack and Walt

will be there. They started this and are entitled to see the end. Colonel Burnside, you coming along?"

"Wouldn't miss it, but I'll fly in one of the DPS planes."

"Before I tell you where we're meeting tomorrow, this is the most important thing I'm going to say. It has the potential to become another Waco. Hear this and heed my warning. It will not be another Waco. We are going after this woman and we are going to take other lives only if absolutely necessary. If we can walk away from there with her, either dead or alive, and everyone else lives, that's what we want. I'll outline my plan tomorrow night."

Jack raised his hand. "Captain, it's very important that we do everything possible to take her alive."

"Understood, Mr. Bryant. We'll do our best. Colonel Burnside has contacted the Midland Police Chief. He's arranged for us to use an empty hangar at the Midland airport for our staging area. It's about an hour and a half from the compound. Tomorrow evening I'll brief you in more detail from there."

"The ground team is leaving from here at 0500. You flyboys can sleep a little later. Be at the helipad at 0900. Any questions?"

"Not a question, Captain, just a comment," Carol Klein, the ground team leader, said. "You're telling us we're going to assault a compound with thirty or so men, armed and ready to die. Your goal may be to walk away with no other lives lost. I'm telling you that is not going to happen. Mark my words."

Several others nodded their agreement.

THIRTY-TWO

By seven in the evening most of the men had returned to the compound. They knew that something was up when they saw the front gate open and Luke Marak's pickup parked beside the road. He told each of them that the colonel wanted a meeting at eight o'clock at the town hall. A few grumbled that they had worked twelve hour shifts and just wanted a beer, some food and a bed. Still, they all showed up.

The men and women drifted into the town hall close to eight o'clock and took seats on folding chairs. They hardly looked like a fighting force. They wore jeans and work boots. Their shirts were streaked with dirt and grease. Most hadn't shaved in days. Nearly all had something alcoholic in their hand. The women at least had clean clothes and sneakers. Two held infants in their arms. The other children were old enough to remain in their trailers, occupied by video games.

Colonel Van Zandt rose from a chair that faced the group.

Miriam sat beside him. "If you all will shut up, I've got some talking to do."

He spit tobacco juice into a paper cup while he waited for silence. "Most of you know that Miriam went out on a mission a couple of weeks ago. Took a bullet in her leg that got infected. She's still limping some, but has put away her cane. Yesterday Sheriff Davis tried to serve a warrant on her. Seems she's wanted for murder and attempted murder in Tarrant County. I tore it up and told him to get the hell off our property. I've been thinking about it for a day now and talking with Miriam and a couple of you guys. We haven't seen the last of it."

"Colonel, I hear she shot the governor and killed some billionaire. Seems like someone didn't think this through very well. Not at all surprising to me that they are coming for her," Sam Carr said from the front row.

Miriam stood to defend herself. "Wasn't supposed to come down this way. I've done enough of these that I know what I'm doing. Yeah, I took a bullet, but that ain't what caused the problem. I got caught on surveillance cameras. That's not unexpected, only, somehow, they tracked me down to here. I didn't leave fingerprints. I changed out the license on my truck. Took every precaution and those sons of bitches still tracked me. We all know that the government is watching these days. Must have had a satellite or something that picked me up between Fort Worth and here. Doesn't really matter now how it happened. We knew it was going to come to this sooner or later."

"I figure we have a couple of days," Van Zandt interrupted. "That means we have a lot to do. You've got tomorrow morning to buy any personal supplies in Pecos. We have to plan for a month long siege. I figure that if we can stall them long enough, they may start compromising. At noon tomorrow we're locking this place down. No one gets in or out."

"Wait a damn minute, Richard," Carr rose as he spoke. "Nearly all of us are working in the oil patch now. Hell, I'm making near a hundred grand a year. Why invite a confrontation? Here's an alternative. Call your friend, Jose. Have him fly that plane over the border and pick up Miriam. He can take her back to Mexico until things cool off. Hell, we can then just invite anyone that shows up to search the property. When they know she's not here, they'll leave. A month or two from now, she can come back."

Van Zandt was turning red because someone was challenging his decision. "Shit, Carr, we can't have cops wandering around in here even if we sent Miriam to drink margaritas on the beach in Cabo. You know how many illegal weapons we have stored in the tunnels. They find those and we all end up in the federal hoosegow. Get a brain."

Carr returned to his seat, obviously agitated.

"As I was saying, we lock this place down at noon tomorrow. Luke will be assigning our best shooters to man the gun ports at the four corners of the property. It'll be twelve hour shifts. If you're working a night shift, don't forget your damn goggles. The gun ports will be manned, starting at daylight tomorrow. Then, we'll have a crew to retrieve the weapons and ammo from the tunnel in front of the town hall. We'll store them in this building along with grenades. Every man will be issued an MP5, Glock 9 mm, body armor, helmet and goggles. And, I almost forgot, six grenades apiece. Only, I don't want those to be used until I give the command. Any of you women that want to join in defending the Alamo will get the same weapons and equipment. If you choose not to or have to take care of your kids, you'll go into the tunnels tomorrow afternoon. By mid-day tomorrow, you will all have your weapons and assignments. Just be glad we had the foresight to build those embankments, trenches and tunnels."

"Colonel, I've got a problem." Zack Gill was one of the newcomers to the compound. "The rig I'm working on is at a critical point. They need me on the job for the next three days."

Several of the other men nodded their understanding.

Van Zandt walked to him and pulled him out of his chair.

"Then, you've got a decision. You can defend the Alamo or you can desert your comrades on the eve of battle. Only, you should know what happens to deserters." He shoved Gill back into his chair stomped back to the front.

After the meeting ended, four men met in a trailer where they popped open beer cans and sat in silence around the kitchen table. "I don't like this one damn bit. It's kind of fun to play soldier and fire all these weapons. I know Van Zandt is all the time talking about this kind of showdown, but I didn't really think it would ever come," the one they called Red said.

"I'm with you," the man across the table joined. "Hell, I'd say we just drive out of here right now, only Van Zandt would have us stopped at the gate and shot as deserters. What do you suggest?"

"I'd say we play along and wait for an opportunity. We know there are others that feel like we do. Who needs another beer?"

THIRTY-THREE

The gray eighteen wheeler with no identification was followed by two black Suburbans, windows tinted and filled with SWAT team members. Jack and Walt rode in the RV, driven by Pat McCombs that brought up the rear. The convoy turned into the Midland airport and was escorted to a far back area where a hangar was open with the helicopter just outside the door. It was one in the afternoon.

Once the convoy was inside, the hangar door was shut and the vehicles emptied.

"Glad to be inside with the doors shut," Jack said has he rubbed his hands. "Winter is already hitting West Texas."

"Now that we have the doors closed, the heaters will start making it a little more comfortable," Captain McCombs replied.

McCombs then turned to supervise the placement of the ramp at the back of the eighteen wheeler and the unloading of the APC and supply trailer. Once he was satisfied, the team stood in line behind the trailer to get their weapons. Some were assigned sniper rifles, some retrieved their sub-machine guns, usually MP510s, and all had semi-automatic pistols. Next they were given grenades...explosive, tear gas, and flash-bang. They had carried their form fitting Kevlar body armor in their packs. Each of them grabbed a sleeping bag and found a place near the back of the trailer where they sat on the floor and began checking their weapons.

"Gentlemen and ladies, we're going to wait for Colonel Burnside before we do our last briefing." He nodded toward a door in the back. "I've arranged to use that room. It's got a projector and I brought my computer. While we wait, there are MREs in the trailer. I'm sure you will be impressed by the wide variety of nourishing and delicious food they contain."

"Come on, Pat," Al Pearson said. "We're still in civilization. I'm sure Dominos delivers here. I'll even put all the pizzas on my credit card."

McCombs smiled. "That would suit me just fine, only this is a covert operation. No one is supposed to know we're here. And that includes the Dominos delivery guy."

Jack and Walt waited in line for an MRE, chose one and grabbed a bottle of water. While they could have slept in the RV, they had already decided to join the rest of the team with sleeping bags on the hangar floor where they returned with their meal.

"Any thoughts, Jack?" Walt asked.

"Just one for now. I'm a little disappointed that I can't be a part of the assault team. I know I'm old and have a bum knee. Still, I'd like to be part of the action."

"I know what you mean." He leaned forward and lowered his voice. "Maybe if I could complete a successful mission I could get this monkey off my back."

Jack nodded his understanding

Walt continued. "We'll be in the command post a couple of miles away but I understand that the APC has cameras mounted and the snipers these days use cameras that will feed to an iPad for each sniper and back to screens inside the command post. We won't be there, but we can see some of the action."

"So, you're saying that the snipers don't even have to show their heads once the cameras are in place?"

"Right, as Pat said, we'll have three on the bluff above the river. They place their cameras and drop down below the bluff and watch the iPads. They can even toggle the cameras to rotate."

The sound of a small plane taxiing up to the hangar interrupted. A couple of minutes later Colonel Burnside came through the door. Captain McCombs had been sitting among the team, talking quietly. He rose to greet Burnside. After they conferred, he turned. "As soon as you have finished lunch, head on back to the conference room. We'll get started as soon as everyone is ready."

When the team was assembled, McCombs turned on his computer and the projector that showed the image on a white wall.

"Fox reports that there has been activity in the compound for the past two days. It appears that they're getting ready for a fight. Again, here's the location of the compound. At 0400 we leave. We're taking I 20 to Pecos and then U.S. 285 north to where it intersects with State Highway 302. That's about two miles from the compound. The RV will be set up there. We'll also drop the snipers at that point. They can hike across the desert to the river. When you snipers see a bluff rising from the desert, you'll know the river is behind it and the compound is on the other side. We'll switch out the snipers every twelve hours. Make sure you have plenty of water. Also, remember that it's November and the desert is cold at night."

"What about the rest of us, Pat?"

"We're driving the APC up to the gate like we were the owners. We'll park there. I'll engage Van Zandt by cell or by bullhorn, if necessary. We may give them some options and wait them out a couple of days before we move in. The fast rope team can stay here until we need you. I'll brief you when the time comes. Any questions? 0400 then."

The hangar lights came on at 0300. The members of the team had laid out their camos, boots, helmets, belts, vests and weapons the night before. After stretching, they pulled on their gear. The fact that men and women were dressing side by side bothered no one. They took turns using the two restrooms by the conference room with some of them brushing their teeth for what might be the last time in several days. They grabbed MREs and bottled water and downed the meal with a sense of urgency. Next they rolled their sleeping bags and placed them along with their packs in the trailer, not knowing when they would be able to use either, They were trained to take cat naps when they could, even when standing if necessary. The fast rope team also arose and did the same, only they didn't store their packs and sleeping bags in the trailer. They would remain in the hangar to be retrieved after the mission. Still, they had to be prepared to go with a phone call from McCombs. They retrieved MREs and bottles of water for several days and stood as the others left.

The hangar doors opened. The APC drove out with eight team members, a driver/machine gunner and Captain McCombs in the passenger seat. Jack, Walt, Colonel Burnside, the six snipers and a driver followed in the RV that pulled the supply trailer. They followed I 20 through Odessa, a city similar in size to Midland and also experiencing an oil boom. Once through Odessa they were soon in the rolling sand hills. Jack remembered reading that, technically, they were not in a desert, but only an ecologist would know the difference. They arrived in Pecos and stopped in the Walmart parking lot to make sure that everyone was still ready to go. They turned onto US 285. It was dark and remained so when they got to 302 where they dropped three of the snipers. They would take the day shift while the other three would relieve them at dark. Once they were gone, the RV pulled off the road where it became the command post. The driver moved to a control station and flipped switches. The screens that lined the walls illuminated. Images would start appearing as the snipers and APC got to their stations. One screen already showed the view from the drone. The APC moved slowly along the few miles to the Pecos and then across it. At the entrance to the compound the APC turned and parked, lights off.

They waited.

When daylight peeked over the dunes in the east and they could barely make out the Alamo façade and gun range ahead of them, McCombs picked up his satellite phone and punched in the number of Richard Van Zandt.

"You're here, are you," Van Zandt said, not a question, but a statement.

McCombs had already decided to refer to him by his adopted military title. "Colonel, this is Ranger Captain Pat McCombs. We're parked at your front gate."

"You think I don't know that? We've got cameras, too. I saw your headlights when you turned in about an hour ago. Best thing you can do now is to turn around and go back to wherever you came from; only, I guess that's not in your plans."

"No, sir. It is not. I know Miriam is your daughter, but she's wanted for murder."

"Dammit, I told Jim Bill that she ain't here. Last I heard, she was somewhere over in Mexico, probably sunning on the beach."

"Colonel, I don't mean any disrespect, but we spotted her just yesterday."

"Shit, you got one of those damn drones? I've been hearing about them. Guess I'll have to go buy us a couple."

McCombs decided to keep the conversation going. "Yeah, it's amazing what they can do. May not be too many years before fighter pilots will be out of a job. We'll just have some kid barely old enough to shave, staring at a screen and releasing bombs from five thousand miles away."

"You planning to do that here?"

"Absolutely not. Colonel, you must understand that we're not leaving. We're prepared to sit right here for weeks, months if necessary. I know that you have supplies in those tunnels, but we'll outlast you."

Van Zandt paced inside the town hall. He had McCombs on a speaker so Miriam and Luke could hear. "How'd you know about our tunnels?"

"Colonel, we've been watching you for years, even before drones started flying. I can give you name, rank and social security number of everyone in the compound. We're not starting anything, at least not yet. I'm going to disconnect now. If I don't hear from you, I'll check back in about mid-afternoon."

"Pat, I've been looking through a scope and see two gun ports at each end of the embankment. There may be two more on the opposite side. I don't see any guns for now, but I think we have to assume they're manned," Carol Klein said.

"Yeah, and there are probably some shooters behind that Alamo façade. Fox, what do you see?"

"Gun ports at each corner of the property, each manned. Behind that façade are four men armed with what look to be AK 47s. I see another dozen or so in the trenches at various places around the property. Most appear to be sitting, waiting for instructions."

"Sniper One, report," Pat commanded. Sniper one was at the corner of the property closest to the road.

"Captain, I'm set up here. I've got the camera in place and feeding back to the command post. I can see the gun port closest to me. The guy in it sticks up his head every twenty minutes or so. I can also see the port to your right. Same activity."

"Two?" McCombs asked.

"Nothing from here, Captain. There's no movement in the compound. I can see the four guys that Fox described behind the façade. They're sitting, smoking and talking."

"Three?"

"I'm like One. I see the guy below me and the one across at the other corner. They seem to have been ordered to check things out about every twenty minutes."

Pat clicked off his mic and spoke to the team in the back. "Okay, we're just going to sit for a few hours. Time is on our side. Anyone needs to take a leak, step out the back. Looks like you'll be safe with the doors shielding you. That goes for you, too, Carol."

Carol smiled at Pat. "Thanks a lot, Captain. Glad I can be one of the boys."

Miriam's hair was once again black. She sat in the town hall, drinking coffee with her father and Luke. "Look, Pa. I'm the cause of this. No one needs to be killed because of me."

Van Zandt shook his head. "Won't hear of it. We promised to defend each other. We don't back down on promises."

"I agree," Luke added.

"Look, I can drop my guns and walk to the front gate. We won't risk the lives of anyone else. We need to be thinking about the children and other women."

Van Zandt rose to face his daughter. "You killed one of the most powerful men in the country and came close to killing the governor. There will be no plea bargain. You'll be headed for the death chamber."

Miriam stood to face her father. "I'm going to obey you for now, but I'm still not ruling it out as a possibility." Determination was in her voice.

"Colonel, I'm going to go through the tunnel to the Alamo and get a better look at what they've got." Luke looked out the windows and cracked open the door. Seeing nothing, he hurried down the steps and disappeared into the compound's main tunnel a few feet away. The entrance had been covered with a heavy sheet of metal until two days before. Wooden steps led down to the floor of the tunnel. It was the largest in the compound. High enough for a six foot man and about the same width across. A string of lights ran the length of the ceiling. Along the wall to the left were shelves, filled with canned goods, MREs and water. Past the shelves were small, two foot wide bunks on hinges. Farther back were camping toilets. The bunks could be raised when not in use. Now five women and six children sat on them. Two of the children were whimpering.

"How long are we going to be down here, Luke?" a short, heavy-set woman with streaks of gray in her hair asked.

"Can't say. Could be a long time." He moved past them and continued down the tunnel. When he arrived at the other end, he paused and hollered. "Roy, it's Luke. Everything clear?"

"Yeah, it's fine. Come on up."

Luke joined the other men. He peeked around one window in the façade and quickly ducked back again.

"Damn, that's a helluva vehicle they've got parked at our gate. You guys ever seen one like that?"

"I did in the army," Roy said. "Earlier version, but does about the same thing. A fifty caliber will bounce right off it. It's got armor plating on the underside, intended to protect it from an IED and grenades. About all we can do is try to figure a way to lure them out into the open."

Luke sat with his back to the façade and smoked a cigarette. "They say that they're not going to attack. They're going to wait us out. That may be a problem. The women and kids have already been in the tunnel for two days. And some of the men are getting antsy about their families and jobs. Waiting long ain't going to work for us."

Luke made his way back through the tunnel. When he encountered the women and children, the woman who complained before blocked his way. "Look, I'm claustrophobic." Her voiced grew louder as she talked. "I can't stand confined spaces. I need to get out of here."

"Mary Jean, calm down, dammit. You start talking like this,

you're going to rile up some of the others. Just hang in there for a while."

Mary Jean turned sideways to let Luke pass. "You just don't get it," she hissed. "I'm trying to control myself, only I don't know how much longer I can."

As Luke stepped around her, the tunnel went black. The kids and women started screaming. Mary Jean grabbed Luke. "Do something," she screamed. "Do it now."

Luke had to shout to make his voice heard above the screams of the women and the wailing of kids. "Everyone calm down. They must have cut the power to the compound. We have a backup generator that will provide electricity to this tunnel and the town hall. It should click on in a few seconds." He pulled a flashlight from his pocket to provide some light. Thirty seconds later the string of ceiling lights came on, thirty seconds of hell for Mary Jean. She had collapsed on the floor and was sobbing uncontrollably. When the lights came on, she looked up at Luke.

"I warn you. I can't take it much more. The Colonel needs to figure out a way to stop this. I don't want to die here."

Luke pushed past her again and made his way to the entrance and into the building.

"Good job, Colonel Burnside. I can see a light in that building, but nowhere else."

Burnside chuckled. "Just a matter of knowing the right people. We were able to shut off their electricity without disturbing any neighbor, not that there are a lot of neighbors to disturb."

"Fox, you see any other lights?" McCombs asked.

"Negative. Of course, it's daylight. I'll tell you if I see any more after dark."

"My guess is that they have a backup generator, probably propane, that will provide electricity for that building, Van Zandt's trailer and maybe a couple of the tunnels. First step in making life just a little more uncomfortable. Even with a big propane tank, it can't be good for more than a few days, a week at most."

Toward sunset McCombs received a call. He glanced at the caller i.d. "Evening, Colonel. How much did you have to pay for your own cell tower? I don't even have to use my satellite phone."

"I'm not calling to make chit-chat. You cut off our damn electricity and it's going to be cold tonight. The trailers need electricity. What do I need to do to get it turned back on?"

"Sorry about that, Colonel. You can surrender your daughter. That's it. Otherwise I suggest you pass out lots of blankets. Think about my proposal more and we'll talk in the morning. And remember, so far, no lives have been lost."

THIRTY-FOUR

Once night fell, Jack discovered that he was not the only person who had armor that could be lowered on an RV. The SWAT team vehicle was even more armored. Steel plates covered the side and back windows and dropped to protect the tires. Now he learned that the metal on the RV was also armor, not quite as heavy as that on the APC, but close. Only the windshield was exposed.

"Pat, we're coming."

"Roger that."

The RV moved slowly along the road in the pitch black of the desert night. When it stopped behind the APC, the interior lights were disengaged. One by one the team left the APC wearing night vision goggles and entered the RV. They made use of the dual facilities at the back and paused for more water and MREs before returning to their vehicle. McCombs was the last to visit the command post. He sat across from Colonel Burnside, Walt and Jack.

"Assessment, Captain?" Colonel Burnside asked.

"So far, so good. Van Zandt doesn't like being without electricity. We'll see how they survive the night. My weather report said it's going to dip into the low twenties. Even if some of them slip back into their trailers, it's going to be chilly. My team is doing fine. Glad we brought the RV on this one. I don't think they're going to start anything. So, we'll see what dawn brings."

Dawn brought the unexpected. Mary Jean had shivered under a single blanket throughout the night. She didn't think she had shut her eyes once. By morning she had come to the end of her rope. She could no longer stay in the tunnel. Van Zandt wasn't doing a damn thing. Her husband was out there somewhere in one of the trenches. He could take care of himself. He wasn't claustrophobic. She was. She would take matters into her own hands. When she could barely make out a change in light at the end of the tunnel near the town hall, she made the decision.

Without saying a word to the other tunnel occupants, she rose from her bunk, put on her sneakers and started walking toward the end of the tunnel that opened behind the Alamo façade. When she arrived at the entrance, she marched up the steps and started running toward the front gate, arms over her head.

The men at the façade were barely awake when they saw her rush past. They hollered at her, but were not about to shoot in her direction since the SWAT team was just beyond. When she approached the gate, she paused to catch her breath and walked to it.

Klein had been on watch for the night. She roused McCombs. "Pat, look what's coming."

Instantly awake, he looked out the windshield to see a short woman, wearing jeans and a T-shirt. He was looking for a bomb vest and concluded that she was wearing none. Further her hands were extended over her head and she was crying.

"I surrender. I can't take it anymore. Please let me out."

McCombs looked at Carol. "What do you think?"

"Not a trap. Woman's had enough."

Pat studied the situation. "Okay, the gate's still locked."

"I got this," Klein said. "I need two men to position themselves on the platforms on the sides to provide cover fire, if need be. Give me two more to help her climb the gate. I can cut the two top strands of barbed wire. Five minutes."

Getting the okay from McCombs, two men followed Klein and two stepped to the platforms, ready to respond if necessary. As it turned out, the extraction was uneventful. Klein calmed the woman down and directed her to climb the gate. One of the SWAT team clambered over the gate and dropped inside. He boosted her up. Carol and the other team member helped her down. Once there, they ran back to the APC. When they were safely inside, they gave Mary Jean water and a MRE.

Carol debriefed her, learning where the tunnels went, how many women and children were in the main tunnel and how many men were in the compound. She was disappointed to learn that Mary Jean knew nothing about the weapons, other than they had a bunch. The day wore into evening. Once it became dark, the RV drove to their back and picked up Mary Jean. McCombs ordered two man teams to keep watch for two hour shifts, one on the platform on either side of the APV. McCombs allowed himself to doze between the shift changes until close to four in the morning.

Four more days went by. In the compound the women and children had to use camping johns in the tunnel in the daytime and could emerge at night to go to their trailers with flashlights to change clothes. They couldn't bath or use the bathroom since the well pumps ran on electricity, and there was none. Otherwise, Colonel Van Zandt mandated that they stay in the tunnel where the smell worsened by the day. The men dozed off at their posts. Once the sun dropped below the horizon, they wrapped themselves in blankets that barely cut the cold desert night.

Van Zandt's phone rang. "Yeah, what do you want?"

"Colonel, a front is headed this way tomorrow. Temperature's going to drop even farther. You need to be thinking about how you're going to end this."

Van Zandt spit into his ever-present cup. "You don't need to worry about us. I've got a plan." He clicked off the phone.

McCombs turned to Carol. "What the hell kind of plan do you think he has?"

"Damned if I know. Why don't you check with Fox and the snipers."

Ten minutes later McCombs said, "They haven't seen anything."

Miriam returned from the tunnel and confronted her father. "We're about to have a revolt down there. Kids are crying. We didn't buy enough diapers. The stench is overwhelming. The women are scared out of their minds. They don't want to die."

Van Zandt dropped into a chair. "So, what the hell am I supposed to do? I knew this day was coming. I'm prepared to die. If our deaths spark a new American revolution, it's worth the sacrifice."

"Dammit, Pa, not everyone thinks like you. Let's go back to that idea about the cartel plane. Call Jose and get him over here at four a.m. when even the SWAT team ought to be sleeping. Tell his pilot there will only be two trucks with lights on the runway. He needs to land, pick me up at the end of the runway, turn around and take off again. Once I'm out of here, you call McCombs and invite him in to search the place."

"But, he'll find our weapons."

"Man up, Pa. You need to take the fall and not cause the deaths of the people in here. You'll serve a few years on weapons charges. You'll still get plenty of publicity. Folks that believe in our cause will be erecting statutes in your honor."

Van Zandt stroked his beard for maybe a minute. "Okay. I'll call Jose. I figure it'll cost us a hundred grand. Damn drug runners won't do anything for nothing. "

Miriam kissed her dad on the cheek. "Thanks, Pa. I'll get Manny and Bud to have their trucks available tonight."

THIRTY-FIVE

"Captain, this is Sniper One. There's a small aircraft approaching from the west. Looks like it's headed for that landing strip."

Instantly awake, McCombs dropped from the driver's side with a scope. He spotted the aircraft just as Sniper One said. *What the hell is happening?* he thought. *That plane's too small to bring reinforcements. Still, we can't let it land.*

Manny and Bud both had black F 150s. They crept to their trailers and drove them slowly to the runway, one on either side. Van Zandt and Miriam drove to the end of the runway and backed up to it. As on all of the other occasions, when the plane approached, they would snap on their lights.

McCombs had anticipated this might occur. He alerted the snipers. "I'm not sure what is happening. It may be an attempt to pick up Miriam Van Zandt. Whatever it is, we can't allow it. You are ordered to shoot to kill. Knock the son of a bitch out of the sky if you have to."

The plane approached the runway and the pickup lights

came on along with those of Van Zandt at the end. The snipers started firing, focusing on the two pickups facing the runway, their weapons on full automatic. Having trained to hit a man at a thousand yards, to hit a small plane at a few hundred was like shooting toy ducks with a BB gun on the midway. The first two snipers shot at the plane. The third aimed for the pickups lighting the runway. Suddenly, like a wounded duck, the plane rolled and crashed into the ground in a ball of fire that bounced down the runway, coming to a stop a few yards in front of Van Zandt and Miriam.

The snipers drew return gunfire from the defenders at the corner gunports who could really only aim at the snipers' gun flashes. Sniper Two took a shot in his right shoulder, his shooting arm. "Captain, I'm hit. Right shoulder."

"Slide back down the hill, Two. We'll send help." McCombs called the command post. "Colonel, you heard Two. Who do you have to check on him?"

Walt Frazier raised his hand. "I'm trained in first aid. Have to be for the governor's detail. Let Jack and me go."

Colonel Burnside sized up the situation. He knew that Walt was correct. "Jack, what about you? You use a cane."

Jack shook his head. "Don't need it most of the time, just carry it. I'm good to go."

Colonel Burnside pondered the situation. "Okay. Both of you get rifles from the trailer. Report when you check him out."

The two men stopped by the trailer and chose rifles. Walt slung a first aid kit over his shoulder. Then they started double timing across the desert with a small flashlight to guide them, knowing it could not be seen from the compound.

After thirty minutes, Walt knew they were close. "Two, it's Walt Frazier and Jack Bryant. Can you see our light?"

"Roger that. Head toward your three o'clock. You'll see me at the bottom of the bluff."

Jack spotted him first. "Over here."

Walt saw the man sitting up, his back to a rock. His left hand held a compress over the shoulder wound. "Sal, how are you feeling?"

"I've been better, but I'll survive."

Walt removed the cloth from the wound while Jack held the flashlight. "Could have been worse. No way to put a tourniquet on it. I can strap a compress there, and we'll get you back to the compound." He opened his first aid kit and retrieved a large compress with straps. He put it in place and pulled the Velcro ends together and secured them. He was picking up his phone when Jack stopped him.

"I'm staying here."

Walt looked at his friend.

"You can get him back to the command post alone. I'll take over here. You know I used to be able to hit a fly at a thousand yards. Can't do that anymore, but I still go to the range and can match any of the team's snipers at five hundred."

Walt nodded and called command. "Colonel, Two took a pretty good shot to the shoulder. I'm bringing him back. You probably need to call an ambulance to get him into Pecos. Jack is going to stay here and observe from his post."

Burnside frowned at the suggestion. "I don't like a civilian in harm's way. Tell him to observe, but nothing more."

The lights on the two black pickups were dark. The Van Zandts drove slowly back to the compound.

"Pat, the pickup at the end of the runway is moving back to the compound. Request instructions."

"Let it go as long as no one is shooting."

Soon, there was nothing to interrupt the night but the crackling and popping of metal in the fire. No one attempted to leave the two vehicles on the sides of the runway.

Van Zandt and Miriam made it back to the town hall, went inside and collapsed in the rockers.

"Shit," Miriam said, "That was a disaster. You think Bud and

Manny are still alive?"

Van Zandt wiped his brow with a bandanna he pulled from his pocket. "We won't know until we can check their trucks. I'll call McCombs."

"Van Zandt, what the hell were you trying to do?"

"Not important now. We failed. Pilot must be dead. Can you hold your fire while we check the men in the trucks?"

"No problem. Only, no weapons. Understood?"

Van Zandt sighed. "Understood. We'll have two men walk to the strip with no weapons. If you agree, I'll follow them in a pickup. We won't move the men or their bodies until I call you back."

Van Zandt recruited two men to walk in front of his truck to the landing strip. Both were more than a little nervous about the assignment. They checked Manny first. He had a pulse. Bud was dead. Van Zandt called McCombs and reported what he had found. Next he called Miriam to report on their status. Miriam let out a sigh of relief that Manny was still alive.

McCombs conferred with Carol and Colonel Burnside back at the command post. "Van Zandt, you want us to get an ambulance from Pecos? We'll cease fire until then."

Van Zandt kicked a sand mound. "Yeah, I don't have any choice. I'll bring them to the front gate."

While they waited, Walt and Sal made it to the command post. Colonel Burnside helped Walt get Sal inside where he checked Sal. "You're going to be fine, son. I've called for a chopper with a medic to take you back to Midland. I doubt if Pecos has a surgeon who can take care of this."

"Thanks, Colonel. Could I have some water while we wait?"

McCombs stood at the gate when Van Zandt drove up. McCombs sized up the older man and concluded that he knew he was losing. Van Zandt climbed from his truck and unlocked the gate.

"Sorry about your loss, Colonel," McCombs said. "You're

going to hear a helicopter shortly. One of our men was hit in the shoulder. We're flying him back to Midland. Let your men know the last thing they want to do is take a shot at that helicopter."

Van Zandt nodded and returned to his truck where he called Miriam to have her alert the defenders about the helicopter. The wail of a siren could be heard in the distance, and an ambulance arrived within a couple of minutes. The EMTs moved efficiently. They had Manny on a stretcher and an IV in his arm in no time. Next they loaded Bud's body beside Manny. Then they were headed back to the hospital in Pecos. While they worked, everyone saw a red helicopter circle once and drop below the horizon a few miles back up the road.

Burnside had chosen not to alert the locals other than Sheriff Davis. Now he had no choice but to call the Pecos DPS office and the Sheriff of Ward County to advise them about what had occurred since a gunshot death would surely attract the attention of local law enforcement. The news would leak from someone in one of the offices. It was only a matter of time before he media started arriving, hoping for another Branch Davidian standoff.

It was afternoon when there was a knock on the door. Miriam was asleep on the floor and her father was dozing in his rocker. He woke with a start. "Come on in."

Brad Mitchell came through the door. He was one of the younger members of the militia, no more than twenty-five, with long brown hair and a matching moustache and beard. His wife and baby son were in the tunnel.

Van Zandt rose to greet him. "Come in, Brad. Need some water? Everything okay on your side of the compound?"

"Water would be fine, sir."

Miriam pushed from the floor and went to a cooler to retrieve a bottle.

Mitchell put his rifle beside the door and took off his John Deere cap. "Sir, I suppose I'm a delegation of one. A number of the guys want this over. We know what happened to Manny and

Bud." He twisted the cap in his hands. "Colonel, this ain't the Alamo. We aren't fighting for our country. This is a little piece of shit desert, not fit for man nor beast." He paused. "When me and Alice showed up here two years ago, we didn't have a pot to piss in. You gave us a trailer. I don't want you to think I don't appreciate that, only things have changed. We have a baby. The fracking boom came along and I've got a good job. So do a lot of the men." He sighed. "I don't know how to say this but direct. We don't want to die. I don't believe in your ideal enough to die for it. A lot of the rest feel the same."

Van Zandt turned red and rose to throw the young man out. Miriam grabbed his arm and spun him around. "Pa, you can't force these men to do what you want. If they want to leave, you've got to let them. You don't want their blood on your hands."

Van Zandt's shoulders slumped and he stared at the floor. Finally, he looked up. "How many want out?"

"I'd say about fifteen men and their families."

"Let them go, Pa. We'll make our stand. Don't matter whether it's ten or twenty. Just like the Alamo, the message of freedom will ring from here."

Van Zandt rubbed his face with his hands. "All right. I'll call the SWAT team and ask for another cease fire. Tell everyone that wants to leave to grab some clothes from their trailers and bring their guns here."

Van Zandt then called McCombs and told him that a number of people wanted out. They would be unarmed but in their trucks and cars. McCombs told him they had an hour. When he put down the phone, he high fived Carol. "We've got them on the run. Get someone to count as they leave. We may be striking sooner than we thought."

He called Colonel Burnside who made hurried arrangements for several local law enforcement officials to get to the scene. When the evacuating families arrived at the front gate, they were met by an assortment of deputy sheriffs, DPS officers and the

RV occupied by Burnside, Jack and Walt. They and their vehicles were searched. Next, they were escorted into Pecos where they were fingerprinted and booked. The men were charged only with resisting arrest since they had no proof of anything more. The women and children were released. The men would remain in the jail until the siege ended and a decision as to their fate would come from the Texas Attorney General.

THIRTY-SIX

When night fell on the desert, the RV slowly made its way to the back of the APC. The only light that came from the compound was in the town hall off in the distance. McCombs and Klein crept to the RV and entered. After sipping hot, black coffee, McCombs said, "How is the one that survived this morning?"

"He's going to live," Walt said. " And Sal's now in Midland and will undergo surgery in the morning."

"What about the airplane?"

"Fox can make out part of a number on the tail. Best guess is it's Mexican registration, probably owned by a drug cartel."

"Interesting," McCombs said. "So, they may have been allowing drug dealers to use that landing strip. Not a bad plan. Out here in the middle of nowhere at night, it probably would never be noticed. Maybe we can charge the old man with drug smuggling, too. I don't think the real defenders of the Alamo would have liked that. How many do they have left in the compound?"

"According to Fox, our best guess is about a dozen," Walt said. "No children and the only woman is Miriam Van Zandt. The old man and Miriam are still in the building. Fox tells us that at dusk there were still four men behind the Alamo façade. That leaves six to either be in the gun ports at the corners or somewhere in the trenches or tunnels. I'm sure the old man has them on full alert, but they've got to be walking zombies by now."

"That's my thinking, too," McCombs said as he yawned. "Sorry. We all could use a good night's sleep. Let's give it until 2200. Colonel, can you call the helicopter and have it hovering twenty miles away at that time. My goal is not to lose any more lives, particularly our team." He clicked on his radio to contact the snipers. When the three of them responded, including Jack, he spoke. "We're going in at 2200. Until I say otherwise, fire over the compound."

"Captain, this is Jack Bryant. It's critical that we take Miriam Van Zandt or her father alive. I don't believe that they hatched these murders in Fort Worth out here in West Texas. Somebody else is behind them. The trail will disappear if they're killed."

"Understood, Jack. That's the plan. Still, you know that plans in a firefight like this often are subject to change."

At 2150 McCombs turned to Wally. "Okay, up into the machine gun turret. We're going to make all the racket we can. I want you firing over the heads of the people in the compound. Go slowly from side to side. I want them thinking that the fires of hell are raining down on them. We'll bust through the gate and stop just this side of the façade. If you can knock some pieces of it off and make them fall on the men on the other side, so much the better. I want four men on the gun platforms on the outside, doing the same thing. Snipers, you're shooting at the building. Aim for the top. Again, we're not trying to hurt anyone. Sniper Three, if there's someone in that gun port down by you, scare the shit out of him. Once we start shooting, the fast rope team will be here. Hopefully, they won't hear it or won't be able to distinguish that noise from World War III we're about to start. The fast rope team will drop behind the building. The helicopter will be in and out in less than a minute. On my mark."

Four men quietly exited to stand on the armor protected platforms, M240B machine guns at the ready. At 2200, McCombs said, "Go, go, go!"

The driver gunned the engine and ripped through the gate. Wally was spraying shells from side to side. The four men on the platforms did the same. Pieces of the Alamo started to fall.

Within two minutes the helicopter arrived. The fast rope team had practiced this hundreds of times. Two booms were swung out on either side and locked in place. A sixty foot, two inch rope dropped from the booms. Six men, wearing gloves, three on each side, seized the rope and wrapped their boots around it. They slid to the ground in seconds. As the last man hit the ground, the helicopter banked and was gone into the night. Like the rest of the team, the six men wore night vision goggles. They did as the others, shooting randomly at the building and popping holes in the roof.

Inside, Van Zandt was trying to peer out the front window without making himself a target.. "We're surrounded. Where did those guys in back come from?"

"I think I heard a helicopter, Pa. We better surrender unless you want us all to die like the men in the Alamo."

Van Zandt rose from his chair. "I will not ask them to surrender. If they do so, it'll be their choice." He paused. "There's one thing that we have to do. They can't get the computers in my trailer and yours. If they do, they'll figure out our bank accounts and who's been paying us." He paused. "We can't have that. I owe it to my friends to protect their identities. I gave them my word."

"Hell, Pa, I just realized that I don't know who your friends are. The money in my account starts with yours and goes around the world a couple of times before landing in mine."

Pa nodded. "I set it up that way. I know a lot more about

computers and wire transfers than most old farts my age. You're lighter on your feet than me. I need you to take two grenades. Toss one under my trailer and one under yours. Then get back here."

Miriam went to a storage bin and retrieved two grenades. She paused to hug her father and was out the door into the night. She slipped off the porch to the right and crawled toward the doublewide. She rose to her knees, pulled the pin and pitched it under the front, toward the kitchen, where she knew the computer would be. She backed away a few feet and watched as the trailer exploded in flames. Debris fell around her.

"What the hell just happened?" McCombs said into his mike. "Anyone hit a propane tank?"

"No, Captain," Jack said. "That was the old man's double-wide. Someone blew it up. I see someone coming around it, heading for Miriam's trailer. Judging from the height, it must be her."

"Dammit, she's about to blow her trailer, too. No telling what they're trying to destroy. Can you hit her in the leg? Wherever you have to hit her, take her down before she destroys her trailer."

Miriam was now on her feet and running the fifty yards between the two trailers. Jack took a breath and held it as he fired. He hit her exactly where he aimed, in the left thigh. He let out his breath, satisfied that she would live but cause no more harm. He underestimated her. Miriam was down but not out. She crawled toward the trailer to get close enough to pitch the grenade from her prone position. She pulled the pin and tossed it underneath. Miriam turned and tried to crawl to safety. She didn't make it. Within seconds the trailer exploded like the double-wide. The blast blew her twenty feet. Van Zandt had observed her from a window. He smiled when she blew his trailer. When he saw her take a bullet in the leg and still toss a grenade under hers, he swelled with pride. When her trailer exploded and knocked her twenty feet, he knew she could not have survived. He slumped to the floor, a defeated old man.

"Shit," Jack yelled. "We've got to take Van Zandt alive."

McCombs ordered a cease fire. He turned on the amplifier. "Drop your guns. This is over. If you want to live, walk slowly to the road."

Jack and the other two snipers came down from their posts, waded the nearly dry Pecos River and joined the others.

One by one the men in the compound dropped their weapons and walked to the road, hands over their heads. McCombs counted eleven. The old man was not among them. He climbed from the APV, and with his team spread out on either side, walked toward the men. As they approached, they heard the sound of one gunshot, coming from the town hall.

McCombs and Carol crept to the house and kicked open the door. Van Zandt was on the floor, a pistol in his right hand and a hole in his head. His left hand was over his chest, The middle finger was extended. He had made one last effort to send a message about what he perceived as freedom.

They heard a shout, coming from the vicinity of the trailers. "She's alive, barely. There's a faint pulse."

Jack heard and ran to her side. A piece of shrapnel protruded from the side of her head. "We need to keep her alive. Colonel Burnside, can you get that medical helicopter back here? She may not make it, but we've got to try."

THIRTY-SEVEN

"Dammit, Joe, you can't do that. I'll be at your office in twenty minutes." Jack slammed the phone, picked up his cane and locked the RV as he left. He made it to the Justice Center in fifteen minutes. Inside the building he shoved onto an already crowded elevator and pushed the button for the eighth floor.

He exited and hurried down the hall to the corner office. When he turned the corner, he felt his knee buckling and almost fell to the floor. He steadied himself with his cane, thinking that he had just recently double timed two miles across the desert in the dark with no problem and his knee craters in a well-lighted hallway. He leaned against the wall and massaged his knee until the pain eased, then limped slowly to Joe's office. Leaning on his cane, he opened the door. Not the entrance he wanted to make. He wanted to show outrage with his voice and body language. Now he would have to settle for the power of words.

The receptionist looked up as he came through the door.

"Morning, Mr. Bryant. Joe said you were on your way over. Your knee bothering you? Probably the change in the weather. I'll call him."

Jack declined coffee and leaned on his cane as he gazed out the window. Joe came through the door. "Come on back. You need some coffee? Come to think of it, a shot of bourbon may be better."

The two friends sat at the coffee table. Jack put his cane on the floor beside his chair. Joe retrieved two rocks glasses and a bottle of bourbon. He poured two fingers in each glass. "I just got a report on Miriam Van Zandt. She survived surgery at Harris, only she may never come out of her coma. I've got her under twenty-four hour guard."

Jack downed his bourbon in one gulp before he spoke. "We've done all we can do for her. It's out of our hands." He stood to make his point. "Whether or not she wakes up, you can't close the investigation. We're not through. We got the shooter, but she couldn't have just waked up one morning and decided she was going to drive three hundred miles to Fort Worth and kill a few Republicans. Someone must have paid her. Someone wanted Hale and the governor dead. Lardner's not safe until we find that person. And, dammit, have you forgotten that someone on the inside shut down the outside surveillance cameras on the afternoon before the event? We retrieved parts of three computers from the trailers. Not much to go on, but forensics is doing what they can. Maybe there's a drive that we can retrieve information from." Jack raised his voice. "Joe, we can't quit now."

"I hear what you're saying, but Colonel Burnside issued a press release, commending the entire task force and, particularly the SWAT team, for bringing down the killers with no loss of life on our side and said the operation was officially closed. Governor Lardner held a press conference and said the same thing, even singled you out for leading the task force and for your shooting at the compound."

Jack paced the room. "I used to crave publicity when I was a plaintiff lawyer. I'm past that time in my life. You gave me a mission, and I'm telling you that I have not completed it."

"Understood." Joe looked at his friend. "Okay, I'll keep an open file. You turn up something, let me know, but the task force has been disbanded."

Jack took a deep breath before he spoke. "Then you better pass the word to Walt and the DPS that they need to double the governor's protective detail. The person behind the attack is still out there."

THIRTY-EIGHT

Jack drove home and found the place empty. He assumed that Colby had a real estate showing. He scratched Killer behind the ears when he entered the kitchen, put his cane in the barrel, and wandered around the house, not really focusing on anything. He understood politics and how the cops worked the media. They wanted to be able to brag that they had pulled out all stops and caught the assassin in less than two weeks. Praise came from all over the country and in the national press. Superb police work led to the identification of Miriam Van Zandt and tracking her to the compound. Loving County had not become another Waco or Ruby Ridge. The old man and one other militia member were killed. Well, that doesn't count the pilot of the plane, but now the DPS was willing to turn that investigation over to the feds. With all of such positive press, Jack understood why the cops and the DPS, hell, even Joe, wanted to take the credit and move on. Only he didn't. He knew his job was not over. He had no idea where to turn, but he would not quit. There was someone out there who wanted these killings done. He would find that person, maybe

197

in a month, maybe a year, maybe two or three years. Meantime, he had no choice but to turn his attention back to his pro bono clients.

He mused that he never would have considered that the hard-charging Jack Bryant of Beaumont would evolve into a lawyer who took great satisfaction out of helping those who had nowhere else to turn. He would start by getting Ike in for a meeting. He had an idea that might get Ike off the streets and set him up for the rest of his life.

Jack's phone rang. "Hey, Walt, how are things in Austin?"

"Couldn't be better. My administrative suspension has been lifted and I'm back on duty. I'm heading to New York with the governor this afternoon. Just calling to thank you for all that you did. And, Jack, I think I'm going to be okay now. I think I snapped out of whatever was bothering me. I apologized to my wife and kids. At first I was sorry that I involved you in this crap, but, at the end of the day, everyone from the governor on down knew I made the right call. The governor would like to invite you to Austin for dinner. That includes Colby, of course."

Jack grinned. "Hell, I told you I was a Democrat. And I'm glad you're back to the old Walt."

"Okay, Okay. We'll sneak you in the back door. The governor really does want to shake your hand and thank you personally. Can I call you when we get back from New York?"

"I suppose. One more thing. You know that this case is not over, no matter what they say."

There was a pause on the phone. "Yeah, I know. We got the killer but not who set the whole thing up and bankrolled it. I've talked to the DPS CSI team. There are no clues as to anyone else's involvement. They did say that the hard drive from one computer was missing. I checked with the guys that searched the compound. They bagged and tagged every damn bit of evidence in the compound. So, we're at a dead end. I've talked to my boss in the protective detail about our concerns, and he understands.

We're on a high alert for the immediate future. I'll call you when I get back. And, thanks again, Jack."

The two friends ended the call. Jack continued to walk the empty house and think about his life and how it had had more twists and turns since he returned to Fort Worth than in all his years of practice in Beaumont. So far, the outcomes had been good. Then, Colby popped into his mind, followed closely by J.D. They were at the center of his universe. Everything else revolved around them. He wasn't looking for love and marriage when he retired to Fort Worth. After all, he had been single for nearly twenty years. Now he couldn't imagine life without Colby. As to J.D., they had a distant relationship from the time his mother moved him to California and for the four years in the Marines. But he made it through as a fine young man who he was proud to call his son. Watching him grow as a scholar and an athlete was worth everything. Now, once J.D. was through with his season, no matter whether it was another game or two or in the national championship, he would do his best to aid J.D.'s decision in what was almost sure to be a successful NFL career. All in all, he was satisfied with his life. No, more than satisfied, he was delighted with it.

The next morning Jack left the house early and was at the RV by eight o'clock. He wanted to be there when Ike and Trousers walked by on the way to his corner. Jack fixed coffee and flipped on the television in the living area to CNBC and watched for Ike. The morning was crisp but clear and the forecast was for temperatures in the low sixties. Nice weather for Ike to stand on his corner. Besides, it was now the holiday season and folks were more inclined to open their wallets and purses. He needed to remember to get a Christmas gift for Ike and, maybe, invite him to the house for dinner.

It was about nine-thirty when he saw Ike walking by, Trousers at his side like he knew he was on the way to work. Jack opened the door and stepped to the parking lot.

"Hey, Ike, we need to talk."

Ike looked over, nodded and waited for traffic to clear before he and Trousers crossed the street. "Morning, Jack. You through playing detective and SWAT team member?"

"Through for now. Sometimes when you agree to help a friend, it turns out to be a little bigger than you bargained for. Can you and Trousers come in for a few minutes? I have an idea about your case."

Ike looked down at Trousers. "He says that we're going to be late for work, but if you have a dog treat, he'll probably be okay."

Ike settled down at the forward table. Jack poured two coffees and pitched Trousers a small bone from a bag he had purchased just for him. He sat across from Ike.

"For now, anyway, I'm through with protecting the governor. Let's talk about your case."

Ike nodded.

"Here are our options. We have a good case, particularly if we can turn up more evidence that you wrote those T-Buck songs. The problem is that I suspect that T-Buck has enough money that even if we win, he can drag this out on appeal for three or four years."

Ike raised his hand. "So, you're telling me that even if we win in the next year or so, I might not see any money for three or four years? What kind of justice is that?"

"Haven't you ever heard that old saying about the wheels of justice turning slowly? Appeals are built into the system. Assuming we win in district court, we'll spend six months on post judgment motions. Figure two years to get through the court of appeals and another couple of years if the Supreme Court takes the case. You'll be making interest on our judgment, but that's not calculated until the end. So, I've got another plan. Am I correct that if we could set you up for life, house with a back yard for Trousers, nice car, enough money to live comfortably, you'd be interested? And, I'm talking in a few months, not years."

"Interested? Hell, yes. You know I never had much. Don't need a lot. What you just described is living like a king. How do we get there?"

"You think you can get your friend, Maurice, up here from New Orleans in the next month or so for a deposition about the songs you wrote. I'll pay his airfare and put him up in a motel for a couple of days. We need to meet with him one afternoon and have him sit for deposition the next day."

Ike smiled at the thought. "Be nice to see my old trombone player again. I think he's living off Social Security. Probably can get up here about any time you want. I'll call him when I get back to the shelter this afternoon."

When Ike left, Jack picked up the phone. When the receptionist answered, he said, "Nicholas Whatley, please."

"Nicholas Whatley's office."

"This is Jackson Bryant from Fort Worth. Is he available?"

"Can I inquire as to the purpose of the call?"

One of Jack's pet peeves: assistants screening calls. "Look, ma'am, I know you're just doing your job, but I don't have to tell you the purpose of my call. I'm a lawyer in Texas. Either Whatley wants to talk to me or not. Just tell him I'm on the line."

"Just a moment, sir. I doubt if Mr. Whatley is available for you, but I'll inquire," came the haughty reply from a voice full of disgust and authority.

Jack had waited nearly a minute and was about to hang up. He would just get the notice out and let Whatley deal with it, but he preferred to be professional.

"Mr. Bryant, how are you today? Sorry to keep you waiting."

"Fine, Nicholas, if I may call you by your first name. We're not much on formalities in Fort Worth."

"Certainly, and make it Nick. What can I do for you?"

"I want to get some facts on the table that may help us resolve our lawsuit."

There was a pause. "I appreciate that, but T-Buck is not going to be interested in settling. He knows he's in the right. Still, what do you have in mind?"

"You've seen that sheet music I produced at the hearing. I'm going to get the guy that had that music to Fort Worth for a deposition. Shouldn't take more than a half a day. Just want to get some potential dates from you."

"That's a long way to fly for such a short deposition."

"Understood, Nick, but you knew where Fort Worth was when you took the case. If you want to appoint local counsel, that's fine with me."

"No, I suspect I better be there. I'll get my assistant to email you some dates before the day is over."

"And, may I suggest that you leave some of your lawyers in Los Angeles. I office in an RV and it might get a little crowded. Oh, and you might want to have your client's agent available by phone. If the deposition goes like I expect, we may need to get him involved in settlement discussions."

THIRTY-NINE

The deposition was scheduled for the Monday before Christmas, the only day that Whatley had available until after the first of the year. Maurice Wilkins flew in on Sunday morning. Jack and Ike met him at the airport. Wilkins was a short, round man whose belly hung over his belt. What little hair he had was curly and white. He made up for his lack of hair with a full white beard that made him look like a black Santa Claus. He even had a twinkle in his eye.

He and Ike talked non-stop from the airport to Jack's RV, bringing each other up to date on their lives and catching up on the whereabouts of old friends and band members. Jack dug into Maurice's somewhat faded memory bank, fishing for as much as he could remember about Ike's songs and other potentially useful information as well as the whereabouts of other band members who would remember Ike writing the songs that T-Buck had recorded. Fortunately, the more Jack probed, the more Maurice remembered. Once he was satisfied that he had extracted all he could from Maurice, he explained how the deposition would go the next day. He intended to drop Ike off at the shelter and take Maurice to the Residence Inn off 7th Street, but Maurice had a different plan. He would stay with his friend in the shelter where they could continue their conversation late into the night.

The next day dawned dreary, cold and wet, not a frog-strangling rain, but a steady drizzle that made the temperatures in the low forties feel ten degrees colder. Jack took Ike and Maurice for breakfast at a café in the stockyards and then drove back to the RV.

Jack seated Maurice at one end of the dining table with the court reporter beside him. He would sit across from Maurice. Whatley could sit at the table. Ike would sit in the driver's chair that now permanently faced the rear. That left the passenger seat or the two easy chairs across from the table for Whatley's associates.

Whatley arrived in an Escalade rental, driven by one of his young associates. He had left his paralegal back in Los Angeles, but still traveled with two lawyers. Jack knew how that game was played. One senior lawyer, one younger partner and a senior associate, all billing by the hour. Must be costing T-Buck twenty grand a day. Jack smiled when he saw them unload from the Escalade. Big firms were the same around the country. Even with his biggest cases and a multi-week trial, he got by just fine with one associate and a paralegal. Jack opened the door and stepped to the parking lot to greet his adversaries.

"Welcome, gentlemen. Hope you didn't have any trouble finding me."

Whatley shook his hand. "No problem. The bellman at the Renaissance seemed to know where you were located. He just said to go out North Main and look for the RV on the left. You remember my two associates, Adam and Paul."

Jack shook their hands and led them in. "Nick, you've met

Ike. This is Maurice Wilkins. I suggest that you join us at the table and your associates can pick a place. I've got coffee, sodas and water on the kitchen counter. You can help yourselves."

When everyone was settled, the court reporter swore the witness.

"Mr. Wilkins, you understand that you have just sworn to tell the truth?" Jack asked.

"I certainly do, Mr. Bryant. And I would add that I would expect the Good Lord to send a bolt of lightning and strike me from this chair if I don't."

Jack smiled. "If you don't mind, please tell the Lord that won't be necessary. The rest of us are sitting a little too close and might not survive. We have penalties of perjury to deal with folks that are untruthful in these proceedings. Now, do you know Mr. Ike Irasmus, sitting over there?"

'Yes, sir. Been knowing him about forty years. Lost track of him after Katrina."

"How did you know Mr. Irasmus?"

Maurice looked at Whatley. "A little background might be helpful. I was born and raised in New Orleans." He pronounced it *Nawleans*. "Started playing the trombone when I was nine. By the time I was sixteen I was pretty good. Started filling in for some bands in the quarter. One of them was Ike's band. Wasn't long before I was full time with him. We were living the good life. Ike was on his way to being a super star. He could play and sing and write music. I thought he would be the next Louis Armstrong and I would be set for life. That all changed when he had that trouble with the law and ended up in Angola. Still, I spent my whole career playing in bands. Would probably still be doing it if I hadn't come down with lung cancer a few years back. I beat the big C but lost a lung in the process."

Jack could see that Maurice liked to talk. Unless he was very specific in his questions, they could be there all day. He got to the point.

"You've already provided us with sheet music to *We Was Doing All Right.*"

"Yes, sir."

"Who wrote that song and arrangement?"

Maurice looked at him with surprise. "I done told you on the phone a couple of months ago that this man right here, Ike Irasmus, wrote it."

"Understand, Mr. Wilkins, I just need you to say it under oath."

"Oath, no oath. Doesn't make a damn. Ike wrote it. I ought to know. I played it until I came down with cancer." He nodded at Ike for emphasis.

Jack reached into a pile of papers in front of him. "I'm handing you Exhibits A through F to your deposition. Can you identify them?"

"Yes, sir. I certainly can. Those are the sheet music to more songs that Ike wrote. See there at the bottom. He signed every page. Little faded now, but even with my bad eyes I can make out his signature."

Whatley had started shifting and a slight twitch appeared in his left eye, the one that always popped up when he realized that a lawsuit suit was not going well.

"Now," Jack continued, "I'm handing you Exhibit G. It's a list of the songs on T-Buck's latest album. Can you identify any of those?"

"Absolutely. There's A through F and *We Was Doing All Right.* Ike also wrote the rest of them. There's still a bunch of the old boys around Nawleans. I've got them looking for the sheet music. I expect to find music for all of them, written thirty-five, forty years ago. But, I can sit right here with God as my witness and swear that he wrote them all."

Whatley had been slowly tapping his pen on the table. With the last answer, he dropped it. "Jack, I see you have an office back there. Maybe we could take a short recess."

Jack smiled his agreement. He winked at Ike as he rose from the table and led the way back to his office. After shutting the door, he motioned for Whatley to take a seat. He went around the desk and leaned back in his chair. "So, what's on your mind?"

Whatley crossed his legs and tried to appear relaxed. "Look, Jack, I checked you out even before we had that hearing. I called a few friends in Texas. I know your reputation. Looks like that if we try this one, you'll be bringing half of New Orleans to back Ike. You haven't heard T-Buck's side of this. He'll also tell a very convincing story. So, let's split the writer's royalty fifty-fifty. It'll be more money than Ike ever thought he would have in his life."

"Not good enough, Nick. You're not going to win in Fort Worth. The jury will find that your client stole from mine. I might add that we will also be seeking punitive damages for the theft of personal property. Case like this, that could be in the millions. Here's what I'll recommend. We'll allow T-Buck to have the artist's royalties. Ike gets the writer's, from the time the album first came out and T-Buck started singing Ike's songs in concerts. We'll drop our claim for punitive damages. And one more thing to sweeten the pot. If Ike can get his personal life settled down, he would like to start writing again. He'll give T-Buck the right of first refusal for five years. We'll want a full accounting of receipts brought current and then monthly, and Ike will be listed as the writer with ASCAP and any other similar agencies. That's a good deal for both sides."

Silence filled the room while Whatley considered his options. Finally, he replied. "I'll need to talk to my client or his agent."

"That's why I asked you to have his agent on standby. I'll step to the front. Jack walked around the desk and stopped at the door. "Oh, and tell the agent that if we leave here without a deal, the next step will be the courthouse. No more negotiations."

Jack made more coffee and made idle conversation with Whatley's two young associates who had no idea what was happening. After a long thirty minutes, Whatley came from the back. "We have a deal."

Jack rose to shake his hand, a confirmation of agreement among gentlemen. "Now, let's dictate the terms of our deal to the court reporter. Then I'll rely on you to draft the papers. I'm not much for drafting contracts, but I can read them to make sure they match our agreement." Ike looked at Jack. His eyes grew big as he listened to the two lawyers dictate the agreement with the final conclusion that the papers would be signed in thirty days. The first accounting and a check to Ike would follow two weeks thereafter.

Once the opposing lawyers and the court reporter left, Ike grabbed Jack in a bear hug. "I think I understood all of that, but go over it for me one more time."

"Maurice, this agreement is confidential. I didn't ask you to step outside, but you've got to keep quiet about this."

Maurice nodded his understanding.

As Jack went through the agreement again, tears welled up in his client's eyes as he thought about buying a house with a yard for Trousers. "You sure this is going to go through?"

"As sure as I can be about any settlement. They don't want to face us at the courthouse. You figure on staying here in Fort Worth?"

No hesitation.

"My life changed completely here. Not going back to New Orleans. I'm going to get with Colby and start looking for a house. I want out of that shelter as soon as I can." He smiled. "Besides, I need to get in a house so I can make you and your family some of the world's best gumbo." Ike got serious. "Jack, there's going to be enough money that I should pay you a percentage as a fee."

Jack shook his client's hand. "Nothing doing. I told you my fee on this case was gumbo. Nothing else."

FORTY

January came and went. It started with a disappointment. TCU made it to the final four and then lost to USC in the semi-finals. Their quest for a national championship would continue next year, only this time without J.D. who had graduated in three and a half years and was training for the NFL combine and looking forward to the draft. He didn't tell Tanya, but he really wanted to play for the Cowboys. He figured that Tony Romo was good for a few more years and he liked the way that Romo ran the offense. Colby sold her house. Jack arranged for his clients to tour it and pick out two items each. That drew a story in the *Star Telegram* since the furnishing were worth well over a hundred grand. Colby showed houses to Ike on the west side of town. He settled on one on Hillcrest, a block south of Camp Bowie, in a neighborhood that had seen several generations of families raise children. The street had been described by more than one person as looking like it had been drawn by Norman Rockwell for the old *Saturday Evening Post.* Ike liked one with a big porch facing west. He hoped it would still be available when he got his money. He pictured himself, sitting in a rocker on that porch in the late afternoon, visiting with the children who roamed the neighborhood and with Trousers either resting under his feet or chasing squirrels in the front yard.

It was a sunny day in early February when everything changed. Jack enjoyed the sunshine as he walked across the parking lot to the RV. He turned off the heat and opened a couple of windows in his office. It was mid-morning when he heard the door open. A familiar face appeared. Jack got to his feet.

"Walt, good to see you. Governor must be in town. If it's another fundraiser, count me out." As he spoke he realized that Walt's face was grim. "On second thought, let me get you some coffee. Looks like you have a problem."

Jack poured a cup and handed it to Walt. So far, Walt had not said a word. They walked back to his office. Walt took a seat and pitched a stack of papers toward his friend. "I'm being sued. In fact, everyone involved is being sued except you. Looks like I did you a favor when I asked you to go to the front to check out that gate crasher; so, you weren't there when the shit hit the fan."

Jack raised his hand. "Hold on, Walt. Let me read through this. Drink your coffee while I do."

Jack did as he always did when reading a complicated pleading for the first time. He put it on his desk, uncapped a yellow highlighter and read slowly, trying to absorb it all. Occasionally, he would highlight a sentence or a paragraph. He took so long that Walt went back to the kitchen and retrieved the coffee pot to refill both cups. After twenty minutes he flipped the petition back to the first page and looked at Walt.

"Let me try to summarize this. The plaintiffs are Maria Hale, Edward's widow, six of his adult children from prior marriages, his estate, and Kevin O'Connell, the fundraiser. The defendants are you and the other members of the detail, the Fort Worth cops, Texstate Guardians, the security service that provided the guards, and the DPS, including Colonel Burnside. They're claiming that all of you were negligent and grossly negligent in carrying out your duty to the public on that night. As to your detail, they say that you abandoned your post when you took the governor and his wife out the back. Particularly, they say that if you had at least left a couple of agents behind, they might have kept the assassin's head down long enough for others to get off the stage. They call it cover fire, probably a reasonable description. They claim that all of the defendants contributed to what's called a 'State-Created Danger' in that you put Edward Hale, Kevin O'Connell and Governor Lardner in a more precarious position by your actions."

Walt stared at the floor and spoke in a barely audible voice. "I told you that there was concern among the detail about what our duty would be to the public if we took Lardner out of harm's way when others were in danger."

"Look, Walt. Just forget that for now. And tell the other members of the detail to keep their mouths shut about that debate. We'll deal with it later on."

"Understood."

"Let me go on. The Hales are claiming physical pain and mental anguish for the loss of their husband and father, standard stuff in this kind of lawsuit. Maria and the kids are claiming they lost billions of potential inheritance. Then O'Connell is saying that his PAC lost millions from pledges that were not honored that night and continuing damages because his PAC has had its reputation damaged. He would have benefited to the tune of millions of dollars in fees if you guys had done your job. Interesting that he didn't name Stepper or SOS. My guess is that he didn't want any lawyer nosing around in their finances."

"Hell, Jack, I make enough to put food on the table for my family and roof over their heads. Same with the rest of the detail and the other cops. It may be time for me to go into some other line of work. You need a private investigator?"

"Calm down and let me talk. First, the state will be providing the detail and the DPS with a defense. You could be defended by the state's lawyers; only I want to be defending you. The attorney general has some good lawyers, but most of them don't know beans about trying lawsuits. And, no, it won't cost you any money. Even if you weren't a good friend, you've seen that sign in the window. I thrive on big litigation and this one is going to be a barn burner.

"Next, they aren't after you. They know you don't have a pot to piss in. The plaintiffs are looking for money from the state, from the city of Fort Worth, and maybe even that security agency has a big insurance policy. So you don't need to worry about losing your house. It's not going to happen.

"Last, lawsuits aren't always about money. For example, O'Connell may figure he can win this case and even if he can't collect a judgment, he can re-establish some credibility with the fat cats in the Republican Party.

"And one more thing. Discovery in a civil case in Texas is fairly wide open. Doesn't mean there aren't some limits, but the rule is that if discovery might lead to something admissible, we can get it. I say that because we still don't know who was behind the attack. Could be our discovery will start us in the right direction. In other words, we may follow the money and see where it leads. That's secondary to getting a verdict in your favor, but that knowledge might help us."

Walt stood and rolled his head until his neck popped. "Gets that way when I'm under stress. Interesting that it never was a problem while we were dealing with the assassination. Would you be willing to defend the rest of the detail?"

Jack crossed his arms and leaned back, gazing at the ceiling as he pondered the question and any potential conflicts. "Yeah, I'll do it if Burnside agrees. It'll just be one less lawyer that I'll have to coordinate our defense with. Now, let me check two things."

Jack went back to the petition and a smile broke out on his face. "We're in Judge Jamison's court. She and I get along well. That's definitely a positive. In fact, I just wound up a case for a pro bono client that was in her court." He flipped to the back of the petition. "Plaintiff lawyer is Cecil Christiansen. He's with a big firm in Dallas that has connections with the Republican Party. He's got a Rambo reputation, like a lot of Dallas lawyers."

Walt looked puzzled. "What's that mean?"

"Means he fights tooth and toenail about every little thing, whether it's important or not. He wants to show how tough he is. Not a problem for me. I've dealt with his kind plenty of times. Just means we'll be spending more time at the courthouse, fighting about discovery and depositions. All the more reason that I'm glad to be in Judge Jamison's court. She'll listen to me. Now, you want to come out to the house and have dinner, or, are you headed back to Austin?"

"I'm heading back. I just didn't want to drop this on you by phone. Mary was worried before. Now, she's in a panic that we might end up living on the street. I'll tell her what you're saying. Maybe it'll calm her, at least a little." Walt hesitated. "I gotta tell you I was worried when I was on administrative suspension, but that's nothing compared to being sued for billions of dollars." He turned and left the trailer without even shaking Jack's hand. Jack watched him walk to his car, head down and hands stuffed in his pockets. He sympathized with Walt. He knew from experience that once someone was entrapped in a big lawsuit, it ate at their insides and never left their mind until it was finally over. Walt and Mary would be no different. Only with Walt it could be worse. Jack worried about his PTSD and whether it would flare up again. He considered trying to get Walt some counseling and quickly discarded the idea. If Walt saw a psychologist, it would be discoverable and PTSD would become another issue that could have impacted on Walt's conduct on the night of the Halloween attack. The only alternative would be that he would have to be Walt's confidant.

FORTY-ONE

Jack turned into his driveway and circled around the house to find J.D.'s truck parked there. He had been on auto pilot as he drove home with his mind on the new lawsuit, styled *Maria Hale, et al, v. The State of Texas, et al.* He would now call it the Hale case. His countenance brightened when he saw J.D.'s truck. He was seeing more of his son now that college was behind him.

He entered the house and found J.D. and Colby talking in the living room. J.D. had a bottle of water in his hand and Colby had Cabernet on the end table beside her seat on the couch. "What a surprise. We're finally using the living room. About time."

Colby got up and kissed him. J.D. hugged him.

"What can I fix you, hon?" Colby asked.

"A beer would suit me just fine."

Jack took a seat on the couch. Colby returned with a beer and squeezed his hand as she sat beside him. Jack took a stiff drink. "Ah, I needed that."

"Tough day?"

Jack hesitated. "Yeah, a little. Looks like I'm right back in the middle of the fundraising fiasco."

J.D. moved forward in his seat. "What's going on now? By the way, my teammates think that you must be one tough mother after that SWAT team assault."

"Walt came by the RV today. He and everyone else involved in security that night have been sued by Edward Hale's family and Kevin O'Connell, the fundraiser. I'll be defending Walt and the DPS."

"They didn't sue you?" Colby asked.

"No. They must have figured out that I was in front when the shooting started." Jack took Colby's hand and turned to look at her. "Hon, I know we were talking about late spring, but with this new case, it may interfere. I'm sorry."

Colby gave him a kiss. "That's okay. I'm not going anywhere. Maybe I'll join the team if this is going to be such a big case."

"This can't go beyond these four walls. I'm worried about Walt again. From the way he is acting, I think his PTSD is fixing to roar back. We'll have to support him and Mary all we can. And, no, I can't let him go to a shrink."

The next day Jack received a call from Walt, saying that Colonel Burnside was delighted that Jack would defend the DPS as well as Walt. He insisted on paying for Jack's time, but Jack declined. Once he hung up the phone, Jack prepared the answer for his clients. In Texas that was easy. All Jack had to say was that the Defendants Walter Frazier and the D.P.S. denied the allegations in the Plaintiff's Petition. He could always go back and amend the answer to allege what are called affirmative defenses. Jack picked the form from the computer data bank and was about ready to e-file it with the Tarrant County District Clerk when he stopped. *Wait a minute,* he thought, *I need to be the aggressor. If there's one thing that O'Connell doesn't want to give up, it's his list of donors. He touted this as a fund raiser for a social welfare organization. He'll go ballistic when he finds out I'm coming after the names and addresses and amounts pledged that night. For that matter, I might as well ask for all of the contributors to all of his PACs. Judge Jamison may not go that far. Hell, maybe I'll even come up with a Constitutional argument that these dark PACs, as most people call them, are a violation of some damn amendment.*

Jack drafted the discovery to O'Connell and filed it with his answer. It would be electronically served on Christiansen who would undoubtedly email it to O'Connell. He decided to wait to serve discovery on Maria Hale and the Hale children until he received responses from O'Connell. One battle at a time. In the back of his head, he kept hearing a voice say, "Follow the money."

Once Jack had efiled the documents with the clerk, he called Walt. "When you can spare a day away from the governor? We need to meet. I suggest you plan to spend the night and we can do some strategizing."

"Hell, I'm off the next two days. I've got a couple of honey-dos in the morning. I'll be at your place about four."

"Perfect. I'll invite J.D. He's interested in being a lawyer after his playing days are over. I presume you still like your steaks rare?"

"You got it."

"Oh, and I'm emailing our answer and some discovery. We're going on attack right out of the gate."

Walt turned into the driveway promptly at four the next afternoon, punched in the code and drove to the back. He was getting his overnighter out of the back seat of his Crown Vic when he heard the door open. He turned to find Jack, Colby and J.D. walking toward him.

"Walt, I'm so sorry," Colby said. "Just when you think you can get your life back to normal, this happens." She gave him a hug.

"Thanks, Colby. Fortunately, I've got the best lawyer in the country." He turned to shake hands with Jack and J.D. "You ready for the combine, big guy?"

"Yes, sir. Counting the days."

When they entered the house, Jack led the way through the kitchen to the living room. "Drop your bag at the foot of the stairs. We have recently discovered we have a living room. Drinks?"

"Bourbon on the rocks for me, a double please," Walt said.

"Cabernet for me," Colby said.

"Miller Lite, here. Getting close to me going on the wagon for the combine."

Jack served drinks from the bar and fixed himself a vodka martini.

"Walt, as you've seen, I've answered the petition and sent some discovery to the plaintiffs. I expect to hear from Christiansen any day now. I'll deal with that. The purpose of this gathering is to put our collective heads together and try to identify anyone who might have bankrolled Miriam Van Zandt. Who the hell would have had a motive?"

"Can I ask a question?" Walt said.

"Sure."

"What does this have to do with the new lawsuit?"

Jack smiled. "As you should know, I have a rather devious mind when it comes to lawsuit strategy. Short answer. If we can pin the attack on someone else, no jury is going to find you and your team negligent for causing the murder of Edward Hale and the wounding of O'Connell. Trust me on that for now."

Colby placed her wine glass on the side table beside her chair. "Back to your question, I'll start. How about Oscar Hale?"

Jack raised his eyebrows. "Why him?"

"Why not? Wouldn't be the first time that one family member killed another over money and, maybe even power. Oscar was the older brother. Maybe he thought that Edward had been riding his coattails, and he wanted it all for himself. Who knows what kind of agreements there were between Oscar and Edward? Maybe when one of them died, his interests in Hale and Hale went to the other brother."

"If that's the case, why was the governor shot and nearly died and O'Connell wounded?"

"Maybe Miriam was a bad shot."

"Nope," Walt said. "The DPS interviewed the others in the compound. Without exception, every one of them said she was the best pistol shot in a hundred miles." Walt rose and went to the bar. "Jack keep your seat. I'm going to fix another drink."

Jacked glanced at his watch. Fifteen minutes to down a double bourbon.

"Maybe a diversion. Did she intend to kill the governor and was off by a few inches and maybe shot Edward to distract attention from her real target?" J.D. added. "Or, maybe her bullets went just where she aimed them. She was only fifteen or twenty feet away. Give me a little time on the pistol range and I could do it. Then the question is why would anyone want to kill Edward, wound the governor and nick O'Connell? Doesn't make a damn bit of sense."

"How about Maria?" Walt asked as he returned from the bar. "Trophy wife, third marriage."

"And I heard she had a roving eye?"

"And, where, Miss Stripling, did you learn that?" Jack asked.

"I'm a realtor. I show houses to rich people. They talk. Other realtors like to gossip about their clients."

"I wasn't going to throw this on the table until I got your ideas, but since you bring up Maria, I just checked the probate records today. She and Edward signed a pre-nuptial agreement. Short hand version is that if she divorces him, she gets a hundred million."

"Not bad," Colby said. "I could somehow manage to get by on that."

Jack nodded and continued. "However, if they are still married when Edward dies, she inherits half of his estate, estimated to be around twenty billion. Edward's sudden death puts her in line for twenty billion."

"Wow," Walt exclaimed. "One of our rules is always suspect the spouse. That damn sure puts her near the top of the list."

"But if she did it, why would she be suing Walt and the others?" Colby asked.

"Maybe, like J.D. said, to divert attention. Maybe she talked O'Connell into joining her."

"How about the kids?" J. D. asked. "Dad, didn't you say that there are six, all from prior marriages and all adults. Maybe one of them didn't want to wait for their old man to kick the bucket."

"But, if it's one of the kids, why wouldn't they kill their stepmother, too, not just their father?"

"Good point," Jack agreed. "And I suppose we can eliminate the governor and his wife. What about O'Connell?"

"I don't think so," Walt said. "Why kill the goose? Oscar had just pledged ten million. O'Connell probably figured that Edward was good for something north of seven figures, too. By the way, while we were chasing Miriam, the DPS interviewed Oscar, his wife and Maria Hale. Took sworn statements. Turned up nothing. And, I should add that Maria appeared to be nothing more than the grieving widow. I suppose it could be an act." He shrugged his shoulders, indicating that he really had no way to know.

"Last, we've got two hundred or more people out in the ballroom, all of whom are potential suspects," Jack added. "Not an easy task we've set for ourselves. And remember that Miriam had an accomplice on the inside who turned off the outside cameras several hours before the party started."

"Dad, are you saying that accomplice is the person who bankrolled the attack?"

"Don't know. Maybe. Or it could be some waiter or cook who took a few hundred dollars. Not bad pay for flicking a switch that no one would notice."

"I agree that we need to find this person," Walt said. "Assuming we do, explain again how does that impact the case against me and the others?"

Jack stood to stretch his knee. As he rubbed it, he replied, "No guarantees, but chances are good if we find the killer, this case will disappear. Best thing we can do is stay on the trail while I handle the lawsuit. Now, who's ready for steaks?"

"I can help with those," Walt said. "Let me fix another drink first."

The next day Jack was unlocking the door to the RV when he heard the phone. He climbed the steps and reached for it on the fifth ring. He glanced at the caller i.d. as he did.

"Bryant, you son of a bitch, what the hell do you think you're doing?" a voice boomed from the phone.

"And a good morning to you, too, Cecil," Jack interrupted. "Am I to presume that you have read my discovery?"

"You're damn right I have. If you don't withdraw it, I'm going to kick your ass all the way into Oklahoma."

Jack smiled at the tirade and responded. "Last time you tried to kick my ass was in that products liability case I filed in Dallas about fifteen years ago. As I recall, the jury awarded my client fifteen million. You took it to the Texas Supreme Court and lost every step of the way. Now that's the kind of ass kicking I like."

Christiansen lowered his voice half an octave. "Okay, you got lucky on that one. This time you're messing in the big leagues. You'll have PACs all over the country intervening in this case, Republican and Democrat both, when they find out that you've asked for the names of all of the donors to SOS and all of O'Connell's other do-gooder organizations. You're not going to win that fight. The big Supreme Court made that clear in the fifties in the *Patterson v. Alabama* case."

"Facts were different. Back then the state of Alabama wanted the names of the members of the local NAACP chapter and the court protected them, saying that they would be subject to retribution if they were made public. The court was right then, but times have changed. IRS Regulation 501(c)(4) was intended to protect social welfare organizations, not fat cat billionaires and corporations. I'm happy to have Judge Jamison make the initial ruling. She's prone to allowing wide-open discovery and come trial time, she'll narrow down what gets into evidence."

Christiansen's voice dropped again, almost to a whisper. "Jack, take this how it's intended. These boys don't abide by the rules of discovery. The stakes are too damn high. No telling what they'll do when they find out that you're trying to expose their political efforts."

Jack spoke through clenched teeth. "If you're saying my life could be in danger, I can handle that. Won't be the first time. I served in Desert Storm. I've been trying cases against big corporations my whole career. I've had them park a couple of goons in front of my house every night during a trial. I had a cartel following me for three months down in the valley. Tell your damn friends to bring it on."

FORTY-TWO

It was late February when Hartley Hampton shut down his computer at the *Star Telegram* for the day and bounded down the back stairs to an entrance close to the loading dock where several tons of newsprint were unloaded weekly. He inhaled deeply as the smell of printers' ink drifted from the interior out onto the street, a smell to be enjoyed only by a reporter. He walked north beside the building in the direction of his car when he heard footsteps approaching rapidly. Suddenly, two men were on him. One of them seized his left hand and forced it behind his back as they shoved him up against the wall. He tried to fight them off, but it was two against one.

"Do not struggle, my friend," one of the men said with an accent. "For now, we are not going to harm you. Consider this a warning. You are to drop your investigation into political funding. No stories about dark PACS. Understand?" He forced Hampton's arm up as he talked.

"Dammit," Hartley cried. "You're about to break my arm."

"If you persist in this investigation, we'll do far worse. Now,

I'm going to release your arm. Continue to your car. Do not look back. Clear?"

Hartley nodded. The arm was released. Hartley continued toward his car, rubbing his left arm with the right hand. He did not look back.

Jack spent the day working on other clients' cases. For the most part, they weren't big ticket items for him, but critical to his clients who lived from paycheck to paycheck or were on Social Security. When they were pushed around by the system or some big corporation, he was there to push back. It had been a quiet day and Jack was about ready to shut down the office and maybe play a couple of games of dominoes when the door opened. Ike climbed the stairs, led by Trousers who knew that this was the place he could expect a treat.

Jack came from the back with his hand extended. "Ike, welcome. Here, let me get Trousers a bone. That your SUV in the parking lot?"

"Yes, sir. Small Toyota, but big enough for Trousers and me and maybe an instrument or two." Ike smiled. "Paid cash for it. That kind of surprised the salesman. I owe that to you."

"It was my pleasure. You deserve to finally have a little good fortune. I hear from Colby that you bought that house on Hillcrest. We're almost neighbors now."

"Well, I'm on the poor side of Camp Bowie, but the neighborhood's really nice. Only two bedrooms in the house, one too many for me. Trousers has made it his goal to catch one of the squirrels that live in those two big old pecan trees in the back yard. But the reason I'm here is to make good on that gumbo dinner I promised."

"You're on. J.D. is off to the combine today. How about next week, maybe Tuesday? Colby will bring the wine. I was about to head next door for some dominoes. Instead, let's just you and me go have a couple of beers."

Jack locked the RV and activated the armor. They walked to

Moe's with Trousers in the lead. They passed the empty tables outside and took one under a space heater that Moe had purchased at a garage sale for twenty bucks.

"I sound-proofed that second bedroom. It's now my studio. I'm trying to renew my skills with the trumpet, the cornet and even a keyboard. Keyboards were just becoming popular back in my day, but I was a decent pianist."

Jack finished his first beer and ordered a second. "You thinking about starting another band?"

Ike shook his head. "Not right now. That's for sure. I couldn't play in a high school marching band, but give me a few months and we'll see."

They were interrupted by Hampton, wearing jeans and a long sleeved blue shirt. The gray in his temples was the only clue that he was around forty. "Jack, I figured I'd find you in here when I saw your truck next door and the place was locked."

Both men rose to shake his hand. "Hartley, this is Ike Irasmus. Ike, this is Hartley Hampton, the best investigative reporter on the *Star Telegram*. Grab a beer and join us."

Hartley returned from the bar with a Lone Star in his hand. When he took a seat, Jack saw that he was worried about something. "Looks to me like you have a problem."

Hartley took a long pull from his beer. "I was just assaulted as I left the *Star Telegram* building a few minutes ago."

"You report it to the police?"

Hartley shook his head. "They roughed me up a little and then they were long gone." He rubbed his left arm. "I think I'll have a sore elbow for a few days."

"Keep going."

"Two men. Foreign accents. Came up from behind me and shoved me into the wall. Somehow they knew that I was researching a series on the big money flowing into politics. They told me to back off or I'd have something more than a sore arm next time."

"You get a look at them?"

Hartley shook his head. "Naw. Happened too fast. After they delivered their message they told me to walk on to my car and not to look back. I did what they said."

"Ike, you need to know that Hartley and I go back a few years. We had a judge in the Dead Peasants trial that started off leaning toward the other side. Hartley wrote some articles that helped me level the playing field." Jack sipped his beer and sat it on the table. "I didn't know you were working on the political money story."

"I was just getting started." Hartley took a deep breath and leaned over the table, lowering his voice. "Somehow I missed the lawsuit that O'Connell and the Hales filed. I ran across the lawsuit and went online to read all of the pleadings and discovery. Jack, you and I are on the same story. My editor approved a series on all of the money in politics and what it's doing to our country. So far, I'm just doing research. I'm a long way from my first story in the series. If fact, I don't even know how those guys knew I was on it."

Jack absentmindedly picked up his cane and tapped it on the concrete floor while he pondered what he was hearing. "I suspect you made a few phone calls. Maybe one of them got back to whoever hired these guys. You worried about your safety or your family?"

Hartley looked around the room again. "Not yet, but we're going to be poking around in the lives and finances of some big players. Shit, Jack, someone almost killed the governor and did kill one of the most influential Republicans in the country. Obviously, the stakes are high, up to and including death. I don't think whoever is behind this would think twice about putting another bullet in the head of a reporter...or a lawyer for that matter. You figure out who was behind that Halloween attack?"

Jack shook his head. "Dead end, so far. Still, like you, I'm trying to follow the money. I've done a little research on these social welfare organizations. Educate me on what you've learned so far." He turned to Ike. "You and Trousers are welcome to stay, but we may be here a while."

"No," Ike said. "This is all new to me. I'd like to listen."

Hartley reached into his backpack on the floor beside his chair and retrieved an iPad. "First, Super-PACs can raise all kinds of money for or against a candidate, but they have to disclose their donors and cannot coordinate with the candidate. That's a meaningless restriction these days. Why bother to use something where you have to disclose your donors? Everything I've read says that they will be little used in 2016.

"The 501(c)(4)s are where the big money is going, so called social welfare organizations."

"Social welfare, like the homeless shelter I used to live in?" Ike asked.

Hartley shook his head. "That was probably the intent a hundred years ago when Congress authorized them. Maybe back in the fifties when the Supreme Court said that the Alabama officials couldn't get the names of the members of the Alabama NAACP. Over the years the line has become blurred to the point of disappearing." He paused. "Over the past several years, the Democrats and Republicans have pushed the envelope. Their ads have become blatantly more political since the Federal Election Commission doesn't regulate social welfare groups. The IRS is probably worried that if they were to do their job, it would piss off both sides of the aisle for them to slow the flow of money. And people like O'Connell are getting rich off their consulting fees. I'll bet what happened out at Oscar's house cost his Stepper group not just that hundred million that probably disappeared after the shootings but cost him millions in consulting fees. Bottom line is the flood gates are now open and no one is going to try to close them."

"For damn sure the Supremes are not about to stop it," Jack said. "Chief Justice Roberts twisted around that *Citizens*

United case to put corporations right in the middle of political campaigns, again with no restrictions. Hell, I'm sure that there are multinational companies just salivating to throw enough money in the pot to have access to the White House and the Congressional leadership, particularly since their names don't have to be disclosed."

"You know the Karl Rove strategy, don't you, Jack?"

"Educate me."

"He's got this outfit called American Crossroads. He has a PAC and a social welfare group. He can get billionaires and corporations to donate to the social welfare side. Then it turns around and funds the Super-PAC. The Super-PAC can use the money however it damn well pleases, for or against candidates in unlimited amounts. Then when it reports its donors, it points to the social welfare arm. When someone asks, he can say that he's not obligated to reveal the names of donors to a 501(c)(4) social welfare organization. Money has been laundered through the social welfare group to the PAC and then for or against candidates. No one can find out where the money came from, no matter how big the amount. The politicians and Kevin O'Connells thank the Supreme Court, particularly Chief Justice Roberts, when they say their prayers."

"You licensed to carry?"

"Yeah, only I usually leave my gun at home. That's changing as of now."

Hartley and Ike rose from their chairs as Jack dropped some bills on the table. "I honestly didn't know what I was getting into when Walt dropped this case on me. Now, I'm beginning to understand." He reached out to shake Hartley's hand. "You and I both try to do the right thing. I want to win this case, but along the way, let's stir up a firestorm of publicity. Maybe there are a few honest politicians out there who will stand beside us. Maybe not. Time will tell. Meantime, we'll both watch each other's backs."

Jack parked his truck and walked in the back door and pecked

Colby on the lips. He went to the bar and poured a large quantity of bourbon on the rocks. He sat on the couch and absent-mindedly scratched Killer's ears while he sipped his drink and gazed off across the room. Colby poured her own wine and sat beside him. Finally, she broke the silence.

"Okay, what's eating on you?"

"Nothing."

"Come on. I know you better than that."

Jack sighed. "It's Walt's case."

"So? It's just a lawsuit, a big one, but big cases are your bread and butter."

"Hartley dropped by this afternoon. Joined me and Ike for a beer. He's working on a series about money and politics, investigating this dark money. He'll probably be covering a lot of the same ground that I will in Walt's case. And he was attacked this evening when he left work."

Colby stared at Jack, then walked to the windows and closed the curtains. "Is he all right?"

"Two guys roughed him up and warned him off the story. He's not about to back off."

"You think that this might get dangerous?"

"Hopefully not, but the stakes are enormous. If I get what I'm seeking, it could change the whole political landscape. Some folks would get upset."

Colby remained standing with her hands on her hips. "Jack, my life was turned upside down with those Dead Peasants killings. He tried to kill me three times. I thought that was behind me. Now, you're saying that we might be living that nightmare again. I can't deal with it." She put her glass on the bar and stormed from the room.

Jack heard their bedroom door slam. She was right, of course. He paced the living room, trying to figure out what to do. He walked to the bedroom, paused and then opened the door. Colby was under the covers. Jack sat beside Colby and put his hand on her hip. She rolled over to face the other side of the bed.

"Look. Nothing's happened yet. Probably won't. If I get threats or anything else, I'll send you away until this is over."

Colby turned to face him with tears in her eyes. "I'll get over it. Only, I'm not going anywhere. If you're here, I'll be right beside you. Now, let me sleep. I promise to be better in the morning."

FORTY-THREE

J.D. burst into the house on Friday evening to find Colby and Jack sitting at the kitchen table. Jack looked up.

"About time you got here. Why'd you go all week without calling? I had to read how you were doing in the paper and on the internet."

"Sorry, Dad. Let's just say I was pre-occupied. Also, I wanted to tell you and Colby in person. "I ran a 4.44, benched two hundred and twenty-five pounds forty two times and scored forty-eight out of fifty on the Wonderlic. Then I caught every pass thrown to me in the gauntlet. In short, I'm not bragging, but I did damn good. And, the Cowboys are interested."

Jack jumped to his feet to hug his son with Colby close behind. "I suspect that calls for dinner at Bonnell's."

"If it's okay, I'd like to pass on dinner. I'm meeting Tanya as soon as she gets out of a night class. I'll take a bourbon on the rocks for my celebration."

"Let's get out of the kitchen," Colby said as she led the way to the living room. "I'm starting to like visiting in here. "

After they were seated, Jack asked, "What's next?"

"Cowboys want me to see them next week. More interviews, maybe one with Jerry Jones, himself. And I've got some other teams interested enough to ask me for a personal one-on-one. What's happening with that case where you're defending Walt Frazier?"

"It's heating up a little. We have a hearing next Friday on my motion to compel O'Connell to turn over his records of contributors and amounts for Stepper and SOS."

"I've got a little time. Can I tag along as your paralegal?"

"Sure. I'm not optimistic that we'll win, but we'll give it our best shot."

Judge Jamison took the bench and beckoned the lawyers and audience to be seated. "Good morning, everyone. In the matter of *Maria Hale, et al v. The State of Texas, et al*, we have Mr. Bryant's Motion to Compel Responses to Discovery. You may proceed, Mr. Bryant."

Jack stood at the counsel table. "Judge, this is really quite simple. Mr. O'Connell is seeking millions of dollars from my client and the other defendants. He claims that his business as a political consultant has been irreparably damaged because of the incident at the Hale mansion last Halloween, that it happened because the defendants were negligent in their security measures. We're not here to talk about liability yet. We're just trying to get a handle on damages. The funds that night were being raised for Mr. O'Connell's Stepper Official Strategies, also known as SOS, supposedly the chief source of income to Mr. O'Connell. All we are looking for is the financial information about Mr. O'Connell's PACs, including the ones he calls Stepper and SOS. It's standard discovery in any case."

Christiansen got to his feet. "That's horse manure, Judge."

Judge Jamison looked over her half glasses. "You need to

watch your language, Mr. Christiansen. You were one word from being held in contempt. I also expect everyone to act professionally. Please respond briefly to Mr. Bryant's argument."

"My apologies, Your Honor. Mr. Bryant is asking you to go against a hundred years of precedent, including the Supreme Court in the *NAACP v. Alabama* case from the fifties. SOS is a social welfare organization. Its donor's names and other information are protected from disclosure."

"Let me interrupt, Mr. Christiansen," Judge Jamison said. "I've been reading about these dark PACs and so-called social welfare organizations. Frankly, the whole concept offends me. Last time I checked, not one had made any donation to my church. And I don't really care that our Supreme Court disagrees. I am ordering you to produce the names and amounts of donations to all of Mr. O'Connell's PACs and social welfare organizations and also how the money was spent. I'm mindful that these so-called social welfare groups are supposed to primarily fund social welfare projects or related issues. If they can't pass that test, it may be another reason to question what your client is doing. I will sign a confidentiality order so the information will not go beyond the lawyers and their clients. I will also expect them to surrender any such discovery at the conclusion of this lawsuit."

"Your Honor," Christiansen said and was interrupted.

"Mr. Christiansen, I'm not through. I know what I am ordering is somewhat unusual. So, I'm staying my own order and giving you an opportunity to take it to the court of appeals before anything is produced. We're adjourned."

Hampton caught Jack and J.D. in the parking lot. "I'm confused. Did you win?"

Jack leaned on his cane. "We won the first round."

"What's this appeal of a discovery ruling?"

Jack shrugged. "It happens. She knows that she's pushing the envelope. If she hadn't certified the question for appeal, Christiansen would have gone to the appellate court to try to have her order stricken, anyway."

Hampton paused in his note taking. "Just remember that our court of appeals is all Republican. Expect an uphill battle."

Jack and J.D. were about to get in the car when J.D. grabbed Jack's arm. "Dad, see those two men in dark suits three rows over."

Jack glanced at the men. Both were wearing horn-rimmed glasses and had hats pulled low in an obvious attempt to conceal their faces now that they were outside. "Go on," he said.

"They were sitting in the back of the courtroom away from the reporters. I went to the restroom while we were waiting for the judge. They were in the restroom, speaking a foreign language and stopped when I walked in. Sounded Eastern European to my untrained ear."

FORTY-FOUR

The offices of Kevin O'Connell and his various PACs and political organizations on K Street in Washington, D. C. could only be described as lavish. He wanted to create the impression that power and money merged at the entrance to his suite. Stepping from the elevator on the penthouse floor, a visitor walked a few steps to oak doors that opened into a sitting area with French antique furniture from the nineteenth century. One wall was for artists who specialized in dramatic American landscapes. The wall across from it was overflowing with photos of O'Connell posing with Republican politicians and influential donors. He was shaking hands and showing sparkling teeth in each of them. In one-on-one meetings, it was obvious that he could overcome his modest looks.

Three doors opened from the entry. One to the left led to a hallway with small offices, ending in a bullpen filled with cubicles occupied by young people enamored with the power and wealth that engulfed them. The second door was directly behind the reception desk. It was the entrance to O'Connell's spacious corner office from which both the Capitol and the White House could be seen. The last door opened to reveal a paneled conference room and a table with sixteen padded leather chairs. Once the door was closed, the conference room was sound proofed. No matter how sophisticated a listening device perched on another building might be, it could not penetrate to hear the secret conversations in that room. And, for good measure, O'Connell had it swept for listening devices every morning. A device had never been found, but when one considered the decisions that were made in that room, it was worth the effort, just in case.

O'Connell has summoned Cecil Christiansen for a meeting. His lawyer had groused at first that they could talk on the phone, but when O'Connell insisted, he decided that if a client wanted to pay his hourly rate of $600 for an overnight trip to Washington, he could deal with it. When he was escorted to the conference room, he was greeted by O'Connell, two of his senior staff and two advisers to the Republican National Committee. After the receptionist served him black coffee, the door was shut.

"Cecil, I asked you to join us because of the ruling that judge in Fort Worth made last week. What the hell is going on down there? I thought you and your firm contributed to every judicial campaign within a hundred miles of Dallas."

Christiansen leaned back and folded his arms, not liking to be called on the carpet by anyone. "We did. People in my firm gave her campaign a total of $25,000 and she's not even up for election. Unfortunately, that doesn't guarantee she will go along with me on every ruling."

O'Connell placed his hands flat on the table while the others observed. "I know Tarrant County is strongly Republican with heavy Tea Party leanings. Maybe we need to run someone against her in the next election, maybe have that person announce early and point to a campaign chest of a couple hundred thousand. I could get that done in a week. Wouldn't that get her attention?"

Christiansen thought. "It might. She was a Democrat until about fifteen years ago when she realized which way the county was going. She held a press conference to announce that she wanted to be among the first of Democratic county officials to acknowledge that the Republican Party was the one of the future. Translate that to her saying that if she wanted to win in the future, she had to join the GOP. Still, I know she has some liberal views. Those obviously came out with the ruling in your case."

O'Connell stood at his place at the end of the table. "That settles it. We'll have a candidate announce against her within a month with a press conference alluding to her ruling. He or she will demand that social welfare organizations must be able to operate without risking that their donors might be disclosed, no matter what the reason. I'll make sure he talks about the Boy Scouts, the Audubon Society, that kind of thing. Now that I think about it, such a candidacy will also get the attention of the judges on the court of appeals who will be grading her papers."

Christiansen agreed. "Yeah, they'll get the message. If they vote against us, they'll face an opponent, too. We'll take some flak from the media, but it'll be worth it."

One of O'Connell's aides spoke up. "Tell us about this guy, Bryant. I hear he works out of an RV. Is he any threat?"

Christiansen shook his head. "Don't be fooled by appearances. He's one of the best trial lawyers in the state. He made a fortune in Beaumont. I hear around a hundred million. Moved back to Fort Worth a few years ago. He doesn't need money; so, he represents people for free out of that RV. The head of the governor's detail, Frazier, is an army buddy of his. They served together in Desert Storm. He's as tough as they come."

"Well, if we can't buy him off, there are other ways to deal with him." O'Connell's eyes narrowed as he spoke.

Christiansen stared at O'Connell for a split second before replying. "I'm not sure what you're getting at. I'm a hardball son of a bitch, but I play by the rules. I may bend one on occasion, but that's as far as I'll go. If you even think about harming him, I'm out. That clear?"

"Cecil," O'Connell said with a wry smile, "I was thinking of no such thing. Besides, when you win in the court of appeals, my donors will be protected and we can move forward with the lawsuit. Money is not the issue. At the end of the day I want the whole country to know that what happened at that fundraiser was the result of incompetence on the part of the law enforcement agencies that were there to protect us all. That ought to clear my name. You accomplish that and there'll be a substantial bonus at the end of the case."

FORTY-FIVE

Jack's phone beside his bed rang at three in the morning. On the fourth ring he realized that it was not part of a dream and groped for it. "Hello."

"Jack, it's Joe. She's coming around."

"I'm sorry. Who's coming around?"

"Miriam Van Zandt. Why the hell do you think I would call you at three in the morning?"

Instantly awake, Jack said, "I'll meet you at the hospital in thirty minutes. What room?"

Jack replaced the phone and threw back the covers.

Colby wiped the sleep from her eyes. "What's going on?"

"Miriam Van Zandt is awake."

"I'm going with you."

"Not necessary."

"I don't care. I want to be there."

Jack was pulling a clean pair of jeans from the closet.

"Forget make-up. We're leaving as soon as we both make a bathroom stop."

When he stepped from the bathroom, Colby followed. Within minutes, Jack was disarming the alarm and choosing a cane. Killer had been sleeping in a chair by the pool and wandered to them, curious as to what was bringing his people out in the middle of the night.

Colby stopped to scratch his ears. "We'll be back shortly, Killer. Take care of things while we're gone." Twenty minutes later Jack parked Lucille in the visitor lot where he found a space on the front row. When they entered the lobby, they found Shannon waiting for them.

"About time you two got here. You know how these comas go. We may have missed our chance by now. Follow me."

Joe led them to the elevator. He punched the button for the sixth floor. When they exited, he led them down a corridor where a Fort Worth cop was seated next to a door. Joe knew him. "Evening, Sam. I hear she's awake."

Sam got to his feet. "She's drifting in and out. Her neurologist is in there with her. He came as soon as he got the word. Name's Reddy. He said you could go in."

They pushed quietly through the door into a room mostly in shadows, with one lamp on a table next to a visitor's chair providing the only light. Various monitors flashed digital readouts and beeped regularly. A doctor with a dark complexion, dressed in a white coat studied the slight form of Miriam Van Zandt, her head still wrapped in bandages, and glanced at the monitors. He turned to them. "I presume that you're Mr. Shannon."

"I am, Dr. Reddy. This is Jack Bryant, the head of the investigation into the events in Westover Hills. Colby Stripling is his assistant."

They shook hands.

"What's her status, Doctor?" Jack asked.

"She started waking a couple of hours ago. At first she didn't even know who she was. When I said she was Miriam Van Zandt, she seemed to understand and nodded off again. She woke a few minutes later and asked what town she was in and what she was doing here. I told her that she had a broken leg and several rib fractures, but the worst injury was to her head. She wanted to know when she could get out. Before I could answer, she was gone again."

"Can I talk to her?" Colby asked. "Maybe she'll respond to another female voice."

Dr. Reddy nodded. Colby walked to the head of the bed and lightly squeezed her hand. At first there was nothing. Then she felt a weak squeeze back. "Miriam, I'm Colby Stripling. Can you hear me?"

While Colby was trying to get a response, Jack pulled Dr. Reddy to the door and in a low voice said, "Doctor, if she wakes enough, can I tell her about what she did at the Hale mansion and about the assault at the compound? I need to do it to try to get some information that might help our investigation."

Dr. Reddy thought for a moment and replied, "Do what you must. She may be awake in the morning or she might never wake again." They returned to her bedside as Miriam opened her eyes.

"Miriam, do you feel like answering some questions?"

She nodded.

"Do you remember being at the compound and the fighting that went on there?"

"I remember I was shot but tossed a grenade under my trailer. What's happened to my dad?"

Colby looked at Dr. Reddy who nodded his agreement. "I'm sorry, Miriam. Your dad was killed."

Tears filled Miriam's eyes, but she didn't lose consciousness. "He died for a good cause. All he wanted was freedom, same as the heroes in the Alamo."

Joe stepped forward. "Miriam, we know that you killed a man at that Halloween party in Westover Hills and almost killed the governor. I could read you your rights, but we don't need your testimony to convict you." Joe spoke softly. "If you'll help us, I can get you life in prison. Maybe you'll get out in thirty years."

The patient stared at the wall. The others worried that she was about to lapse back into the coma before she spoke. "Pa's dead. What about Manny?"

"If you're talking about Manford Donley, he'll be standing trial along with the rest of the defenders that stayed to fight."

"I don't know much."

"Who paid you?" Jack asked.

Miriam was quiet while she searched her memory. "I don't know. Money was wired to Pa's Cayman Island account. He put some of it in mine. All the transactions were on the computers. I never knew who put up the money. Neither did Pa. Money came from a Vietnam War buddy of his. That's all I knew. I was trying to blow up those computers when I was hurt."

"You succeeded, Miriam," Jack said. "The computers were blown to smithereens. You know the name of your dad's friend?"

Long silence.

Miriam closed her eyes.

"Miriam," Colby said, "who was your dad's friend?"

Her eyes opened. "Pa called him Cross. Said he got a tattoo of a black cross on the side of his neck when they were on some R and R in Taiwan. That's the only name I ever knew. Pa said he lived in New Orleans or somewhere around there. Now I need to sleep."

Joe thanked Dr. Reddy and asked that he be notified when she woke again. They stepped out into the hallway. "Let's go downstairs to the cafeteria. I'm buying."

They rode the elevator to the basement in silence. The cafeteria was just opening, and they were able to fill mugs with hot, fresh coffee. They had the place to themselves and chose a table away from the door.

"So, Jack, what have we got?" Joe asked.

"Looks like a dead end, doesn't it?" Jack said. "Chances of finding an old man in New Orleans with a cross on his neck are pretty damn slim, maybe next to impossible."

"If he's ever been arrested, we document tattoos these days," Joe said.

"For that matter, if he re-upped in the army or any branch of the military, it would have been recorded, just like scars. We can have Walt check with the army, but I don't know how they track that kind of thing."

Colby was stirring her coffee with a plastic spoon. "Are we sure that the compound was searched thoroughly? Maybe they overlooked some piece of the computer."

"No way, Colby," Joe said. "I talked to Colonel Burnside. They looked under every rock and grain of sand, not to say they didn't also search the tunnels and trailers. Found weapons that Burnside confiscated. They're now stored in Austin. Found lots of other stuff, kid's toys, MREs that could have lasted for months. They did find fragments of computers but the DPS forensics guys couldn't do anything with them."

FORTY-SIX

Cecil Christiansen immediately put his appellate partner to work, drafting a petition for the Fort Worth Court of Appeals, seeking to overturn Judge Jamison's decision to require disclosure of the donors to O'Connell's SOS committee, which, of course, was characterized as a social welfare organization.

When Christiansen demanded to depose Walt, Jack agreed. Walt arrived at his RV early on the day before the deposition. Jack thought he detected alcohol on his breath. Not a good sign, particularly so early in the morning. Walt sat at the table with both hands wrapped around his coffee cup. He refused to look Jack in the eye. Jack had prepared hundreds of witnesses for deposition and trial, and he recognized that his usual tactics would not work with Walt.

"I know this is going to be difficult for you. You're going to be asked questions that may make you re-live the whole night. If you start having another flashback, immediately ask for a break.

Understand?"

Walt continued to stare at his coffee cup. Jack did not recall ever yelling at a client while preparing him for deposition, but there was a first time for everything. He pounded his fist on the table. "Dammit, Walt, I'm your friend and lawyer. If you won't talk to me, tomorrow will be a disaster."

Walt blinked his eyes and focused on Jack. "I'm sorry. I got an anti-depressant and something for anxiety from my regular doctor, not a shrink." He reached into his pocket and retrieved two bottles, extracted a pill from each and washed them down with coffee. "I've been trying not to take them, but I suppose now's the time. I promise I'll do better."

"State your name," Christiansen said.

"Walter," He broke out in a cough and had to take a sip of water before continuing. "Frazier, Jr."

"Mr. Frazier..."

"It's Sergeant Frazier."

Christiansen nodded. "Sergeant Frazier, you just raised your hand and took an oath administered by the court reporter. Did you have any difficulty understanding it?"

"No, sir."

Jack kept his poker face, but realized that Christiansen was going straight for the weakness in their defense when he began with a question about oaths. He and Walt had spent the whole day rehearsing answers to the kind of questions that were about to come. He only hoped that Walt remembered and could execute their plan.

"How long have you been with the DPS?"

"Fourteen years. I was a deputy sheriff in Wharton after I was discharged from the army and then joined the DPS as a trooper."

Christiansen folded his hands in front of him and took off his glasses as he stared at Walt. "Do you remember taking an oath as a trooper back then?"

"Yes, sir."

"Do you remember the words, 'preserve, protect and defend' in that oath?"

"I do, Mr. Christiansen."

"What were you swearing to preserve, protect and defend?"

"The Constitution of the United States and the State of Texas?"

Christiansen raised his voice. "Keep going, Sergeant."

Walt hesitated and looked at Jack. "And the laws of this state."

"In fact, you swore to protect and defend the people of this state, didn't you, Sergeant?"

"I suppose so."

"Not suppose. You knew that was part of your oath as a state trooper, didn't you?"

Walt looked down at the table and murmured, "That's correct."

"You continue to be a DPS officer even though you are now protecting the governor?"

Walt hesitated and took another sip of water while he thought about his answer. "That's correct, sir."

Christiansen smiled at the answer. "You became part of the governor's protective detail when?"

Walt paused to think, staring up at the ceiling. "It'll be ten years next month."

"What are your duties now?"

"Protect the governor at all costs."

Jack didn't like the way that answer came out.

"And, sir, I have to be willing to take a bullet for him. I wish I had been the one shot that day."

Christiansen thought about that last answer. "What did you do when the governor was shot?"

Jack could see that his client was blinking his eyes and knew that he was flashing back. "I think we need to take a break. With so many people in this RV, it's getting stuffy. Let's take five. Walt, step outside with me."

They walked across the parking lot and leaned against Jack's pickup, out of hearing from others who also stepped out to stretch their legs. "Did you take your meds?"

Walt nodded.

"I saw you were having a flashback. Can you stay in the present and answer the questions about that night? I'll interrupt again if I have to."

Walt took a deep breath. "Yeah, let's get this son of a bitch over. I'll be okay." They returned to the RV. Jack had the court reporter read back the question.

"We followed procedures to the letter. The detail went into crisis mode. We pulled the governor off the stage. We also hustled Petal, I mean Mrs. Lardner, off the stage and out to the limo. Well, it's a Suburban, but it's still called a limo."

"And you ignored that oath you took fourteen years ago to protect the public, didn't you?"

Walt gazed into the camera without answering.

"Didn't you, Sergeant Frazier, you and the rest of the detail." Christiansen was raising his voice. His face was turning red. "You know that about eight seconds elapsed before the second round of shots that killed Edward Hale and wounded Kevin O'Connell, don't you?"

Jack slapped his palm on the table. "Dammit, Cecil, quit shouting at my client and asking multiple questions, or we'll stop this deposition right now."

"Don't like how this is going, do you, Jack? I'll break up my questions. When the first shot was fired and the governor went down, you made no effort to protect the other people on the stage or, for that matter, in the audience?"

"One of our men took a shot at that woman from the back."

"And then he bailed and ran for the limo, too."

"Sir, we had to get the governor to the hospital as quick as we could. If we hadn't, he almost certainly would have died."

"How many men does it take to drive that limo?"

"One."

"And he was already outside by the car, wasn't he?"

"Sir, it took two of us to pull the governor off the stage and out to the limo and one for Mrs. Lardner."

"Come on, Sergeant, you're a big man. You could have dragged him out to the car, couldn't you? That would have left one of your men to fire at the assassin, maybe keep her head down long enough for the others to get off the stage. You also could have told the man at the back to stay, right? You know that Edward Hale was following right behind you as you left the stage. Five more seconds and he would have been out of the line of fire. Five seconds, Sergeant Frazier."

"I can't speculate, sir."

"Fact is, you didn't think about anything other than protecting the governor."

Walt's voice got stronger. "Mr. Christiansen, there were three Fort Worth cops on the balcony who could have been doing just what you said. They definitely had the high ground."

"Sergeant, I don't want to talk about the Fort Worth police today. I'll depose them and the security company later," Christiansen sneered. "The fact is that Edward Hale might still be alive if protecting the public had even crossed your mind."

"I can't answer that, sir. My team and I did the best we could."

Christiansen motioned to his associate and abruptly rose. "No more questions. I'm out of here."

FORTY-SEVEN

Jack and Walt hardly spoke on the way back to Jack's house. They said their good-byes in the driveway, and Walt headed back to Austin. Both knew that it had not gone well.

Jack entered the house and found Colby in the living room, studying some documents. "How'd it go?" she asked after she stood and kissed Jack.

Jack shook his head. "Not good. Cecil knew exactly what our weak point was and blew it wide open in less than an hour. Walt had to fight off his PTSD. It didn't go well. It's only going to get worse when he questions the rest of the detail."

"But Walt saved the governor's life. That was his job."

Jack opened a bottle of water and sat across from Colby. "Yes and no. Walt and I talked about this at the start. He took an oath to protect the public. That oath didn't go away when he became a part of the governor's detail. It's an impossible conflict of interest."

"Wait a minute. Doesn't the Secret Service have that exact

same conflict when someone attacks the president?"

"Issue hasn't really come up. Certainly not when Kennedy was assassinated or when Reagan was shot. And I don't think that the Secret Service has any duty to the public. On top of that, the president travels with a whole army of agents. The governor travels with only four or five. We're already going to be making law with these Dark PACs. Now it looks like the court is going to have to decide the role of the detail when the governor and the public are both in danger. I can handle it, but I'm worried about Walt. He's having flashbacks again. He's drinking way too much. I just hope he's sober when he's driving. I wouldn't be surprised if he has a flask stashed in his glove compartment."

"Do we need to talk him into some counseling?"

Jack shook his head. "I'm trying to avoid that. His medical records could be discovered. I certainly could spin them so he looks like the war hero he was, but Christiansen would be arguing that the DPS never should have hired him and his flashback impaired his judgment that night. Now, what do you have spread all over the couch?"

"I was walking by your desk and saw the inventory of what the DPS collected at the compound. I hope you don't mind if I looked at it."

"Of course not. I'm happy to have another set of eyes and your smarts studying the evidence. You find anything interesting?"

"Maybe. You remember I had questions about the computers when we had coffee with Joe after visiting Miriam. By the way, how is she?"

"She woke up a couple of times. Said something about her father, and then drifted back to sleep. Dr. Reddy says that the fact that she is still waking up, if only for a couple of minutes, is hopeful. She's not getting out of the hospital any time soon. That's for sure."

"Well, that inventory has all of the evidence that might be related to computers on two pages. I looked them over and didn't really know what I was reading. So, I emailed them to J.D. He says that there are parts of three computers, but the hard drive on one of them is missing. Well, it's not actually the hard drive. It's some thingamabob that fits in the hard drive that is the memory. It's gone. Also, it's small enough that it might have been missed by all of those boots on the ground stomping around the compound. I think that you and me and Walt, and, particularly J.D. since he's our in-house computer geek, need to take that beautiful drive to West Texas to do another search."

Jack remained silent while he went to the bar to retrieve another bottle of water. He turned and leaned against the bar. "Probably won't find a damn thing, but worth a try, and it would be good to give Walt something to do. I'm worried about this lawsuit. We won a round with Judge Jamison and lost one with Walt's deposition. Not a damn thing he could have done different. He was caught up in a situation he couldn't control. So, let's go for it. Only, we'll have to wait a week. J.D. leaves for New York tomorrow for the NFL draft. He's high enough up the list that they want him there on draft night. I need to give him a call and wish him well. Hold on."

"Hey, Dad. I was about to call you."

"I've got you on the speaker."

"Hey, big guy," Colby said. "We've got our fingers crossed for you on Saturday night. Enjoy yourself. You've worked hard to get to this point."

"I join in those sentiments," Jack said. "And, when you get back we're going to take a little drive out to West Texas for a look around. Colby told me you think there's a piece of the puzzle missing."

"Yeah, it may be blown all to hell or they might have missed it because it's small. I'll be available on Monday. Just let me know. And, expect a call from me on Saturday night."

FORTY-EIGHT

J.D.'s call came early on Friday night, and it had nothing to do with the draft. He was staying at the Grand Hyatt, just a few blocks from Radio City Music Hall where the draft was to take place. He had been invited to dinner by Jerry Jones and had declined the offer to ride in his limo back to the hotel, saying that he would enjoy the short walk and fresh air. He was a block from the hotel when he saw two men cross the street while he waited for a light to change. They seemed familiar but he could not place them as they stood behind him. When the light turned green, it hit him. They were the same two men who had been in the courtroom and the parking lot. Stepping to the curb on the other side, he considered what to do. The street was surprisingly empty, particularly for a city that never sleeps. He thought about just walking to the hotel entrance a half a block away, then changed his mind.

He took a few more steps and whirled to confront them.

"What can I do for you gentlemen?" he said as he moved toward them until he was only about a foot away. They were not expecting his response. He was four or five inches taller than either of them and outweighed them by at least fifty pounds. He thought back to his days in the Marines and figured that if he had to take both of them down, he could do it without breaking a sweat.

They looked at each other before one spoke with a foreign accent. "We don't know what you mean, sir. We're tourists, just out seeing the sights in New York."

"That's bullshit," J.D. said as he moved to stand chest to chest with the one that spoke. "I saw you in Fort Worth less than two weeks ago. For some reason, you're following me and my dad. You want to tell me why? Otherwise, I'm tempted to wipe the pavement with your asses. If you've got weapons, I'll take those in the process. Carrying one in New York will get you to prison in a hurry. It's not like Texas."

"Sir, we wish you no harm. If you don't make a scene, we'll be on our way. You won't see us again."

J.D. backed up a half a step and kept his eyes on their hands, ready to take them down if they reached for a pocket. "All right. Here's what I'm going to do. I'm reporting this to NFL security who'll certainly involve the New York cops. I suggest that you get out of town, maybe even back to whatever country you came from." J.D. turned and walked to the hotel where he asked for NFL security and explained what had happened. Once in his room he called his dad.

Jack sensed some concern in his son's voice. "What's going on? You all right?"

"Yeah, Dad, I'm fine. I just had a little incident in front of the hotel." J.D. described what had happened.

Jack had him on the speaker so that Colby could listen. When J.D. finished, he said, "Look, Son, you're big and strong and fast and a former Marine, only that doesn't help much if they had a gun." "I know, Dad. Believe me, I had them intimidated as soon as I turned to face them. And, it's definite that they are from somewhere in Eastern Europe, some former Soviet Union country."

The next night Jack and Colby were glued to the television. Colby had stocked the room with enough food for a week. They drank and munched and watched as the draft unfolded. The order was determined by the place the teams finished the prior year, last team first. The Cowboys were drafting twenty-sixth. Each team was given ten minutes after the last draft choice to announce its selection. After the twenty-fifth selection, J.D. was still on the board. The commissioner moved to the podium. "Next up is Dallas. You are now on the clock."

Other teams might have their general manager or head coach announce their choice. Not the Cowboys. Jerry Jones never saw a television camera he didn't like. As soon as the commissioner stepped away from the podium, Jones approached with a grin. "The Cowboys don't need ten minutes. One is more than enough. The Cowboys are delighted to select a former combat Marine, an All American from the great Texas Christian University and a future Hall of Fame tight end, Jackson Douglas "J.D." Bryant."

Jack and Colby were on their feet, cheering and hugging each other when J.D. stepped from off stage to shake Jerry Jones's hand and accept a Cowboys jersey and cap. After a few words of thanks to the Cowboys, he and Jones left the stage. No one, including J.D., noticed that when his name was called, eight additional security guards in plain clothes came to attention and studied the audience. Fortunately, everything went smoothly.

J.D. met with the national media in New York on Sunday and flew back to Fort Worth on Monday. The Dallas and Fort Worth media were waiting outside of the security area. The airport police escorted him to a conference room where he fielded questions for an hour before a member of the Cowboys media department ended it, saying that J.D. had slept little in the past two days. Further questions could wait. From there he went to the

TCU locker room where he visited with his old teammates and thanked Coach Patterson and his staff. The last stop before he went to his dad's was at Tanya's apartment. J.D. kiddingly apologized for not being drafted by the Chargers, but promised that part of his signing bonus would go toward buying a condo on the beach in San Diego. Finally, he drove to his dad's place where he met Jack and Colby.

"Now, I can have one of those 10th Mountain bourbons you seem to like so much."

Jack poured each of them a double and a glass of Chardonnay for Colby. "Let's go out back. It's a nice, spring evening. Should be a fine sunset. I've got steaks marinating."

Once they settled into patio chairs and Killer had made the rounds to have his ears scratched, Jack raised his glass. "A toast to my son, J.D. You've come a long way from that time I had to convince a young assistant D.A. in Los Angeles to drop those assault charges to a misdemeanor so you could join the Marines. I couldn't be prouder."

J.D. acknowledged the toast. "Thanks, Dad. With the help of you, the Marines and Coach Patterson, I made it. Next is a ten year career, a couple of Super Bowl rings and, maybe, the Hall of Fame."

"I like you setting your sights high," Colby said.

"Since we now know more about the start of your NFL career, I did more research and talked to a friend who has been an agent for some pros. I figure that you're looking at a three to four million dollar signing bonus with a total contract in the neighborhood of twelve to fifteen million for four years. Make it to the end of that one and then, we'll get you some really big bucks."

J.D. choked on his drink and launched into a coughing fit. "Dad, that is big bucks. And, I want to give ten percent of all I earn to the Wounded Warrior program. I'm lucky I'm here and not in some V.A. hospital. It's the least I can do."

Colby looked at her almost-stepson with admiration. "I think you should announce that."

"I'm not looking for publicity."

"I know you're not, but if you get out in the front with your favorite charity, it'll encourage others to step up."

J.D. looked off into the setting sun. "I'll think about it. Now, Dad, what time are we leaving tomorrow?"

"I'd like to be up and out of here at six. We're meeting Walt at a truck stop east of Midland around two."

"Then, I guess you better put those steaks on. I want a big one, rare. Then I'm ready to call it a night."

FORTY-NINE

Colby had breakfast ready at five-thirty. She put a two day supply of food and water out for Killer, then paused. "Wait a minute, Killer." She walked back to the kitchen. "Hon, are we taking the Hummer?"

"Yeah, I've been in the compound. We may need four wheel drive."

"Then, can we take Killer? Maybe another nose will help us."

"Okay with me, assuming we can find a pet friendly motel in Pecos."

"Well, we'll either find one, or Killer and I will sleep in the Hummer." Colby smiled.

Jack pitched the keys to J.D. as they walked to the garage. "Here, I want to brag that I had a millionaire chauffeur." Jack rode in the passenger seat. Colby motioned for Killer to join her in the back. The shepherd bounded to his place in one leap and settled himself so that he could look out the window. Once seat belts were fastened, they were off to I 20 West. At stops for gas and food, J.D. spent much of his time sending and receiving texts from old friends and teammates along with new teammates. His new teammates were ecstatic to have a tight end with his skill set. They were already calling him Gronk, Jr. J.D. accepted that as a compliment since Gronkowski was the Patriots' all pro tight end.

Between texts J.D. asked, "Dad, I understand that sometimes agents loan their clients some money until they sign. You think you can loan your new client a few bucks. I'd like to buy a new pickup and start looking for a nice condo over close to the Cowboys training facility."

Jack looked at him. "How much are you thinking about, client?"

J.D. thought and said, "How about a hundred grand?"

"You think you can pay that much back?"

"If my agent's any good, I can for sure."

"Fortunately, you've got one of the best. I'll write you a check when we get back to Fort Worth."

They turned into the truck stop in Midland at a quarter of two. Walt's Crown Vic was parked alongside the convenience store. He was talking on his cell when they stopped beside him. He clicked off his phone. Jack saw him tip a flask to his lips. It remained on the floorboard when he climbed from his Crown Vic. Everyone made pit stops and bought sodas. Jack had already loaded a cooler in the back with bottled water that would be needed in the afternoon sun at the compound. Colby shooed Killer to the back seat which didn't please him until he discovered he could wander from one side to the other. Walt sat beside Colby.

Back on the road Walt asked, "J.D., first, tell me again what we're looking for."

"There's a small drive inside the hard drive that has the computer's memory. Amazing how much data it can store. Can't say exactly how big this one would be, but roughly about the size of your little finger, well, maybe Colby's would be more accurate. It's not very big. I could see how it might have been blown into the dirt or under a rock. Who knows? If we can find it, I just hope I can retrieve the data from it."

As they drove into Pecos, Colby pointed at a motel and said, "I booked us two rooms in that La Quinta with my iPhone. Killer is welcome."

They turned north on Highway 285. After thirty minutes Jack pointed to 302 and directed J.D. to take a right. They crossed the Pecos and turned onto the compound road. The gate had been restored and locked by the DPS, but now it was lying to one side, under a sign that said "No Trespassing, Texas Department of Public Safety." The sign served only to highlight the location of the Alamo Defenders. The road to the back was littered with beer and soda cans. The trailers were gone. Only the town hall remained. Windows were smashed. The door hung from broken hinges. They parked in front of it. Previously, campers and others had taken up residence in it for a day or a week or more. Now it was deserted. When they opened the door, the smell of sweat, urine and feces was overwhelming.

"Let's leave it open. Maybe some of that odor will dissipate," Jack said. "I doubt if we'll find anything. The DPS damn sure would have searched it from floor to ceiling. I'll venture inside later when the smell may not be quite as bad."

"How do you want to do this?" Walt asked.

Jack pointed to where the two trailers that were blown up had been. "Right about there, wouldn't you say, Walt?"

Walt nodded.

"J.D., it's been a while since Walt and I have been pitching grenades. Assuming one is under a trailer, what's the diameter of the debris field?"

J.D. walked over to study scorched sand where the double-wide had once been. "Little hard to say. Fifty to a hundred yards is my best guess."

Jack looked at his watch. "We've got about three hours of daylight. Let's walk a grid, say five feet apart. Everyone get your hats and a bottle of water from the back. The DPS has walked this repeatedly and, no doubt, a bunch of sightseers have been looking for souvenirs. Maybe we'll get lucky. We'll start with the area around the old man's trailer and then try to get Miriam's area done before dark. If not, we'll come back early in the morning. And everyone watch out for rattlesnakes. They're starting to wake up from their hibernation. With a nice, sunshiny day like this one, they may be out getting a suntan. Colby, don't let Killer stray too far."

They all wore hiking boots. Jack carried his cane. They kept their eyes down and methodically kicked at any rock or limb that was in their path. Killer picked up on what they were doing and followed along until he flushed a desert rat. He was a hundred yards away before he responded to Colby's calls and turned to trot back to the group. After two hours, they finished what they considered to be the maximum blast area around the double-wide. It overlapped some into the area of Miriam's trailer.

It was long past time for a break. They chose the scrub oak that had been close to Miriam's trailer. It provided a little shade and maybe cut the temperature by five degrees. Colby carefully checked around a rock about a foot tall and satisfied herself that there were no snakes or spiders in residence and took a seat. She took a long drink of water that emptied her bottle. Jack and Walt leaned against the tree trunk.

Walt poured water on a handkerchief and wiped his face. "This PTSD is strange. I was thinking back to when we were here before. I never had a problem. Even when I had to help Sal get back to the RV, it never hit me that is what I was doing at the barracks."

"Yeah," Jack said. "I've read up on the syndrome. No one can predict what will trigger the symptoms and when."

J.D. walked to the house and took a brief walk through it. He returned with four bottles of cold water from the Hummer and reported, "Nothing inside. I can't imagine anyone spending the night in that place."

Again, around Miriam's trailer, they were meticulous in their work, missing not a single inch. They stopped when they got to the river bank.

Jack looked at J.D. "You figure there could be something down there?"

J.D. looked back at where Miriam's trailer had been. "Not likely. Way out of the blast area."

Jack shook his head in disappointment and looked at the sun as it was fading into the west. "Let's call it a day. For good measure we'll come back here in the morning for a couple more hours."

They were walking back to the car, getting close to the scrub oak when Colby exclaimed with excitement in her voice, "I think we may have been looking the wrong way all this time. What's that reflecting the setting sun up in the tree?"

They looked to where Colby was pointing. Something metallic was caught in a branch and could probably only be noticed just before sunset.

"Dad, I'm going to drive the Hummer down here. If I climb on top, I think I can reach it."

"Move it, Son. We're about out of daylight."

J.D. returned with the Hummer and followed Jack's directions to position it under the tree. He climbed to the roof and extended himself. His outstretched hand was two feet from the object. "No problem," he said. 'My vertical leap in the combine was thirty-three inches."

"No," Jack said. "Take my cane. That ought to work and we won't have to worry about you falling off the damn Hummer and ruining a promising NFL career."

He handed the cane to his son who pushed it to the metal object. On the third try, it dislodged and fell to the top of the truck. "I'll be damned," J.D. said. "It's what we were looking for.

It's banged up and burned some, but maybe I can salvage the memory."

Jack laughed. "Everyone who searched this place before was looking down just like we were. Sometimes when you want manna from heaven, it pays to look up. Let's check into that motel and order pizza. I want to get an early start in the morning." He pointed to J.D. "The magician here needs to get started with his magic. The sooner the better."

FIFTY

The day after they returned from West Texas, Jack got the bad news. The Court of Appeals had reversed Judge Jamison, saying the IRS had accepted its 501(c)(4) status, and he had failed to prove that SOS was not a social welfare organization. The Court of Appeals would not permit him to have the list of donors. Jack knew that he could appeal to the Texas Supreme Court, but also knew that was a waste of time since it was a court of nine justices, all Republican. Further, deep down he knew that the court was right. He had not really proven anything about SOS or where it spent its money. He only hoped that he had not tarnished his reputation with Judge Jamison. He had convinced her to rule his way and now she had been slapped down by the court of appeals, something no trial judge wanted to happen.

Jack had been staring at the computer for at least an hour, trying to figure out his next move when the door opened and Hartley entered the RV. "Hey, Hartley, grab a cup of coffee and come on back."

Hartley did as he was directed and settled into a chair across the desk from Jack.

"You had anyone threatening you or following you?" Jack asked.

"Not lately." He smiled and reached under his coat to put a Sig Sauer next to his cup of coffee on Jack's desk. "I saw what the court of appeals did to you. Dammit, I was hoping that we could pull back that curtain that's hiding the dark money donors. Looks like we'll have to go in a different direction. You have any ideas?"

Jack shook his head. "I've been staring at the wall for an hour. I haven't come up with a brilliant strategy."

"Hell, why don't you just depose O'Connell. No telling what he might say. I hear he has a temper. Maybe you can get under his skin."

Jack gazed at the computer screen and looked back at Hartley. "Might as well. I was waiting on those donor names. In hindsight, that was a foolish wish on my part. No use waiting any longer."

"I'll run an article in the paper tomorrow about what the court of appeals did. My sense is that most people don't like political contributions hidden from the public. I'll also revisit what the Supremes did in *Citizens United*. I just can't believe that our country is going to be run by the fat cats and a few rich labor unions. I'll get out of your hair. Let me know if you turn up something interesting."

Jack chose to take a different approach. If he couldn't get the donors, he would get every bit of data from O'Connell about how he spent the money. That had to be made known even by the welfare organizations. The problem often was that they could dodge having to produce even that information until after the election was over. He didn't have to wait for their filing. He could subpoena the records and try to prove that SOS was not even close to a social welfare committee. He served a notice of O'Connell's deposition for Christiansen's office in Dallas and attached a sub-poena, requiring him to produce copies of every video, audio and scrap of paper having to do with his political campaigns and social welfare campaigns for the past three years. He also demanded any emails generated by or received in his office about them along with documents establishing the money spent on any such campaign. Once he received the information, he would have someone analyze every penny spent to evaluate whether SOS was primarily a social welfare outfit or not. It was a long shot, but, as far as he knew, no modern court had ever defined social welfare as it related to political spending. He was willing to take a shot at it and maybe take a new issue back to Judge Jamison. He knew he would either have a roomful of documents or several CDs, crammed full of materials. He also expected an-other call from Christiansen.

It didn't take long for the call, less than twenty-four hours. "Jack, you son of a bitch, I just finished whipping your ass in the court of appeals and here you go again."

Jack smiled. "Can't blame a guy for trying. You can black out the donors' names and claim privilege. I won't object. I'm after something different now."

"You care to elaborate?"

"Now, Cecil, why would I want to educate you? I'll see you in three weeks." Now, he would start looking for an expert, a media consultant or professor who could review all of these materials and offer opinions as to which of the expenditures were political and which really were seeking to push a social cause. He didn't think Christiansen would see this coming. And, while he was thinking of experts, he realized that he had neglected to line up an expert to testify that what Walt and his team did was in keep-ing with their oath. A retired Texas Ranger would be perfect. He pictured one, long and lean, white hair, bushy white mustache and white eyebrows outlining piercing blue eyes. His voice would rumble like thunder. His demeanor would command respect.

Jack picked up the phone and called J.D. "You have anything yet?"

"Come on, Dad, I just started working on it this morning. Tanya and I drove over to Frisco where the Cowboys new training facility is under construction to scout condos."

"You and Tanya have something to tell me?"

"Not quite yet, but if you and Colby don't get a move on, you may be the second Bryant man to be married this year. As to the computer drive, it's going to take me a few days, but there's hope."

"Good, now here's what I called about." Jack described what he was subpoenaing from O'Connell and explained that he needed a credible political science professor to review the materials to determine if O'Connell's dark groups were primarily engaged in social causes. J.D. said he would check around since political science was not a course he had taken.

As they ended the conversation, Jack said, "And, as to you and Tanya, I think I'm ready to start spoiling some grandkids. I vote for a granddaughter first, followed by a couple of football players. Call me when you've got something."

Three nights later Jack and Colby were about to turn in when the phone rang. "Dad, you in bed, yet?"

"Just headed that way."

"Stay up. I've got something. I'll be there in twenty minutes."

Jack turned to Colby. "I haven't heard him that excited since he scored his first touchdown for TCU." Twenty minutes later a buzzer announced that someone was opening the driveway gate. A minute later J.D. burst through the back door and into the living room. He handed copies of computer printouts to Jack and Colby.

"You don't really need to look at the spread sheets. I know what's in them. The old man and Miriam both had bank accounts in the Caymans. Not easy to break through bank security in the Caymans, but I managed it. For people living in trailers out in the middle of nowhere, they had a truckload of money flowing in and out of those accounts. A couple of times a year, two, three hundred thousand would be deposited in the old man's account and he would immediately transfer fifty or seventy-five thousand into Miriam's. My guess is that those were all murders for hire. Right now she's sitting with half a million in her account. The last deposits were two weeks before the attack. He received $300,000 and transferred a hundred grand to her. You would think that he would have been a little more generous with his daughter since she was taking all of the risks, but that's not for me to judge."

"That's a good start," Jack said. "Only tell me more. I need to know the source."

"Hold on. I'm not through. I traced the money through two more accounts in the islands and then to an account for a Cayman corporation that no longer exists. That's where the trail ends. Looks like the corporation was set up just for this transaction and closed as soon as the money was transferred. There was originally $750,000 in that account. In addition to the $300,000 that went to Van Zandt, there were two cashier's checks for "cash", one for four hundred thousand and one for fifty thousand. Then the account was closed. Best guess is that someone had those two checks overnighted somewhere. As I said, it's a dead end as far as anything more I can do."

"Shit," Jack exclaimed. "I can't subpoena an offshore corporation to trial and blame it for causing the shootings. And it's impossible to get cooperation from a bank in the Caymans."

J.D. interrupted. "Hold on. There's one more thing. Van Zandt was also wiring smaller sums to an account in New Orleans. They aren't as big, ten, fifteen, twenty thousand once or twice a month. Only that adds up to some real money."

"Wait a minute, Jack," Colby said. "Miriam said that her dad talked about someone he called Cross who lived in New Orleans. You think he's somehow tied in with Van Zandt, maybe even the attack. Maybe he's the money man."

"Good idea. I doubt if some ex-army buddy of Van Zandt's

put up $750,000, but he could have been the go-between to set up the attack. Again, we have to keep following the money. I'll check with Walt about Cross first thing in the morning to see if they have anything on a veteran or criminal with a tattoo of a cross on his neck. Then, we'll go from there."

The next morning Walt picked up on the first ring. "Walt, you doing okay?"

"I'm good. I see we lost in the court of appeals on that discovery. Is that going to hurt our defense?"

"I don't think so. I have a new strategy. You turn anything up on that guy Miriam called Cross?"

"I did. I got a verbal report, but I'm still waiting on his file. We went to the army and got a break with his tattoo. His name is Adam Crossmore. Went by the nickname, 'Cross.' Tattoo of a black cross on the left side of his neck. Spent thirty years and never got above a buck sergeant. Seems like he was always in trouble for one thing or another, fighting, drinking, AWOL a time or two. Every time he'd get three stripes, he would do something that would get him busted. Never married, no kids. He mustered out at Fort Hood. Hell, he even served in Desert Storm. We might have run across him. And one more thing. He served in Vietnam at the same time as Cross, even the same damn platoon. After he got out, the army lost track of him. Only, his retirement check is wired to a bank in New Orleans."

"That confirms what the old man told Miriam. And we've just turned up some other evidence that may tie Van Zandt to Crossmore. It's possible he may have been the go-between and arranged for the attack. Now, we've got to find him. We may be heading to New Orleans in a few days."

"You want me to go with you?"

"No need. I'll ask J.D. He's got a license to carry. I'll also get my client, Ike, to go along. He seems to know half the people down there. I'll fill you in when we get back."

FIFTY-ONE

Walt came through. It took a few calls to Fort Hood and to the records center in Missouri. A week later, he received an email attachment with the records and a photo of Sgt. Adam Crossmore. The photo was faded, but close study identified a man in his late-forties with a craggy face and sandy brown hair. A portion of the tattoo on the left side of his neck was barely visible. He had a nose that appeared to have been broken numerous times and a two inch scar above his right eye. Another scar extended down his left cheek. He had a cauliflower left ear. Without knowing his age, one would have guessed it as somewhere north of sixty. Walt had his forensics department modify the photo, adding varieties of facial hair, showing him as bald and with long gray hair hanging down to his shoulders and then pulled back into a pony tail. When they were done, Walt emailed the package to Jack.

Jack took it home that evening and called J.D. He also asked Ike to drop by. They assembled around the kitchen table and spread the photos out to study. Jack had seen them when he was at the RV; so, he pored through the personnel file one more time.

As he flipped the pages on thirty years of the man's life, he said, "Seems like anytime someone looked at Cross the wrong way, he'd cold-cock them. Spent more time in the stockade than anyone I ran across in my day."

"Looking at that photo, it looks like he may have lost a few fights along the way," J.D. said. "If he'd been in the Marines, they wouldn't have put up with his crap. Maybe things were different back then."

Jack turned to Ike. "Any of these photos ring any bells?"

Ike shook his head. "I'd suggest we make a bunch of copies of all of these and start showing them around in New Orleans. Colby, some of the areas I'm going to suggest we visit aren't very safe. Maybe you ought to stay back here with Killer."

Colby paused before answering. "I've been thinking about it. I like New Orleans, but after my last experience there, I think I'll stay home. You can bring Trousers over for dog sitting. He and Killer haven't met, but Killer loves small dogs."

Ike laughed. "Actually, the issue may be with Trousers. He's been a street dog all of his life. No one would ever convince him he doesn't weigh two hundred pounds and is five feet tall."

Jack turned to J.D. "You got time to join us? Your size just might intimidate someone."

"Wouldn't miss it. I like New Orleans, too. I'm just sorry that I can't drag Tanya along. I'll invite her to stay with Colby. She can referee any altercations between Killer and Trousers. When are we going?"

"Day after tomorrow. We both need to carry our guns, just for good measure. You still have that Glock?"

"I do. It's my favorite."

"Okay, tomorrow I'll make plane and rental car reservations and book three rooms for a couple of nights at the Sonesta."

"Oh, my favorite." Colby faked a pout.

"I'll go by the gun store over on Camp Bowie and get a TSA approved hard case for two pistols and fresh ammo in the original cartons. I'll email both of you when I get the reservations." He turned to Ike. "You figure out that new laptop you bought?"

"I'm getting there. I can definitely send and receive emails. I'll contact my friends and let them know we're coming."

FIFTY-TWO

Several years earlier at the Fort Hood station, Cross walked to the back of the bus, tossed his bag on the overhead rack, and sprawled out on the rear seat. As the local bus pulled away, he raised his right hand in a middle-finger salute to the army. The bus dropped him at the Greyhound station in Killeen. He surveyed the outgoing buses and picked the one headed to New Orleans, as good a city as any to begin civilian life. He knew no one there, but really had no friends anywhere, and the last of his family had died years before.

Once in New Orleans, he found a cheap hotel and spent three days riding local buses around the city. At night he wandered the bars in the French Quarter. On the second night he paid for a prostitute. Each morning he bought the *Times Picayune* and studied the rooms for rent. He had a limited budget, $2,000 in his pocket, a credit card with $10,000 maximum and a monthly benefit of about $1,200. It was the third morning that he spotted a room uptown in a house a block from the streetcar stop. The mansion was run down and in need of paint. Weeds filled the flower beds. When he knocked, an old lady appeared at the door, wearing a housecoat covered in faded flowers.

"Morning, ma'am. I'm here about the room you have for rent. Is it still available?"

The woman looked him up and down. "Don't allow no drugs or loud music. Won't hesitate to call the cops. Done it before."

Cross tried to hide the exasperation on his face. "Can I see the room?"

The woman shut the door and returned with the key. "Follow me."

She held the rail and inched down the steps from the porch and walked a brick path to the right side of the house and around to the back. "Got its own private entrance. Used to be servant's quarters," she said as she approached a door on the ground level and unlocked it.

The room was musty. The two windows were grimy. It was furnished with an old brass four poster, a couch, a coffee table and a scarred mahogany dresser that must have been a fine piece fifty years ago. A door with a mirror glued to the inside opened to the bathroom that contained a sink, shower and toilet, all with rust spots. Another door opened to a closet with a light that didn't work. The floor was covered with a stained and frayed brown carpet.

"How much, ma'am?"

"Seventy-five dollars a week with a fifty dollar damage deposit."

"Not much to damage. I'll take it for a month. He reached into his back pocket and pulled out a wallet from which he extracted $350. If I decide to stay longer, I'll let you know."

The woman sized up her new tenant as she handed him a key. "I suppose I ought to know your name."

"Adam Crossmore. I answer to Cross. And, ma'am, I just got

out of the army. I always wanted to grow a few vegetables. Would you mind if I worked on one of those beds here beside the house, get it in shape and plant a few tomatoes and beans and such? I'll share with you."

The old woman smiled for the first time. "Well, that would be nice. Use as many of the beds as you want. I don't do anything with them anymore. And, you can call me Rose." She looked down at the floor and back into his face. "And, I wouldn't mind it if you planted a couple of red rose bushes in the front." She turned to walk out, then looked back. "Oh, the house is old and a little run down like me, but I do have wireless internet that I think works in this room. You're welcome to try it. Password is *gardenrose.*"

Cross took the key and walked the block to the streetcar stop. When he boarded it, he again admired the stately old mansions that lined St. Charles. He got off at Canal where he hoofed it the few blocks to his hotel, retrieved his suitcase and checked out. On the way back he stopped in an electronics shop and bought a Dell laptop on sale for $399. Just before he got back to St. Charles, he found a small grocery where he purchased some cleaning supplies. Back in his room he first cleaned the grime from the windows, then tackled the bathroom. He was walking the carpet, trying to figure out what to do about it when he noticed a corner that had been pulled up sometime in the past. When he jerked on it, he discovered it covered a fine hardwood floor. The more he pulled back the carpet the more he liked what he saw. He fired up his laptop and typed *gardenrose.* He was on the internet. He searched discount furniture and hardware stores that would deliver, buying three throw rugs, a new box spring and mattress, a couch and two chairs, a television, a new bathroom mirror, a small desk and chair, a microwave oven, a small office-sized refrigerator and a coffee pot. Total expenditures: $980. The only things that would remain would be the brass bed and the coffee table which was slightly scratched but useable.

He walked around to the front of the house and climbed the steps to the door. He rang the doorbell and waited. Rose came to the door, still dressed in the same faded housecoat. "Ma'am, I mean, Rose, what day is heavy trash pickup?

Rose looked puzzled. "It's this Friday. Why?"

"I've ordered a few things for my room and want to replace some of that old stuff. By the way, I think I'll be staying indefinitely. So you've got a renter for a while."

"Trash is picked up in the alley behind the house."

"Yes, ma'am. Nice thing about these old neighborhoods is that they have alleys so trash doesn't have to sit out at the front curb. Once I get everything done, I'll show you the room. Meantime, if any deliveries come knocking, please send them around. Oh, and I'll be starting on that garden in a few days." He smiled. He received a smile in return.

Cross ripped out the carpet and put it in the alley, behind a fence that had more holes than boards. While he waited on the other deliveries, he rented a floor sander and a polisher and sweated his way through the grime that hid the ancient oak beneath it. Doing so, he was reminded that the room was not air conditioned. That led to another session on the laptop to order a window unit. Two days later his purchases started arriving. He tossed the mattress, spring and bedding, along with the other furniture and replaced them as the new furnishings arrived. At the end of the week a pile of old stuff was in the alley. The room looked almost new, with the microwave on a new dresser, a 36 inch HDTV on a stand, the small refrigerator, a desk for his computer and a new bed along with brown Naugahyde couch and chairs. When it was done, he invited Rose to have a look.

He opened the door ahead of her and stood aside to allow her to enter. "Why, it's beautiful, Cross." She admired the floor that now gleamed. "You think that you could do that to my floors? I can pay you." She hesitated, not wanting to be too bold with her tenant. "And, if you like, I can make some curtains for those two windows."

Cross shook his head. "Tell you what, let me get my garden in and then I'll take care of your floors. No charge, but maybe you can knock a little off my rent. As to the curtains, I accept. No hurry, though."

Over the next several days, Cross slept late and then spent the afternoons working on weeding, spading, tilling and fertilizing three of the old flower beds at the side of the house. Once he was satisfied the beds were ready, he put tomato plants in one, potatoes and green beans in the second and squash, onions and a few black-eyed peas in the third. As he worked, it occurred to him that he needed to buy a small electric cooktop to go next to the microwave. Next, he moved to the front yard and did the same with the beds along the house below the porch, planting red roses in them. While he was doing so, the old lady came out to sit on the porch, now dressed in black pants and a flowery yellow blouse. She even wore a little lipstick.

When Cross had finished, she invited him to join her in a second rocker on the porch and fetched him a glass of sweet tea. They said little as they watched the shadows grow at the end of the day.

Each evening Cross boarded the streetcar to Canal and walked to the French Quarter where he trolled the bars, observing the people as he had several drinks, knowing that even if he drank too much he only had to make his way to the streetcar stop. He had never been a jazz fan. On the other hand, he had never heard jazz quite like that in the French Quarter. While he began by hitting the strip clubs, his tastes quickly evolved and he found himself hanging in a variety of clubs that featured local bands that played jazz and blues. He would sit quietly in a corner, sipping a beer and soaking in the sounds of music until it was time to make the last St. Charles car.

After two weeks, he was low on cash and realized that he needed to open a bank account where he could have his retirement deposited. He picked a branch on Canal, close to St. Charles and continued to care for his garden in the daytime and spend evenings in the Quarter. He also refinished Rose's floors, upstairs and down. Then it was summer and the Gulf Coast heat smothered the Garden District. He and Rose had little in common. She was old enough to be his mother. Still, they enjoyed each other's company, particularly in the late afternoon when the sun had dropped below five o'clock and the temperature finally slipped below ninety. It was then that Cross would go to the front porch and sit until Rose brought two glasses of sweet tea.

The old lady and the craggy veteran rarely talked. She didn't care about jazz or baseball. He had learned all she cared about were her departed husband and two children who had abandoned her for the west coast. She used to get cards on her birthday and at Christmas, but the last had been more than ten years before. Still, over the months they became evening fixtures on the porch, sometimes sitting for two or three hours, watching the streetcars and acknowledging the passers-by. Once it was dark, Rose would retire to her bed, and Cross headed for the Quarter. One evening Cross was evaluating the flaking paint on the porch and sides of the house.

"Rose, it'll be getting to be fall here before long. Temperature will be getting tolerable. If you'll buy the paint and rent me a scaffold, I'll scrape all this old stuff off and repaint the outside of the house."

Rose rocked and sipped her tea without saying a word.

"What, you don't want your house painted?"

"Of course I do," she choked. "It's just that I've never had someone offer to do such a thing for me. You do that, you can forget about paying rent."

"I wasn't trying to get out of rent. I just have time on my hands and restoring this old mansion to how it looked a hundred years ago would give me some satisfaction."

"How about white with red trim that'll match the roses

in the spring?"

"Deal. Give it a few more weeks to cool off and I'll get started."

It was right after Labor Day when Cross arranged to have the scaffold delivered along with scrapers, an electric sander, brushes and fifty gallons of paint which he had the delivery guy take around to the garage that backed up to the alley. As he helped the driver unload, he realized the garage would be next. Like almost any project started by man or woman since the beginning of time, this one took far longer than Cross had predicted. He started by pulling up a few obviously rotted boards on the porch and ended up ripping all of them out and replacing them. Once the porch floor was done, he started the restoration at the front of the house, first climbing the scaffold to the top and slowly working his way down. When he began to scrape off the old paint, he discovered that there were three and sometimes four layers that had to be hand-scraped and sanded. Of course, once he had exposed the bare wood, he couldn't leave it exposed to the elements; so, every so often he would get to a point where he would put down the scraper and sander and paint the fine old wood he had uncovered.

Every two hours or so Rose would appear with sweet tea and demand that he take a break or risk a stroke or heart attack. At first she tried to invite him in for lunch. He declined, saying he was too big a mess and would track all over her new floors. So, she quietly began bringing a platter of sandwiches, covered with cellophane, out to the porch and set them on a small table, available for whenever he was ready to eat.

The work was backbreaking. Cross was up and down the scaffold all day. His legs ached. His neck and arms joined in the chorus with his legs. He thought he was in fine shape for a man nearing sixty. Wrong. He started taking more and longer breaks where he would just sit on the porch. His trips to the French Quarter became fewer as he looked forward to a beer and bed. Since he had begged off the invitation to eat with Rose, when she saw him cleaning his brushes at the end of the day she came out with a wooden tray of hot food for him to take back to his room.

During the ordeal, as he now called it, Wednesdays were the only day he caught the streetcar to the Quarter since he wanted to avoid the crowds and drunks that frequented the area on weekends. There was a time when he would have been right there with them, but that was twenty years ago. One of his favorite jazz bars was Trombone's. He tried to visit it regularly, but, lately, his project had interfered. It was on a dark side street off Bourbon. Many tourists were loath to venture down what appeared to be a dangerous alley. The only sign was a small neon trombone in the window. Inside it occupied a narrow space, maybe twenty feet across with light coming only from the bar. The band was in the back. The musicians appeared to be more interested in entertaining themselves than the customers that found their way to the bistro. Cross usually sat at a table against the wall, close to the band. Armand, the bartender knew him by name and that his favorite beer was Sam Adams from the tap. When he took a seat, the musicians nodded to him and Armand would soon arrive with his beer. Cross became enough of a regular before he started his painting project that the band members would often join him on their breaks, particularly once they learned that the beer was on him.

It was Wednesday, and Cross arrived at Trombone's around nine, just in time for the first set. The band marched in from a side door, instruments blasting. The piano player took his seat as they did. Cross sipped his beer and tapped his foot in time with the music. After forty-five minutes they put down their instruments. Bernard, the cornet player, drifted over to Cross's table.

"Hey, Dude, we ain't been seeing much of you lately. Thought maybe you found some other bar."

Cross smiled. "Have a seat. Naw, I've been painting my landlady's house in Uptown. Been too tuckered out at the end of the day to get over here very much."

Armand brought a Sam Adams for Bernard.

Bernard started with small talk. "You think the Saints can make the playoffs?"

Cross finished his beer and motioned for Armand. "Depends on Brees as always. He may have lost a little distance at his age, but he's still one of the top two or three in accuracy."

Bernard sipped his beer. "I hear there's a hurricane brewing out in the Gulf."

"Saw that. I'm watching it to see if I have to board up my landlady's house. Looks like it's heading for Corpus, but you never know."

Bernard took another sip of his beer and sized up Cross over his glass. When he put it down, he reached into his jacket pocket and extracted a gold necklace. He laid it on the table in front of Cross. "You ever buy any fine jewelry?"

Cross picked up the necklace and studied it. "Can't say that I have. Never had a girlfriend that deserved anything more than what I could buy at Walmart."

"I've been told that this has retail value of $5,000."

Cross pulled out his cell phone and turned on the light while he studied it. He turned off the light. "Hell, I don't know why I'm doing that. Costume jewelry and the real thing all look about the same. Why are you showing it to me?"

Bernard leaned in. "Bought it off a guy I know. I don't want to mislead you. Let's just say it may be a little warm, if you get my drift. I paid $500. I'll sell it to you for a thousand."

"Play your next set and let me think on it."

Bernard rose and, in a show of good faith, left the necklace on the table when he returned to the stage. Close to an hour later he was back and took a seat facing Cross. "What's the decision?"

"If you'll trust me for a day, I want to have it appraised. If it's real, we'll try to make a deal. I'll be back with it tomorrow night."

Bernard looked Cross in the eye. "Hell, I gotta trust some-one, sometime. I guess you're as good as any. I'll see you tomorrow night."

The next day Cross took the necklace to three pawn shops, giving each of the owners a story that he and his wife were breaking up and he needed to sell the necklace to settle up with her. Knowing that pawn shops low-balled value, he was surprised and pleased that the offers were all between $5,000 and $7,500. That evening he went back to Trombone's, satisfied that he could negotiate a profitable deal. After all, Bernard had already offered to sell it for a thousand bucks. He would pay that if necessary, but decided to bargain.

When they were seated at his table after the first break, he said, "I shopped it around a little. It's damn sure not worth five grand, but I think I can make a little money if the price is right. I'll pay you $650."

"No way, dude. Maybe I'll consider $900. That's it."

Cross hid a smile. "Okay, $800. Take it or leave it."

Bernard smiled and extended his hand. "Deal. You got the money on you?"

Cross had visited his bank that day and pulled a roll of one hundreds out of his pocket. When he peeled off eight of them, Bernard said, "I may run across more of these from time to time. You interested?"

Cross took a napkin and wrote some numbers on it. "Here's my cell. Call me when you have something."

Cross left Trombone's and caught the streetcar back to his room, having no idea about what to do with the necklace. He could try to pawn it, but he knew enough about pawn shops to know that if he didn't find the right one, he might get a visit from the NOPD for selling a stolen necklace. Leaving the streetcar, he had an idea.

When he took a lunch break the next day, he took his sandwiches back to his room and picked up the phone. He hadn't talked to Richard Van Zandt in at least a dozen years. Still, Van Zandt's cell was in his contact information. He punched in the number and hoped Richard hadn't had a heart attack out there in West Texas. After several rings, a voice said, "Cross, you son of a bitch, is that you?"

"Damn right, Rich. How the hell you been?"

"Just out here stocking up for the fed's attack. Expect it any time now. Of course, I've been saying that for twenty years."

"You ever dealt in gold, Rich?"

"You mean bullion? Probably a good investment with what the feds are doing, but I haven't done it."

"No, I'm talking about buying and selling gold jewelry. I've run across a fine gold necklace, appraised at ten grand. I need to unload it."

Van Zandt thought. "This line ain't tapped is it?"

"Not as far as I know."

"I work with a few of the cartels over across the border. They have more money than the damn Mexican government. If it's really worth ten grand, I can probably get twenty from one of their kingpins. He can give to one of his senoritas. Tell you what, send it to me at the convenience store in Pecos where my daughter works. Fed Ex won't deliver to my compound. I'll call you when I get it sold and we'll split the profit. Deal?"

"Deal."

Thus began the criminal career of Adam Crossmore.

FIFTY-THREE

Cross finally finished painting the outside. He and Rose asked a passer-by to take a cell photo of them standing proudly in front of the gleaming white Victorian with red trim. Rose insisted that he hold a paint brush across his chest as a badge of honor. She had the photo blown to twelve by eighteen, framed it and placed it on the wall in the entry.

The two of them were sitting on the front porch one evening, Cross with a beer and Rose with her sweet tea. Neighbors strolled by and complimented them on the transformation of the old mansion. Rose took a sip of tea and rocked before she spoke.

"Cross, the outside is beautiful. Only now I need to figure out what to do with the inside. You've seen it. Paint's old. Wallpaper is beginning to peel…" Her voice dropped off.

Cross also sipped and rocked. "Tell you what, Rose. That's a lot of rooms and walls. It's going to be about as big as the outside. I'm not willing to do it for free. If you'll buy the paint and pay me

$10,000 up front, I'll do it."

More sipping and rocking.

Rose said, "Okay. I'll go through the rooms and pick the colors. I'll go online to buy the paint and put a yellow stickie on the wall in each room so you'll know the color. I have a little money in the bank but I prefer to buy the paint a room at a time. Let me know when you want to start."

Within a couple of days Rose handed him a check for the ten grand. Cross was feeling pretty damn good about his finances. Only a few days before Van Zandt had called, saying he sold the necklace for $27,000 and wanted to know how to wire his share to him in New Orleans. Suddenly, Cross had close to $25,000 in the bank, an unheard of sum when he was in the military. He started the new paint job. Rose wanted light colors, sky blue, emerald green, pale yellow, carnation pink for her bedroom. He took his time. There were a few streaks on the outside that only he would ever notice. He wanted the inside to be perfect. After six weeks, he was close to being finished. When he retired to his room, he had a message from Bernard. It was cryptic but clear. He had some merchandise that he wanted Cross to see. Cross texted him that he would be there that evening. He showered and took a short nap before warming up a TV dinner in the microwave.

It was near the end of the second set when he entered Trombone's and took a seat at his regular table. Bernard nodded at Cross. When the set was over, Bernard almost rushed over to the table to be sure that no other band member got to Cross first.

"I was worried that something came up and you couldn't make it."

Cross shook his head. "I told you I would be here."

Bernard fished in his pockets and came out with diamond ear rings and a diamond tennis bracelet. "I want two grand. Should sell retail for ten times that. You interested?"

"Same as before. Let me check them out. I'll be back tomorrow night."

Cross needed a couple of different pawn shops. Fortunately, New Orleans was a tourist and gambling destination along with it being a major port with sailors looking to sell what they had picked up overseas for a few bucks; so, pawn shops were a dime a dozen. Both shops offered $15,000 on the spot. Of course, Cross declined, knowing he could find a buyer across the border for three times that.

So he did. Cross paid $1,350 and called Van Zandt. In a matter of weeks, he had another $22,500 in his bank account. Cross smiled when he got the call about the wire transfer from Van Zandt. He sized up the situation and concluded that while it might be a criminal enterprise, the chances of getting caught were minimal as long as he was careful about what he purchased and from whom. Certainly, there was little to no chance that on Van Zandt's end a problem could occur that would be traced back to him.

He finished the interior painting and moved his painter's gear to the garage, which would be his next project. Rose was effusive with her praise and thanks. He would never pay rent again. He knew the garage could wait and started spending more time at Trombone's.

One evening the third set ended and Bernard joined him. After talking sports, Cross said, "Look, Bernard. I want you to be careful who you tell, but I'm willing to consider fine jewelry from someone other than you. If you can vouch for a seller and send him to me, you get ten percent on top of whatever I pay."

Bernard broke into a grin. "Boss, you best plan to be here several nights a week."

Cross stared across the table. "Don't bring me anyone you can't vouch for one hundred percent. If I get in trouble, I'll hunt you down like a gut shot deer. You understand?"

FIFTY-FOUR

Over the next two years Cross became one of the biggest fences in New Orleans, maybe the Gulf Coast. He established a routine and sat at his table at Trombones on Tuesday, Wednesday and Thursday nights. Not on the weekend when the joint was close to capacity with tourists. Bernard was his gatekeeper. Bernard put out the word on the street that he knew a fence who would pay top dollar. Whether it was a second story artist, a pickpocket or a gambler down on her luck, if the seller couldn't get past Bernard, there was no meeting with Cross. Cross located a pawn dealer who would appraise anything for a flat fee of three hundred bucks, knowing that there would be no sale. Cross watched his bank account grow and decided it was time to buy some wheels. Nothing fancy. He settled on a silver Toyota Tundra pickup with a crew cab. That forced Cross to take another look at the garage. He talked to Rose who agreed that he could tear it down and replace it with one that would hold his new pickup. And about once a week he took Rose for a ride, wandering the streets of the garden district in the early evening. Rose pictured herself as a princess, riding in a carriage of pure silver. Cross was just trying to be nice to the old lady and get her out of the house and off the front porch on occasion. He had no idea what was coming.

One evening about five o'clock Cross knocked on Rose's front door. He hadn't seen her in three days and thought it was time for another drive. When there was no answer, he took his key and let himself into the front foyer. He called her name.

"Rose, it's Cross. Where are you?"

His voice echoed through the silent house. Now be became worried and called again. Still, no reply. It was too early for her to be in bed. He started up the stairs and sniffed the stale air. There was a distinctive odor, one that he had encountered several times in the army. The odor of death.

He knocked on her bedroom door. There was no response. The door creaked as he opened it. Rose was crumpled on the floor. He didn't bother to check for a pulse. Probably a heart attack. He picked up the house phone and dialed 911 and reported the death. He walked back down the stairs and took a seat in one of the rockers on the porch. *Nice old lady,* he thought. *She just needed a friend. I'm glad I could fill that role for the last couple of years of her life.*

Cross heard the siren before he saw the cop car with lights flashing. It stopped in front of the house. He rose to greet the officers.

They climbed the stairs to the veranda. "I'm Cross. I found the body."

"You live here?" the older officer asked.

"Yeah, around the corner in the back. I rent a room."

"Why did you go in the house?"

"I have a key. I haven't seen Rose in two or three days. Figured I better check on her. She's about eighty. I served thirty years in the army. I know the smell of death. It was coming from the second floor. I checked her room. Left her as you'll see her. Probably dead a couple of days."

The officer turned to his partner and spoke to Cross. "You stay here while we check it out."

The two officers entered the house just as an ambulance, a second siren disturbing the quiet of the evening, stopped behind the police car. Neighbors began to gather on the sidewalk. Cross knew a couple of them and walked down the stairs to report what had probably happened. Still they stayed and more joined them. Cross shook his head. They wouldn't leave until they saw the stretcher with a body covered in a sheet being placed into the back of the ambulance.

The two officers appeared on the front porch and motioned to Cross. He joined them.

"No sign of foul play," the older officer said. "Looks like her heart just stopped beating. Or maybe it was a stroke." He motioned to the EMTs. "Body's in a bedroom at the top of the stairs. No need for an autopsy." He turned to Cross. "She have relatives?"

"She told me she had a couple of kids, boy and a girl as I recall. They both moved to California. She hadn't heard from them in ten or fifteen years. If it's okay with you, I'll look through the house to see if I can find phone numbers or something."

The older cop nodded. "That's fine. Here's my card. Let me know if you turn up a way to locate them. She'll be in cold storage at the morgue for a few days while you look."

The EMTs came out with Rose's body covered and on a stretcher, placed it in the back of the ambulance, and then were gone. The crowd finally dispersed and the cops left. Cross went to his room and poured large bourbon over rocks and returned to the front porch to listen to the sounds of the night.

Cross drank two cups of black coffee the next morning and walked around to the front of the house. He unlocked the door and paused. He glanced to the left of the entry to a small den that contained a butler's desk pushed up against the wall. He rarely saw Rose use it but decided to start there before rummaging through kitchen cabinets and drawers and her bedroom. The desk had a writing piece that was pulled down to reveal a dozen small drawers, about four inches by four inches, maybe ten inches deep. Under the writing surface were three large drawers. Rose had an old oak straight back chair beside it that she could move in front when she lowered the writing surface. Cross started with the small drawers. They were stuffed with canceled checks, doctor bills, receipts, articles clipped from magazines, some twenty years old. If there was rhyme or reason to the hodgepodge, Cross could not determine it. Certainly, there was nothing from Rose's children.

He closed the writing surface and, one by one, went through the three large drawers. Still nothing to or from any children. At the back of the bottom drawer Cross found a heavy manila envelope with "Last Will and Testament of Rose Beauregard" written on the front. He opened the envelope and found the will. He skimmed it and stopped when he got to the bequests. Rose had willed everything to him. The house, the furniture, her bank account, everything. She had her lawyer put in the will that Cross was her only true friend. Her children had abandoned her. She wanted Cross to have everything.

The old veteran teared up as he read. He wasn't looking for this when he helped the old lady. Still, he was pleased that he inherited the house. He found New Orleans to his liking and particularly liked Uptown. He would make sure that the roses in front stayed in bloom in honor of their namesake.

FIFTY-FIVE

Cross filed the will for probate. The clerk told him that the probate court was swamped and it would be several months before even a simple will would get to the top of the docket. Until then he could not transfer the house to his name. Rose's bank account held less than $10,000 with deposits coming monthly from Social Security. He did get permission to use the money in her account to buy a burial plot at a small cemetery in Metairie out close to the airport. He asked the funeral home associated with the cemetery to arrange for embalming and a minister to say a few words at a funeral that only he attended. He tipped the minister with a hundred dollar bill, thanked him and drove back to what he now called his house where he continued his very lucrative career as a fence.

It was late on a Thursday evening. Bernard had not brought him any clients, as he now called them. The band was winding up its final set. He sipped the last of his fourth beer and was rising to leave when Bernard motioned him from the stage.

"Cross, can you stick around for ten more minutes. I wanted to wait until the place had cleared out to talk to you about another business opportunity."

Cross nodded and returned to his seat. Bernard left the stage to sit across from him and leaned over the table, his voice barely a whisper. "This is big. I've got a lead on a contract. There's a big event coming up in Fort Worth. Someone wants a multibillionaire named Edward Hale killed and the Texas Governor wounded, not killed. Fee's a half a million. If you can arrange it, I'll take fifty grand. The rest is yours."

Cross glared at Bernard. "Not interested. I'm making a very good living. Killing is not something I want any part of, not now, not ever." He rose to leave.

"No, no. Hear me out. Money can't be traced to you. I suspect you can make a few calls and get it done."

"Dammit, Bernard, you're talking about the Texas governor and some rich guy. Cops will be all over it like flies on a rotting carcass."

"Cross, it'll be a clean. I know the guy that is putting out the contract. He comes in here three, four times a year, whenever he's in town. He likes our music. He's not a criminal. Not the Mafia. It's strictly a business deal."

"What's he do?"

"I don't know. I don't even know his name. Dresses nice, Rolex watch with diamonds all around the face, Matching diamond ring. Well spoken. Pretty ordinary looking guy. Very big tipper. Usually slips the band a grand at the end of the evening."

Cross drummed his fingers on the table while he thought. "Tell him it's going to cost $750,000. That leaves me $700,000 after paying you. I'll set up an offshore corporation just for this. Money flows into the corporation. I don't want to know his name. He doesn't know mine. We'll have one phone call, if I do it, just to get the information on what he wants done. If he'll do it on my terms, we've got a deal. If not, you better be looking for someone else."

Bernard rose and shook his hand. "I'll be back in touch in a couple of days."

FIFTY-SIX

Two days later Bernard called Cross at home. "We're set. Can I give him your cell number?"

"Not yet. I need to incorporate a business. Then open a bank account for that corporation. Give me a couple of days. I'll call you."

Cross clicked off the phone and walked out to the veranda with a cup of dark black Community coffee. He sat in one of the rockers and remembered all of the hours he had sat in that same rocker with Rose beside him, neither of them saying much. He had grown fond of her and missed her rocking quietly beside him as the district coasted into darkness. Then he thought about the proposal Bernard had dumped in his lap. If he were caught, he would probably die in prison. He had heard that Angola was not the place to spend your last days. On the other hand, if he could get Van Zandt to fulfill the contact for $300,000, that would put $400,000 in his hands, tax free. And what were the chances of getting caught? This guy wouldn't know his name. The money would go into and out of his new corporation; then he would close down the account and the corporation. That would leave Bernard as the only link to him. If Bernard had to be eliminated, he could do it. Still, that decision could be postponed. He rose from the rocker and went inside. He sat at his desk and searched through his cell phone until he found a banker in the Cayman Islands. He told the banker he wanted to establish a corporation on an expedited basis and open an account in that corporation's name. The banker put him in touch with a lawyer who stream-lined the process. In forty-eight hours he had a corporation he named Kathouse Properties, Inc. a name no one else had used, and an offshore bank account in its name.

Next, Cross drove down Canal and stopped at one of the tourist shops that lined the street. He bought a burner phone, good for about ten hours. He returned to his house and sat at the kitchen table to call Bernard. He didn't identify himself. "I'll do it. Have your man call me on this cell at five today. Only you and him have this number."

"Got it. He'll identify himself as Zero."

"I don't give a damn about zeros as long as there are four of them with a dollar sign and seven-five at the front."

Cross was sitting at the butler's desk with the phone in front of him. When it chimed, he waited until the fourth ring before he clicked it and put it to his ear. "Yeah."

"This is Zero. We're about to do some business. Here's what's coming down. There's a big Republican fundraiser in Fort Worth in a few weeks." Zero described the event, including the fact that the attendees would be in Halloween costumes. He would arrange for one of the side doors to the ballroom to be open. Next he explained what he wanted done once the shooter ac-cessed the ballroom. Cross confirmed the amount of the con-tract and gave him the wire transfer instructions for the offshore account, warning that the funds had to be in that account in twenty-four hours or the deal was off.

Before Cross ended the call, Zero said, "Look, this has to be a really fine shooter. I don't want the governor killed, only badly wounded. Your shooter will have photos of everyone on the stage, with names on the back. My instructions have to be followed to the letter. Clear?"

"Yeah. It'll be done like you say. I'll check that account about mid-morning tomorrow."

The funds arrived. When he verified on line that the funds were there, he called Van Zandt and explained the mission. There was a long pause after Cross finished talking.

Cross could hear Van Zandt spit into something. "My best pistol shot is my girl, Miriam. She enters competitions all around out here in West Texas, even over into New Mexico. She shows up and everyone else, male or female, knows they're going after second place. She can do the job. Wouldn't be the first time. What's it worth to you?"

Cross thought before he replied. "I'm not sure what the going rate is for a hit. I figure something in the range of $25,000."

Van Zandt coughed and spit again. "That's about right for most, say a wife wants her husband eliminated. Here, you're talking about the top of the food chain. "I'd say it'll take a half a million."

Cross offered a hundred thousand. They settled on $300,000, just the number Cross wanted all along. Van Zandt asked more questions about the party, security, access and escape routes. Cross said he would call his contact for more information, explaining that he had never done this before. Van Zandt gave him his Cayman account information. That brought a laugh from Cross.

"Seems like everyone has accounts offshore these days."

"I damn sure do. Can't trust the government. I ain't being paranoid, believe me. They could confiscate folks' onshore accounts any time. I'm surprised it hasn't happened by now."

"Look for the money in your account by tomorrow."

They ended the call. Cross then used the burner phone to call the banker in the Caymans. He arranged for a wire transfer to Van Zandt and was about to wire the rest to his account in New Orleans when he hesitated and thought. No one would probably ever try to trace the money. Still, he was now involved in a murder. The thought of Angola again flitted across his mind. Out of an abundance of caution he requested two cashier's checks, payable only to cash, to be overnighted to him, one for $400,000 and one for $50,000. It wasn't foolproof, but nothing was. Still, it would be one more obstacle to overcome if anyone ever tried to get information from the Cayman bank. Once the checks were in his hands, he would put his in another account, again, probably offshore. Once the banker verified the transactions would be done that day, he closed the Kathouse Properties account. He made one more call to Zero and a second call to Van Zandt to relay more information. Two nights later he went to Trombone's and put a smile on Bernard's face when he handed him his check for fifty grand.

FIFTY-SEVEN

The three men retrieved their bags from the luggage area at Louis Armstrong Airport in New Orleans. Jack claimed the guns and ammo. They were bussed to the Hertz lot where Jack had reserved a small SUV. J.D. took the driver's seat with Jack beside him. Ike was in the back.

As they made the thirty minute drive into New Orleans, Ike could hardly conceal his excitement. "Man, is this bringing back memories. I haven't been back since Katrina blew me all the way to Fort Worth. Now, explain once more what we hope to get done if we find this fellow, Crossmore?"

Jack turned to face Ike. "We know there was $750,000 in a Cayman account with a dummy name. $300,000 went to old man Van Zandt. Two checks, one for $400,000 and one for $50,000 were written to cash and the account was closed. We know that Van Zandt and Crossmore had some business dealings. Now that we know that until a few years ago Crossmore was a buck sergeant in the army, he couldn't have been the one funding the attack. Our guess is that he got the $400,000 for setting it up. We want to find him, may have to bluff, but threaten him with jail or even the death penalty to learn who provided the money."

Ike thought for a few seconds. "I understand. What about the $50,000?"

"That's another unanswered question we'll pose to Crossmore if we can find him."

Ike sat back and tried to absorb all that he had heard.

"J.D., you packed plenty of those photos of Cross, didn't you?" Walt asked.

"Come on, Dad, of course I did. We could tack one on every utility pole in the French Quarter and still have a bunch left."

"Then, we'll head to the Sonesta, check in, and maybe take a nap since we may be out late tonight."

When they entered the Quarter, Ike gazed from side to side like he was a tourist.

"You recognize anyone yet?" J.D. asked as he looked in his rear view mirror and saw what Ike was doing.

"Not yet. Recognize some of the clubs, though. I played some of them a long, long time ago."

"J.D., turn onto the side street there beside the Sonesta. There's a basement parking garage entrance right around the corner."

J.D. parked in a spot close to the elevator on the second basement level. When they rose to the lobby, they exited. Ike stopped and took in the scene. "I'd forgotten how beautiful this hotel was. I would have a drink here from time to time, usually when I could talk someone else into buying. I'm glad that Katrina didn't do any serious damage to her."

"Did it flood the French Quarter?" J.D. asked.

"Nothing serious. The land here is a little higher than the surroundings. So the hotels and bars and strip clubs and restaurants and jazz clubs were mostly saved. Once the water went down in other parts of the city, life went on in the Quarter like nothing had happened."

Jack approached the desk and presented his credit card and identification. "Welcome, Mr. Bryant. We haven't seen you since that Sugar Bowl game four years ago."

Jack complimented the desk attendant for checking on his last visit. That was when J.D. was a freshman, and T.C.U. won the Sugar Bowl, defeating the Florida State Seminoles. He thanked the attendant and declined any help from a bellman since they each had a wheeled bag. "I've got three adjoining rooms. The one in the middle is mine and should have a large living area where we can meet and discuss strategy." J.D. pushed the elevator button for the fourth floor. When they exited, Jack looked at the sign that directed guests in the direction of their room. Jack motioned left, and they walked down the hall. "Here's our first. Ike you take that one. Unlock the adjoining door when you're ready." He and J.D. walked a few steps farther. "This one's mine. Yours is next. Come on over when you get unpacked."

The men assembled in Jack's suite that included a living area with a door opening to the balcony and Bourbon Street down below. "J.D., there's your Glock with some ammo on the coffee table. Ike, we have these rooms until Friday. How do you suggest we go about the search?"

Ike thought for a moment. "We start with Bourbon Street and walk it from one end to the other. Early evening is going to be better to get anyone to talk, before the crowds hit. We can keep trying when the tourist invasion occurs. That's usually starting about nine every evening, but it'll be a little harder to get someone's undivided attention. That's when they're making their big tips. After Bourbon Street, we start on the side streets and over to Jackson Square. A little like finding a needle in a haystack."

Jack shook his head. "Not quite. We know he has his army retirement deposited here."

"Shouldn't we pay a visit to that bank?" Ike asked.

"First thing in the morning," Jack replied. "Since we have a couple of hours, I'm going to take that nap."

"Sounds like a good idea to me," Ike said.

"While you guys take a nap, I'm going to start checking Bourbon Street. Maybe I'll check out a couple of the strip clubs." J.D. grinned as he went through the adjoining door to his room to retrieve several photos of Cross.

J.D. rode the elevator down and walked through the lobby with its white tile floor and gold pillars. He took a detour to the left into the courtyard, took a deep breath and smelled the aroma of the flowers that surrounded a fountain that cascaded its water to the lilies floating below. When he walked to the entrance, two doormen dressed in blue waist coats with gold trimming opened the doors. He stopped and reached into the manila folder he carried.

"Afternoon, gentlemen." He handed one a photo of Cross. "Either of you seen this man? He might look more like this now." He handed them two more photos, one with Cross bald and one with long, gray hair.

Both men studied the photos and shook their heads. "Nope," the first said. "I've been working this door for fifteen years. Don't recall seeing him. Henry, you've been here longer than me."

"Sorry. I'm not any help either."

J.D. thanked the men and replaced the photos in his folder as he turned left into the crowds and noise that was Bourbon Street. He crossed the street to a courtyard where a band played and people sat outdoors, drinking and listening to the four musicians on an elevated stage. When the host saw him standing there, she approached and asked if he would like a table. He showed her the same photos of Cross and received a shake of the head in return.

He turned up the street and walked a block until he was confronted by a young, black man. "Hey, there, big dude. Come right on in. Buck naked women dancing for your pleasure."

J.D. hesitated and then showed his photos with the same negative response. He stepped into the near darkness of the dimly lighted dive and stood at the entrance until his eyes adjusted. To his right was a bar, behind which was a walkway with a bleach blonde swaying up and down it. She was nude. Lights from the walkway reflected from her eyes. The eyes were bloodshot and glassy, obviously comprehending very little. J.D. figured she must be high on something. To his left were tables, mostly empty at that time of day. A few were occupied by men about his age and at least one dancer per table, wearing a bikini bottom, high heels, and nothing else. The men were buying champagne for the dancers that probably cost a buck and a half a bottle and sold for twenty dollars a glass. So much for checking strip clubs. J.D. turned and walked out into the sunlight. He tried three more restaurants, two tourist stores selling T-shirts and such, and one voodoo store before returning to the courtyard across from the hotel. This time he took a seat and ordered a Bud Light. He sipped it slowly while he enjoyed the jazz. When the band finished its set, he placed a twenty in the tip jar and returned to the hotel.

An hour later the three men walked up Bourbon Street a few blocks. When they passed the strip joint that J.D. had briefly entered, he said, "That place cured me of ever visiting a strip club again. Women have vacant eyes, boobs pumped full of silicone. They might as well be slaves."

"They are, J.D.," Ike said, "slaves to heroin. I knew their grandmothers back in the day."

When they arrived at Galatoire's, Ike continued. "I used to know the host here. He played in my band when I was a youngster. Name's Louis. Maybe he's working tonight."

The host, dressed in a dark blue suit and a red bow tie, was greeting guests and picking out sport coats for men who didn't have one. After five o;clock, men had to be dressed properly. That meant a coat. He glanced up as they entered. "Ike, I'll be damned. Sorry I couldn't help you with that sheet music. When I changed careers, I tossed all that."

The two men hugged and sized each other up. 'You're looking

good. Who are your friends?" Louis asked.

"The man with the cane is Jackson Bryant. The big one is his son, J.D."

Louis turned to a closet and picked out three coats. "I hope this one is big enough for J.D. It's a triple XL. Put them on and I'll escort you to your table."

J.D.'s coat had sleeves that were two inches short and he couldn't button it, but he was now appropriately attired. Louis escorted them to a table by the window, looking out on Bourbon Street. Louis snapped his fingers, and a waiter appeared to take drink orders. He hovered around until the waiter hurried to the bar.

"So, what brings you to New Orleans? Did you do any good with that issue about our old songs?"

Ike nodded. "Sure did. Jack was my lawyer. Thanks to him, I'm pretty well set, only Fort Worth is my home now."

"Louis, if I can interrupt, we're here for a reason," Jack said. He took photos from J.D.'s folder. "We're trying to find this guy. You ever seen him?"

Louis studied the photos. "Yeah. He comes in here every once in a while. Calls himself Cross. Looks more like this one." Louis pointed to one with the hair long and gray. "Hair comes down below his neck, but I've seen a tattoo that looks like a black cross on one side."

"When was the last time you saw him?" J.D. asked, trying to hide the excitement in his voice.

Louis gazed up at the ceiling while he thought. "I'd guess a couple of months."

Jack handed him a card. "Do us a favor. When he comes back, try to strike up a conversation, maybe find out where he lives. Call me at that number any time, day or night."

Louis took the card and placed it in his pocket. "Must be something important."

Jack nodded. "We're investigating a murder."

Louis's eyes grew big as he fished in his pocket and took another look at the card before returning to his post at the front of the restaurant.

After dinner they split up, with Jack taking the south side of the street and J.D. and Ike on the north side. They stopped in every establishment and met at each corner to compare notes. Three blocks past the hotel and two hours later, they were striking out. Jack got to the next corner first and was standing, leaning on his cane when a street person, obviously strung out, accosted him. "Hey, man. I bet you have five bucks to spare."

Jack ignored him and continued to stare across the street, waiting for J.D. and Ike to catch up. The street person persisted. "Look, man. I'm not kidding. In fact, it's going to cost you a twenty now." He pulled a switchblade from a frayed pants pocket and flicked open the blade. Jack backed up a step to open the space between him and his attacker. "If you had ever seen *Crocodile Dundee*, you'd know what is about to happen." He raised his cane and pushed a button on the handle. A ten inch dagger suddenly appeared in the end. He stuck it in his attacker's stomach, not breaking the skin, but pushing enough for him to know what would come next.

"I suggest that you drop that knife in the gutter and get the hell out of here, or I'll shove this knife all the way through until it comes out your ass."

The man's face filled with fear. "Look. I didn't mean no harm. Wasn't going to hurt you."

"Drop it," Jack said.

The knife clattered to the sidewalk. The man turned and took off. J.D. and Ike had stepped from a shop across the street and saw the last of the altercation. J.D. ran to his dad. "You all right?"

"Just fine. You've seen me use one of these before."

"Yeah, back in that Hispanic bar on the north side of Fort Worth. How'd you get that on the plane?"

Jack smiled. "Different cane. It's ceramic, housing and blade.

Blade won't cut a steak, but it'll damn sure punch a big hole in a man's gut."

FIFTY-EIGHT

The men were finishing the last of their breakfast coffee in the hotel dining room.

"What I learned from last night is that about eleven o'clock, maybe twelve, is about as late as we should be out, particularly if we're going to hit some of those bars on the side streets," Jack said.

"If it's later or on one of those dark streets, the three of us need to stick together," Ike added. "Where do we start this morning?"

"Like I said yesterday, we're going to Cross's bank over on Canal," Jack said. He glanced at his watch. "It ought to be opening right about now."

They left the hotel to find the sidewalks and pavement wet. "Did it rain last night?" J.D. asked.

"Naw," Ike said. "Street gets littered every night with beer cans, broken bottles, needles, human puke, you name it. About four every morning, a water truck comes through, spraying everything down, followed by a street sweeper. City doesn't want tourists to walk through the filth from the night before. There may be some drunks sleeping it off in doorways. Cops will leave them alone until the shops start opening. Then, they'll roust them out and send them off to streets where tourists are not likely to trip over them."

"We're going to go down Bourbon to Canal and then hang a left. Bank should be in the next block," Jack said.

After a ten minute walk, they were in front of the bank. "J.D. we don't want to intimidate the manager with three of us. You stay out here and talk to a few of the shop owners. Ike and I will go inside."

Jack and Ike entered the lobby and stood, surveying the bank. Jack spotted a glass enclosed office with "Manager" stenciled in gold letters on the door. They walked to the office and saw a young man sitting at the desk working on a computer. Jack tapped on the door. The young man smiled and motioned them to enter. "Morning, gentlemen. Name's Dean Babineaux. Have a seat. What can I do for you?"

"Mr. Babineaux, I'm Jackson Bryant. I'm a lawyer and a deputy sheriff from Fort Worth. My friend is Ike Irasmus, formerly a resident of your fair city. Now Fort Worth claims him. Here's my card." He handed his deputy sheriff card across the desk. The banker studied it and placed it on the desk.

"Again, what can I do for you?"

"We're investigating the murder of a prominent Fort Worth man and the near fatal wounding of Texas Governor Rob Lardner."

"I remember that. Didn't I read that they caught the killer somewhere out in West Texas?"

"That's true, but it didn't end the investigation. You have a bank customer named Adam Crossmore." Jack handed him a wire transfer slip that Walt had obtained from the army.

Knowing he could not evade the question, Babineaux

answered, "I recognize the name. I, uh, don't deny that he is one of our clients."

"What can you tell us about Mr. Crossmore?" Jack asked.

The banker stood behind his desk. "Mr. Bryant, we have a very strict policy of confidentiality regarding our customers. I told you he was a customer because you presented me with that wire transfer slip from the army. That's all I can confirm. You'll have to get a warrant if you want more information. So, if you're finished, I have work to do."

Jack rose and shook the banker's hand, realizing they had hit another dead end. As of this visit he had no basis to get a warrant from any judge, state or federal, regarding Adam Crossmore. He and Ike walked out onto Canal. They walked a few doors down and saw J.D. coming out of a pawn shop.

"You do any good?" J.D. asked.

"Struck out again. Couldn't even hit a foul ball," Jack said.

"What do you suggest, now, Ike?"

"Let's try Jackson Square. Place will be overrun with tourists, starting about now. Worth knocking on a few doors, anyway, maybe talking to a cop or two."

As they made the short walk over to Jackson Square, Jack told Ike about Colby being pushed into the river near the Natchez and his having to dive in to save her. Rather than stop in every shop, at random, one of them would step inside a shop or bar and return in a few minutes with an empty look on his face. It was a big city with hundreds of shops, restaurants and bars. The haystack was looking gigantic. That evening they sat at the bar at the hotel and re-traced their steps.

"Hell, Dad, we could spend a month, maybe a year, and never find the son of a bitch."

"Let's spend one more day. If we come up empty-handed, we'll catch our flight back on Friday. We know he's here, but it's a big city."

"Can't we get the New Orleans police involved?" Ike asked.

Jack shook his head. "That would take some Texas law enforcement agency to make the request. They all agree that the case is now closed. They damn sure won't admit they closed it too soon. Dead end there. I've already been through that analysis when I considered trying to get a warrant to serve on the bank."

They started trying hotels and casinos on Thursday. They even went to the other side of Canal and talked to bellmen and desk clerks. At the end of the day, they stopped at NOLA's for dinner. Ike addressed his two companions. "When we're through with dinner, I'm going to take you to some out-of-the-way places. Tonight we stay together. I don't want Jack having to use his dagger again."

Jack nodded his agreement. "You lead. We'll follow. J.D. and I do have our guns."

Ike's choices were several jazz clubs, off the beaten path, but with incomparable sounds drifting through open doors. The men took their time, enjoying a beer and the music at each stop. Soon it was pushing toward one o'clock.

"You figure it's time to call it a night?" Jack asked.

"One more stop down this way," Ike said as he took them down what appeared to be little more than an alley. Halfway down the block, they came to Trombone's. "I used to work here. Usually not crowded during the week. We'll see if any of my old friends are still in the band."

He led the way to a seat near the front. The six piece band played to an almost deserted club. The bartender was sitting in front of the bar, drinking a beer since there were virtually no customers to serve. When they took seats, the bartender moseyed over and took drink orders, returning to place them on the table before again taking his seat.

Ike surveyed the musicians and turned to his friends, excitement in his whisper. "I know the piano player."

J.D. had been looking at the few patrons and settled on one. "Dad, go find the restroom. When you come back, take a look on the other side of the room at that one guy seated by himself at the front."

Jack nodded and headed toward the restroom. When he returned, he stood at the bar for a minute, as if to let his eyes grow accustomed to the dimly lighted room. He moved to the table and took a seat. "It's pretty damn dark, but he fits the description. Long gray hair, craggy face. Couldn't see the tattoo or scars on his face in this light."

"What do we do?" J.D. asked.

Jack thought a moment. "We're going to wait until he leaves and follow him until we can get a better look. We'll figure something out."

An hour later the band concluded its last set. As the last wail from Bernard's cornet sounded, Cross put a twenty on the table and walked toward the front door. When Jack saw him leaving, he said, "Ike, stay and talk to your friend. See what you can learn about Cross. J.D. and I are following him." Just as he finished speaking, the overhead lights came on, improving the visibility, but it was too late. Cross was out the door.

Ike walked to the stage as Jack and J.D. beat it for the front door. When Al, the piano player turned, he did a double take. "Ike, is that you? You done got old on me."

Al stepped from the stage and hugged his friend, then stepped back. "Well, on second thought, you don't look so old, just got white hair now. Matter of fact, it looks good on you."

Al was six feet, two inches with a prominent nose and pencil thin black mustache. "Thanks, Al. You're still tickling those ivories with the best of them. Like the sound you guys are producing. May be I'll write some music for you one of these days."

"I heard you were living in Fort Worth and made a killing on some damn lawsuit. What brings you here?"

"No killing, but some young rapper stole some of my old songs, and he's having to pay for it. I'm pretty comfortable these days." Ike turned to point to where Cross had been sitting. "What do you know about that gray haired fellow that was sitting over there?"

Al glanced at the empty table and nodded his head. "Oh, you mean Cross?"

Ike felt a shiver flow through his body as he heard the name. "Yeah, what can you tell me about Cross?"

"Comes in here two, three nights a week, rarely on weekends. Doesn't like tourists. Likes our music, though. He's good for a beer on breaks. Bernard over there knows him best." Bernard was bent over, putting his horn in its case. "Hey, Bernard, come over here and meet an old friend of mine."

Bernard closed the lid and walked over to the piano. "Bernard, this is Ike Irasmus, one of the best horn players New Orleans ever saw."

The two men shook hands.

"Ike is asking about Cross. I told him you knew more than anyone else about him."

A flicker of concern crossed Bernard's face. He looked around to make sure that Cross was gone. "Can't help you. He's just a regular in here. I have a beer with him on occasion. That's about it." He looked around again. "I, uh, I've got to go. Got to meet a guy over on Bourbon in ten minutes." He hurried to grab his horn and rushed out the door.

Al shook his head. "That's a little strange. You're not a cop these days, are you? I don't want to get Bernard in no trouble."

"I'm definitely not a cop. You know how many years I spent in Angola? I want nothing to do with cops."

Al lowered his voice. "Yeah, I forgot about that. Okay, you didn't hear this from me. Word on the street is that Cross buys jewelry. I've seen folks come in here and sit in the back until a break. Then Bernard motions them to Cross's table. Even seen the flash of gold or silver once in a while. My guess is that Bernard is getting a piece of the action. That's probably why he didn't want to talk to a stranger about Cross. Why are you asking?"

"My friends and I are investigating something big. May involve Cross. That's all I can say. Not looking to get Bernard in trouble. One more question. You know where Cross lives?"

"Uptown, big house from what I hear."

Ike stuck out his hand. "Thanks, Al. I'll bring a crowd next time I'm in town. I'm working my music back into shape. Maybe you'll let me join you for a couple of numbers."

Al smiled as Ike turned toward the door, wondering why he was asking questions about Cross. He hoped he didn't say too much.

FIFTY-NINE

Jack and J.D. were met by a storm that had blown in from the Gulf, driving rain in their faces when they stepped from the door of Trombone's. "Helluva time not to have a raincoat," Jack muttered.

"Which way?" J.D. hollered to make his voice heard above the wind and rain. Jack looked both ways and at first saw nothing. Then he pointed to the left.

"I think I saw someone turning up that next street. Let's give it a try." J.D. took the lead, like a blocking back, breaking the storm for his dad. They arrived at the corner and looked down the street.

"I think I see him, up there about a half a block. Son of a bitch! Two men just stepped out of a doorway behind him. I'm going ahead. Catch up when you can."

"Be careful, son," Jack tried to caution J.D., who was already sprinting through the storm.

Cross heard something behind him as he pushed through the rain with his arm crooked over his eyes. He looked back to see two men closing on him. He took off in a run. Thirty years before it would have been a sprint. Now, with old legs and a slippery surface, it was no more than a slow trot. Two shots rang out. Cross was down. J.D. had closed the gap and pulled his weapon, firing at both of the men as they ran by Cross's prostrate body. One of them turned and fired a shot over his shoulder, not coming close to J.D. Still, J.D. ducked and lost a few feet. The men turned the next corner. J.D. fired several shots in their direction as they disappeared.

J.D. stopped at the corner and crouched as he peered around it. One of the men was down. The other was nowhere to be seen. J.D. walked up to the man on the ground and felt for a pulse. There was none. As he rose, Jack huffed around the corner. "Cross is dead. I checked his wallet and confirmed his identity. What about this one?

"No pulse. This is one of the guys I saw in Fort Worth and again in New York. What the hell is going on?"

Jack shook his head. "Just another part of this damn mystery we have to solve." He reached into his pocket and retrieved his gun, firing it one time into the air. "Now I have gunshot residue on my hand. Trade guns with me."

J.D. stared at his father. "I don't understand."

"I'm a licensed law enforcement officer, about to call 911. I have a reason for killing him. You don't. Now, check his pockets."

J.D. did as he was told while his dad reported the shootings. "I found a cell phone, a wallet, and his passport. Shit, he's Chechen."

Jack glanced up the block. "I see a trash can up there. Go dump that stuff in it. We'll need to be back here by dawn to retrieve it. Let's hope the cops don't delay us too long."

A police car could be heard with siren wailing. It wheeled around the corner, lights flashing. Two cops leaped out with guns in hand. Jack and J.D. made a display of laying their guns on the sidewalk and rose with their hands turned out.

"Officers, I made the call. I'm Jack Bryant, a deputy sheriff in Tarrant County, Texas. That's Fort Worth. This is my son, J.D. Bryant. We've been on the trail of that man around the corner and were about to apprehend him when two men stepped out of a doorway and shot him. His name is Adam Crossmore. I suspect he's dead. We chased after the men. I shot this one. You'll find a gun under him. I know he's dead. The other one got away."

"Let me see your creds, Deputy Bryant." Jack reached into his pocket and opened his wallet. He handed his laminated sheriff's identification to the officer who had "Sergeant Peavy" on his nametag. While he studied the card, his partner was checking the body. "No identification. Sig Sauer is under his chest. No pulse. You want me to go back to check the other one?"

Peavy nodded. "I'll keep this card for now. You understand, Deputy, that we don't take kindly to someone, even a deputy sheriff from Texas, coming into our parish with guns blazing. You better have a good reason."

"How about the attempted murder of Texas Governor Rob Lardner and the killing of Edward Hale in Fort Worth back in the fall. We believe that Crossmore was involved in that attack. Could I suggest that we get out of the rain, maybe go back to the station? I can give you a couple of numbers to call."

That got Peavy's attention. His partner came from around the corner. "Other guy's dead, too. Bryant's right. I.D. on him says he's Adam Crossmore. Lives in Uptown."

"Call for backup and a CSI crew. I'm taking these two back to the station. See if we can't clear up a few facts."

Peavy elected not to handcuff two cooperative suspects. Once they were in the back, he locked the doors. They drove the few blocks to the French Quarter station. Once inside, Jack and J.D. were put into an interrogation room. In a few minutes Peavy returned with two coffees. "Hope you don't mind if it's black."

Jack nodded. "Not as long as it's hot." He and J.D. both sipped for a few moments before Peavy began. "Let's back up to the start. I did hear about what happened in that mansion in Fort Worth.

Your card says you're a reserve deputy. How'd you get involved?"

"Got to go back a little further than last fall. About three years ago J.D. and I tracked down and brought the Dead Peasants killer to justice in Fort Worth."

Peavy rubbed his hand together as he searched through his memory. "Now I remember. He killed twenty or thirty people, even some over around Shreveport. You telling me that you caught him?"

"With J.D.'s help."

"You a police officer, young man?

Up until then, J.D. had done what his father told him: Don't speak unless spoken to. "No sir. I'm a football player. I just signed with the Cowboys."

Peavy's eyes lit up. "You're shitting me. J.D. Bryant, I was hoping the Saints would draft you. Sure would have been nice if you were on the receiving end of Drew's passes. That's okay. Cowboys are my second favorite team." He turned back to Jack. "Keep going, Mr. Bryant."

"I'll try to make this brief." Jack told of his relationship with Walt Frazier and being persuaded to lend a hand at the fund-raising party, his appointment by the district attorney as special prosecutor and how they tracked the killer to the compound in West Texas.

Peavy interrupted. "I'm a backup on our SWAT team. We've studied that assault on the compound. Went off textbook perfect. You telling me you were involved in that?"

"Not quite perfect. We had one of our team hit and the head of the Alamo Defenders died. We wanted him alive." Jack paused as he thought back to that night. "I was just supposed to be an observer, but one of our snipers took a slug to the shoulder. I took his place. I brought down the assassin."

Peavy sat quietly as he allowed all of this to sink in. "Wow. You think I can get you back over here to talk to our SWAT team. First, though, why were you chasing Crossmore? You already had the one who pulled the trigger."

"Trail didn't end there. We followed it to Crossmore. We believe that he was involved in the money that changed hands to arrange for the killing. We were so close and then this had to happen. That guy that I killed or his partner killed Crossmore. Not sure what their involvement is in all of this."

Peavy thought for a minute. "Okay, I believe every word you've said, but I need to get confirmation."

"Can I give you my cell phone?" Jack handed it to Peavy. "Joe Shannon, the D.A. I mentioned, is on speed dial. He won't like getting rousted out of bed, but he'll calm down once you tell him what it's about."

Shannon answered, "Dammit, Jack, this better be important."

"Mr. Shannon, this is Sergeant Peavy with the New Orleans P.D. I've got Jack Bryant and his son sitting across the table from me. He gave me his phone to call you. I just want to verify his story."

Joe was instantly awake and swung his feet over the side of the bed. "Go ahead."

When Peavy finished the story and described the events of earlier that morning, Joe said, "Everything he told you is gospel. I knew he was looking for this Crossmore. I didn't know he was in New Orleans. If you want to release him and J.D. to my personal custody, that's fine with me."

"Not necessary, sir. We're going to get a tape recorder and have them repeat the events in more detail. Should have them on their way by dawn. I don't anticipate any charges being filed. If that changes, I'm sure they'll cooperate. I hope you can go back to sleep."

"Thanks, and tell Jack to call me as soon as he gets back to Fort Worth."

Jack and J.D. walked out of the police station just as light was beginning to show in the east. Their guns remained in police custody. They walked casually for two blocks until J.D. said, "I'm going to run from here. I'll meet you at the trash can."

When Jack arrived at the corner, J.D. had the Chechen's wallet, cell phone and passport in hand. "What do we do now?" he asked his dad.

"We're going back to the hotel, bring Ike up to speed, see what he learned, shower and have breakfast. Then we're on the next flight back to DFW. We'll sleep when we get home. The sooner we can get out of New Orleans the better I'll like it."

SIXTY

Jack had leaned back in his chair in the RV and was snoring quietly when phone rang.

"Jack, this is Mary Frazier."

"Mary, nice to hear from you. How are you doing these days?"

"Is Walt in Fort Worth?"

"Not that I know of. I haven't talked to him since last week."

"Then, I'm getting worried. He's gone. Missing."

"Tell me what's going on," Jack said as he walked to the front of the RV to retrieve a bottle of water.

Mary struggled to get her emotions under control. "It all started at that Halloween fiasco last fall. You know he had a hard time getting over what happened in Desert Storm. For years he couldn't get past it. Oh, he finished college and got on with the sheriff's office and then made it into the DPS. For eight or ten years he had nightmares, woke up in a cold sweat. I can't tell you how many times I woke up with him yelling, 'Incoming.'"

"Mary, Walt told me about most of that. I know he was able to put that behind him over time until this past Halloween. He told me that something that night triggered the PTSD again. I've been trying to talk him through it, as much as he'll let me. I know you've done the same. Tell me about Walt disappearing."

"This isn't the first time. Over the past six or eight months, I've gotten up in the morning to find him nowhere in the house and his truck is gone. Usually he comes back by dark. Never tells me what he's been doing. Now he's been gone two days. He doesn't answer his cell. Jack, I don't know what he might do. He's told me that he doesn't want to spend years again, fighting this PTSD."

"Have you notified the DPS?"

"This morning. They're on the lookout for his truck, but after two days he could be in Mexico or Colorado. Who knows?"

"You just need to stay there with your boys. I'll have the Tarrant County Sheriff put out the word to sheriffs around the state. We'll find him."

Walt hadn't intended to disappear that morning. He had found in the past when the demons were filling his mind that driving through the hill country west of Austin calmed them. He usually would wander the backroads that meandered through the cedar covered hills and over low water crossings through dry creeks that only occasionally would be flooded by spring storms. When he found a stream with water, he would usually stop, find a rock under the shade of a tree, and immerse his mind in the water that rushed by. After an hour or so, he would climb back in his truck and continue his odyssey. The hills and water seemed to bring some peace to his tormented mind. On this day, he found himself following the Pedernales River to Johnson City and paused to study the memorial to President Lyndon Johnson who most Texans thought had served his country well. Walt wondered how Johnson endured watching President Kennedy die with a bullet to the brain. Was he tormented by re-living the event? If so, Walt didn't recall reading about it in history books.

Walt stopped in Fredericksburg for lunch at a German restaurant and was soon headed west again. When he arrived at I-10, he knew he should turn back, but something pulled him onto the interstate and he continued west. After three more hours he realized where he was going. Something in the back of his mind told him he needed to re-visit the compound. He could just make it before dark. The small towns on the interstate flew by at eighty miles an hour. He stopped for gas and a cup of coffee in Ozona. At Fort Stockton he turned onto 285, a highway he knew well by this time. As he passed through Pecos his mind turned to their assault on the compound. He realized he was no longer thinking about the barracks but about their success in capturing Miriam Van Zandt with a minimal loss of life.

He turned right on 302 and stopped where the command RV had been stationed. He wanted to retrace his steps to where he and Jack had rescued Sal and also have a look at the compound. Looking to the west at the setting sun, he would need a flashlight for the walk back to the truck. He took one from the driver's door pocket and started the walk, his mind full of the events after the attack that led up to this time in his life. Nothing about them caused nightmares. He, Jack and the others had accomplished their mission. He spotted the bluff above the Pecos and started walking through the twilight. He found the rock that Sal was leaning against and paused to think about him. Then he climbed to the top of the bluff and was surprised to find that the Pecos had water flowing through it. Then, he reminded himself it was spring and the water was to be expected.

He glanced around the remains of the compound, remembering their latest trip where Colby had spotted the memory drive. "Nice job, team," he said to no one but whatever varmints were starting to come out as night fell. He had no desire to wade the river and set foot on the compound. Seeing it again was enough. Mark up two successes there, both of which he was a part of. He made his way down the bluff as the stars began to appear and walked toward his truck, remembering the last time he had walked in that direction, he had been supporting Sal. Again, no bad memories.

After spending the night in the LaQuinta in Pecos he turned on his phone to find that Mary had tried to call him eight times, the last being an hour ago. He thought about calling her back but was not ready to explain his actions. In fact, he was not sure what he was trying to accomplish, only that he was feeling better. He made his way to I-10 and turned east, back toward San Antonio. After a few miles a sign pointed to Highway 277 and Del Rio. He thought of Fox and his contributions to the mission. On the spur of the moment he turned south to Del Rio and Laughlin Air Force Base. It wasn't a long drive, less than an hour on the mostly deserted highway. When he approached the base, he stopped at the guardhouse.

"Morning, Corporal. I'm looking for Colonel Floyd Foxworth. Could you direct me to his residence?"

The corporal shook his head. "Sir, I'm not permitted to do that."

Walt dug into his pocket and pulled out his i.d. "I'm a sergeant with the DPS. I've worked with Fox on a couple of missions but never met him. I was hoping just to say hello."

The corporal studied the i.d. "I suppose I can call him. Wait here." He stepped back into the guardhouse and returned a minute later. "He said he would be delighted to see you. He's off today." He handed Walt a yellow stickie. "Here's his address. Turn around and go back to the light. Take a right. His is the fourth street. Take a left and you'll find his house."

Fox was waiting in his front yard when Walt stopped at the curb. Walt stuck out his hand in greeting and got a hug in return. "Walt Frazier, welcome. I recognize you from my camera that's in the video room in Austin. Come in, come in."

When they walked through the door, a middle-aged woman

greeted him. "I'm Flo. Fox has told me over and over about the compound mission. It was the most fun he's had since he started flying that drone. Let me get you some coffee."

Walt followed her to the kitchen where there was a fresh pot of coffee. Flo reached in the cabinet above it and handed him a large mug. "How do you take it?"

"Black, thank you, ma'am."

Fox refilled his mug. "Come on out to the back patio. It'll be pleasant out there until the sun hits about eleven o'clock." They walked out a glass door into a back yard, filled with a large pool and surrounded by spring and summer flowers. "Have a seat. I swim fifty laps in that pool every morning. Then, I work in the flower beds on the days I'm not flying the drone."

"Beautiful yard, Fox."

"Thanks. It gives me pleasure and my grandkids love the pool when they visit. This is not on the way to anywhere. So, why am I honored by this visit?"

Walt absent-mindedly scratched his nose while he thought. "Damned if I know. I left Austin yesterday morning, intending to take a drive in the hill country. I ended up at the compound. I was headed back this morning when I saw the sign to Del Rio. Here I am."

"Something about our mission bothering you?"

Walt shook his head. "Not that one."

Fox had been around the military his entire life. He suspected something. "Were you in the military before you became a trooper?"

"I was a young grunt in Desert Storm."

"Go on," Fox encouraged.

"I, uh had some experiences there that stayed with me for a while after the war." And then the story came tumbling out. After thirty minutes and another mug of coffee, he described the recurrence of his PTSD at the Halloween attack.

When he finished, Fox rose to pull a weed from a rose bed

and turned. "Let me tell you, there's nothing good about war. Maybe the generals like playing their chess games. They're never on the front lines where the killing is happening. For the rest of us, it's about death, mangled limbs, nightmares and terrible memories. For those of us who have been in real combat, we don't even like to talk about it. Just brings back those memories. What I'm about to tell you I've told to very few in my life, but you need to hear this.

"I was flying fighters in Desert Storm. In fact, I was a major and led a squadron. Our mission was to soften up Saddam's forces before you guys advanced on the ground. Was a damn good plan in my opinion. Saddam had a few fighters. Their pilots shouldn't have been flying a Piper Cub. We strafed artillery. We bombed tanks. We strafed troops. They were the enemy and we were doing our job." He paused as he thought back to the time. "Then, one morning our assignment was to bomb a village occupied by the Iraq army. We pretty much leveled it. When we returned to the base, we learned that our intel was wrong. Civilians were in that village, including women and children." He put his arms on his knees and clasped his hands as he stared at the patio deck. His voice dropped. "We killed them, Walt, women and children." The he looked up to stare into Walt's eyes.

"I never wanted to climb into a plane again. But I did, in spite of nightmares that left me bleary-eyed every morning. Fortunately, our part of the mission was over shortly thereafter. You guys took over and the war ended with Saddam running back to Iraq with his tail between his legs. Only it didn't end for me. I rotated back to the United States and was put in command of several squadrons on this training base until I retired. I suffered from about everything you described. Slowly the memories faded." He raised a fist to his head. "Knock on wood, they haven't come back like yours did."

There was silence for a long minute. "Thanks, Fox. I appreciate you telling me that."

"Look, whoever said war is hell didn't come close to describing the horror of it. We all react differently to what we saw and did. I can only imagine what that scene at the barracks did to a nineteen year old like you were. But, Walt, it's over. You need to put it behind you. It's been a long time. Move on with your life."

"I'm trying, Fox. Somehow, I think that I was drawn here just to hear your story. It's going to help for sure. I'll be heading out now. I see some weeds in that bed on the other side of the pool that need your attention."

Walt stopped on the edge of Del Rio. He was about to head back to Austin when he changed his mind. He had one more stop first. After filling the truck and getting a Big Mac at McDonalds, he headed northeast through central Texas, actually enjoying the small towns that dotted the highways. It was late in the day when he arrived on the outskirts of Fort Worth. He found his way to Westover Hills, then to the Hale mansion where he cut the engine and rolled down the windows as night descended. He stared at the mansion and forced himself to re-live the experience, hour by hour and, at the last, minute by minute. He forced himself to look at the costumed freaks below him when he was on the stage. He breathed a sigh of relief when they did not turn into a mass of bodies at the barracks. He remembered carrying the governor from the stage and the wild ride to the hospital. Finally, he accepted all that occurred on that night as well as what he went through in the barracks. He was about ready to leave when a Westover Hills cop on patrol drove up and lowered his driver's window.

"Something I can do for you, sir?"

"No officer. Name's Walt Frazier. I'm a DPS officer. I'm reaching for my wallet now."

The officer tensed as Walt's hand dropped below the window and relaxed when it appeared with a wallet. Walt extracted his DPS creds and handed them to the officer. "I was part of the governor's protective detail when the attack occurred here last

Halloween. I was just trying to put a few things in my mind to rest. If you'll give me my creds, I'll be leaving now."

It was almost dark when Walt pushed the code to open Jack's gate and drove to the back. Colby looked out when she heard the gate buzz, expecting to see J.D. When she saw Walt instead, she rushed out to greet him. After a hug she stepped back. "Where the hell have you been. Mary's been out of her mind."

"Sorry. I had some soul searching to do and had to do it alone. Let's go inside. I'll call Mary. I suspect someone has called the DPS. I'll call and report that the prodigal has returned. Jack here?" "I'm calling him now. He'll be here in twenty minutes. And, let me be the first to say that you need a shave and shower. Jack's clothes are too small for you, but I suspect you can wear a pair of J.D.'s shorts and one of his T-shirts. I'll pitch them on the bed while you're in the shower. You'll find a clean razor and a toothbrush in there, too."

When Jack arrived, they sat around the kitchen table while Walt explained his last two days. When he finished, he said, "For the first time in months, my head is clear. This two day odyssey was somehow therapeutic. At least something I did worked. Fox was a giant help. Anyway, I'll head back to Austin in the morning."

Jack smiled at his friend. "And I'll be taking O'Connell's deposition tomorrow."

"Can I attend? I feel like I'd like to face that son of a bitch now. I'll let Mary know I'll be home after the deposition."

"I'll find the smallest pair of J.D.'s pants and a dress shirt," Colby said. "You may have to cinch them up with a belt, but the dress shirt should fit about right."

SIXTY-ONE

"State your full name for the record"

"Kevin O'Connell.

"Mr. O'Connell, you understand that we are here in your lawyer's office in Dallas to ask you questions about your injury at the fundraiser and to obtain documents? With me is my client, Walt Frazier."

O'Connell was dressed in a $5,000 suit, a $500 shirt and a tie equal in price to the shirt. "I understand."

"Mr. O'Connell, you also understand that the court reporter is recording everything that is being said and we also are making a video. Further, either of them may be used at the time of trial."

"I do."

"I'm handing you a subpoena that requires you to produce certain documents and financial records, personally and from the Stepper PAC as well as Stepper Official Strategies, Inc., also known as SOS." Jack stretched his arm across the table and

O'Connell did likewise to take the subpoena.

"Your lawyer has shown this to you before today, hasn't he?"

"Yes, sir."

"Jack, if I can interrupt, I'm handing you a flash drive that contains the financial records of the PAC and the list of contributions made by SOS. We have eliminated the names of the contributors to SOS, pursuant to the ruling from the Court of Appeals. They are accurate up to last month," Christiansen said.

"Thank you, Cecil. Am I correct that they are in searchable form?"

Cecil nodded his head.

"Then, Mr. O'Connell. we'll turn to your damages. I know you were wounded. In fact we visited with you in your hotel a couple of days after the shooting. Did you recover from that bullet to your arm?"

O'Connell nodded. "Pretty much. It was painful for a few weeks and gradually improved. I wouldn't be here if it was just that."

Jack made a few notes on his legal pad. "What are your other damages?"

"First, SOS had pledges that night before the shootings of nearly a hundred million, by far my most successful one-day fundraiser ever. Afterwards, we ended up collecting less than five million. My consulting and other fees would have been in the range of five million dollars. After the shootings, the consulting fees basically evaporated. Then, SOS and Stepper have become persona non grata in Republican circles. I was expecting to springboard from that night during this election cycle. A billion dollars was not out of the question. Bottom line is it's not happening."

Jack tapped his pen on the table as he thought. "Any explanation?"

"Mr. Bryant, I don't know why. Frankly, one of the reasons I filed this case is to, hopefully, convince the Republicans that this fiasco wasn't my fault."

Jack nodded. "We're going to trial next month. So you and Mr. Christiansen will have your chance. No more questions."

Jack and Walt returned to Fort Worth. When he arrived home, he shook Walt's hand in the driveway before Walt departed for Austin. "Looks to me like whatever you did has worked. Let's hope it continues."

"I really think that I'll be okay. Keep your fingers crossed." Walt was smiling as he drove away.

Inside, he told Colby about the deposition.

"Are you going to depose Maria Hale and the Hale children?"

Jack shook his head. "Nope. She was interviewed by the DPS for hours a few days after the shootings. We can use that statement about what she saw and heard that night. I've got her financial records and we can analyze her claimed losses. I'll just cross her during trial. As to the Hale children, they weren't at the party. I'll just cross-examine them at trial. I suspect that there will be a big probate fight between her and the adult kids from the prior marriages. They're probably postponing it to put up a united front in this case. Meantime, they're just riding Maria's coattails. You'd think that with an estate worth forty billion, that pie could be sliced so that everyone was happy, but the rich are greedy just like the rest of us."

He speed dialed J.D. "Hey, Dad, how'd the deposition go?"

"Nothing exciting. I have a flash drive that supposedly has the financial information of the Stepper PAC and SOS, only not the contributors to SOS. I'll make a few copies. Can you drop by later today to pick up one for yourself and one for our professor. Tell me his name again?"

"Cagle, Calvin Cagle. He's a political science junkie and eager to take a look inside these organizations. Did you see that the Texas Legislature had a bill to make these dark money organizations disclose their contributors? Damn thing was killed in the Senate. You were right. The politicians don't want us to know who is funding them."

"You got that right. Still, I may be able to use what happened in Austin in our case. We'll see. Tell Professor Cagle we need his opinions in about a week. We have to list him as an expert and give a brief summary of his opinions. I want to be vague so that Cecil won't be interested in deposing him. If the professor finds what I think he will, we'll set a nice trap that we'll spring during trial."

Jack ended the call and pressed another button on his cell, this call to Walt. After they returned from New Orleans, he forwarded the i.d. information on the guy J.D. killed in New Orleans to Walt. "Walt, I'm sorry to bother you even before you get home. I forgot this. Your guys find anything on that guy we had to shoot in New Orleans?"

"Not much. The guy worked security for the Chechen delegation to the United Nations. At least, that was his cover. Could have been a government assassin for all we know."

Jack gazed out the window to the old bomber plant across the Trinity River. "I've been racking my brain, trying to figure out why some Chechen would want to kill Crossmore. We know he had ties to Van Zandt. He probably was in the middle of the payments to Van Zandt for the attack, only now that can only be an educated guess."

"Yeah," Walt replied. "We've contacted the Cayman bank and even the government. Been stonewalled at every turn. We may eventually dig up something, but not before trial. That's for damn sure."

"But why the Chechens? Were they behind it? Lardner was only one of about ten potential Republican candidates. If he had been killed, it would have left plenty of right wing Republicans. As to Edward Hale, was that an accident? If someone wanted to cut off the Hale brothers funding of right wing causes, he needed to kill Oscar, too. He was right there at the front of the stage. Easy shot for someone like Miriam. For some reason she wasn't after him. And I have to believe that if Chechnya wanted someone killed, they wouldn't have gone through Crossmore and Van Zandt. We damn sure know they have trained killers. These days, I'm sure some of them could pass for Americans and even speak Texan like they grew up on a ranch in West Texas. They killed Crossmore to cover something up. Damned if they didn't succeed. Now, we'll probably never find out. Shit."

SIXTY-TWO

When Jack was close to trial, he rarely went to the RV. Instead, he moved the trial case materials home to spread on the dining room table, and the dining room became his war room. He, J.D. and Colby sat around the table, iced teas in hand, on the Thursday before trial started the next Monday. Jack looked glum and out of sorts.

"Dammit, here we are a few days from trial, and we don't have any more idea who paid to have this attack done than we did months ago."

"Yeah," J.D. said. "We were so close at Trombone's. Then we let the answer get away from us."

"Maybe, maybe not. I suspect that he never knew who was paying him the money. His cell phone didn't have any calls around the time of the attack except to Bernard and Van Zandt. Still, I would have liked to have grilled him."

"You think that he had one of those burner phones I hear

about on the criminal shows?" Colby asked.

"Good a guess as any. If he had lived, maybe we could have gotten our hands on it. The New Orleans cops searched his house and didn't find one." Jack pounded the table with his fist. "Dammit, our strategy was to find the real killer. That was a great plan at the time. Unfortunately, we've we put all of our eggs in one basket. Now all we have to show for it is a bunch of broken eggs. Last time I saw a strategy fail this badly was probably twenty years ago."

"So, what do we do now?" J.D. asked.

"We try a straight up negligence case. We convince the jury that no matter how good the security is, you can't always stop an assassin. We've had four presidents who have been assassinated. Like Walt said, they have a small army protecting them. All it takes is some idiot who gets off a lucky shot, Lee Harvey Oswald for example. So, that's our backup plan. If that army of Secret Service agents can't protect presidents, how could Walt's detail and a few cops have changed the outcome?"

"I read Walt's deposition," Colby said. "He didn't do very well. Neither did the other members of the detail."

Jack shook his head. "Yeah, I know. I have Walt driving up here tomorrow. J.D., you'll have company upstairs for the duration."

"I've already moved into my room. OTAs are over. I've got a few weeks to be your legal assistant. What about the other members of the detail?"

"St. James is preparing them. He's the DPS lawyer. I will be defending them at trial, but I haven't had time to work with them. St. James is pretty sharp. He knows our game plan and can get them ready. And I suspect that Christiansen is going to try to unload on Walt as head of the detail that night. If I'm right, he won't have much for the others, may not even call them."

"We were talking about cell phones," J. D. said. "Didn't you mention that Mr. Nichols was going to subpoena the cell records of the plaintiffs?"

Jack picked up his cell and called Nichols's office. When the Fort Worth attorney got on the phone, he said, "Brian, Jack here. Just checking in. You got the Fort Worth cops squared away?"

"Sure do. They'll be singing from the same hymnal as the DPS, and Keith says he has the security company boys ready, too."

"One more question. Didn't you tell me you were subpoenaing the cell phone records of the plaintiffs?"

"I did. They haven't gotten here yet. I had to go through lawyers for three different phone companies. They were a pain in the ass. Dragged it out for months, but they finally agreed. Should have them early next week. You think we'll find anything?"

"Damned if I know. We've all gotten in the habit of subpoenaing cell records and mountains of emails. Most of the time we spend a hell of a lot of hours and turn up empty handed. Still, if you get them, email them to me. We'll both start looking for anything unusual. Otherwise, I'll be working on the case between now and Monday. Call if you want to talk."

"You do the same," Nichols said as he hung up.

Walt pulled into Jack's drive about ten-thirty the next morning. Jack met him as he exited his car. J.D. was close behind to take his bag from the trunk.

"I brought three suits. Is it okay to wear them more than once and then get them cleaned next weekend?"

Jack laughed. "I'll tell you a funny story. One of Houston's best plaintiff lawyers always wore the same suit and tie and a white shirt every day of trial. He said that he only had one suit when he tried his first case, won it, and decided not to mess with a good thing. So, when I started practicing, I did the same thing. You'll see me in the same dark, charcoal suit every day. I do wear different ties. Oh, and fresh underwear every day. So, with three suits, you'll look like a fashion plate.

"J. D., if you'll carry Walt's suitcase up to his room, we'll grab some tea and sit out here under one of the umbrella tables until it gets too hot. Walt, have a seat and I'll retrieve my notes. I presume you've got your deposition and the depositions of the other security detail in that briefcase in the back seat."

Walt nodded and took the briefcase. Before they could enter the house Colby came out with a tray containing a pitcher of iced tea and glasses. "Welcome, Walt. Wish it could be under better circumstances."

"You're not the only one. At least we're going to get this SOB over. Maybe then my life can return to normal."

Jack went to the house and returned with an arm full of papers and depositions. He made one more trip to retrieve his laptop. J.D joined them at the table.

"First, I've made a deal with the other defense lawyers that I'll take the lead. They understand that if all of us go into lengthy questions with each witness, it's going to get the jury confused. I don't expect Burton to ask much of anything. Brian Nichols may be the exception. He's a damn fine trial lawyer. If he wants to cover something I may have overlooked, I've had a private conversation with him and encouraged him to do so."

Then they started. Jack had prepared witnesses hundreds of times. His routine rarely varied. He explained the order of trial, discussed what types of jurors would be ideal and then started going through Walt's deposition and the other depositions, line by line.

The sun was dropping over the horizon when he finally said, "Okay, remember the old Chinese saying: *The mind can absorb only so long as the seat can endure.* I suspect your mind and your butt have had enough for today. How about a beer?"

"Can you make that a double bourbon on the rocks?"

Jack looked at his friend. "Okay, further advice. I know you've been hitting the hard stuff since all this shit happened. Now, we're about to start trial. A couple of beers a night will be fine, but that's it. Clear."

Walt stared down at his feet, then rose and extended his hand to Jack. "Agreed. After my recent self-imposed therapy, I may be content with iced tea."

SIXTY-THREE

Jack expected a media trial. For that reason he, J.D., Walt and Colby loaded the Hummer with their files and supplies the night before. They left the house at seven o'clock on Monday morning. Colby was enlisted to join the team to offer a female perspective on everything from jury selection to how the witnesses were being perceived by the jurors. Probably the most important device was J.D.'s laptop computer. Every surveillance video was loaded on it. Jack wanted to use the videos of the event to demonstrate the impossible situation presented to those trying to protect the attendees as well as those who were on the stage.

Jack was wearing his charcoal trial suit and carrying what he called his Bat Masterson cane, the straight black one with a gold knob on top. It reminded him of the legendary lawman and gambler. Jack knew that to be a successful trial lawyer, it helped to have the personality of a riverboat gambler. That was Jackson Bryant in spades. His only weakness was that he rarely wanted

to fold his cards and walk away from a trial. When he started, he was almost always all in.

Once at the courthouse, they parked on the side near an entrance close to an elevator where Walt and J.D. unloaded the Hummer and used a dolly to make the several trips necessary to move their trial materials to the second floor. Jack and Colby parked the Hummer on the lot in front of the courthouse and climbed the steps to the main entrance. Inside, the deputy sheriff manning the metal detector knew Jack and waved them around it. On the second floor they went to a conference room adjoining Judge Jamison's courtroom which would be the home away from home for the defendants and their lawyers for the duration of the trial. Once satisfied all of their trial materials were in the room, Jack walked into the courtroom, briefcase in one hand and cane in the other. As planned, they were the first to arrive and took the table inside the bar closest to the jury.

While Jack was unloading his briefcase, Ernest Rios, the deputy sheriff and bailiff, came from a door near the judge's bench. "Jack, nice to have you in our courtroom," Rios said.

Jack walked over to shake his hand. "Always my pleasure, Ernie. You know we have a lot of parties in this one. What do you suggest?"

Ernie nodded toward the jury box. "For jury selection, I'm going to put the parties in the jury box. If we need more than fourteen seats, I can find a couple more chairs. We have a panel of fifty-six. That's all this courtroom will hold. Any reporters will just have to line the walls during jury selection. As you know, Judge Jamison doesn't permit cameras in the courtroom. So that eliminates one problem. Once you pick the jury, we'll reserve the first two rows for the parties. Others, including the media, can sit in the next six."

Jack nodded his head as he surveyed the courtroom. "Works for me." He studied the old courtroom, recently refurbished with the intent to maintain its majesty. The contractor had succeeded.

The bench was solid Texas oak, burnished to an auburn sheen. It placed Judge Jamison at least three feet above everyone else. The ceiling was twenty feet tall with recessed lighting. Paneling covered the walls. The chairs for the jury were on swivels, with cushioned leather seats and high backs. Each counsel table was outfitted with a computer hookup. Monitors were on the tables and in the jury box, one between each two jurors. The last monitor was mounted on the witness box. At the push of a button a large screen dropped to the side of the jury to also display exhibits. "They did a nice job. Installed all the modern technology and maintained the old feeling. Just like a courtroom ought to look," he said to Ernie.

Ernie excused himself as other lawyers and parties started drifting in. Cecil Christiansen burst through the door at about eight-thirty, trailed by two lawyers, one male and one female, and a legal assistant. "Jack, I knew you were going to get that table. I left Dallas early, intending to beat you to it. Damned if I didn't get tied up in a traffic jam caused by some eighteen wheeler jack knifing."

At nine Ernie returned to the courtroom. By then, all of the lawyers and parties were in attendance. Hartley Hampton and three other reporters stood against the wall behind the last bench. Hampton intended to be there every day, hoping that that Jack might find a way to lift the veil of secrecy that shrouded dark money in politics. The court reporter, Annette Slack, had set up her equipment at her table in front of the witness stand. Ernie surveyed the room. "Everyone here and ready to go?"

When all of the lawyers nodded or stated their agreement, he picked up the phone on his desk and called Judge Jamison who left her chambers and took the bench in less than a minute. Then something unexpected happened.

"Judge, before we go any further, I've been evaluating my case against the various defendants," Christiansen said. "We've deposed them all. I now believe that neither the Fort Worth cops nor the security service did or failed to do anything that could have prevented this tragedy. So, I am nonsuiting them, leaving only the DPS and the governor's protective detail as defendants."

Judge Jamison removed her glasses and quietly wiped them with a tissue before she spoke. "Mr. Bryant, do you have any objection?"

Jack knew that Christiansen's decision was a wise one. He preferred to have other defendants who would all profess they did all they could to prevent what happened, but he saw no basis to object. He rose. "None, Your Honor, as long as I get assurance that those defendants will be made available to testify on a day's notice."

Nichols and Burton readily agreed. Nichols walked over to Jack, shook his hand and whispered, "I was looking forward to defending this with you. Let me know when you need one of my cops."

The judge and the remaining lawyers spent the next hour and a half, going over pre-trial motions. Once finished, she turned to Ernie.

"Judge, I've got the panel lined up in the hall."

"Get them in here. We'll go until a reasonable time and then take a lunch break. I want this jury seated before the end of the day."

The jury selection was unique in one way. Neither the judges nor the lawyers had ever found themselves needing to ask about the politics of prospective jurors. Judge Jamison handled it right from the start. "This case involves a murder, and attempted murders at a Republican fund raiser in Westover Hills. Most of you have probably read or seen something about it, particularly since Governor Lardner was shot. A juror's personal political opinions are not something that would normally be appropriate for questions by the lawyers. I've thought long and hard about how best to deal with it. Here's what I have decided. I'm going to let the lawyers ask you questions about any political affiliations you may have, whether you usually vote Democratic, Republican or otherwise."

The judge saw several members of the panel with looks of disagreement and raised eyebrows. Some turned to stare out the window, obviously upset that anyone could delve into their political leanings. She continued. "However, while I am going to let the lawyers ask such questions, if you choose not to answer them, you can so indicate either verbally or with a raise of the hand, if appropriate. I must tell you that I've never been faced with this situation. And for the benefit of the record and some appellate judges who may grade my papers later on, I believe that I have made a decision that should permit the lawyers to try to get answers that may be critical to their selections and also protect your rights as voting citizens. Mr. Christiansen, as counsel for the plaintiff, you may proceed with voir dire. You have two hours."

"Oh, one more thing. Mr. Bryant's son, J.D. Bryant, is his legal assistant. I've seen several of you glancing at him. He was an All American at TCU and recently signed with the Cowboys. I want to get that out on the table. In this courtroom, he's not an All American anything. Do you all understand and agree that you'll now set it aside? If so, raise your hand."

Fifty-six prospective jurors raised their hands. "Now, Mr. Christiansen, you may begin."

Jack observed the jury panel's responses to Christiansen with even more care than usual. The usual trial lawyer rules of thumb for picking jurors were tossed out the window in this case. When a number of jurors declined to discuss their party affiliation, Jack could not determine if it was because some folks thought how they voted was nobody's business but their own or, in the Republican stronghold of Fort Worth, did some not want to admit that they voted Democrat? When the plaintiff lawyer finished, they broke for lunch. Jack and his team retired to the conference room.

"You see that coming, Dad?" J.D. asked.

"No, but it's a good move on Christiansen's part. He had a weak case against the other two defendants. Now he can focus on us and that perceived conflict of interest. We can still call some of those cops and guards, if we need to. Now, let's look at the jury panel and evaluate them in light of Christiansen's questions and their answers." After studying what they had learned so far, Jack pitched his pen on the table. "This is nothing but a giant crapshoot. We might as well take the first twelve and be done with it."

In spite of his comments, Jack was not going to pass up the opportunity to conduct his own voir dire. He spent an hour and a half, seeking more information, with no more success than Christiansen. Still, at the end of the day Judge Jamison got her wish. They had a jury of twelve with two alternates. After the jury was excused and the courtroom was nearly deserted, Hartley approached Jack. "So, what do you think of your jury?"

Jack blinked his eyes and thought before he spoke. "Damned if I know. Ask me again in a couple of weeks, after they have returned a verdict."

SIXTY-FOUR

In his opening statement the next day, Christiansen immediately seized the attention of the jury. He moved to the front of the jury box and said, "I'm going to start my watch now."

The composition of the jury was a reasonable cross-section of the citizens of Tarrant County. Seven Anglos, three African-Americans, Two Hispanics. Ages ranged from eighteen to seventy-three; seven male and five female. The two alternates were one white male and one Hispanic female. Their occupations ranged from mechanic to accountant to housewife to waitress.

The jurors watched the plaintiff lawyer push a button on his Timex. All fourteen wondered what he was up to. Time seemed to move slowly. Silence filled the courtroom, broken only by the click of the seconds ticking from the clock on the wall over the door to the hall. Several jurors watched it, wondering what Christiansen was trying to prove. The lawyer clicked his Timex again and looked up at the jury, still letting the silence fill the court. Even Jack squirmed a little when he saw it had been eight seconds.

"That was eight seconds. Long enough for Usain Bolt to run about eighty meters from a dead start. Long enough for Peyton Manning to take a snap, survey the defense, spot his open receiver and throw a touchdown pass sixty yards down the field. On the night of the Halloween attack, it was the length of time from when the assassin fired her first shot that nearly killed Governor Lardner and her second shot that did kill Edward Hale, leaving Maria here a widow, followed by a third shot that wounded Kevin O'Connell. Rather than keeping the killer down behind the bar where she had taken refuge after that first shot, the governor's security detail abandoned their duty to the public and rushed to get the governor and his wife off the stage. If only one of them had continued cover fire in the direction of the killer, she would have been forced to remain behind the bar, giving Mr. Edward Hale and Mr. O'Connell and the others on the stage a chance to escape. The detail, and particularly its lead, Walt Frazier, were derelict in their duty to anyone other than the governor and his wife. We expect you to so find and make them and the DPS pay for the damages they caused to Mrs. Hale, the Hale children and Kevin O'Connell."

Three of the jurors looked at Walt who wanted to disappear if some genie could only wave a magic wand. Instead, he turned to gaze out the window. The remainder of the detail stared straight ahead, their faces looking like some of the masks that were worn at the fund raiser.

Christiansen next backed up and described the event, its purpose and briefly touched on the various witnesses that he would call before focusing on the multi-million dollars in damages suffered by his clients. He thanked the jury for their attention and returned to his seat.

Jack stood and walked the few steps behind J.D. and Walt. The members of the detail were seated in the chairs immediately behind them. He glanced at the benches where Colby now sat on the first row, taking notes. The plaintiffs occupied the same row but across the aisle and behind Christiansen. The remainder of the benches were now filled with reporters from local and national media. He leaned on his cane slightly as he spoke.

"Easy for Mr. Christiansen to say, isn't it? He wasn't there. You'll see what Sergeant Frazier and the other members of the detail were faced with. Understand, they didn't choose this scenario. If it had been up to them, Governor Lardner would have appeared on closed circuit television. They were outvoted by the politicians. Instead, three of them were standing on the stage with one in the back of the room, trying to evaluate any danger that might pop up suddenly from a room teeming with two hundred and fifty people in costumes, many with weapons, either real or fake. You will see on the videos that they had already dealt with multiple balloons bursting, corks popping, blanks being fired at the ceiling.

"Each time they had to decide if Governor Lardner and others were in danger. When the shot was fired that nearly killed the governor, they couldn't immediately determine which of the revelers fired it. Finally, Wyatt Kamin, one of the governor's detail who was stationed in the back of the room, spotted someone dressed as a cat burglar who had what appeared to be a real gun in her hand. He fired several shots at her in rapid succession, forcing her to duck below the bar. Knowing there were cops on the balcony, Kamin made the decision to go to the aid of the governor. The assassin took that moment to pop from behind the bar and fire two more shots, killing Edward Hale and wounding Kevin O'Connell. Once you hear the evidence and see the videos, you will agree that my clients performed up to the highest standards. But for their efforts, more people probably would have been killed."

Jack paused to allow what he said to sink in. "And one last thing. We know the name of the killer. The DPS tracked her to a compound in West Texas."

Two jurors nodded as they remembered reading about the assault on the compound.

"She is Miriam Van Zandt. She's still alive in Methodist Hospital. She rarely awakens but on one occasion she admitted that she was paid for what she did that night. As of now we don't know who paid her. Maybe this trial will bring that person to the surface and we can finally have justice done." Leaving that unanswered question floating in the air, Jack returned to his seat.

Christiansen glanced over at Jack, wondering if Jack knew something that he didn't.

"Mr. Christiansen, call your first witness," Judge Jamison said.

Christiansen had pondered throughout the weekend about his order of proof. He finally settled on Oscar Hale as the first witness. It was his house. He was host of the party. Even though his brother had been killed, at least he did not carry the bias of a plaintiff seeking damages. And he was known to be a generous benefactor to nearly every civic cause and charity in Fort Worth. Even though a man of enormous wealth, he had the image in Fort Worth of a benevolent grandfather.

"Your Honor, Plaintiffs call Oscar Hale."

The billionaire walked slowly to the witness stand and stood while the court reporter swore him in. Ernie brought him a cup of water. He took a sip and looked at Christiansen. "I'm ready, Cecil."

Christiansen took him through his early days, growing up in Fort Worth. Edward was younger than he by three years. They rarely saw their father since he spent weeks at a time, nosing around the Permian Basin and what would later become known as the Eagle Ford shale play in South Texas. When he found a working interest in a well at the right price, he would offer the land owner cash on the barrel head to buy a piece of that interest, leaving the owner as the biggest holder of the minerals, but putting cash in his hands to buy a new truck or send a kid to college.

Over the years, the old man bought hundreds, maybe thousands of such interests. By the time he died, Oscar and Edward inherited mineral rights worth several hundred million dollars.

Oscar had gone to Texas A & M. Edward opted for the Ivy League, Yale to be exact. When their father died, they made decisions together. Both bought mansions in Westover Hills, but Edward always maintained an apartment in New York. They were wealthy, but not in the billionaire class, that is, until George Mitchell, another Aggie oil man, perfected fracking and gave his technique to the world. With that the Hales moved well into the ranks of the billionaires.

Having talked about Oscar Hale's background, Christiansen moved into his interest in politics. "You see," Hale said, "I'm a self-made man." He ignored the fact that he inherited a few hundred million. "I never asked the government...he pronounced it "govment"...for a penny to develop my business..."bidness." Don't want anything from any government and want them just to leave me alone. Early on in my career I realized that I couldn't ignore politics. As a young man, I voted Democrat, supported Lyndon Johnson, John Connelly, Jim Wright and others. Then a bunch of us realized that we were getting shoved aside in the Democrat party. We became Republicans. So did Texas." He turned to look at the jury. "Hell, you folks know we haven't had a Democrat in a statewide office in twenty years."

Three of the jurors on the front row nodded their understanding of Texas politics. Christiansen could see his witness was about to mount the stump to lead a political rally and wanted to stop it. "Let me interrupt, Mr. Hale, Let's get to the current times. Why did you agree to have this big fundraiser in your house?"

Hale turned to the jury. "Money. I've learned through the years that money is the grease that makes the political wheels turn. More and more in every election cycle. Kevin O'Connell here," he said as he pointed to the man at the plaintiffs' table, "came to my house and explained this *Citizens United* decision from the U.S. Supreme Court and a couple of others that came after that one. He made me understand that the price of poker just went up big time. If we conservatives were going to stay in the game, we had to up the ante. That's why I agreed to host the fundraiser and invited every rich conservative I could think of. It's time to get the damn Democrats out of the White House."

"Why a costume party?"

"That was Kevin's idea. Halloween was coming up. The money being raised was going into this social welfare fund. I call it a dark PAC. That may not be technically right, but it's easier to say. Costumes and masks were intended to convey the message that no one can look behind the mask." He shook his head. "In hindsight, it probably wasn't a good idea."

Christiansen sucked in a breath at that statement and let it out slowly when he realized he had to follow up. "Meaning what, Mr. Hale?"

"Maybe if every damn fool wasn't in a costume, someone might have noticed that woman sooner. A few seconds might have saved my brother's life."

Christiansen grabbed onto that thought. "A few seconds?"

Hale pounded the witness stand with his fist. "Yes, sir. Damn right." His face was turning red. "If someone had spotted her a few seconds sooner, Edward would still be here."

Christiansen had several pages more of questions, but he knew to quit at a dramatic moment. He barely hid a smile when he said, "Pass the witness, Your Honor."

The judge looked at the clock. "Let's take our mid-morning break. Please be back in the jury room in fifteen minutes."

When the jury was gone, J.D. turned to his dad. "Not now, son. Let's go back to our conference room. He turned to Walt and the rest of the detail. "You guys take a break."

Jack led J.D. and Colby back to the conference room and shut the door. "Okay, now talk."

"I didn't know that testimony about a few seconds was coming."

"Neither did I. I doubt if Cecil did either. Damn sure plays well since they're talking about seconds. We can still deal with it."

"You going to do it now?" Colby asked.

"Not now. We'll get back to it. I've got other matters to cover with Oscar."

SIXTY-FIVE

"Mr. Hale, you and your brother were equal business partners, correct?" Jack started.

Hale shrugged his shoulders to suggest that was no surprise. "Yes, sir. Dad left us each fifty percent of his estate. With his Yale degree and my Aggie degree, we did pretty well by him."

"Am I correct, sir, that you were each worth around forty billion dollars at the time of his death?"

Their net worth was published every year in *Forbes* magazine. Again, he shrugged his shoulders. "More or less, maybe a little less now that the price of oil is down, but it'll come back."

"It's also true that up until a few years ago you and Edward jointly contributed to Republican and conservative causes?"

A puzzled look flitted across Christiansen's face.

"True, Mr. Bryant."

"That changed after Edward married Maria, didn't it?"

Hale looked at Christiansen and remained silent.

"You have a problem with that question, Mr. Hale?"

"Objection, Your Honor. Argumentative and vague."

"Overruled. Answer the question, Mr. Hale."

Hale took a sip of water, swallowed and paused before he answered. "Mr. Bryant, I'm very fond of Maria. She's a fine, cultured lady, very intelligent and loved my brother."

Bryant rose. "Objection, Judge. Non-responsive."

Judge Jamison looked over her glasses. "Sustained. Mr. Hale, please answer the question."

Hale realized he had no choice. "As much as I respect Maria, she's a Democrat. After they married, she had my brother's ear. They spent more and more time in New York. Damn city has too many damn liberals for me."

Bryant remained standing. "Let's get back to the question. Eventually, Edward told you that he was no longer going to contribute to your right wing causes. Your Honor, may I approach the witness?"

Jamison nodded.

"J.D. please put Exhibit 22 up on the overhead."

"Mr. Hale, I'm handing you Exhibit 22 that is also being shown on the overhead. Can you identify it as your pledge of ten million dollars on the night of the fundraiser?"

Hale read it and turned to the back where he read the fine print.

"That's signed only by you, not your brother, correct sir?"

The witness thought for a few seconds and answered, "Correct."

"You got your brother and his wife to attend your fund raiser as some kind of show of solidarity, but he was not going to contribute to O'Connell's PAC, or whatever you call it."

Hale folded his arms. "He had apparently been convinced by his wife that our country needed to go in a different direction. I don't know for sure."

Jack returned to his table and retrieved Exhibit 23. "You see this. It is from the tax returns of Edward and Maria which we subpoenaed. Look at this line. There's a contribution to a 501(c) (4) organization called Citizens For A Moderate Republic for twenty-five million. You know about that? Let remind you that you are under oath."

Hale's shoulders slumped. "I heard that they were talking to some organization like that. I tried to talk Edward out of it. I didn't know what they were contributing."

"Certainly, he had the means to contribute a billion dollars to moderate or liberal causes, if he chose."

"He could. So could I. Neither of us would have missed it."

"Pass the witness."

Christiansen was at a crossroads. He could pass the witness and act as if nothing happened or he could take the bull by the horns. He stared down at his table long enough that the judge was about to say something when he looked up. "Mr. Hale, because of what Edward was doing politically, did you have him killed?"

Hale stood at the witness stand and looked at the jury. "Of course not, ladies and gentlemen. We had developed some political differences, but we were still family."

SIXTY-SIX

Maria Hale walked to the stand in a black Dior dress, gold necklace, matching earrings and two thousand dollar Jimmy Choo heels. At forty-nine she had maneuvered carefully to get to her position of luxury in life, and she saw no reason to hide her wealth. She grew up in Athens, in East Texas, the only daughter of an auto mechanic and a Dairy Queen waitress. When she graduated from high school, she escaped the small town and landed in Fort Worth where she worked at Macy's in women's shoes and attended community college. It was at Macy's where she met her first husband, a handsome thirty-something with a chiseled face and raven black hair. When she learned he was a plastic surgeon, she turned on the charm. A year later he had divorced his first wife, and they married. He had three children with his first wife and wanted no more. Maria was fine with that. Along with the marriage came a membership in Shady Oaks. She spent her time playing tennis and golf and having discreet affairs with pros in both sports.

Unfortunately, word of the affairs eventually drifted from the women's locker room to the men's grill. A divorce soon followed. After a second marriage ended in a similar fashion, Maria found herself financially secure and traveling in the upper levels of Fort Worth society. It was at a charity ball that she met Edward who was sitting across the table. That evening she checked him out on the internet and decided he was the grand prize she had been looking for. She literally stalked him, learning where he had lunch, when he played golf, where he went on business trips. She even arranged to stay at the Ritz in New York and feigned surprise to run across him in the bar. Once she set her sights on him, the sixty year old man never had a chance.

They married, but only when Edward demanded a pre-nuptial agreement that left her with only a hundred million dollars if they divorced. Over the years they spent more time in New York while they maintained their official residence in Westover Hills. Edward had an office in New York and spent the day on conference calls with his brother and oil industry executives. He and Oscar had heated arguments over politics when Maria convinced Edward that the country needed to come together in the middle. When she took the stand, she was confident that she could sell herself to the jury and defend whatever attack Jack threw her way.

"You lost your husband last fall at the fund raiser at your brother-in-law's house?" Christiansen asked.

Maria Hale thought she was in control, but choked up as she thought back to that night.

"Yes, yes, sir."

"Do you need a tissue?"

"I'm okay."

"You and Edward were married how long?"

"I'm forty-nine now. We married when I was forty. So last fall it was eight years."

"Before I get to the events of that evening, I want to cover something that Mr. Bryant brought up. At first you and Edward didn't see eye to eye about politics, did you?"

She turned to look at the jury, knowing that the white jurors were probably all conservative Republicans. The blacks and Hispanics were almost surely Democratic. She chose her words carefully. "Edward was a staunch conservative like his brother when we met. I was a Democrat. We regularly discussed politics and the state of our country, both in Fort Worth and with friends in New York. After several years, we decided that the only way we could move our country forward was to end the sharp divides between Republicans and Democrats, African-Americans and Anglos, you name it. We compromised as moderates and have given generously to both Democrats and Republicans as long as they are not on the fringes. We had enough money that we thought we could make a difference."

Christiansen pointed to Oscar who was now seated in the back row. "How did your brother-in-law take that?"

"We had several heated arguments over the years, but finally decided to set politics aside and keep family together."

"Still, you showed up at Oscar's house that night, knowing it was going to be a fundraiser for conservative Republicans."

Maria Hale nodded her head. "We did, Mr. Christiansen. Again, we wanted to show the world that family was more important than politics." She reached for a tissue as she teared up. "In hindsight, it was as bad decision."

Christiansen moved to the podium in the middle of the room. "I know this is difficult for you but I just want to cover briefly the events of that evening. Let's skip to when you were seated on the stage beside your husband. What do you recall?"

"First, I was pleased for Oscar and Mr. O'Connell. I don't agree with them, but I still love Oscar. The pledges were even better than expected. There was a lot of noise. People were having a good time. A few were drunk. I heard a popping sound and saw Governor Lardner collapse. In my mind, time just stopped. I saw his security detail pulling him and his wife from the stage. Edward grabbed my arm to follow them. Then he was shot in the head, close to his left temple. He fell backwards into my arms. My first thought was about Mrs. Kennedy and the assassination of President Kennedy. I, I held my husband in my arms." She paused to wipe her eyes. "I don't know if he was still breathing or not. Right after he fell I heard another shot and Mr. O'Connell fell to the floor. Then there was pandemonium."

The courtroom was silent as everyone, including the jurors, took in the events as described by the widow.

"Mrs. Hale, just one more question about that night. How long between the first and second shots?"

Maria Hale wiped her eyes. "I couldn't tell you from my own memory. I've seen the video."

Jack rose to his feet. "I'm sorry, Mrs. Hale, but I object, Your Honor. If she's going to tell what she saw on the video, that video itself would be the best evidence."

"Sustained, Mr. Bryant."

"We'll save the video for a later time. Thank you, Mrs. Hale. Oh, one more question about your damages. What are you claiming?"

"I don't need money, Mr. Christiansen, but I'm going to go through my life with this horrible memory and without my husband. I blame the protective detail for that and they should be found responsible."

"No more questions, Judge."

"Mrs. Hale, I'm going to be brief. Take yourself back, one more time, to that night," Jack began. "When you got to the stage and looked out, what thoughts went through your mind?"

"Objection, Your Honor. Vague," Christiansen said.

"Overruled. You may answer."

The witness rubbed her eyes as she thought back to that night. "I'm under oath; so, I'll tell you exactly what I thought. There was this mass of humanity, all in costumes and masks. There was a lot of drinking. The noise was deafening. Corks were popping constantly. I heard a few shots that must have been blanks because none of the cops or security did anything."

"Anything else?"

The witness blew out a breath and looked at the jury. "I actually turned to Edward and said that I don't like this situation. Something could happen. Maybe it was a woman's intuition, but I, I was frightened. I had never seen anything like it."

"I'm moving on, now, Mrs. Hale. May I approach the witness, Your Honor?"

Judge Jamison nodded.

"I'm handing you Exhibit 9 for the defense. Can you identify it as the pre-nuptial agreement that you and Mr. Edward Hale signed before you were married?"

The witness glanced at the exhibit and flipped through the pages. "It appears to be. Do I need to read every page?"

"Your choice. Can you confirm that is your signature on the last page?"

"Yes."

Jack stood at the podium, leaning slightly on his cane. "Please turn to page 14, paragraph 34. J.D., please put that page on the overhead and zoom in to paragraph 34. I'm not going to read all of the legalese, but it says that the agreement is binding in the event of a divorce. If that occurs, you are to receive one hundred million dollars. If the marriage ends because of the death of either spouse, the marital estate is to be divided according to any valid will. Correct, Mrs. Hale?"

The witness hesitated long enough that Judge Jamison said, "You need to answer the question, Mrs. Hale."

The widow's face became hard. She glared at Jack. "That's correct, Mr. Bryant."

"Edward's will has been filed for probate in this courthouse. Under the terms of that will since your husband died, you stand to inherit twenty billion dollars with the rest going to his children, right, Mrs. Hale?"

"Mr. Bryant," the witness erupted, "If you are insinuating that I would have had my husband killed for any amount of money, that's outrageous and I resent it."

One of the jurors on the back row turned to the man beside him and whispered, "I don't know how much it would take for me to have my old lady bumped off, but I believe twenty billion would be enough." The seatmate nodded his agreement.

"Mrs. Hale, I'm just bringing out the facts. The jurors can draw their own conclusions."

At the lunch break Jack had arranged for sandwiches and soft drinks to be delivered to their conference room. While they were eating, there was a knock at the door.

"Come in," Jack said. It was Hartley.

"Can I take a minute of your time?"

"Sure. Have a seat."

"I'm only eating half my sandwich," Colby said. "You want the other?"

"No thanks." Hartley turned to Jack. "I didn't see this coming. Two witnesses and you have two suspects, or at least two people who had a motive for killing Edwards."

Jack nodded as he chewed on a chip.

"I didn't know that there was such a big riff in the family. You think that Oscar was pissed enough that he had his own brother done in?"

"Don't have any evidence of it, but I'm laying out the facts."

"And, Mrs. Hale. I'd read the will that was filed for probate, but I never saw the pre-nup. She had twenty billion reasons. Going to make an interesting story in tomorrow's *Star Telegram*. You have any more suspects?"

Jack remained noncommittal. "Maybe another one or two. You'll just have to stay and watch."

SIXTY-SEVEN

"My name is Kevin O'Connell. I live in Washington, D.C., but, I spend so much time in Texas that I'm beginning to talk like you folks."

"Your occupation is what?" Christiansen asked

"My umbrella organization is O'Connell Communications, Inc. I've got various other PACs and advertising companies and such within OCI."

"One of those is called the Stepper PAC?"

"Yes, sir."

Christiansen smiled at the jury. "Kinda an unusual name for a political action committee. Where did you come up with that?"

"I think I heard the saying sometime in my Texas travels. Some old boy said, 'That ain't no hill for a stepper.' So, I incorporated it and the motto became *Washington's no hill for a stepper.*"

"Then there's something called Stepper Official Strategies?"

O'Connell nodded. "That's a 501 (c)(4) social welfare

organization. We call it SOS."

Christiansen rubbed his chin, as if in thought. One of his associates took notes on a yellow legal pad while the other was staring at a laptop screen. Jack idly gazed off into space as if there was nothing that Christiansen could asked that could possibly interest him. Judge Jamison was on her computer, probably exchanging emails with other judges while she listened to the testimony. Christiansen knew that he had to confront the secrecy of the SOS donors, knowing that some of the jurors would find it offensive that they could not learn the identity of large donors.

"This SOS, why do you call it a social welfare organization? You're a political operative. Do you really give a damn about social welfare?"

Jack kept his poker face but quietly admired his adversary for facing this issue head on.

O'Connell rubbed his hands together as he gathered his thoughts. Then he turned to face the jury. "First, I am a strong believer in social welfare. I also believe that the government wastes far too much money and the private sector should play a bigger role, but that's for another day. SOS can maintain its status as long as it is primarily engaged in social welfare which can be about political issues. For example, Mr. Christiansen, let's say you are a senator from Texas. SOS could run a series of television commercials complaining about the lack of attention paid by Washington to environmental issues and end it by asking that the viewer call Senator Christiansen and tell him folks are concerned about the environment. The rule is fifty-one percent social welfare issues. The rest can be contributed to political campaigns."

Christiansen moved to the podium to make sure he had the jury's attention. "Does SOS have to report its spending?"

"Absolutely."

"What about contributors?"

"No, the government doesn't require us to reveal our contributors."

Several of the jurors were leaning forward, not liking what they were hearing. Christiansen noted their attention.

"But, Mr. O'Connell, that can't be good for the country. You can have billionaires and corporations and labor unions and such giving tens of millions of dollars to your organization and nobody but you knows their names. And the Democrats can do the same damn thing. Come on, now."

O'Connell accepted the challenge thrown at him by his lawyer. "Mr. Christiansen, wouldn't you agree that it's more important to know how the money is spent than where it comes from?"

Christiansen cast a sideways glance at the jury and didn't like what he saw. "I suppose. We'll come back to that another day." Christiansen knew that other day would not come. He hoped the jury would forget the issue by the end of trial. "The jury's heard about the fundraiser that night. You went to Oscar Hale to set it up?"

O'Connell crossed his legs and relaxed. "I did. I knew he was a strong conservative and knew most of the wealthy people in this area. I was trying to raise a hundred million dollars that night. We were close when the shooting started."

"All these costumes and masks and guns, you agreed with all of that?"

"I'm sorry to say that the costumes were my idea. I didn't want guns at the party, but I was outvoted by Mr. Hale and Governor Lardner."

Christiansen nodded. "In hindsight, I think we would all agree that the costumes and masks were poor choices, too. We've already heard from Mr. Hale and Mrs. Edward Hale. I don't want to re-plow any ground. Let me ask when you first realized there was trouble."

The witness momentarily got a faraway look in his eyes as he thought back to that night. "We were approaching that one hundred million in pledges. I was confident that we were going to blow right through the number. Then there was a pop, turns out it was the first shot." O'Connell hesitated. "The governor went down. Then it was an eternity. His detail was trying to get him off stage. I heard some shots from the back of the room. Then two more shots rang out. One hit Edward in the head and one got me in the arm. Edward died in Maria's arms. My wound was minor. I, I was fortunate."

"Are you making any claim for your injury?"

"No, sir. In the overall scheme of things, it was not important."

"How about any monetary losses?"

O'Connell sucked in his breath. "It has almost destroyed me financially. Those pledges for that night virtually disappeared. Personally, I would have managed that money and put it to good use. My fee is usually five percent. I should have a half a billion dollars in my various social welfare organizations and PACS now. Instead, I can't get phone calls returned. I've lost at least twenty-five million personally." He turned to the jury. "This wasn't my fault, ladies and gentlemen. If the governor's protective detail had done their job, of course, the governor still would have been wounded, but he made a full recovery. No one else would have been shot by that woman."

Christiansen turned to confer with his associates and said, "No further questions, Your Honor."

Jack rose, buttoned his coat and said, "We'll reserve our questions for this witness for our case in chief."

The judge looked over her glasses. "Well, Mr. Bryant, I haven't had a defendant do that in a civil case in years. Of course, it's your right. We're adjourned." She rose and told the jury, "See you in the morning. Remember not to talk about the case. And since we seem to have the media's attention, please avoid reading anything about it. If something is on television, please mute that part of the news."

Jack loaded his roller briefcase as did J.D. Colby was waiting for them in the first row. "Okay," Jack said. "We know a bunch of those reporters and cameras are going to be waiting for us at the steps when we walk out the door. I haven't talked to them so far, but now's the time. Just may be that a couple of our jurors choose to ignore the judge's admonition. Might as well give them a little something to chew on."

Jack was right. Cameras were rolling. Reporters were jostling one another with microphones in hand. Jack stopped on the first step. J.D. stood beside him. Colby backed away.

"It's about time I broke my silence. I've got a statement. You just heard from Kevin O'Connell today. He described what most of us are calling a dark PAC. We all know it's got a more formal name with the IRS. None of us know where the money comes from but it's a huge number. He and his lawyer and the other plaintiffs want to blame my clients, Walt Frazier and the other members of the protective detail, for what happened that night. You folks need to remember that because of the DPS and its SWAT team, we captured Miriam Van Zandt in an assault on the Alamo Defenders compound in West Texas. The authorities called an end to the investigation, but we know that she was not acting alone. Someone paid her. Just as these dark PACS have hidden donors, we know that somewhere out there lurks a money man who wanted this to happen. We are going to win this trial, but this case will never be over until we know who paid for the trigger woman."

"Jack," Hartley asked, "are you suggesting that one of these dark PACs paid for the killing of Edward Hale and the shooting of Governor Lardner and the wounding of O'Connell."

"Don't know. I can't rule it out, but, so far, I can't prove it. Still, this trial is only just beginning."

As Jack pushed his way through the reporters, Ike Irasmus drifted away from the fringes of the crowd. He had listened to the evidence all afternoon and chose not to let Jack know he was even in the courtroom. Jack had too much on his mind, and he was just an interested observer. Until now. He thought about Crossmore and how Bernard avoided talking to him, claiming that Crossmore only bought them drinks. But Al said that Bernard and Crossmore did business together. He probably should have told Jack, but they were dealing with Crossmore's killing, and It didn't strike him as important at the time. Now he realized that Bernard might be the only person left who could lead them to the money man, as Jack just called him. He couldn't bother Jack or J.D. in the middle of the trial. He would do this himself.

SIXTY-EIGHT

Ike walked out to his backyard where he found Trousers sleeping on the porch of the doghouse he had built for a pet that spent the early part of his life sleeping on the street. He overfilled the dog's food bowl and made sure that the automatic control worked to continuously refill his water. "I'll be gone tonight, Trousers," he said as he stooped to scratch the dog behind the ears. "I'll see you tomorrow."

Ike drove to DFW airport and boarded a flight to New Orleans. Once there he took a cab to the Marriott that bordered the French Quarter on Canal. After a nap and dinner at NOLA, he walked to Trombone's. He entered the club at about eleven and sat at the bar where he ordered a Miller Lite. The club was nearly full, something a little unexpected on a Thursday night. Between numbers, he saw Bernard look over the crowd. When he looked at the bar, his eyes passed Ike by, then returned to gaze at him briefly before turning to talk to the trombone player.

At the next break, Al spotted him and walked to the bar. "Ike,

I didn't see you come in. You bring your horn?"

Ike smiled. "I'm not ready for prime time, yet, Al."

"Nonsense." Al turned to the stage. "Bernard, you bring your spare cornet?"

Bernard glanced at Ike. Reluctantly, he said, "Yeah. It's here behind the stage."

"You mind if Ike borrows it?"

Knowing he had no choice, Bernard stepped behind the stage and walked over to the bar, horn in hand. "Here you are, sir."

"No need to call me sir. I'm just an old, worn out jazz musician. Al, can I go back to your dressing room and warm up a couple of minutes?"

Al nodded and walked Ike to the back. When he returned, he saw Bernard hurriedly packing his horn. "Where the hell you going, Bernard?"

Bernard looked at him and glanced at the door back to the dressing room. "I figure that you have another horn player for the evening. I have better things to do."

Al studied him for a minute. "I know. You're worried that he's going to ask you some questions about Crossmore. If he does, so what, Crossmore's dead. You stay right where you are. You might learn something from Ike. He was the best back in his day."

Resigned to staying, Bernard took his cornet from the case and resumed his place on the stage. In a couple of minutes Ike came from the back and joined him.

"Ike, we'll play some of the old stuff. You'll probably remember. Just join in whenever you feel like it."

They started with *Basin Street Blues*. Ike listened quietly for a minute and then tentatively joined in, quietly at first and then matching Bernard, note for note. Next came *Birth of the Blues*. Ike felt comfortable enough to cut loose about half way through the number. The rest of the band stopped and listened as he played the borrowed cornet like he owned the song. When he finished, the band members clapped while the audience got to their feet, crying for more.

"Ike, can you do *We Was Doing All Right?*"

Ike nodded. The other band members lowered their instruments as Ike played the opening bars. Half way through, he starting singing the lyrics, sounding as close to Louis Armstrong as anyone since Sachmo died. When he finished, the audience was again on their feet. Ike did a little bow, acknowledged the band, handed the cornet to Bernard, and moved through the audience to his seat at the bar. Thinking he must be a celebrity, several people in the audience stopped him to sign napkins.

After the last set, the lights came up. Ike walked up to Bernard. "We need to talk."

Bernard refused to even turn his eyes toward Ike. "Got nothing to say."

"I only need ten minutes."

"Don't matter. I'm scared to even step out on the street. I have a taxi waiting for me every night out front when we're through. I ain't about to walk anywhere around here at night."

"Look, Crossmore is dead."

"Yeah, but two guys killed him."

"One of them was killed by my friend out there on the street. We've learned the other one left the country the next day."

Bernard shook his head. "May be more coming behind them."

Ike raised his voice. "Just a damn minute. Get over here and sit your ass down. If you don't tell me the truth, I'll go to the police. You were involved with Crossmore. From what I hear, you had quite a profitable operation going with him."

Bernard tried to maintain his composure, but did as Ike directed. He took a seat across from Ike. "Look, keep your voice down. Okay, I sold him a little jewelry from time to time. So what?"

Ike remembered the conversation with Jack when they were last in New Orleans. Jack had said he would bluff Cross into talking. Ike rose to the occasion. "Two weeks before Halloween last year he gave you a check for $50,000, a cashier's check from a bank in the Caymans. And it was for introducing him to a man who wanted that attack in Fort Worth. Admit it and I won't go to the police."

Bernard slumped his shoulders and sighed. Somehow Ike had figured it out, even down to Crossmore's check coming from the Caymans. "Okay. Let's make it fast. Cross started coming in here a couple of years ago, maybe three. Bought all of us beers between sets. I spent a lot of time at his table. I showed him a gold necklace one night and asked if he knew anyone who would buy it. That was the beginning. He bought necklaces, diamond earrings, fancy bracelets, expensive watches, all that kind of shit. I made a few bucks. Suspect he made a lot more, but I did all right."

"What about the check? And remember NOPD can get a warrant for your bank statements."

Bernard looked around the room to make sure that there were no customers in earshot. The seats were empty. Most of the band members were packed up and headed out. Only the bartender stayed behind. It looked like he was counting receipts. Bernard lowered his voice to a whisper.

"There was this customer. Didn't live around here, but did business in New Orleans. Came in maybe three or four times a year. In fact, he usually sat at this very table. Fancy dresser, expensive suits. Wore a Rolex with diamonds all around the dial and a diamond ring. Must have been two or three carats in that diamond. Once in a while he would have some other businessman with him, but usually he came alone. The band loved to see him. He tipped a grand in cash at the end of the evening."

"What did he look like?"

"Nothing about him to pick him out of a crowd. Medium height, a little overweight, somewhere in his fifties. Kind of a prominent nose. Always pleasant to me and the band." Bernard searched his mind. "One interesting thing. He was right handed.

Most of us that are right handed wear our watch on our left wrist. He had his on his right wrist. Maybe he wanted to show it off more when he shook hands."

"You never knew his name?"

"He never gave it and always paid cash."

Ike placed his hands flat on the table and leaned over until he was only inches from Bernard. "And about the fifty thousand."

"This same guy called me one evening. I learned later that the bartender gave him my cell. He wanted someone to do a contract. He said that he presumed I knew what a contract was. It was worth a half a million to him." Bernard looked at the ceiling. "Understand, I've never been involved in anything like this. I told him so. He just asked if I could put him in touch with anyone."

Ike saw that he had Bernard on a roll and pushed him. "Keep going."

"I thought about it. Figured I could make fifty grand or so. Next time Cross came in here I raised the idea with him. He thought about it. Couple of days later he gave me a burner phone number for this guy to call. I called him and put him and Cross in touch. That was the last I was involved."

"Not quite. You got fifty large delivered to you by Cross."

Sweat was breaking out on Bernard's face. "Well, there's that. Only, I didn't know any of the details. Honest to God, all I did was arrange a phone call between Cross and this guy. I didn't even know the contract was done until you guys showed up that night and Cross was killed."

Ike thought for a minute and had one more question. "You have any cell phone record of the calls with that guy?"

"Naw, man. That was last September, maybe even August. Besides, I never even see that bill. It just gets paid from my checking account every month."

Ike figured he had gotten all the information he could. It wasn't much, but he would report it to Jack. He had last parting words for Bernard. "Okay, I'm not going to the NOPD. My friends and I are on the trail of the killer. Here's my card. You remember anything else, call me. Understood?"

On the way to the airport, Ike called Jack. He explained what he was doing in New Orleans and his conversation with Bernard. He could tell that Jack's mind was on the trial. When he said that Bernard admitted receiving $50,000 but couldn't provide any more information, Jack lost interest. "If that's all he has, I don't have time to deal with him right now. I'll mention it to Joe after the trial to see if he wants to do anything."

SIXTY-NINE

Back in Fort Worth, Jack rose, dreading the day and expected evidence. Christiansen told him the night before that Walt would be the first witness on Thursday. When Walt learned that his time had come, he declined even a beer, saying with a smile that he would stick with water.Before they went to bed, once again Jack walked Walt through the expected questions and how he could answer them. He explained, as he always did with clients and witnesses, that with a good lawyer on the other side, he would not go unscathed. Christiansen would score a few points, but that always happened. "Look," he said, "there's never a day in trial that I don't get home and mentally kick myself in the butt because I either asked the wrong question or forgot to ask a key question or even asked one question too many that led to some damaging testimony. Walt, it's not a movie or a damn play. Nothing's scripted. You do your best, and I'll deal with it."

"Easy for you to say," Walt replied. "The audience is full of reporters. Whatever I say will be all over the country by tomorrow night. Hell, my job could be on the line. I've got a wife and family. I'm not trained to do anything else. Still, I'll give it my best shot. That's all I can do."

The next morning there was silence in the Hummer when the four made their way to the courthouse. Colby was the only one to break the silence when she said that it would be good to have a three day weekend since there would be no trial on Friday when the judge handled motions in other cases on her docket.

Walt's name was called by Christiansen. He rose, trying to hide his nervousness, and moved to stand in front of the bench. As was her custom, Judge Jamison, swore him in. He settled into the chair, poured a cup of water and smiled at the jury before turning to face his adversary. Nice touch, Jack thought.

"You are Walt Frazier?"

"Actually my full name is Walter Frazier, Jr. Neither my dad nor I have middle names."

Knowing that Jack would like to cover his background, Christiansen elected to do it first. He established that Walt had joined the national guard upon graduation from high school. He served in Desert Storm where he met his lawyer. Upon his return he chose to remain on active duty. He was stationed at Fort Hood in Central Texas and took courses working toward a college degree. When he was discharged, he was a cop in Wharton for a number of years, finding time to complete his degree. He had been with the DPS for fifteen years, the last ten with the governor's protective detail.

"Sergeant Frazier, you agree that when you became a state trooper, you took an oath to protect the public?"

Walt looked him right in the eye. "I did."

"Even though you were transferred into the protective detail, you did not abandon that oath, did you?"

Walt turned to look at the jury. "No, I did not, and neither did the rest of the detail."

Christiansen tapped his pen on the table. "So, what you're telling this jury is that if the governor was in danger, you could ignore your oath?"

Walt's face hardened. He deflected the question. "When we accepted the responsibility to protect the governor and his wife, we accepted an added responsibility. It was clear from our training that, if necessary, we had to take a bullet to protect the governor."

Christiansen could sense that the jurors were looking at Walt and the detail members seated behind Jack in a new light. Very few, if any, of them had agreed as part of their job description to accept death. Christiansen pondered his next question. "In your training, did you have any instruction on what to do when both the governor and citizens of this state were in danger from the same event?"

Walt hesitated. "All we were told was that we had to use our own judgment. We were experienced law enforcement officers."

"Yet, you had four members of your detail in the ballroom and one out at the Suburban. Once the governor was shot, your only concern was to protect the governor and his wife, wasn't it?"

Walt shook his head. "Not true. Wyatt Kamin, seated there on the front row, spotted the shooter and laid down cover fire for several seconds."

Christiansen looked down at his watch. "Wasn't long enough, was it, Sergeant? Took a few shots, then he hightailed it out the door at the front and met you guys back with the governor. You didn't even need a fifth man to take the governor to the hospital. You already had four. If he had continued to shoot at the woman, maybe Edward Hale would still be alive and Kevin O'Connell wouldn't have been shot."

Walt said nothing but only stared out the window, unsure how to respond.

"I need an answer, Sergeant Frazier."

Walt looked at Jack and then at the jury before forcing himself to focus on Christiansen. "Sir, there were other law enforcement officers present along with armed security guards. We assumed that they would do their job."

"Proved to be a wrong assumption, didn't it?"

Walt fumbled for words. "That's hindsight, sir. We reacted the best we could in only a matter of seconds. If we had done something different, like you suggest, the governor probably would have taken a second bullet and be dead now."

Christiansen stood at his table, knowing that he was finished. "You failed that night, didn't you?"

Walt whooshed out a breath, gripped the arms of his chair and said nothing.

"Didn't you, Sergeant?"

"Sir, we saved the governor's life."

Christiansen looked at the jury and turned to the judge. "No more questions for this witness." He turned his back on Walt and walked to the window to gaze outside, as if nothing that Jack could do could possibly overcome the damage he had just inflicted.

"Time for a morning break. See you in fifteen, ladies and gentlemen."

Back in their conference room, Jack shut the door.

"I blew it, didn't I Jack?"

"No, you answered the questions the best you could. I'm going to play some videos. We'll put things back in perspective. Just follow my lead."

While they were talking J.D. was checking his iPhone. "Dad, Nichols has sent us the cell phone records he subpoenaed. I'm going to bring my laptop back here and check them. I'll tell you what I find at lunch."

"Good. Colby, you'll be playing the videos."

"Your Honor, at this time we are going to ask Sergeant Frazier to describe what happened that night, using the videos from the cameras inside the ballroom. First, Sergeant Frazier, were there cameras focusing on the premises outside?"

Walt was now more relaxed since his lawyer was doing the questioning. "Yes, sir. Only, for some reason, the outside cameras had been turned off at 3:38 that afternoon. We have no feeds from then until sometime after the shootings when we discovered they had been shut down."

"Let me cover that just a minute before we move on. Where were the controls to the security cameras?"

"There was a closet off a hallway in the house. Various switches controlled the cameras."

"Who had access to the house at that time of the afternoon?"

Walt saw where he was going. "Access was limited, but included a lot of people. There were security guards at each entrance. If a person's name wasn't on the list, he couldn't get in. Of course, that list was pretty long--family, O'Connell Communications staffers. Later the governor showed up, security guards, a few Fort Worth cops, cooks, caterers, waiters."

"Still, someone had to be on that list at 3:38 in the afternoon to switch off those outside cameras?"

"That's correct, Mr. Bryant."

Jack picked up his cane, more as a prop than a crutch and stood behind the podium. "Before we get to the videos, what were your feelings about this whole costume fundraiser even before that night?"

"I tried to talk everyone out of it. I even went to the governor's office at the capitol and told him that this was an impossible situation. He wouldn't listen. I asked him to appear on closed circuit television. My advice fell on deaf ears. We had to deal with the situation."

"Now, I've got my legal assistant, Colby, rolling the video. The first one is from behind the stage. Was that your view on that night?"

"It was."

The jury saw a sea of people, dressed in costumes and masks.

"Any way you could pick out an assassin in that group?"

Walt shook his head. "Impossible, sir."

Jack thought he could see a couple of the jurors nodding in agreement. "Now, we're showing the video from the back of the ballroom, facing the stage. I'm eliminating everything except for a few seconds before the first shot." Colby put up the video and paused it. "We're looking at the stage. The governor is there. You're to his right and Ryan Fitzpatrick is to his left. Jeff Foster is behind him just in front of the curtain. What are you doing?"

"We're looking for what we call tells among the crowd, any sign of a potential problem. With that crowd wearing costumes and masks, it was wasted effort."

"Now, we're going to show the shooting of the governor."

Every juror had moved to the edge of his or her seat.

"We hear a faint popping. Is that the shot?"

"Yes, sir, a pistol doesn't make noise a whole lot different from a popgun or even a balloon in that crowd."

"Now, watch the video," Jack said, "and the timer at the top. How much time elapsed from that shot until the governor went down?

"Looks like one and a half seconds."

"Then, you are there using your microphone on your sleeve."

"I'm saying that Wolf's down. We need to get him and Petal out. Wolf and Petal are code names for the governor and his wife."

"How much time elapsed while you alerted your team to what had happened?"

"Looks like another second and a half."

Jack motioned to Colby to start the video. "So, we're down to five seconds. During that time, can you hear shots that were later identified as coming from Wyatt?"

"I can. They cover another four seconds."

"So in that one second, the killer jumps up and fires two more shots, killing Edward Hale and wounding Mr. O'Connell. Could you have prevented those shots?"

Walt turned to the jury. "In my honest opinion, no sir."

Jack could have done more but decided to quit.

Christiansen spent the rest of the morning, briefly calling the other members of the detail. He elicited the same basic information. He spent only fifteen minutes each on the Hale children. Jack elected to ask no questions of the detail or the children.

When they broke for lunch, Jack, Colby and Walt hurried back to the conference room to talk to J.D. After they shut and locked the door, Jack asked, "You find anything?"

"Nothing in Maria's records or the Hale children, but there's something interesting in O'Connell's."

"Keep going."

"There are calls by O'Connell to the New Orleans area code within a couple of days of each other last September. I called both numbers. One was a recorded voice, saying the person at the number was not available and to leave a message. I hung up. Two calls to and from that number. The second number was disconnected and no longer in service. There was also a second call from that disconnected number to O'Connell."

"I'll be damned."

Colby looked at Jack. "Are you thinking that O'Connell set this up?"

Jack tapped his cane on the floor while he thought. "Maybe."

"No, Jack. That makes no sense. Why would he get himself shot?"

"Colby," J.D, said, "He was just barely wounded. Maybe he wanted the governor and Hale killed. Hell, maybe just Hale. What better cover than for him to be wounded. We already know that Miriam was the best pistol shot in West Texas, and she was only about fifteen feet from the stage.

"We can't draw any conclusions right now. We've got to tie it together. J.D., round up Ike. You remember he said that Bernard paid his cell phone direct from his bank. You and Ike need to get back to New Orleans and sit Bernard in front of a computer to find his cell records for last September. We're looking for O'Connell's number. The judge won't care that you're not in the courtroom. Colby will cover for you."

After the lunch break Christiansen rose and told the judge and jury that his last witness would be William R. Ringer. When Ringer followed Bailiff Rios through the hallway door, the jury sized him up. In his sixties, he had once probably been in very good shape. No longer. He had a slight paunch that caused him to pull up on his pants as he walked the middle aisle. His hair was white. He wore gold rimmed glasses. There was little about him that was impressive until he began to talk. Then, he commanded attention with his voice.

"I'm Bill Ringer. I retired ten years ago after a career in the Secret Service. The last twenty years I was on the presidential detail."

Jack glanced at the jury and found that just the mention of the Secret Service and presidential detail had their attention. Christiansen established his credentials, Texas A & M, member of the Corps, service as an officer in the military police for six years, then joined the Secret Service. Now he consulted with major corporations on matters pertaining to security.

"Mr. Ringer," Christiansen said, "I have asked you to evaluate the conduct of the governor's protective detail on the night of the Halloween attack."

"Correct."

"Did they deviate from appropriate standards in their handling of the events at the Hale house on the night of the fundraiser?"

Ringer straightened up in his chair and swiveled to face the jury. "I can make this brief. They were sworn peace officers. That was their primary duty. They had a second duty to protect the governor. I've watched the videos of the event. They had four officers on the inside. Three would have been sufficient to get the wounded governor and his wife off the stage and out of danger.

That would have been the three on the stage. The fourth, Kamin I believe was his name, was positioned at the back. He did the right thing to fire in the direction of the killer. He managed to get her to drop below the bar. Then, ladies and gentlemen, he took off and circled around the ballroom to meet Sgt. Frazier and the rest of the detail. That enabled the killer to rise up from behind the bar and get off two more shots. I might add that she was one helluva shot. Two shots and she killed Edward Hale and wounded O'Connell. Then she rushed out the door. Must have been just ahead of the rest of the detail who had to drag the governor down the stairs and out to the Suburban. Someone in the DPS should have trained the detail to keep up the cover fire until others could respond. They didn't. That was negligence and caused the death of Mr. Hale and the injury to Mr. O'Connell."

With that he paused and looked at Christiansen.

"No more questions, Your Honor."

Jack almost jumped to his feet and walked to the podium, cane in hand, a slight smile on his face. "Mr. Ringer, let's clarify a few things. First, you've never worked on a protective detail where only five men had the responsibility to protect a high ranking public official, have you?"

"I have not, sir."

"When you were protecting the president, you did not take an oath to protect the public. Your only duty was to the president and the first lady."

Ringer nodded his agreement.

"So, if that had been the president on that stage that night, and the detail did exactly what you saw on that video, you would have no criticism, would you?"

Ringer hesitated and finally answered, "No, sir."

"Another difference between you and your work in the Secret Service is that you folks would have had dozens of agents arriving days before the event and maybe even as many as a hundred on the grounds that night."

"You're probably somewhere in the ballpark, Mr. Bryant. The president always travels with a large number of agents."

"If it had been the president up on that stage, a half a dozen agents certainly could have gotten him and the first lady out of the ballroom, leaving several dozen to lay down cover fire in the direction of the assassin, right, Mr. Ringer?"

The witness was beginning to feel uncomfortable now. He poured a cup of water and his hand trembled slightly when he took a sip. "No doubt we would have had much more firepower than four agents."

Jack saw that the answer led very well into his next and last series of questions. "You agree that no matter how many agents are available to protect the president, a lone assassin can still succeed?"

"That's unfortunate, but true."

"There were three presidents, including Lincoln, gunned down in the nineteenth century. And they all had a protective detail of some kind, didn't they?"

Ringer rubbed his hands on his pants to wipe sweat from them. "That's true, but I don't know how many were protecting those presidents."

Jack nodded. "Then, let's go to more modern times. President Kennedy was killed by a lone assassin even though he had a large contingent of Secret Service agents in the area and around him."

"Some of us believe that Oswald may have had some help, but you are correct that the official conclusion of the Warren Commission was that he acted alone."

"And what about President Reagan? He had only been in office for a couple of months when John Hinckley wounded him, probably brought him close to death. He didn't lack for protective agents, did he?"

One of the jurors closest to the witness saw his right leg bounding up and down, obviously a nervous reaction to the questions.

"He did not."

"And, in fact, three others were shot by Hinckley before he could be subdued, including James Brady, Reagan's press secretary. That's four people shot, all in a matter of a few seconds, one more than what happened at the Hale house, correct?"

Ringer took in a big breath and exhaled. "That's all true, Mr. Bryant."

"So the conclusion we draw is that no matter what a crew of four agents did on that night, even if Kamin had laid down that cover fire for ten more seconds, we can't conclude that anything would have changed."

Ringer looked down and back up at Jack. "I can't disagree with you, sir."

Jack returned to his table. "Nothing further, judge."

Judge Jamison looked at the clock. "I understand that this is Mr. Christiansen's last witness. We're making good progress. Let's call it a day."

Jack jumped to his feet. "Your Honor, I have one witness. It's is very important that I get him on today. It's one of our experts, Calvin Cagle. I can be brief, but I need his testimony to prepare for next week."

The judge looked over her gold rimmed spectacles and said, "Very well. You know the jury is tired at this point. I suggest you keep your pledge. Call Mr. Cagle."

SEVENTY

The jury saw a string bean with a yellow polka dot bow tie just below a prominent Adam's apple enter from the hallway. He wore a blue blazer, gray slacks and somewhat scuffed black penny loafers and carried an old soft-leather briefcase. If Hollywood wanted someone to play Ichabod Crane, he would be first choice. Clearly, he was not trying to make a fashion statement.

After he took the oath and settled into the witness stand, Jack said, "Tell us a little about yourself."

Cagle smiled as he turned to the jury. "Good afternoon, ladies and gentlemen."

"Good afternoon," several replied, taking an instant liking to the witness.

"You heard my name. Never much cared for Calvin as a first name, but I wasn't given a vote."

Most of the jurors smiled.

"I'm a professor out at TCU. I have a PhD, but I don't really like to be called doctor. Cal suits me just fine. I teach political science. Been doing so for twenty plus years."

"Professor," Jack asked, "have you written any books about politics?"

Cagle nodded. "Last time I counted it was twenty-two. Plus a bunch of journal articles. I also appear on national news programs when there's some political event that might be worth my two cents."

"Sir, you're familiar with 501(c)(4) organizations, are you not?"

Cagle sighed. "I'm sorry to say I am. After what the Supreme Court did to us in the name of free speech, I worry about the damn things every day."

Christiansen rose. "Objection, Your Honor. Non-responsive."

"Sustained. Professor, please just answer the question with no editorial comment."

Cagle shrugged his shoulders as he looked at the jury. "Sorry, Your Honor. My opinions occasionally just slip out, particularly when they are strongly held."

"Professor, I asked you to study the contributions of the Stepper PAC and SOS, the ones that have been provided to us by Mr. O'Connell's lawyer. Have you done so?"

"I have."

"Have you formulated opinions as to the percentage of expenditures from SOS that went to social welfare organizations?"

"Wait a minute, Your Honor," Christiansen almost shouted. "There's nothing in the designation of this witness about any such opinions."

"Not so, Judge. In the designation, I wrote, and I quote, 'opinions about the status of Mr. O'Connell's various organizations.' If Mr. Christiansen wanted more detail, all he had to do was ask."

"Mr. Christiansen," Judge Jamison ruled, "I agree that is global and very skimpy. Still, I'm going to let the testimony in. Proceed, Mr. Bryant."

Christiansen bent over to whisper something to his associate who had the laptop, then turned and walked to the rail where he leaned against it as he listened.

"Can I answer, Judge?" Cagle asked.

Jamison nodded.

"Pardon me. Mr. Bryant, can you hand me my briefcase?"

J.D took it from their table and handed it to him. Cagle opened two buckles and extracted a large file, overflowing with papers. He turned to look at the jury.

"Don't worry, I'm not going to read all of this stuff to you. I have a summary on top, but wanted to have my backup data in case one of these smart lawyers wants to challenge any of my opinions." The way he said it, the jurors could tell that he was eager to be challenged by the plaintiff lawyer. "Now, here's my summary, just three pages. First, I took a hard look at what is called SOS. It's supposed to be a 501(c)(4) social welfare organization. That means that fifty-one percent of its money has to be spent on social welfare issues. Now, the first part is easy. Forty-nine percent over the past election cycle and up to now has gone straight to the Stepper PAC."

"Is that okay?" Jack asked, primarily just to break up Cagle's lecture.

"I don't like it, but it's all right, according to various federal regulations and the United States Supreme Court." He grimaced when he said the name of the court.

Christiansen started to object but decided to let it go.

"What about that other fifty-one percent?"

"That gets interesting. Most of the money is spent on ads about guns, the environment, immigration, fracking, the Keystone pipeline, nearly any hot button political issue you can think of. Are they issues important to our society? Of course. The problem is that the commercials take, in the case of SOS, a decidedly conservative, Republican view of the issue and then take shots at some liberal or Democratic politician. You know,

'Tell Governor so-and-so" to vote for the right to carry or against more environmental regulation. Oh, there may be a little money spent by SOS, supporting Boy Scouts or the Audubon Society, but that's a very small percentage. Now, I don't mean to be just taking shots at conservatives and Republicans. The Democrats do the same things."

Jack saw that the jurors found this all very interesting. He spoke softly. "In your opinion, are these ads and commercials supporting social welfare?"

"Objection, objection, Your Honor," Christiansen said as he saw that O'Connell was turning red with anger. "He's not the one to decide if a campaign is for social welfare or not."

Jamison looked at Jack for a reply. "He certainly is, Your Honor. I've qualified him as an expert. We've researched the issue, and it is not currently defined by the courts nor the IRS. We've got to start somewhere. Might as well be here."

"Mr. Christiansen, your objection is noted. Professor Cagle may continue."

Cagle had turned to face the judge. With her last pronouncement, he faced the jury as if he were lecturing to a freshman class in political science. "You see, that's the problem. No one has defined what a social welfare organization is. The Federal Election Commission is composed of three Republicans and three Democrats. They are gridlocked. Can't even agree on what time to start their meetings. The designation 501(c)(4) is an IRS regulation, but they have had a hundred years to define it and haven't done so. The Supreme Court actually took a shot at it back in the seventies and then reversed itself in *McConnell v. FEC* in 2003. The IRS is not about to incur the wrath of Congress. Our good Senators and Representatives like all that money rolling in. So, I'll be the one to go on record that most of these kinds of organizations are not qualified as social welfare organizations under the Internal Revenue Code. That definitely goes for SOS. In addition to that forty-nine percent that admittedly goes to Stepper, of the remaining fifty-one percent, all but two or three percent go to promote politicians or political causes, absolutely not social welfare issues. In short, there's no way it's an organization formed to promote social welfare. And if it is not qualified, then it can't hide its contributors. After all, ladies and gentlemen, don't you want to know who is spending the billions of dollars to elect your officials?"

Christiansen shook his head. "Objection to the last comment, Your Honor."

"Sustained. It will be stricken from the record and the jury will disregard it."

Jack smiled, knowing that the objection and the judge's ruling would only go to reinforce Cagle's comment.

Jack bent over to whisper to Colby who nodded. "No further questions, Judge."

Christiansen stood at the back against the rail with his arms folded while he thought. Finally he said, "Judge, this line of questions and answers is so clearly improper that I am not going to dignify it with cross-examination."

The judge stared at the plaintiff lawyer. "Mr. Christiansen and Mr. Bryant, please approach the bench." The lawyers moved to the side of the bench away from the jury. "Mr. Christiansen, that last comment put you very close to contempt. I will not tolerate your questioning my rulings in front of the jury. Do I make myself clear?" she said. "Now, I'm going to strike your sidebar comment and accept your decision to forego cross-examination of this witness. The witness may be excused. And one more thing, Mr. Christiansen, consider yourself warned." She turned to face the jury. "As I told you at the first of trial. I have to deal with other lawyers fighting about discovery and motions on other cases on Fridays; so, you are dismissed for the weekend. Remember not to discuss the case or read or watch anything in the media about it."

Jack stood. "Your Honor, after the jury is gone, I have a motion."

Jamison nodded as Ernie escorted the jury out. When they were gone, she said, "Let's take fifteen, and then I'll hear what Mr. Bryant has on his mind."

O'Connell practically dragged Christiansen back to their conference room.

"Dammit, Cecil, I see what is about to happen. He's going to ask the judge to order me to produce my list of SOS contributors and their amounts. You have to stop it," he almost shouted, pushing his index finger into his lawyer's chest.

"Keep your voice down and get your damn hands off me. First question is can you produce that kind of data?"

"Of course. We just have to hit a few keys on the computer."

Christiansen thought. "Okay. I'm not going to say that. I'm going to say that you will need a few days. That'll give me a chance to get a ruling from the court of appeals early next week. I just pissed the judge off, and I don't expect any rulings in our favor when we reconvene. If we can get it to the court of appeals, we'll be okay."

SEVENTY-ONE

The lawyers reassembled in the courtroom just before the judge opened the door to her chambers. They rose. "Keep your seats. The jury's gone. However we are still on the record, and I see the media is still in attendance. Mr. Bryant, what's on your mind?"

Jack moved to the podium. "Your Honor, early in the development of this case, you ruled we could get the names and information on contributions to SOS. The court of appeals reversed that decision. Now, I re-urge that motion. We have established through Professor Cagle that SOS is a welfare organization in name only. Based on the only proof before you, it's clear that the SOS money is being spent to promote political candidates and causes with maybe a small percentage actually going to social welfare. I can tell you that there is currently no appellate case on this issue and no IRS ruling or regulation since the politicians seized on 501(c)(4) as a means to hide donors. We've got to start somewhere. It might as well be here. We request that the court order Mr. O'Connell to provide the names of persons and organizations that have contributed to SOS or have pledged to do so. That information certainly must be readily accessible on a computer. So, we further request that the order be for no later than ten a.m. tomorrow. That will give us sufficient time to analyze the information over the weekend."

O'Connell looked as if he might have a stroke as Christiansen rose. "Judge, first, let me apologize for my comments before we dismissed the jury. I was completely out of order."

"Apology accepted. Move on."

"Judge, what Mr. Bryant is asking for will set the political system in this country on its ear. There is no precedent for what Mr. Bryant asks. It's a Pandora's box that once opened will cause havoc for both Republicans and Democrats."

"Mr. Christiansen, I told you during the discovery hearing that I saw nothing wrong with transparency in political contributions. You can call SOS a social welfare outfit, but the only testimony I have before me contradicts that conclusion."

"Judge, there's another issue. You said this had to be produced by ten tomorrow." Christiansen chose his words carefully. "I don't believe we can get that volume of information together before Monday at the earliest."

The judge stood and fixed her eyes on the plaintiff lawyer. "Mr. Christiansen, I understand computers. I also understand that you would like to get this to the court of appeals where you would seek another reversal of my ruling. You can take your best shot, but my order stands. Ten tomorrow morning. By the way, if you want a record of these proceedings for the appellate court, my reporter will be tied up with me on my motion docket, probably until about mid-afternoon tomorrow. And, Mr. Bryant, I'm entering a confidentiality order on whatever Mr. Christiansen produces. That will remain in effect until we re-convene on Monday and we can evaluate the relevance of what is produced. That's all. I'll see you on Monday."

Christiansen and his entourage along with his clients packed and moved from the courtroom to their conference room, Hartley Hampton pushed his way past the phalanx of reporters and through the swinging gate. He approached Jack. "Shit, man, do you know what you just did? It'll be on the front pages of every newspaper in the country tomorrow."

Jack nodded while he and Walt packed their trial materials to haul them back home for the weekend. "We'll see. I don't think that Cecil will risk a contempt order. And he really can't get to the court of appeals without a record of today's proceedings."

"I presume the contribution information will be on a disc or a flash drive. Where will it be delivered?"

"My office is on North Main. You know that. I plan to get there by about nine-thirty tomorrow. You're welcome to join us, if you like, only I can't let you see the information. You heard the judge."

"Wouldn't miss it. Wow, what a story. I've said it before. I just ought to spend all my time hanging around you. I might win a Pulitzer."

Jack turned to the members of the detail who had been standing quietly. "You guys can head back to your hotel. I'll call if I need you. I sent J.D. off on a project. Walt and I will do some strategizing tonight and will let you know if we need anything."

When O'Connell got to the privacy of his car, he placed a call. The voice that answered spoke English but with a decidedly Eastern European accent. "It was understood that we would not communicate until after this trial."

"Something has come up," O'Connell said. He explained the problem.

The man responded very firmly. "You promised that if my organization contributed a hundred million to SOS, it would be absolutely secret. You also guaranteed discrete access to the White House once your candidate won. Are you going back on your promise? If so, we have long memories. It could be very bad for you and your family."

O'Connell tried to calm the panic in his voice. "No, no. Certainly not. My lawyer is ordered to send a flash drive to the defense lawyer, that one who offices in an RV on North Main. It will have the names of all of the contributors to SOS, including your organization."

"I know that RV. We have watched it off and on since this lawsuit began. We will deal with this problem. However, let me make it very clear, if another issue such as this occurs, we will conclude that you are the problem. Understood?"

SEVENTY-TWO

J.D. climbed into his new pickup, a Toyota Tundra quad cab, with an emblem designating it as a "1794 Edition" on the side. As he drove away from the courthouse, he admired his new truck. The cab was big enough for even him, and the interior looked like it belonged in a Mercedes. Maybe he and his dad could negotiate an endorsement deal. After all, J.J. Watt with the Texans was paid to drive a Ford F-150.

Using the hands free feature, he called Ike. "You got anything pressing going on this afternoon?"

Ike smiled at the thought. "Nothing that won't wait. What do you need?"

"I'm on my way to your house. Pack an overnight bag. We're catching the next flight to New Orleans. I'll explain more when I get there."

It was nearly eight when they landed in New Orleans. After renting a car, they drove to the Marriott where J.D. had reserved three rooms, expecting to need one for Bernard before the night was over. After dinner at the hotel, they walked to Trombone's, arriving just as the ten o'clock set was nearly over. They chose a table in the front row and ordered two Bud Lights and listened to the last of the set. When it ended, Bernard spotted them. A frown appeared on his face.

He put his cornet down and walked to their table. "Look, Ike, I done told you I ain't doing anything more to help. What don't you understand about that?"

Ike pointed to an empty chair. "Have a seat. We'll talk a minute and then we'll enjoy your music until the place closes. You told me about how you paid your cell phone bill. If you can get online, we want to check a couple of numbers from early September last fall. You know your log-in and password?"

Bernard raised his hands in protest. "Why should I be helping you?"

"Damn you have a short memory," Ike said. "You already forgot about that fifty grand you got from Cross. You just have to play ball a little longer and we'll be out of your hair."

"That log-in shit is stuck to the wall back at my apartment."

"That's okay," J.D. said. "While Ike stays here, I'll go back to the Marriott and retrieve my rent car. We can visit your apartment as soon as you're off work."

Bernard shook his head in disgust when he walked back to the stage. J.D. left the club, remembering what had happened on these streets before and watched as he passed every entry and alley. On this night his vigilance was unnecessary. While he was gone, Al walked over to visit with Ike. Ike declined his invitation to join them on stage.

It was an hour before he returned to Trombone's. He sat down beside Ike and refused another beer. When the set was finished, Bernard put his cornet in its case and shuffled over to their table. "Okay, let's get this done."

"One more thing," Ike said. "You better let Al know you may

be gone a few days."

"That wasn't part of the deal," Bernard shot back.

"We'll pay for any money you lose. We may need you in Fort Worth," J.D. said.

"You can sleep on my couch. We can do a little jamming in my studio. You'll like it," Ike added.

Bernard returned to the stage where he talked to Al and pointed to J.D. and Ike. Al nodded. When they strapped themselves into the rent car, Bernard directed them out of the Quarter and across I-10 to an apartment close to the Fairgrounds Racetrack. Bernard occupied a one bedroom in a sixteen unit complex, probably built in the sixties or seventies. He unlocked the downstairs unit and flipped on an overhead light. J.D. was surprised to find that it was neat, clean and tastefully done. Bernard placed his horn on the small kitchen table and went to the back where he returned with his laptop and a yellow sticky with writing on it. Sitting at the table he clicked on the computer and typed in his password. A browser appeared. He looked at the writing and went to the site where they hoped to find his cell records. Once there he looked at the writing again and typed in a user name and password. When his cell records appeared, he motioned J.D. and Ike to stand behind him as he scrolled back by the months to September.

"Now, tell me again what we are looking for?" he asked.

"We're looking for this number. That should be the person who called you about the contract."

As he scrolled through September, J.D. said, "Stop. There it is twice. Someone at that number called you and you called back two days later. Do you see a call to or from Crossmore?"

By now Bernard was all in. "No, that's not his regular number. See here." He scrolled to July and August. "That's the number I would call when I had, uh, something I wanted him to look at." He scrolled back to September. "Just a minute. Now I remember. He said he bought one of those burner phones. I think that must be it."

"Okay, let me check these phone records for that burner phone number," J.D. said. He flipped through several pages of paper until he found September. "Son of a bitch, there it is. We've got our suspect calling you twice and twice to Crossmore's burner phone." He glanced at his watch and turned to Ike. "It's too late to call my dad. He's had a long week. Besides," he smiled, "I'd like to see the look on his face when we show him what we found. Bernard, pack clothes for about four days. You're spending the night with us at the Marriott. Oh, and print off those cell phone records. We're flying to Fort Worth in the morning."

"I don't need to stay at the Marriott. I'll be right here."

J.D. shook his head. "Look, Bernard, We've already had too many killings, two right here in New Orleans. I don't want to take a chance that we've been followed and find you dead in the morning. Get your stuff."

SEVENTY-THREE

Jack turned his pickup into the RV parking lot at 9:30, figuring that Cecil would have the information delivered at the last minute. Getting there thirty minutes early should be plenty of time. He checked his rear view mirror and noted that Hartley was behind him. Might as well have the press witness the occasion. As he parked, he looked on the steps of the RV. No package. No surprise. He presumed that someone would have to sign for it. He climbed down from his pickup, took his cane from behind the seat and patted Lucille on the fender like she was a member of the family. In fact, she was.

Hartley was walking toward him when it happened. The RV was hit with an explosion that lifted it off its wheels. The front windows blew out. The armor panels were blown away like missiles. He and Hartley had to duck as a large piece of one flew at them. A second explosion erupted, strong enough to lift the RV off the ground several feet and lay it on its side. The second blast knocked Jack and Hartley to the ground with more pieces of debris clattering around them like a giant hail storm.

Jack moved to a sitting position and removed a piece of metal from his leg. "Dammit. That was my good leg."

Hartley sat up, his face bleeding from a nasty cut on his forehead. They both struggled to their feet. Jack's cane was nowhere to be found. "Here, let me look at that cut," he said to Hartley. He wiped the reporter's hair away and pulled a handkerchief from his back pocket, to wipe the blood from his forehead. "I saw a ton of these in my army days. Forehead wounds bleed even when they're not serious. You'll be okay. Here, hold this handkerchief over it for now."

"You okay?" Hartley asked.

"I'm going to have a sore shin for a few days, but that's all. Sure could use my cane right about now." Jack limped over to survey the RV. "Shit. Damn thing is destroyed." He bent over to pick something up. "Look here." He showed Hartley the cardboard sign that seemed to be the only thing that survived intact. *LAWYER; NO FEE.* "Looks like I'll be out of the pro bono business for a while. Takes months to outfit one of these damn things with armor."

"Jack," Hartley asked, "what about the SOS contributor information?"

"I suspect that's the reason for the explosion. Someone didn't want us to have it."

"Only, you just said that someone would probably have to sign for it."

"Maybe I'm wrong. That's how I would have done it. Christiansen might have thought differently."

"How would they know it got here?"

"Haven't figured that out. I suppose the delivery service could report it was done by cell or text."

"Christiansen?"

"No. He's a tough bastard, but he wouldn't do this. Someone

on that list didn't want to be known."

Jack heard a noise and looked up to see Moe stepping through the debris, coming from the ice house. Sirens could also be heard coming up North Main.

"Jack, you all right? Anyone hurt?"

"We're fine. I banged up my shin and Hartley has a cut on his forehead. All things considered, that's not bad."

"I haven't seen you in a couple of weeks. I've been reading about your big trial."

"I moved home until that one is over. I came down here today because there was supposed to be a delivery by ten this morning."

"Wait, wait. I'll be right back." Moe turned to pick through the debris to his icehouse as a firetruck turned into the parking lot, followed by an ambulance.

An assistant chief jumped from the passenger side. "Anyone hurt here."

"Nothing serious, Chief."

He asked Hartley to remove the handkerchief from his forehead. "We'll get a compression bandage on that. You feel light-headed, dizzy? You lose consciousness, even for a few seconds?" He motioned to an EMT.

"Naw, Chief. I know about concussions. I don't have one."

The other firefighters had pulled hoses from the truck and hooked one up to a hydrant on the corner in front of Moe's. "If you'll back up, we're going to put out those fires, throw water on that gasoline that's leaking from the back and soak everything to make sure there are no hot spots." As they did, two cop cars arrived, followed closely by reporters and televisions trucks, the ones with telescoping aerials.

Moe dodged the spray from the hoses and joined Jack and Hartley. "Here, this was delivered about nine this morning. I was just setting up for the day. The delivery guy said that someone had to sign for it. Asked me to do it." Moe handed him an envelope. Jack looked at the outside and ripped it open and extracted a flash drive. A smile enveloped his face when he did so. He turned to Hartley. "I'm going to set a little trap for Christiansen. I'll use the media and then place a call to him. You're in on this; so, you can't let on what I have in my pocket."

Hartley nodded his understanding as reporters and cameras circled around. "Mr. Bryant, what happened here?"

"It's pretty obvious. Someone blew up my RV."

"Couldn't it have been a fuel leak or something?"

Jack shrugged his shoulders. "Anything's possible, but some of you were in court yesterday. You know I was supposed to get the information about SOS and Stepper this morning. Now I got nothing but a blown up RV. Now, if you'll excuse me, the Northside police are waiting to talk to me." Jack went with them to a police car and sat in the back while they questioned him. After thirty minutes, they excused him. As Jack got out of the car, he could hear one of the officers calling in the bomb squad.

Jack made his way through the reporters with a series of "no more comments," climbed in his truck and wove through the maze of firetrucks, police cars, media vehicles and debris to the street. Once on it, he picked up his cell phone and dialed Christiansen's cell.

"Jack, you get my delivery this morning?"

"You'll be seeing it on the news in a couple of hours. My RV was blown all to hell. Your delivery was probably in it. Can I get you to send me another flash drive?"

Silence on the other end.

"I've got a text message from the delivery service, saying that someone named Moe signed for my delivery at nine this morning. Once is enough. I've complied with the court's order. If you want to take it up with the judge, do so on Monday. Have a good weekend."

Jack grinned. Christiansen had stepped into his trap. Next, he pulled to the side just as he passed the courthouse. He figured that J.D. was on the way back and didn't want him to worry once he landed and heard the news. He sent a text. All he said was, "I'm fine. See you at the house."

When he arrived home and parked, Colby rushed from the house and wrapped him in a bear hug. "You all right? I just saw it on the news."

Jack shook his head. "I have another banged up leg. It should be all right in a few days. Otherwise I'm fine. Boy, those reporters get the news out fast these days."

"I saw what was left of your RV. I'm sorry. But, if you had gotten there five minutes sooner, you wouldn't be standing here." Tears came to her eyes.

Jack kissed her. "I'd wipe those tears away, but last I saw my handkerchief, Hartley was using it as a compress on his forehead."

"My God, is he hurt?"

"He's fine. May have a slight scar. That's all."

As they walked across the driveway, Jack's cell rang. He took a look at the caller i.d. and said, "I'm fine."

"I got your text," J.D. said. "Ike and I just landed. We've got Bernard with us. I'm dropping them by Ike's house. Then I'll be home. You're going to be even better when you see what I have."

Driving from DFW, which was halfway to Dallas, it was forty-five minutes before J.D. arrived at the house.

Colby handed him coffee in a giant mug when he came through the back door.

"About time you got here," Jack groused goodnaturedly, "I brought your laptop down to the dining room." He handed him the flash drive and told him what had happened, including his slight lie to Christiansen.

J.D. took a sip of coffee before he sat in front of his computer. "Wait a minute. Before we start searching for stuff about contributors, look at this."

He pulled Bernard's cell records from a manila folder. "Check early September last year and compare the records with O'Connell's."

Jack studied them, flipping back and forth. He finally looked up with a smile on his face. "Son of a bitch."

"Well said. I've got Bernard holed up with Ike. We can put him on the stand, if you need him."

Jack high-fived his son. "I'll have to call Joe and work out some kind of plea if we do. Let's cross that bridge when we get to it. Now, let's see what we can find on this flash drive."

SEVENTY-FOUR

Jack decided to start the day on Monday with Governor Lardner. When called, he strolled in from the hallway, a politician overflowing with confidence, no matter what the situation. He stood in front of Judge Jamison and raised his hand for the oath without prompting and then turned to the jury. "Good morning, ladies and gentlemen."

The jurors, most of whom voted Republican, were thrilled to be so close to the governor and potential presidential candidate, replied in unison, "Good morning, Governor Lardner."

Jack had a more noticeable limp as he walked to the podium, still feeling the effects of the weekend bombing. He took the governor through the events of the day that led up to the fundraiser. Jack didn't know until he asked a random question that there was a pre-party reception for a number of the high rollers in the governor's suite on the second floor. O'Connell wanted to make sure that the big dogs got a little face time with the governor, figuring that it would pay off in pledges later in the evening.

"Governor, what was your reaction when you entered the ballroom that night."

Lardner smiled ruefully. "I was overwhelmed. I thought 'Walt tried to talk me out of this and now look what I've got myself in for.'"

"Were you worried?"

The governor paused while he took himself back to that night. "All of these people in costumes and masks. I knew some of them had real guns. So, damn right I was, but I couldn't turn and walk away at that point, so I smiled and started shaking hands as the detail led the way to the stage.

"Once we got there and I made my speech, I started thinking that these are all fine Republicans. Not likely to be any problem. Boy, was I wrong."

"Do you remember much about being hit?"

Lardner again thought for a few seconds. "Not really. I felt the pain in my left side and then I was going in and out. I remember voices and bright lights and being dragged off the stage. That's about it."

Jack knew the jurors wanted to have an answer to the next question. For that matter, Lardner wanted to make it clear himself. "Have you made a complete recovery from your injuries?"

No hesitation. "Absolutely. I lost a lot of blood. That was because the bullet went in my left side and punctured my spleen. In case you don't know, ladies and gentlemen, when the spleen is traumatized, you're going to lose a lot of blood."

Several of the jurors nodded their understanding.

"I actually lost my spleen, but it's one of those organs you can do without. So, I still run five miles a day and go to the shooting range every weekend. With my pistol at twenty-five feet, I'm damn near as good as that woman who shot me."

"That brings up an interesting question, Governor. Since you're a marksman yourself, if that woman had wanted to kill you, you figure she could have done so."

"In a heartbeat. She was apparently a trained killer and also had studied human anatomy. I suspect she was told to wound, not kill me."

Jack said nothing for several moments while the jury absorbed what the governor had just said. "Pass the witness, Your Honor."

Christiansen tapped his pen on the table while he thought. This was the governor. No way should a lawyer attempt to impeach him. "No questions, Judge."

Jack called his retired Texas Ranger next. Bart Scurlock removed his ten gallon white hat as he entered the courtroom. He was not long and lanky. In fact, he was somewhat overweight, for which he apologized when he took the stand. He blamed it on too little activity in retirement and his wife's good cooking. He did have that bushy white mustache that Jack had visualized.

Jack had him describe his forty years in law enforcement, the last twenty-five as a Ranger. He was a captain, overseeing South Texas when he retired. When asked his opinion of the events of the night in question, he turned to face the jury, his sky blue eyes and demeanor capturing their attention. In fact, if asked, most of the jurors would have had a difficult choice as to whether it was more exciting to see the governor or a real, live Texas Ranger up close and personal.

He explained that no member of the protective detail or, for that matter, the Fort Worth cops or even the security guards should bear any responsibility for the tragic events that unfolded that night. Whoever arranged for the shootings had to have known it was going to be a costume party. Whoever made the decision to have all those people crowded into the ballroom with masks and even some carrying guns, that was the person to blame. Once the decision was made to hire an assassin, the die was cast.

His words carried the authority of a Texas Ranger. In the eyes of the jury, his opinions were powerful. Christiansen knew he had to do something to attack his credibility. About all he could do was establish that the Ranger was being paid $300 an hour for his time as an expert and, as a Ranger, he had also been a member of the DPS. The Ranger conceded both points, shrugging his shoulders and saying that neither impacted his testimony. As he stepped down from the stand and picked up his hat that had been carefully placed in front of him, something happened that Jack had never witnessed.

He walked past the man in the first chair on the front row of the jury. The juror stood to honor one of the most revered lawmen in the state. The man behind him did the same. And as he walked past the rest of the jury, they all stood in silent homage to a Texas Ranger.

Jack shook his head and said to himself, "Take that, Cecil, you son of a bitch."

After the mid-morning break, the jurors were escorted to their places by Ernie and stood until the judge took her bench.

"Your Honor, our next witness is in a wheel chair in our conference room. May J.D. go with the bailiff to bring her into the courtroom."

"That'll be fine, Mr. Bryant. You mind telling us the witness's name?"

"My apologies, Judge. We call Miriam Van Zandt."

Suddenly, there was a buzz of whispers in the jury box and among the reporters and others in attendance. *Wasn't she dead? Wasn't she in a coma? Do you think she will remember anything?*

"We'll have order in this court. Any more such outbursts and I'll clear the courtroom. Is that understood?"

J.D. followed Ernie out the doors. When they opened again, Ernie held one of them while J.D. wheeled Miriam down the aisle. They were followed by a nurse who was there to lend assistance to her patient, if necessary. The nurse stood at the back of the courtroom. As she was wheeled down the aisle, Joe Shannon stepped into the courtroom and stood next to the nurse. Van Zandt looked tiny in the wheelchair. She wore a simple black skirt and white blouse. She had a black wig to hide the indentation in her skull from the shrapnel and surgery. Her only make-up was a hint of lipstick. She looked straight ahead, but her eyes were darting from side to side. J.D. wheeled her to the front of the bench. When the judge administered the oath, she answered in a voice almost too quiet to be heard. J.D. turned her chair to face the jury and then returned to his seat.

"Miss Van Zandt, are you able to hear and understand my questions?"

Pause.

"I can hear you just fine. If I don't understand, I'll tell you."

Jack nodded. "Excellent. Let's get some information about your current condition."

"I'm still a patient at Methodist. I've been there since the attack on our compound several months ago."

"Did you have brain surgery?"

"Yes, sir. And I was mostly in a coma for a long time after that."

"Are you doing better now?"

"I'm awake more. And I'm starting to do some physical therapy. I hope to be walking soon."

"I'm going to make this as brief as possible. You killed Edward Hale, seriously wounded Governor Lardner and grazed this man here, Kevin O'Connell on that night?"

Van Zandt looked down at her shoes and slowly raised her head to face the jury. "I did, sir. I admit it."

"Were you paid?"

"$100,000."

"Who paid you?"

The jurors moved to the edge of their seats. They were disappointed.

"I don't know, sir. Someone wired some money to my dad

and he wired that $100,000 to my bank account. I heard him mention someone named Cross at one time, but I don't know who he was or who he worked for."

"Were you given specific instructions about that night?"

The witness gazed off into space and didn't respond.

"Miss Van Zandt, were you given specific instructions?"

"I was told to wound the governor, kill Edward Hale and shoot O'Connell in the arm."

That answer caused another stir in the audience with several jurors whispering to one another until the judge banged her gavel and called for order.

"How did you get in the party?"

"Climbed the back wall. There was a guard on the patio that I had to eliminate. Someone on the inside was supposed to have left a key in a flower pot. It wasn't there. I went around to the back came in through the delivery entrance."

"How did you identify them?"

"Knew they would be on the stage. Had photos of everyone on the stage. Knew the governor would be the Lone Ranger and O'Connell would be in a clown outfit. I knew where Edward Hale would be sitting. I also knew what kind of costume he would be in." Pause. "I forget now his costume."

Jack moved to the end of the jury rail, across from the last juror and leaned against it so that the witness would be looking at the jury as she answered the remainder of his questions. "Were you a good enough marksman that you could carry out those instructions?"

A slight smile crossed the witness's face. "Before this happened I used to put up four targets and empty my weapon, firing at them randomly. All my rounds were in the bullseye. What I was asked to do was easy."

Jack looked at the jury. One last question. "Did you have any reservations about killing?"

Van Zandt pursed her lips and lowered her eyes. "I suppose

my answer should be that I did. But, I'm under oath. Truth is the Alamo Defenders were soldiers. We knew the government was coming for us. I did it because we needed more weapons and to recruit more defenders. So, I did what I had to do. It was war."

Silence now enveloped the courtroom.

"Nothing further, Your Honor."

Jack glanced at Christiansen who was quietly staring at the witness, obviously contemplating whether she had really done any material damage and what he might gain by cross examination. Sitting behind him was O'Connell, who was folding and unfolding his arms, blinking furiously, sweat showing on his forehead, and breathing rapidly, almost like he was about to have a heart attack. Finally deciding that he could really do nothing to damage this witness--after all, she had admitted to being a murderer--he told the judge that he had no questions.

After lunch, Jack announced, "The defense re-calls Kevin O'Connell."

O'Connell looked at his lawyer who motioned for him to take the stand. He moved around the table and stood in front of the bench, raising his right hand to take the oath. "That won't be necessary," Judge Jamison said. "You have already sworn to tell the truth and are still under that same oath. Please be seated."

Colby was watching carefully when O'Connell walked to the bench and raised his right hand. While Jack started his questioning, Colby scribbled something on a yellow stickie and slipped it to J.D. He read it, opened his laptop and started scrolling through pictures.

"Mr. O'Connell, let's establish a couple of preliminaries. First, people contribute to political campaigns because they want something."

O'Connell saw it as a throwaway question. "Yes, of course."

"A person, or these days a big corporation or a labor union may want to push for or against some issue, say national defense or women's rights or government spending or a dozen others, correct?"

"I agree."

"Second, they may want to obtain access to a Congressman or a Senator or, maybe, the President and the more they give, the greater the potential access."

O'Connell was now feeling more comfortable. He could handle these questions. "Not always true, Mr. Bryant, but no doubt that big money does talk in Washington."

"Now, the way you set up Stepper and SOS, SOS doesn't have to disclose its contributors, at least not until this trial, and Stepper can just file a report, saying that it received, say a hundred million, from SOS and the buck stops there."

"Provided you don't succeed in changing the law. I might add that we have filed an emergency appeal to try to stop your disclosure of the SOS contributors."

"I'm not surprised, but I suppose I best hurry if we want to get this information in front of the jury and the public before some appellate clerk walks in the back door with an order. Let's start now. Your Honor, am I now permitted to go into what was produced on Friday?"

Judge Jamison looked puzzled. "I understood from the media that your RV and its contents were destroyed. Are you saying that you have that information?"

"I do, Judge."

O'Connell twisted in his chair as he glanced from the jury to Christiansen, to the bailiff and to the door and windows. He reached into his pocket for a handkerchief and wiped the sweat from his forehead, then used it to dry his hands.

"You may use what you have been provided, assuming, of course, that I don't get a call from the court of appeals."

"We've reviewed all of your spreadsheets of contributors, their contact information and amounts. Without going into detail, you would agree that you have several hundred contributors in SOS with about $500,000,000 raised or pledged so far."

O'Connell could no longer hide his nervousness. His voice cracked. "If, if that's what it shows, I don't disagree."

"So, SOS has collected much more than what you said just a couple of days ago, including tens of millions from the costume fundraiser."

"Like I say, you have the numbers. I could have been off on my math. I have a staff to keep up with that."

"There's one contributor I want to focus on for a moment. It's called *Mosaic Council of Americans and Eurasians*. You're familiar with that council, are you not?"

"Not particularly. I don't keep up with all of them. That's what I have a staff for."

"Wait a minute. This Mosaic Council contributed a hundred million to SOS and you don't know who they are? Don't you have an obligation to check into contributors, particularly large ones like this?"

"My staff in Washington will eventually get around to that."

"Mr. O'Connell, J.D. did some checking over the weekend and found that this Mosaic Council is a front for the Chechnya government. He had to backtrack through several dummy corporations, but he finally figured it out."

Christiansen rose. "Objection, Judge. Whatever the younger Mr. Bryant figured out is not in evidence."

Jack decided to bluff. He picked up a folder from his table. "Judge, I have all of the documents right here. I can put J.D. on the stand later if necessary." In fact, the folder contained various pleadings that had long ago been filed in the case.

"With the understanding that you'll tie it up, I'll let you go forward, Mr. Bryant, subject to being stricken if you don't."

Jack nodded his understanding. "Mr. O'Connell, you know that it's a violation of federal law for a foreign government to contribute to our elections, don't you?"

The witness looked to his lawyer for guidance, now beginning to regret that he had ever decided to file the lawsuit.

"Don't be looking at your lawyer. He can't help you now. Fact of the matter is that if the judge hadn't ordered you to turn over these records, the Chechens would have a hundred million dollars' worth of access to the White House if your candidate won. That might even get them a couple of nights in the Lincoln bedroom."

"Objection, Your Honor. Argumentative."

"Sustained. Move on, Mr. Bryant."

"Very well, Judge. At this time we offer as Defendant's Exhibit 44 the cell phone records that Mr. Nichols subpoenaed from Mr. O'Connell's cell phone company."

"No objection, Judge. They were listed as a potential exhibit before trial. We just didn't see them until last week."

"Then, Judge, we have other phone records from a gentleman named Bernard Batiste from New Orleans."

When he heard the name, the blood drained from O'Connell's face.

"Judge, we are offering these for impeachment. They have not been authenticated, but we have Mr. Batiste in the hallway to be called as our next witness."

"Objection, Your Honor," Christiansen said as he leaped to his feet. "We've never seen these."

The judge as well as the jurors were now eager to see where this was all leading. "This is impeachment, Mr. Christiansen. Overruled. Carry on, Mr. Bryant. Again, with the admonition that I may strike some of this testimony if you don't connect it."

"Understood, Judge." Jack walked to the witness stand and handed copies of each set of cell phone records to the witness. At the same time, J.D. split the overhead screen so that he could display both. "On the right you will see your cell records with the 202 area code. That's your phone, isn't it?"

O'Connell's eyes moved up and to his right briefly before he answered. "I better explain something, In early September last year, I left my cell phone in a taxi. I reported it to the D.C. police.

I thought it was gone, but it turned up in a bar about a week later. I don't know who used it or what calls were made during that time."

"Then, you must know where I'm going with this. You've been in a club called Trombone's in New Orleans a number of times, haven't you?"

"Name sounds familiar. I visit New Orleans in my job and like jazz."

"You heard me mention Bernard Batiste. You know him, don't you?"

Realizing he could not dodge the question, he said, "Name sounds familiar."

"In fact, if we look at your cell records, there are calls going to New Orleans during that week you claim your phone disappeared. If we look at your records, where I've highlighted two calls to one cell number and look at these records from Mr. Batiste's cell phone, there's a call from yours and he's calling you back two days later."

O'Connell was now squirming in his seat. "Like I said, I lost my phone." His voice dropped to a whisper as he ended the sentence.

"And, if we look at two other calls, they are to and from a burner phone that Mr. Batiste will identify as that of Adam Crossmore, the middleman in the killing done by Miriam Van Zandt. Do you deny talking to Crossmore?"

The witness didn't respond and didn't move a muscle. The judge was about to order him to answer when Jack continued.

"Mr. O'Connell, can I get you to step down in front of the jury?"

Almost in a trance, the witness did so.

"Will you raise your right sleeve and display your Rolex to the jury?"

O'Connell did so.

"J.D. will you put clip 88 from the security camera exhibits on the overhead?"

An image appeared. It showed a suited right hand and arm. A diamond studded Rolex was shown with a large diamond ring on the hand. The hand was reaching to switch off cameras at the mansion. The digital display was 3:38. Even if the jurors didn't understand all of the testimony, the sight of O'Connell's right hand in front of them with the clip on the overhead was the final nail in his coffin.

Suddenly, O'Connell became animated. He started coughing violently and holding his chest. "I need air, right now."

His eyes bounced around the courtroom and settled on the door where the jury went out the back to the jury room. He turned and ran for it.

"Ernie, you better go after him," Jack said.

Ernie sprinted to the door, followed by Walt and the rest of the detail with J.D. close behind. When O'Connell burst through the door, he found a hallway and headed to the jury room. Beside it was another hall which he assumed led to the outside corridor. As he rushed down it, he heard the door to the courtroom open behind him and realized there were multiple footsteps close behind. He bounded down the stairs two at a time. Jack had come from the back of the courtroom and joined in the chase, albeit at a fast limp.

O'Connell hit the front doors of the courthouse and went down the stairs and across the street, dodging traffic as he did. When he got to his rented Lexus, he clicked open the doors as the men in pursuit were crossing the street. Instead of getting in the driver's side, he opened the passenger door and reached in the glove box. His hand came out with a Glock in it.

He put it to his head when the men were about to get to his car. They stopped on the other side. "Put that gun down," Ernie said, his own gun drawn.

With panic on his now-red face, O'Connell gasped, "Don't you understand? I had to do it. Edward Hale had told me that he would not help in my campaign. He was going to the other side. No matter how much money I could raise, he could write a check for that much and more. He was hell bent on neutralizing all I had fought for all these years. We couldn't afford to have a moderate or a Democrat in the White House again. It was for the good of the country." He hesitated. "Besides, after what happened in court just now the Chechens now will kill me."

The gun went off with a deafening explosion and O'Connell disappeared behind his Lexus. The last Jack remembered of him was the Rolex and diamond ring on the hand holding the gun.

EPILOGUE

Jack, Colby, J.D. and Walt sat on the back deck, watching a majestic sunset, full of reds, blues, oranges and greens. They sipped their drinks in silence. Finally Walt spoke. "I never thought it would end this way."

"None of us did. It's the law of unintended consequences," Jack said.

"Meaning what?" Colby asked.

"Blame it on the Supreme Court. They have screwed up our political system in the name of the First Amendment. With so much money now in the political arena, the stakes have gotten too high. O'Connell knew what Mosaic was. He didn't give a damn as long as he thought he could keep their involvement hidden with SOS. He knew that Edward was no longer drinking the same Kool-Aid as his brother. One carefully planned and executed murder would solve his problem. He was willing to arrange it to get rid of someone who could destroy what he was building. If it had worked, he would have been the puppeteer, quietly pulling the strings in the White House. Imagine the power."

J.D. downed his beer. "Yeah, Dad, and he might have gotten away with it if you hadn't tracked down the evidence."

"I appreciate that. I did what you've heard so often. I followed the money. I couldn't have done it without you and your computer skills, but, you know, what really put the icing on the cake was when Colby remembered that photo of the hand on the camera switches. That's when he knew the jig was up."

"We've gotten a pile of publicity," Colby said. "The media is finally waking up to all of this dark money in politics. I know you're getting calls every day. You think what we did will change anything?"

Jack popped another beer. "For once, I'm taking calls from reporters and agreeing to interviews. J.D. and I are going to New York for a round of news shows in two days. Is that going to do any good? Probably not. Like I said once before, the Supreme Court doesn't recognize what they've done. The Senators and Congressmen are like pigs at the trough. They're not about to shut off the flow of money. Still, we're going to make our case to anyone who will listen."

Dear Reader,

Thanks for taking the time to read Dark Money. I hope it grabbed your attention and you enjoyed it. If that's the case, I have a favor to ask. Reviews are extremely important to an author. In the world of e-publishing, reviews can make or break a book. If you liked my story, it would be greatly appreciated if you could take a couple of minutes to go to your favorite e-book websites and write a short review to let others know they, too, would enjoy it.

Thanks for your help and be sure to watch for my next novel.

Larry D. Thompson

About the Author

Larry D. Thompson was first a trial lawyer. He tried more than 300 cases throughout Texas, winning in excess of 95% of them. When his youngest son graduated from college, he decided to write his first novel. Since his mother was an English teacher and his brother, Thomas Thompson, had been a best-selling author, it seemed the natural thing to do.

Larry writes about what he knows best...lawyers, courtrooms and trials. The legal thriller is his genre. *Dark Money* is his fifth story and the second in the Jack Bryant series.

Larry and his wife, Vicki, call Houston home and spend their summers on a mountain top in Vail, Colorado. He has two daughters, two sons and four grandchildren. He is a staunch believer in *Elmore Leonard's Ten Rules of Writing*, particularly number ten: *Leave out the parts that the readers tend to skip.*